MASKED

G.A. FINOCCHIARO

WRITING BLOC

INDIE PUBLISHING TEAM

ISBN: 9798986554310

First Edition September 2022

writingbloc.com
www.gafino.com

Edited by Cari Dubiel
Cover Illustration by Rachel Perciphone
Book Design by G.A. FinocchiaroInterior Comic Book Illustration by Lisa K. Weber - lisakweber.com
Author Photo by Ashley Griffin Photography

This story is part of the
SCALES SEQUENCE.
The sequence can be read in order or as individual series within. <u>You decide</u>.

Each book is marked with a roman numeral within a circle.
This is where it exists in the SCALES SEQUENCE.

For more information, please go to
gafino.com and click on SCALES.

PROLOGUE

"WELCOME TO A WORLD OF EVIL. I'M RHEA RAMSEY."

Behind the television host was a burned-out building on Wonder City's north side—it was a war zone, or maybe Doctor Insane-O had finally blown himself up in a lab experiment gone wrong. The surrounding lot was scorched, and a tower beyond a rusty chain-link fence had been toppled.

The host was dressed in red—bright and vibrant, unlike the overgrown landscape littered with broken glass and fragments of concrete. Her hair was cut into a fancy bob, blonde streaks frozen in place by only the strongest hair products. Likely part of the Warrior Princess line—named for the supe from South Africa.

"Insanity. Depravity. Lawlessness. Greed. Bloodthirsty villainy," she continued while pacing toward the camera, gracing viewers with a close-up of her Botox-ed features, the rubble over her shoulder. "Three weeks ago, this was the secret lair of the nefarious Dope Gang. What happened here, who are the Dope Gang, and what lurks inside the minds of lunatics? This week on *Supes-Roundup*."

SUPES ROUNDUP

with *Rhea Rhamsey*

Supes, or Supers—the affectionate terms for super-powered individuals with do-gooder intentions—had been an ongoing national obsession for decades. It was a phenomenon about the phenomenal and a ratings cash-cow.

Rhea Ramsey was the host of America's highest rated TV magazine, *Supes-Roundup*. Two years ago, it replaced *60 Minutes*, the hard-hitting investigative news-journalism television show, with trashy supe interviews, puff pieces, supe re-enactments, and live footage of actual super violence. The show traveled throughout America, sometimes to more exotic locations, interviewing supes and gathering first-hand footage for *The Best Slobber-Knocker Battles*™ *of the Week*. They focused less on the solving and prevention of crime than they did the blood-fest, often opting for scenes of destruction and death instead of, for example, the time Optimum Overdrive rescued a bus full of kids. The transmission had broken as the bus drove through a rocky mountain pass on a field trip to All-Star City—the man beneath the mask was a hero, but much less popular than the brawny-brawlers without the brains. Blood, as it had been since the days of Rome, was a persistent crowd pleaser.

"Crimson Justice," said Rhea, sitting in a dark room with a spotlight shining on her surgically enhanced smile. "Welcome. Can you tell us, from your perspective, what transpired on that fateful day, at the abandoned warehouse, in the old train yard on Wonder City's north side?"

Over the next ten seconds rolled grainy live footage—a combination of aerial shots from ZepNews® Balloons and drones, to shaky handheld cell phone clips depicting all six members of the Dope Gang at their worst. A montage of the disturbances was cut into short vignettes, each violent display edited from various appearances across their five years of terror—from Tin

Men marches to high profile burglary to their infamous scuffles with well-known supes like The Cossack Kid and Major Rager.

The camera cut back and forth between Rhea, the vignettes, and Crimson Justice. If Crimson Justice was asleep, one wouldn't know the difference. You couldn't see his eyes beneath the red hood, and he sat there motionless, a giant man on a small wooden chair.

From head to toe, Crimson Justice was fitted with skintight, textured red leather that covered every inch except his burly chin. Upon his massive chest was a symbol that struck terror into the hearts of villains and thugs alike. All in all, he was more than six-foot-five inches tall, and his shoulders were half as wide.

When the violent clips ended, and he still hadn't answered, Rhea added, "Can you tell us anything at all about your bloody confrontation with the Dope Gang?"

The camera slowly zoomed into Crimson Justice's face. It was only when the camera stopped zooming that the audience realized he had turned his head to face the lens, peering directly into the souls of every viewer—his menacing eyes piercing the shadows beneath his blood-red hood.

"They fought the law," said Crimson Justice, followed by a five-second pause, "and the law won."

"Wow," said Rhea. "So breathtaking. So emotional. We'll be right back after a word from our sponsor."

When the screen faded to black for dramatic effect, it immediately rose into a brilliant white and sharpened. Shades of gray dissolved into blasts of color and music with hints of the Star-Spangled Banner and God Bless America rising to crescendo. The melody was interwoven with patriotic imagery before the announcement: "This week on American Supe!"

Scott Rio, the D-list television actor, stood beside Ted Nougat, former hillbilly rock star. They stepped forward in colorful, star-spangled suits, their eyes bulging like they had inhaled a whole kilo of cocaine before filming the commercial.

Rio announced, "It's finals week on *American Supe!*"

"Welcome to Thunderdome!" added Nougat, black tobacco chew spittle flying from his wadded lower lip.

"The stakes have never been higher," the narrator began. "From Greenville, Tennessee, the mighty Apollo will face off against the sweetheart of America's heartland, Cowgal Jezebelle, for the chance at being this year's *American Supe* champion."

A chiseled man, bronzed and blonde, stepped out from behind a star-spangled cloth in nothing but a toga and sandals, backlit by blinding white light and wisps of dramatic fog. He appeared to glow as he flexed his muscles and winked at the camera. Cut scene—a girl in daisy dukes, pigtails, cowboy boots, and a knotted, red-checkered shirt. She came dancing into view, her hands rippling with mystical blue energy that sparkled for the camera. Her beaming smile and brilliant white teeth—her all-American freckles drawn on, and strawberry blonde from a bottle—dazzled viewers. She sauntered up to the camera, brandishing finger-guns, and blew a kiss to the audience.

"With their choice of four top-notch supe-city-licenses hanging in the balance, these two will square off in the American Supe Arena with the chance to become the newest defender of truth, justice, and the American way. Tune in to witness history! America's next fully licensed supe is just hours away from being crowned! The stakes have never been higher!"

"And we all know what that means, Scott!" said Nougat.

"That's right, Ted," said Rio. "It means you better get ready for a bloodbath!"

"The stakes have never been higher!" shouted Nougat.

Across the screen flashed a brilliant display of guns, fireworks, flags, eagles, and explosions. "Tonight, following *Supes-Roundup*," said Rio, "join us for America's highest rated sports program!"

"Only on *Patriot*!" said Nougat, followed by, "The stakes have never been higher!"

From Ted Nougat's sweaty face came a quick fifteen-second spot for *Supe-Burger,* home of the Triple Patty Gut Buster, and the new *Justice Broiler—an all-beef quadruple patty phenom with six slices of cheese and onion straws—on sale now for just $9.99, plus tax, without drink or fries.

*Serving size = Two Bites. 1600 Calories per serving.

The broadcast cut for a local news update.

"Hi, I'm Sandra Song with tonight's top news stories. Earlier today, President Haines announced his plans for supe-justice reform."

"I will be signing an executive order," said the President, "to position this country for a new American future. A future where every supe has the god-given right to use their abilities to keep us safe."

"Mr. President! Sir!" shouted a reporter. "What about your comments from last week? You said *'the only good criminal is a dead criminal.'* Do you believe that, sir?"

"What an awful question," scoffed the President. "Do you disagree?"

Sandra's smile returned and broke the tension as she continued her update. "Amycus Industries announced a breakthrough in cybernetic intelligence." B-roll of scientists placing a human brain into a robot body cut to grainy footage of an old police investigation.

A group of kids were being ushered out of the woods, wrapped in blankets, and into the back of an ambulance. "And today we remember the Mum Murders, twenty-seven years later. We discuss the significance of the first supe-serial-killers with the leader of the F.B.S.I. task force, Codename Phantom. Agent Jonathan Graeber joins us for a discussion. What happened to the Grace Falls Seven, and a new lead on the killer who got away."

An old police sketch of a gaunt man in a wide-brimmed black hat and vacant eyes appeared on screen before fading back to Sandra's permanent grin. "Earlier this evening, a small gathering of Tin Men marched on the nation's capital, forcing the White House to erect a ten-foot barbed wire fence down Pennsylvania Avenue." Footage from the event displayed, as the men dressed in gray, with tightly tied hoodies over their heads and sunglasses, silently marched in protest. Some carried simplistic signs with big Xs over images of supes, including The Vigil and Crimson Justice. "Fortunately, there was no reported violence of any kind despite the V-Boy presence, who arrived claiming to keep the peace." The aforementioned V-Boys carried semi-automatic long guns and were dressed in army surplus fatigues barely covering their beer-bellies.

"I'm here to make sure those Tin Men don't do nuffin' dumb," said a V-Boy into the camera. "These idiots bring their fists to a gun fight. Shows how smart they are."

The interview cut to another reporter attempting to interview a Tin Man, who sat silently, staring off into the distance behind his sunglasses—the hoodie pulled so tightly over his face he was just a nose and a pair of lips. "Sir, can you tell us why you're here? Can you tell us anything?" But he didn't—the man did not even flinch.

"Tonight," returned Sandra, "following *American Supe*."

The screen faded to black, and the TV-MA warning appeared at the top right corner of the screen. Supes-Roundup returned with Rhea Ramsey walking toward the camera.

"What's it like inside the dark criminal underbelly of society?" Rhea asked the audience. "Come with us as we step inside the madness."

Each week, a new set of unknown actors staged campy, over-acted dramatizations. The writers, producers, and police consultants had no knowledge if the events depicted on screen were true or not, which didn't matter to the viewers—so long as the villains were evil and the heroes were good, all was right with the world.

"Welcome to the Dope Gang's hideout," said the narrator as a camera flew through the halls of the burned-out warehouse. "Inside these walls was an asylum of depravity. Come with us, as we introduce you to the notorious—the vile—the maniacal—Dope Gang."

Next, the show cut to a horribly disguised sound stage—a sleazy alley with fluorescent strip-club signs, brick walls slathered in graffiti, and flickering streetlamps. "The Dope Gang were named after various forms of illegal narcotics. Their powers reminiscent of their individual effects on the human body. These are their members."

"Moll-E." The narrator spoke her name like he was introducing a professional wrestler known for cheating and flipping off fans. Through a fog came a woman with fire-engine red hair. She wore leather pants and a bustier with a yellow smiley-face pin conveniently placed next to her bosom. Her face was painted like a sugar skull, and her mouth was an exaggerated smile. "Named after the illegal drug ecstasy, Moll-E's stare will infect you with extreme pleasure before igniting into a flaming inferno."

Moll-E punched an innocent man strolling through the fog, then grabbed him by the hair and said, "I'll make you feel good, punk!"

"Next, *just say no* to these evil twins," said the narrator. "Oxy and Perc."

Through the fog came two men in trench coats, assailing random innocents with fists and spit before tossing them to the ground. Their faces were partially obscured by a single Tragedy mask broken in half—the top portion covering Oxy's eyes, the bottom half covering the mouth of Perc, like two parts of a whole. After beating an old lady walking her dog through the seedy alleyway, they struck a pose for the camera. "Named after powerfully addictive opioids, this evil duo plunders your life-force, feeding off joy and happiness, then expels those emotions in terrible eruptions of power." The duo pointed their fingers at a pair of cops, who flew and tumbled away attached to high-tension wires.

The camera spun and caught up with the next member charging out of the fog.

"This is Annie Phetamine. She's a real live wire," said the narrator. Annie sauntered through the fog with a baseball bat, dual French-braided blonde hair, and skimpy shorts, dramatically clobbering cops while red and blue lights flashed off-camera.

"I'll give ya a spark, hon," she sneered from behind a domino mask, then placed an outstretched finger on an officer attempting to arrest her. There was a flash of light, and the officer fell to the ground like he had been shocked with a powerful zap.

"Named after the oft-abused stimulant, amphetamine, Annie's touch carries a powerful charge. And don't even try running. Annie will track you down with short bursts of super speed."

Annie looked like she belonged at the roller derby rink, with fishnets and a patched-up denim vest over a black tank top.

Behind Annie traipsed a similar, if not a more sinister, figure sporting pigtail-buns of blonde curls with streaks of blue. A streaky smudge of black makeup covered her eyes, with bright, electric blue eye shadow creeping out from beneath. She wore ripped jeans and combat boots and cackled like a witch enjoying a terribly unfunny joke. Red fingerless gloves adorned both hands. A ripped t-shirt spray-painted with an anarchy symbol rested beneath her denim vest, which was covered in patches and buttons.

She took the bat from Annie and began bashing cop heads, beating some of them over and over like she was lost on a sea of rage.

"Say hello to Crystal Beth," said the narrator. "Named after the illegal form of methamphetamine, this drug decays everything it touches." Beth struck a pose, gazed at all the injured cops on the ground, then laughed. "She's quick, she's strong, she's ferocious, an absolute maniac—and she's a killer."

The camera hung on Crystal Beth for a moment, allowing the flashing police lights to illuminate the crazy in her eyes before it panned away, and the mood darkened.

The fog suddenly overwhelmed the set and the lights refocused, casting a dark, ominous silhouette at the mouth of the alley. Out of the mist came a tall man, wide shouldered, wearing a short leather duster. He had dark hair, blue eyes, and a Japanese war mask with a wicked smile and curling fangs covering the bottom half of his face. His heavy brow hung low over his eyes, casting a brooding shadow.

"Their leader, the mastermind behind the Dope Gang's violent spree of crime and terror. Meet Dust." Several cops and even a few colorful supes tried to take Dust down, but he went toe-to-toe with them all, beating down three or four men at a time. Then he roared into the sky like an animal howling at the moon. "Named after PCP, NMDA, or phencyclidine—Dust is a rage machine. Gifted with super strength and invulnerability, he only gets more dangerous when angry. Stay away from Dust, or you'll surely end up dead."

The five members of the Dope Gang then came together for a psychotic cast photo, striking lewd poses before the show cut back to Rhea Ramsey, on location of the destroyed warehouse—formerly the Dope Gang hideout—with the Wonder City police commissioner.

"Commissioner Dudley, welcome to *Supes-Roundup*."

"Thank you, Rhea, it's a pleasure," said Dudley. In her fancy red heels, Rhea towered over the small man. They were pacing through the ruins of the warehouse, carefully stepping through debris.

"Commissioner," said Rhea, "can you tell me what transpired here that fateful evening?"

"At 7:15 PM, we received a call from neighboring businesses about a disturbance," said the commissioner as he wiped his white mustache to keep it from tickling his nose. "By the time we arrived on the scene, it was chaos."

"Mmmmm," said Rhea, nodding along. "Crimson Justice had already engaged the Dope Gang?"

"Yes," said Dudley. "There wasn't much we could do except stay back and let the supes duke it out."

"Yes, because your department decided against having a supe on staff," said Rhea, as if this were controversial. Several supe-cities had upgraded their police departments with supes and enhanced humans to battle the rising threat of supervillains.

"Who needs supes on staff when your city is…" said Dudley, who took a big gulp mid-sentence, "…protected by Crimson Justice."

"Great point," said Rhea. "What happened next?"

"Well," said Dudley as they paced through a section of the warehouse with an obliterated kitchen and a scorched, upended sofa. It didn't look like the asylum that had been described at the outset, and Rhea gestured at the camera crew to aim their focus at the commissioner standing by the rubble. "Six against one doesn't sound like good odds unless it's against Crimson Justice. The Dope Gang threw all they had at him, but in the end, he was too much."

The broadcast broke away to a reenactment. The word "dramatization" flashed on the lower portion of the screen as the six actors portraying the Dope Gang sat around in their hideout, snorting and shooting up drugs while Moll-E made out with both Oxy and Perc on the couch.

Annie Phetamine was dancing out of sync to death metal playing on the stereo while serenading two bottles of champagne, one in each hand.

Crystal Beth and Dust were arguing over who was going to snort the last line of coke when the door burst open and Crimson Justice walked in.

"It is I, your worst fear," said Crimson Justice, holding up his left and right fists. "Law and Order."

"Oh no!" screamed Annie Phetamine. "We can't go to The Cooler!"

"Don't worry, Annie," said Dust. "They can't put us in jail. We're too powerful to be locked up."

"Yeah!" cackled Crystal Beth as Moll-E ran over and kissed her too.

"Oh, I'm not taking you to jail," said Crimson Justice. "I'm sending you where you belong."

"Where's that?" asked Moll-E.

"Hell." He ran into the room, punching and kicking everything that moved. There were even cheap special effects to replicate Crimson Justice's extraordinary powers: The Red Death—a red mist-like tear gas, and the Justice Beams—a power blast that erupted from his mouth.

When it was over, a spatter of computer-generated blood splashed onto the television screen, wiping away to Rhea Ramsey and the commissioner.

"Why were the charges dropped against the Dope Gang following this incident?" Rhea asked.

The commissioner bent down and grabbed a stuffed teddy bear from the ground. It was charred on one side with fluff spilling out the other.

"We have laws in this country," said the Commissioner. "The Constitution gives people the right to live their lives as they choose."

"That doesn't answer my question, Commissioner," said Rhea, who was on the offensive. "If the law can't hold the Dope Gang accountable for their reign of terror, then why should supes like Crimson Justice respect the law?"

"Reign of terror?" questioned the commissioner. "You can spin it any way you want. They've committed crimes, sure. But that does not give Crimson Justice the right to murder."

"Murder?" questioned Rhea. She sounded aghast at the accusation.

"A young woman was murdered," said Dudley, "and another seriously injured. She's currently in police custody in a medically induced coma."

"The machine keeping that lunatic, Crystal Beth, alive should have the cord cut immediately," sneered Rhea. "And Annie Phetamine died while in the act of depravity and indecency."

"She was in the act of making macaroni and cheese," said Dudley with a humorless chuckle, pointing toward the kitchen opposite the camera. The camera panned toward a pot on the oven and an open box of mac & cheese on the counter.

Rhea's face twisted in shock and disgust as she quickly stepped aside to block the camera's view. Anything that painted supervillains as human was against the whole premise of *Supes-Roundup*.

"Are you actually the commissioner of a supe-city?" she asked as her eyes lit up, imagining the ratings. "Or are you a snowflake Sympie?" When things got political, ratings soared, and she was eyeing an Emmy nomination—not for Investigative Reporting, but for non-scripted—though *mostly* scripted—Reality TV.

"I'm an old man," sighed Dudley. "An old man who's tired of seeing needless death and destruction."

"Hmmm. Sounds like a Sympie—an anti-law, anti-supe, anti-patriot sympathizer to me," said Rhea with a wicked smile. "When we come back, we go to Metro City to remember the life and times of The Bolted, who tragically passed away a year ago this month—Next! On *Supes-Roundup*!"

The program faded to black for commercial break.

MASKED

CHAPTER 1

FIVE YEARS AGO...

WEDDINGS WERE FOR ASSHOLES. THAT'S RIGHT, DEAN SAID IT—weddings were for assholes. Well, truthfully, he didn't actually say it, but he was thinking it. If his thoughts had volume, they'd roar, and he'd chase that angry hot take with dueling middle fingers, spraying the room with big F-Us to every smiling wanker in the room.

Yeah, weddings were for assholes.

"Dean," said Peter with a patronizing tone reserved for deeply concerned friends. "Do you think grinding your teeth is the best way to spend the next three hours?"

"Three hours?" asked Dean incredulously.

"Yeah," replied Peter, again with the patronizing tone that made Dean want to wipe his face in the dirt. "When was the last time you were at a wedding?"

"You and Tammy's wedding," said Dean.

"Right," replied Peter. "That was six years ago."

"Fuck, has it been that long?" asked Dean. "Wait, how old is lil' Pete?"

"Six," said little Peter, sitting between his mom and dad and staring at the man who wouldn't stop using all the naughty words.

"Jesus," said Dean.

Peter said, "You know, nobody made you come to this."

Yeah, yeah. But he couldn't exactly miss it, could he? It was the principle. It was a statement—

—It was fucking torture.

"Pete, how long have we known each other?" Dean was having a hard time with the math. His head throbbed from the awful perfume radiating from the burly woman in the purple dress with the big hat that came scooching in beside him. It was summer. It was hot. The lawn was recently mowed, which made his eyes water just a little, and the tiny fold-out white chairs crammed them together like chickens in a tiny crate. Wasn't that what this was? A butchering? A throw-your-life-away party?

Fuck weddings.

"Nine, ten years, give or take," replied Peter.

Dean looked at him for a moment before realizing that his dear friend of a whole freaking decade was answering his question. Math was always Pete's subject—he was an accountant, after all—and he delivered. It suddenly dawned on Dean that the crowd was comprised of mostly people he had attended college with, just like Pete, Tammy, and Brie.

Twenty-eight years. He was twenty-eight. That was so depressing. Where did all that time go? All those days of playing ball at the park, goofing off at bars, and chasing after...*the one that got away...*

"Oh, I just love weddings," said the purple-people-eater sitting beside him. A mouthful of her rotten perfume hit him square at the back of the throat.

"Me too!" he replied sarcastically and a bit too loud. She turned away, squealing with glee.

"You know," said Peter, "you really could go. I could tell Brie you already left."

"You can't," replied Dean.

"Why?" he asked.

"Because I haven't told her I'm moving," said Dean.

Tammy leaned across her son and husband and glared at Dean. "You haven't told her?" It sounded meaner than she probably intended, but Tammy had been Dean's first love—Then one of his best friends after she woke up, dumped him, and started dating Pete. And look how that turned out? Her scolding was the kind you could only get from family, and that's what they were—family.

Dean shrugged as Tammy eyed her husband up and unsaid words were exchanged. Peter elbowed Dean politely for a private aside, which consisted of the two men leaning toward one another awkwardly and speaking in lower-than-usual whispers.

"You haven't told Brie?" whispered Pete.

"No," replied Dean matter-of-factly.

"Are there other things," started Peter discreetly, "you haven't told Brie that might have been important to discuss?"

"Why, Peter," said Dean theatrically, "I have no idea what you mean."

Peter's jaw dropped in sync to the musical rise of the procession theme, cutting off any additional commentary between them. This was typical, wasn't it? Peter giving him the third degree over something that really wasn't any of his business? Dean wasn't being an asshole. He had his reasons for not telling Brie.

Everyone stood. When it appeared Dean wasn't going to get up, Peter grabbed Dean's collar and yanked. He probably wouldn't have, if nobody made him.

Some moments come and go, fleeting like passing cars on a nighttime road—just lights zipping by. Other moments, the ones that land with a thud, happen to be the moments that pass like slugs across fresh tar. They linger, sometimes painfully, transmitting not-so-secret messages, unmasking the thinly veiled truths.

Brie in her dress was everything Dean hated about weddings.

She was blonde curls and pearls—a sparkling white dress that twinkled in tune to her blue eyes as much as they did to the diamond on her finger. The high slit in her dress exposed a tan thigh as she marched achingly slow up the aisle. Her aging father on her arm, blushing twice as much as she was—his eyes passed over Dean as if they were strangers.

She was radiant, a star, a daydream memory of days gone by—of things that were once within reach.

The thing was, seeing her made Dean realize that weddings weren't for assholes. He was just an asshole at a wedding that should have been his.

A prayer. Vows. The kiss. The proclamation of man and wife. The long march from the gazebo to the reception. The beer. Two beers. A shot and another beer. The food. The dancing. It all went by in a blur. Dean made sure to sit with his back to Brie and her husband, Lawrence. He couldn't bear to see them. In fact, he had already settled on one more drink until he would finally work up the courage to wish Brie well—a simple congratulations, nothing more—then storm out and off to start the next phase of his life.

"Want another?" asked Dean. He was sitting at a round table with a centerpiece so big, he couldn't see lil' Pete on the other side, which was probably arranged on purpose. Tammy seemed to think Dean was a bad influence, which was something of an overreaction. Dean had been staring at the centerpiece for the better part of an hour. It was an odd arrangement of cinnamon sticks and colored glass with a huge fan of peacock feathers that didn't exactly fit the wedding's motif. It was clearly a Pinterest abomination gone horribly wrong, and Dean laughed at Brie's horrible taste…in centerpieces, of course…among other things.

"How many have you had?" asked Peter.

"Slow down, bro," said Teddy. Dean hadn't seen Teddy since college graduation, and now this guy, Teddy the Tank, was going to tell *him* to slow down? Jake used to pick up a case of beer for Teddy every week back in college—whatever happened to ole' Jake?

"I'm fine," said Dean.

"Are you sure?" asked Madison, Brie's old roommate. She and her husband rounded out the seven of them, at one of three "college friends tables" directly behind a "high school friends table" in the back by the exit. A mini-reunion. Though Dean was still trying to understand why Teddy was invited—and Madison? She'd always been a chirpy nag. "I mean, you've like, literally had like, literally six of them."

"Literally had six?" questioned Dean. "I've had five, so it literally cannot have been six." His tone was angry. Probably a little extra vinegary than it should have been, but he didn't care. Was he really going to see Madison and the "Tank" ever again?

"I'll have one," said Peter. "C'mon, let's go."

They left before Tammy could protest. Peter always had Dean's back.

"You know, Tammy was fun once," said Dean after they were out of earshot.

"People tend to grow up when they settle down and have kids," said Peter.

Dean wanted to respond, but everything he wanted to say would just come out wrong. Everybody seemed like they were moving so fast. The world was spinning, and he was a fixed point in time and space. That needed to change. But why did he feel so awful about it? He was frustrated, and it was manifesting in vomitous social miscue after miscue. Everything sucked, and all he wanted, all he needed, was a ray of sunshine. An opportunity. A little hope.

"How did you know?" asked Dean when they approached the queue at the open bar as a couple of shoeless kids went charging through the line, howling with laughter.

"How did I know what?" replied Peter. There was a time, once, when the two of them could have communicated in shorthand. A nod and a half-formed sentence could mean all kinds of things—from "steer clear of the bathroom, I just nuked the toilet" to "sleep somewhere else tonight, I have a lady friend over and the landing gear has been deployed."

"How did you know Tammy was the one?" Before Peter could spill on what was sure to be a mushy litany of reasons that Tammy was the love of his life, Dean needed to clarify. "I mean, you and Tammy never made sense to me. She was a type-A sorority girl, and you were a—"

"—video game junky that probably killed half his sperm drinking Mountain Dew from noon till midnight?" Peter said, finishing Dean's thought.

"Yeah."

"I don't know, man. Opposites attract, I guess."

"Is that it? Is that your entire explanation?" asked Dean. "Look at her, Pete." Dean gestured back at the table where Tammy was wiping gravy off lil' Pete's face after licking a cloth napkin. "How did you end up with her?"

It wasn't a mean comment. It was actually a fair point. Tammy was beautiful. Smart. Charismatic. The breadwinner. She took charge. Heck, if it wasn't for Tammy, both Dean and Peter would have probably failed their last semester. Once she and Peter started dating, Dean reaped the benefits of having Tammy kick his ass into gear without the downside of being attached to a relationship that inevitably was going to implode.

Peter shrugged and said, "I got lucky, I guess."

"Why am I so unlucky?" asked Dean after a short pause. It was a moment of clarity hidden away behind all the frustrated banter and anger Dean had been wielding as a shield all day.

"C'mon, man," whined Peter, "You're not unlucky. You've just been…" Peter tried to find the correct phrase. Then he settled, unfortunately, on "…unlucky."

"Thanks," groaned Dean as they moved up in the queue. One step closer to adding another beer on top of the previous five. Then he could tell Madison she was now "literally correct."

"I can't explain it," said Peter. "It's not like I tried. Tammy just sort of fell into my lap."

"From mine into yours." It was harsh. It was the alcohol talking. "Sorry, I didn't mean to say that."

"It's okay," Peter chuckled. "You're not wrong. If she didn't date you, she would've never met me." Then Peter said something so profound and awful that Dean wanted to throw up. "If you and Brie weren't friends, she would've never met Lawrence."

Dean stewed on that for a moment.

"You know he has a sesame seed allergy?" said Dean. "Only point-two percent of people have it. The guy just touches one and his whole body swells up like a marshmallow."

"So?" said Peter, shaking his head. "I have a dog allergy."

"The point is…" said Dean, then double clutched and repeated himself. "The point is, if Brie was going to settle down with someone, I expected him to be perfect for her. I expected him to be that impossible soulmate that nobody could compete with. That girl loves herself a sesame seed bagel with cream cheese in the morning."

Peter sighed—not because he agreed or disagreed. It was admonishing, wishing his friend could move on.

The line was moving quickly, just one person left in front of them, as the song changed. One moment people were getting rowdy to Bel Biv Devo's "Poison," when a new melody queued up—something vaguely familiar. But it wasn't until someone yanked Dean's arm that his brain registered the song.

"C'mon, Puppy!" yelled Brie, her unbreakable grip on his arm dragging him across the room.

"Where?" yelled Dean as they arrived at the one place he'd rather not have been.

The dance floor.

"When I gave the DJ the song list," said Brie, all smiles and glowing like a movie star, "I snuck this one in. My way of saving us a dance."

Before Dean could comprehend what was happening, Brie had her arms around him, and they began swaying. It was their song.

Dean wanted to be anywhere but here. He wanted to be staring down at the empty bottom of one more bottle. "What is this?"

"'Angel,'" said Brie, glaring at him like he was suffering through a bad case of amnesia. "By Aerosmith."

"No," replied Dean, quickly adjusting to the music. "I mean, what is *this?*" It was amazing how Brie could grab him like that, thrust him into the spotlight, throw her hands around him, and suddenly he was more worried about stepping on her toes than he was at the fact that he was with her on her wedding day. "I mean, why are we dancing?"

"What do you mean, Puppy?" The smile hadn't worn off her face. Somewhere in Brie's world, she thought she was doing Dean an honorable thing—giving him a dance with the bride.

"Stop calling me that." Was there anything he hated more than that silly pet name? Especially now. "It's your wedding. Shouldn't you be dancing with Lawrence?" The man was the first Lawrence he had ever met that didn't go by Larry or Lar—the man preferred Lawrence, and somehow that didn't sit right with Dean.

"I have already, and I will again," she said. "But I planned this just for us, Puppy."

"Why?"

"What do you mean, why?" she asked with a smirk. She made everything seem like a game. And this wasn't a damn game. He was feeling awful, awkward—even guilty!—for the fact that he was staring at this beautiful woman who was now married. She wasn't his—and never would be. "You're my best friend. We're aces, remember?"

Was there anything worse than hearing that phrase come from the mouth of someone you dreamed would say something else? *We're best friends* was right up there with getting your cheeks pinched by your overzealous aunt on your fifth birthday.

"Yeah," groaned Dean.

"What's wrong?" asked Brie. "It's my wedding day." She said it like she was trying to get him into the spirit. Like he was being Grinchy with her own personal holiday.

"Nothing," said Dean.

If only she knew how many times he was standing at the edge of this moment—on the cusp of reciting paragraphs upon paragraphs of text and subtext that needed to be expelled from his soul—and yet he said nothing. He held onto it. Swallowed it like a poison pill. All because he didn't want to say something he might regret. They had a real bond. It had gotten them both through tough times—how could he ruin that? Even if it meant he would never be happy?

"It's something," she said—a super-sleuth in a white dress. "I know you, Dean. I know you better than anyone else in the world. Now spill!" It was a demand, and if there was one thing he couldn't do, it was hide something from Brie once she knew there was something being hidden.

"I'm moving."

"When?"

"Tomorrow," he said.

"What? Where?" she asked.

"Wonder City," he replied.

"But," she said, shaking her head, her face contorting into a wrinkled mass of confusion, "That's a supe-city. You hate supes."

"Yeah," he replied.

"Then why?" she asked.

"Because I need to start over," he said.

"I don't understand, Puppy—"

"—stop calling me that."

"…Dean."

They had stopped dancing. She was looking at him like he was breaking her heart, and he kept wondering, how did she not know that she had been breaking his for eight years?

"Congratulations, Brie," said Dean just as the music ended.

"Ladies and gentlemen," shouted the DJ, "it's time for the bride and groom to cut the cake!"

"Where are you going?" asked Brie as Dean backed away from her.

There were tears in his eyes. He couldn't hide them anymore. This wasn't what he wanted. He had no intention of doing this now...

"I always thought things would work out one day," said Dean. Brie's maid of honor grabbed her by the waist, laughing, then realized something was going on. Soon, everyone was watching them, the dance floor as quiet as a crime scene.

"I never knew," said Brie, like she was choking. She looked mortified.

"I thought it was pretty obvious," said Dean. "You were my everything."

Lil' Pete said, "What's happening, mommy?"

"Nothing, baby," said Tammy. "Uncle Dean's making a scene."

What was once a raucous party, with music and laughter, alcohol and shoeless children playing tag, was reduced to the quiet intensity of a wake. All eyes were on him, and Dean could feel the sudden closeness of a looming figure behind him.

Brie's eyes were the size of planets. Her irises whole oceans. Her tan, suddenly obvious that it came from a can, became a sickly orange color as she paled several shades beneath.

This was not how Dean had envisioned this moment—a moment he should have taken years ago, long before her special day.

"I have to go," said Dean, "because I can't bear to be near the *married* woman I love, any longer."

Dean didn't wait for Brie. He spun on his heel, narrowly avoided Lawrence, and strode for the quickest way out.

"Congrats, Lawrence," said Dean, aiming for the exit like an astronaut pod re-entering the atmosphere. He passed Madison and the Tank, mussed lil' Pete's hair, and gave Tammy a quick peck on the cheek before stalking over to Peter standing by the door.

Peter handed Dean a fresh beer and said, "I'm proud of you, bud."

"Thanks," said Dean, even though he didn't feel like anyone should be proud of what had transpired.

"Good luck," said Peter, who patted him on the shoulder as Dean stepped out into the night.

TODAY. FIVE YEARS LATER...

This parking garage at 7:30 on a Saturday morning was the last place Dean wanted to be. He would've preferred to be in bed, even if it meant wrestling with the chaotic dreams that invaded his sleep each night.

Squealing tires corkscrewing up the ramps from level to level were just annoying enough to keep his groggy mind at bay while he wrestled with a series of pre-dawn yawns. They were the kinds of yawns that snuck up when he least expected them—like the ninja assassins that attacked Wonder City last year.

Now that had been a shitshow.

Dean was unloading boxes out of the back of his Jeep while chugging on Pow!™ Energy Drinks like an alcoholic pounding double malts. The label promised to:

- "zap you up!"
- "level up concentration!"
- "power up strength!"

...but Dean had already swigged one can, was swiftly guzzling another, and was still struggling to concentrate on the uneven stack of boxes teetering on the hand truck. For whatever reason, that stack was as mind-numbing as long form division, and he barely reacted when it finally started to tip.

Just like Dean's life. A haphazardly stacked hand truck full of boxes waiting to fall.

He caught it after a last-second lunge, preventing them from spilling out all over the garage—and jammed his finger in the process.

"Goo—guh, mutha—fummmmm…" he groaned. He was too tired to curse.

His cell phone buzzed...*again*, followed by a recording in Rudy's voice. "Answer me!" Dean had tried to remove the recording from his phone, but Rudy knew more about that shit than he did.

Every five minutes, on the freaking dot.

Rudy's texts graduated from polite, to sans-punctuation, to ALL CAPS within a fifteen-minute span. Rudy's latest—an abomination to grammar—was a veiled threat hidden directly behind the nicety of "HEY BUTT FACE"—and it only got worse from there.

Dean was supposed to meet Rudy a half hour ago. If it wasn't for Rudy texting Dean with a "psychic feeling" that he had overslept, Dean would've blissfully snoozed through the morning, having only found comfort sometime between the hours of 5 and 6 AM.

"In the garage. Coming…" texted Dean before he took a last hearty sip of Pow! and prayed for it to extinguish his anxiety.

A car pulled into the garage with the stereo blasting as Dean closed the Jeep hatch and gave the hand truck a push toward the entrance. A familiar tune belted out a familiar chorus, and if Dean had something heavy in hand, he would've tossed it at the asshole for having the nerve.

"That fucking song," he groaned under his breath.

If Dean ever met Steven Tyler, which was a long shot, he was going to give that old crooner a piece of his damn mind—even if he was a supe.

It was like the universe wouldn't let him stop thinking about Brie. It was a goddamn conspiracy. Not like the @NON quacks and their loony theories—this was real. He couldn't get away from her, even when he closed his eyes.

Every few days he was cursed with dreams of Brie. He saw her face—shocked, aghast, stunned, offended, *appalled?*—her sparkling wedding dress and the crowd of onlookers glaring at him like he had just evacuated his bowels on the dance floor. That's what had happened, right? He *did* evacuate his bowels on the dance floor—he left a big, stinking, steaming load as he backed away from her after professing a love that had all but disappeared in the five years since—five long years of radio silence. A due punishment for a big stupid mistake.

It also didn't help that in his dreams he literally took a dump on the dance floor. A figurative reimagining of his literal dump…a literal reimagining of his figurative dump—both applied depending on the point of view.

His phone buzzed…*again.* "Answer me!"

The Wonder City Convention Center was a fresh new hell, and nothing was going to change, not this day, not ever. Every time the doom clouds overhead parted with a sparkling ray of sunshine slicing through, it evaporated before he could even feel its warmth.

Hope felt so fleeting.

Why was that? Why was he defeating himself before the day had even begun? Why was every obstacle in his path? Why was a gatekeeper standing in front of every opportunistic door?

"Pass," growled the security guard. "Sir, your pass."

Dean flashed his vendor pass, which hung from a lanyard around his neck, and expected the guard to step aside. That was how this worked, wasn't it? Provide a pass and ye shall enter—only this big lunk of beef wasn't budging.

"Hey," he said, his posture softening after a quick scrutiny of Dean's face.

Dean had seen this before, from a very specific crowd with very specific interests. One little selfless deed, and three years later, he'd still get people stopping him on the street. He would have humored the man if he wasn't already running late.

"Hey yourself," replied Dean with an awkward finger-gun gesture that made the security guard smirk.

"Don't I know you?"

"I don't know," said Dean. "I don't know you."

"Yeah." The guard beamed. "You're that hero guy." Dean nodded along, feigning embarrassment with a twist of bashful theatrics worthy of a daytime soap. It was one thing to have a quasi-famous face, it was another to have his 15 minutes of fame extended within the dregs of internet chat rooms. "Drew? Dan? Drake?"

"Dean."

"Dean! Yeah, Wonder City's own powerless hero," he said, taking Dean's unwilling hand and shaking it by force. "Man, you're a true inspiration."

"Nah," replied Dean, swatting at the air. "I did what anyone would do. Even you!"

"Not true," said the security guard, his white earpiece audibly crackling with static. "That was some fire, bro. We could all use a bigger set like you, if ya know what I mean?"

"Oh hey!" Dean laughed. "Watch it! This is my set, big guy."

Dean only wanted to go inside the convention center and start setting up for the day, and this guy wanted to pal around and discuss Dean's balls. It was only a matter of time before he…*wait…there it is…*

When the security guard's eyes glanced over something shiny on Dean's collar, his whole mood soured, like someone had soiled his protein shake with almond milk.

"Do you know where you are?" he asked.

"Excuse me?" Dean replied politely.

"Do you know where you are, bro?" This time with more aggression.

"Physically?" asked Dean. "Or are we talking, like, metaphysically?" It was too early in the morning for this kind of shit. The guy looked like one of the Khaki Klan, or a V-Boy—groups of vigilante wannabes that dressed up at night, armed from head to toe to the very tip of their small peens, while patrolling the streets looking for trouble. Many of them ended up in a holding cell, drunk, until the feds evaluated them. Vigilantes were illegal in most states, but the Ministry had other ideas. It was one of the many things Dean hated about the country—everyone wanted to be a supe.

Everyone but him.

"Bro, you're wearing a *Tin Men* pin on your jacket." He pointed at it with a big meaty forefinger like Dean had no idea where his collar was located.

Dean had forgotten all about it. Yeah, he pinned it onto his collar—*on purpose*—just a simple, silver Tin Men pin that usually went unnoticed. Most people didn't know its meaning, which gave more credence to the idea that this guy—this bald-headed brute with cauliflower-ear—was almost certainly a V-Boy—a Supie—defender of supes. Armchair criminal justice experts that learned everything they knew about law and order from watching *Law and Order*.

"Oh hey," said Dean, "look at that. I forgot that was even there."

"I thought you were one of *us*?" he asked. "A patriot."

"I am a patriot," said Dean, shrugging. "Just not one of *you*."

"I heard on FriendSpace that Tin Men were being funded by the Reformist Deep State CIA and that they've been putting fluoride in our water. Manipulating us for years."

"That's one *theory*…" said Dean. He wasn't about to argue unsolicited conspiracies with a V-Boy.

"Do you know what fluoride is?"

"No," Dean lied.

"It's a toxic agent that was designed by the CEO of FriendSpace to make us compliant idiots so we'd go along with all the Reformist plots to ruin this country."

Dean's head hurt. It may have been the Pow!™, but there were few things he could stomach less than this dipshit doubling down on idiotic conspiracies. Dean could have just shrugged and said, "I don't know, bro," but he didn't.

Instead, Dean said, "So, the CEO of FriendSpace created a toxic-stupid-chemical, which most dentists use to strengthen tooth enamel, that he gave to the Tin Men, and the CIA, to put into our water supply, and you heard this breaking news on his own platform, *that he created*?"

"Yeah, it all adds up."

"Does it though?"

The guard glared at Dean, his eyebrow twitching.

They were at an impasse.

"You do realize you're walking into Supes-Con." The brute looked more bewildered than angry, like he wasn't going to stop the chicken from walking into the lion's den. If Dean was a supe-hater, let him enter a world full of supe-loving-fanatics.

"Huh," said Dean. "Here I thought I was walking into a Star Trek convention." The look on the security guard's face morphed from *civil warning* to *miffed* in a blink, but Dean didn't let up—sometimes he didn't know how to take his foot off the gas. "Damn, I was really looking forward to meeting Jeri Ryan. I totally had a crush on Seven."

"Do you think I'm stupid or something?" asked the security guard.

Yes.

"Define *something*," said Dean.

Dean had never been in a real fight—though he had been blindsided a few times in high school. They were always lopsided affairs that couldn't have accurately been defined as an actual fight, though he probably could if he needed to. He wasn't weak or uncoordinated, but Dean had a sharper, blunter weapon than his fists—his cleverness—and he reserved his nastiest bits of repartee for bullies, especially those who belittled others.

"You think you're cute or something?" sneered the security guard.

"*Define something*," asked Dean in the same tone as before, followed by an "Answer me!" shouting from his back pocket.

It was Rudy, obviously, and his texts were getting belligerent. When Rudy swore, it was definitely going to be a fun day.

"You know what I think—"

"—I don't," said Dean, cutting him off, "and I have to go. I'm being summoned by a hyper-attentive morning person with a positivity complex that I have full intention of ruining someday."

Then, before the security guard could catch up to the first half of Dean's comment, he had already whisked away into the convention center with a shit-eating grin splitting his face.

"One of these days, Dean," he said under his breath, "you're going to piss off the wrong asshole." Then he chuckled to himself. "Not today."

He couldn't have been more wrong.

MASKED

CHAPTER 2

10:45 AM

MEN WERE ASSHOLES. THAT'S RIGHT, TORI SAID IT—MEN WERE assholes. Well, truthfully, she didn't actually say it, but she was thinking it. If her anger manifested, it would melt whole faces clean off the bone. She'd follow that critical assessment with a bellow of fuck-yous, making every offended ear bleed like they were being assaulted by nasty word boners.

Sitting on the edge of the bed, she stared across her room—her little slice of life. The framed photos of Grammy and Grampy, her music degree, and the childhood photos of times gone by were all collecting dust. The acoustic guitar in the corner had been left unplayed for months, and her dreams were circling the drain.

This wasn't the life she wanted.

She had dreams. Big dreams.

Recording her first album. Inspiring others with her music. Playing for a stadium full of people. Accepting her first Grammy award and dedicating that Grammy to her Grammy in her acceptance speech while wrapped in a feathered boa—just because. Finishing the tall stack of books on her nightstand. Eating pizza in Sicily. Marrying a handsome man and having a kid or two, if that was her destiny. Visiting the Giant's Causeway in Northern Ireland because it looked so 'effing cool. And last, but not least, conquering her fear of rodents and tiny dogs in costumes.

So where exactly had her life gone wrong?

Three weeks ago, she and Amanda were sitting at their favorite spot atop the old train-yard water tower at the edge of the city. Their feet dangled over the edge, scouring the skies for shooting stars—a childhood tradition they'd carried into adulthood.

They were always confused, and at times accused, of being sisters. Both tall, blonde-haired, blue-eyed—but the accusation was mostly levied at them when they were laughing. They always laughed so much, to tears if something particularly funny occurred. To the point that people just assumed they were related. And that's the thing, they weren't related, but they *were* sisters—and their relationship had been through hell and back time and time again.

But they survived. Together. Finding their way back to each other, their bond growing stronger every time. And so, that night, three weeks ago, they returned to their very first tradition—talking, laughing, and scouring the skies for shooting stars.

"I bet Cinderhella and Robo-Lad get it on all the time," said Amanda, making Tori laugh even harder than she already was. "Do you think he's packing something mechanical in those tiny shorts?"

Tori nearly spat out her beer—Amanda always had a way of saving the funniest, most stupid stuff while Tori was drinking. For her efforts, Amanda had gotten showered in alcohol many times over.

"What is up with you and supe romances?" asked Tori. "Did you get bored in the checkout line again? Browsed a copy of Supes-Weekly?"

"No," grumbled Amanda. "I mean, yeah, but I can't help but feel hopeful, you know? If a cyborg dude and a princess of hell with creepy horns can find love, then why can't I?" Tori could sense her impending backpedal to append her comment. "Why can't *we*?"

"Jordan and I are over," said Tori. She wasn't even wearing his ring. "For now." She took another swig and stared up into the starry sky, feet dangling over the edge of the tower, and sighed. "Even after all this time, after all you've seen, you still like supes?"

Amanda shrugged. "Supes have always represented hope to me."

"That isn't reality, though," said Tori. "They're nothing but a bunch of twisted dickheads."

"Twisted dickhead," she giggled. "I bet Robo-Lad's packing that."

"Shut up!" said Tori, laughing so hard it hurt.

When things got quiet, they doubled their efforts at watching the stars.

"Supes are human, Tor," said Amanda. "Maybe one day, supes will represent the hope, the dream, the impossible ideals—just like in the comics."

Tori wanted to argue. She felt the urge building but then spotted something streaking across the sky. "There!"

They had spotted no less than five shooting stars together—including the one Tori had sighted over Red Rocks, Colorado when they were on spring break. Amanda was too busy laughing at Tori's bad impressions of famous people, like De Niro, Pacino, and Pee Wee Herman, to see it—but it still counted. By the rules established on Amanda's fourteenth birthday, it counted so long as both their faces were angled at the sky. However, that did not include the two Amanda saw when she was on shrooms—for obvious reasons.

Then came lucky number six. A brief flash as it crossed the heavens in a brilliant fiery streak—there one moment, gone the next.

"Six!" shouted Amanda.

"Lucky six!" shouted Tori. "I knew tonight would be the night!"

"Five-second rule!" yelled Amanda. "Make a wish! Make a wish!" She'd heard that phrase once when they were kids and applied it as if it were an actual rule—a wish must be made no more than five seconds after seeing a shooting star, or it would never come true.

In the history of Tori and Amanda's friendship, all five previous wishes had come true for each of them. Ten total wishes that manifested, perhaps, not in the way they wanted, but the way they needed.

—friends forever—

—a dynamic duo—

—two-of-a-kind—

—A combo—like their first shooting star—both girls wishing for exactly the same thing. Two ten-year-old girls, staring at the starry night sky from the roof of Amanda's childhood home. A wish that had come true, through thick and thin—

—That they'd be together to see every falling star for the rest of their lives, followed by a pinky-swear that would last a lifetime.

"What'd you wish for?" asked Amanda after chasing her wish with a heavy sip of beer.

"I can't tell you that," scolded Tori. She was already feeling contented and buzzed and never wanted to come down—both from the buzz and the water tower. It was her happy place.

"Why not?"

"Because," said Tori. "You can't go around telling people what you wished for. It won't come true. Same rule applies to all wishes." Then, to hammer home her point, she listed every wishful thing she knew. "Thanksgiving turkey wishbones, leprechauns with four leaf clovers, birthday candles, white horses, fallen eyelashes, wishing wells, *shooting stars*." She should have stopped there, but another example popped into her head, and she mentioned it without thinking. "Magic lamps…"

"How are you going to wish on a magic lamp if you don't speak the wish out loud for the genie?" There was sass in Amanda's voice, like she had blown Tori's argument apart with the simplest loophole.

"You can tell the genie, but you can't tell anyone else," said Tori, "Obviously."

"Okay." Amanda sounded like she was giving up, but Tori knew better. She was scheming. She was pivoting to something else to get what she wanted. "Hypothetically, if you had three wishes, what would they be?"

"Easy," said Tori. "To record a hit song."

"That's one."

"Play to a sold-out crowd."

"Two," said Amanda, holding up two fingers.

Tori held onto the last one, as if she was unsure of its importance. Was this last desire worthy of a third genie wish?

"To find someone who loves me unconditionally."

"You already have that, dummy," said Amanda, shoving her playfully with her beer hand, amber droplets sloshing out of the bottle.

Tori smiled, then turned away to look at the stars. She hoped for another shooting star to change her wish. Nothing like wishing for something she knew would never come true.

"Wait," said Amanda. They had known each other for twenty-seven years, and there were nuances in the way they moved, in the micro-expressions that could be deciphered into whole thoughts and phrases. "Was that your wish?" When Tori didn't move, Amanda started laughing. "Oh my god, that was your wish."

Amanda always got what she wanted out of Tori.

"And now you know, and it won't come true," scolded Tori.

"I thought you were done with love."

"I am done with it," said Tori, "but it's not done with me."

"Sounds like your last breakup."

"It does." Tori nodded in agreement. Her love life was the gift that kept on giving. "What about you? You know my wish. What's yours?"

Amanda shook her head. "Nope, I guessed yours. Samesies or nothing."

"You're such a dick," said Tori.

"Shithead," said Amanda, firing back.

"Twatwaffle."

"Jerkoid."

"Shitastrophic Arsebadger," said Tori, her bottle next to her lips.

Amanda nearly choked on her beer, and they fell into a giggle-fit that made them sound like they were already drunk.

"Fiiine," groaned Tori after catching her breath.

Tori eyed up her friend as she kicked her legs back and forth over the ledge. It was a hundred-foot drop, at least, to the ground below, and it was so dark you couldn't see it. It was just a big black void of nothing, like staring into an abyss.

"Waiting," sang Amanda.

"You…" sang Tori.

"Uh huh." Amanda nodded.

"…wished for free pizza from Giordano's? On me?" said Tori, finishing with a cheesy grin worthy of one of Giordano's five-cheese slices.

Amanda shook her head dramatically from side to side. "No." Then she changed the direction of her head shake into an exaggerated nod. "But yeah! I'm starved!"

"Let's go!" said Tori. "I need validation from a nine-hundred calorie slice of cheese and carbs to fill the emptiness left behind by my invalidated wish."

Amanda laughed and brushed herself off as Tori started down the ladder first.

The two girls descended the water tower together. Going up was so much easier than going down. Going down always felt like they were playing a game of Russian roulette—would the next rung be rusted through?

They were halfway down when Tori's foot slipped. For a half second, she was weightless, as if she could fly, before she started to fall away—the black void below calling her home. Three rungs whipped by before she caught herself. The whole ladder tolled like a muffled bell as she grappled to it with a white-knuckled death grip.

She thought she heard his voice—the old man with the black hole eyes. *"Close your eyes, child."* It was a nightmare from her past that whispered into her ear when things seemed out of control. She shook off the dark thought and the shiver that followed, scolding herself for drinking that last beer.

"Are you okay?" asked Amanda from above. She hadn't seen Tori's fall. Amanda often missed things, just like that fifth shooting star—too distracted by her surroundings to see what was really going on.

"Yeah, I'm fine," said Tori. She took a deep breath and continued down. "Be careful. It's slippery tonight."

Once at the bottom, Tori found herself surrounded by chirping crickets, and the glowing eyes of a stray cat watched them from beneath an abandoned rail car. A streak of red zipped overhead, and Tori got excited—she almost called out *lucky number 7*, until she realized that wasn't a shooting star. That was something else.

"What's wrong?" asked Amanda as she hopped onto solid ground.

"Nothing," said Tori. "I wish this would all be over soon."

Amanda glared at her. Startled, her face blank and blinking.

"How did you know?" she asked.

"How'd I know what?" asked Tori.

"How'd you know what I wished for?"

Three weeks later, and the only thing that made Tori get out of bed was the fact that today was for Amanda. These were Amanda's plans, and she wasn't about to let her best friend down. Not now. It was Supes-Con Weekend, and Amanda never missed a chance to dress up, see all the costumes, hobnob with Supes, and grab a few comics for nighttime reading before bed.

If there was a reason to get out of bed at all these days, it was to do it for Amanda. It would make her happy. But just because it made Amanda happy didn't mean that Tori would be happy doing it.

She connected her phone to the Bluetooth speakers and thumbed the volume angrily until it maxed out, then thumbed it some more for good measure. Every gesture, every thought, every motion was an exaggerated push or pull—as if she wanted to punish everyone and everything around her, including herself.

"The Warrior" started playing. It had been their anthem.

But it wasn't until the lyrics *shooting at the walls of heartache bang, bang* blasted through those speakers, rattling her bedroom mirror, that her heart was truly in it. She pulled out finger guns, firing imaginary bullets at every man she had ever met. Why did they always let her down? Why did she always give them the opportunity to let her down?

"I am the warrior!" she sang in perfect pitch, jumping onto her bed like she was ten years old all over again, and she felt truly alive for the first time in…*forever*—

—until the gut-wrenching pain returned and she doubled over. Her very soul was bleeding, and she sobbed beneath the music until she gasped for air.

When the song finished, she grabbed her phone and put the song on repeat, then relived the torture all over again as she slipped on a pair of ripped jeans and combat boots, then slathered her face in makeup.

There was a knock on the door, followed by three angry bangs when she didn't answer. Someone yelled, "We're leaving in ten!" through the door, over the music.

Tori was almost ready. She pulled on her fingerless gloves and admired herself in the mirror. Her costume was complete—her platinum curls tied up in a wave, her makeup on point—but she felt hollow. This badass gal was just a shell.

When she opened her door, Cyndi was waiting for her, twisting her gum around her forefinger before slurping it back into her mouth. Cyndi's wig and makeup made her look happy, thought Tori, but she knew better.

"What's up with you today?" asked Cyndi.

Tori thought it was obvious, but some arguments that were better left unfought.

"I'm in a mood," replied Tori.

"No shit," said Cyndi.

Tori followed Cyndi down the hall, then down the stairs toward the glowing exit sign. Once beyond the door and into the light, Tori realized just how bright and cheery the day had bloomed. It felt strange to be storm-clouds and rain on the inside when the outside was sunny.

She was so distracted that she never saw the car pull up to the curb.

"Get in," said Grant, and they loaded themselves into the crap-bucket on wheels. It was a beat-down sedan with a muffler that dragged when the car dipped below thirty-five miles-per-hour.

Dream big, live small, Tori thought to herself—but all of that faded as they merged onto the highway, the skyline coming into view. Wonder City was beautiful, especially from a distance. She could see the rising towers and the ZepNews Balloons drifting over the city. It felt cathartic until Grant put the rap equivalent of death metal on the radio, blasting her calm into oblivion.

"You're late," said Grant. "Now we're gonna hit traffic."

Grant sucked the fun out of everything. He was a fun suck. A real fucking fun sucker.

"We're late?" questioned Tori. "You *just* got here." Every detour over the last few weeks felt like her skin was being dragged across a cheese grater. "When are we meeting the others?"

Cyndi checked her watch. "Two hours."

Tori sighed.

"Are you moaning already?" asked Grant, giving Tori the side-eye through the rearview mirror. It was the last thing she felt like enduring—being teased by Grant Gross.

"Trust me, Grant," said Tori, "you won't ever hear me moan."

Cyndi laughed. "Damn. This is going to be a such fun day."

When Tori was mean, people listened. When she was mean, people showed her respect. When she was mean, people left her alone. Maybe she just needed to hold onto this pain forever. Maybe this world was all about making yourself bulletproof. In a world full of supes, her strongest power against the harsh truths of reality turned out to be a broken heart.

CHAPTER 3

12:10 PM

"OH HONEY," SAID RUDY, "YOU'RE TALKING TO THE KING OF fiction! The mastermind of blow your mind! The breath-taking, scene-stealing, heart-beating Einstein of horror."

"The Einstein of horror?" questioned the kid, like he wasn't buying any of it—and that wasn't limited to Rudy's sales pitch.

"Have you heard of Stephen King?" asked Rudy, his eyes flaring with passion. The kid nodded, and his baby-double-chin wagged a moment behind the rest of his head. "He's better." Rudy's outstretched finger wagged in Dean's direction.

Dean had an impassive look on his face as he attempted to ignore Rudy's ridiculousness. Rudy made over-the-top underwhelming. He was the hype-man Dean never wanted.

"If he's the *king of fiction*," said the boy, "what are you?"

Rudy blurted, "Boy! I'm the queen of—" then paused, suddenly struck by the verbal snare the kid had trapped him in. "Oh, I see! You weasel. Get outta here! Shoo! Shoo!" The kid ran away with a grin that made Dean smirk.

"Stop scaring away the customers," said Dean as he sat back into his chair.

"Oh, that boy wasn't gonna buy nothing," scoffed Rudy, slapping the accusation from the air as he slipped on his Gucci shades to block out the fluorescent lights. He claimed they gave him migraines—but Dean theorized it was more fashion than function.

Dean checked his watch. It was already noon. At this rate, with the cost of admission and setting up a table, he might just make his lunch money back. A small portion of the five hundred bucks he didn't have.

"What makes you so sure he wasn't going to buy anything?" asked Dean.

"Dean. Deano. Dean-Dean lady machine," said Rudy, "You're a horror author trying to sell books without pictures at a Supes Convention. These people don't read novels unless they're ushered by the word *graphic*."

Wonder City was never more popular than during Supes-Con weekend. It was the tenth annual convention honoring superheroes, and there were going to be real-live Supers in attendance. The explosion of super-powered humans over the last few decades had taken over the populace and become a sensation unlike the world had ever seen. Comics, toys, action figures—these were no longer considered kids' stuff, as people collected hordes of memorabilia for their office or mantle. People were even buried in replica costumes of their favorite supe.

"On the Flamboyant-meter," said Dean, "you're at a zillion right now."

"Honey," sassed Rudy, "you noticed!"

Dean glared at him. "Stop calling me a lady machine."

"How are you ever gonna meet someone if you don't start thinking like a winner?" replied Rudy. "I'm your best friend, Dean-Dean lady machine. And I'm gay. That makes me the world's greatest Dean-hype-man."

The convention center was filling up, and Dean decided to ignore Rudy. Their table was along the far wall, opposite the entrance, which meant any new arrival would take at least an hour to make it all the way over to their section, and Dean had to be ready. Presentation, however, was everything—something they could both agree on. After Dean checked his inventory, he straightened out the six-foot banner with his name in big bold letters, then began fidgeting with a stack of postcards and picking imaginary lint from the tablecloth. With nothing more to futz over, he sat back down and checked his watch again.

Then…he checked his phone.

Rudy saw it, and Dean knew he saw it, but Rudy didn't say anything…*yet*.

When he was done, Dean tossed his phone face down onto the table and leaned back in his seat. Before long he found himself counting the number of Crimson-groupies that wandered by, losing track at a full dozen—including a shirtless guy who had carved the scales logo into his chest hair.

In Wonder City, there was no supe more popular than Crimson Justice.

The Red Knight. The Scarlet Guardian. He was the reason for the dramatic drop in petty theft—but also directly responsible for the rise in violent crime and property damage as villain syndicates, like the Dope Gang, arrived in the city to make a name for themselves.

In the United American States, not all cities had supes, and not all cities with supes were Supe-Cities. Most cities had outlawed vigilante justice, and it was only those cities obsessed with "law and order" that welcomed the help and put them on the payroll—along with a healthy influx of federal money and sponsorships. Thus the birth of Supe-Cities. Then came the obvious political split: those that supported supes—Supies—and those that did not—unaffectionately called Sympies. The names had originated from somewhere deep in the bowels of 5Dud, an internet message board known for subhuman opinions, repulsive male behavior, conspiracy theories, and other delinquencies.

Throughout the convention hall, from children in strollers to elderly in motorized carts, more than half the attendees were dressed as their favorite supe, and most of those wore their crimson proudly. Though, there weren't just Crimson Justice costumes or gender-bent takes—there were B-level supe costumes too and even a few villains here and there. Most notable were members of the Dope Gang and even a Savage Roach costume that was turning heads, if only for the supe's obscurity.

"I don't get it," said Dean.

"Hmmmm?" replied Rudy.

"I don't get why supes are still so popular."

"Yeah," said Rudy, "gorgeous men and women with perfect bods in skin-tight spandex—I don't get it either. What's there to love?" It was sarcasm at its finest, punctuated by an eye-roll Dean could see from behind Rudy's $500 designer shades. A dazzling display of wit and charm by the talented Oscar Rudolph, but only his mother called him Oscar.

"No," grumbled Dean. "I mean, look at the devastation? Look at all the death? The dismemberment? There's a nightly curfew because being out past 10 PM could become a death sentence."

"You know I don't disagree, Dean-Dean lady machine," said Rudy. "I know why you hate them, but it's the way the world works right now." A group of potential customers made eye contact with Rudy, then shuffled away before he had the chance to give them a sales pitch. "Sure! Walk away! Miss out on the next Stephen King! I don't care!"

But Rudy did care. He had just as much tied up in this endeavor as Dean. They both had day jobs, but it would've been so much better to do something they loved, together, rather than drone away at a nine-to-five that slowly murdered their souls.

Dean checked his phone again right after an Electro Girl cosplay waltzed by.

"Check that phone one more time, Deano, and I'm going to bitch slap you so hard, you'll taste nothing but my lavender-scented hand sanitizer for the rest of the day."

"That's aggressive," groaned Dean as he eyed up the surrounding tables. Most other merchants consisted of artists, writers, and craftsmen, too busy engaging customers or talking amongst themselves to witness their drama.

"I'm serious," said Rudy, this time more sympathetic. "You obsessively check your phone and it's not healthy. I don't even know her, and I hate her."

"Who?" said Dean incredulously.

"The creature!" replied Rudy. "The life-eating demoness? The one that visits your dreams at night, sucking your life away?"

"What?" scoffed Dean. "Are you talking about a succubus?"

"That's her!" said Rudy, pretending to forget her name. "Brie."

"Don't. Don't call her that." Dean was exhausted with the subject, especially after the last time they'd discussed Brie.

The first Dean-Brie-Intervention was initiated by Rudy and his partner, Arthur. They had him cornered in a bodega between the Benadryl and the Doritos—which made sense, since Dean was both irritated and depressed. Rudy and Arthur took turns playing good cop/bad cop, and Dean caved under the pressure, deleting her number from his phone and removing her from his FriendSpace account.

"Has she called you since the wedding? Has she sent you a text? Has she attempted to show she cares about you in any way, whatsoever, over the last five years?" asked Rudy.

"No." Dean looked down at his hands, then at the stacks of books on the table with his name printed on the cover. He had become an author because of Brie. She always told him he was good at telling stories, and he decided it was time to make some moves. He spent hours at night after work, typing away at his keyboard in a dark room, putting together his masterpiece only to send Brie an early copy she never read. Every time he asked if she had a chance to read it, she told him she was too busy planning the wedding.

"Well, I don't really read fiction, or books for that matter, but I'll get to it," she said, followed by, "Congrats! I'm so proud of you for chasing your dreams."

But what good was reaching for a dream when there was no one there to share it with?

When it came to Brie, Dean had a huge blind spot. He always gave her the benefit of the doubt, even when she didn't deserve it.

"Then why," professed Rudy, looking into the rafters of the convention center as if speaking to the gods, "why, why, why do you keep looking at that phone? Why do you keep hoping she will magically remember that you were an important part of her life? That she suddenly realizes she cannot live without you and comes crawling back?

Dean shrugged. He knew it was awful. Every time his phone beeped, buzzed, or trilled, his heart fluttered at the potential—the chance, however miniscule, that it might be Brie. It never was. In five long years, the only interaction he had with her was liking an updated profile photo she uploaded onto FriendSpace—her first ever since the wedding without smooching Lawrence. It was like they kept taking the same photo—lips mashed together— and Photoshopped over a new background each time.

"I don't know," grumbled Dean.

12:15

The convention center was in the heart of downtown Wonder City. This was the good section of town, where the streets were prowled by licensed supers like Crimson Justice. A dozen blocks away, past Monaco Park and the art museum, things got rough—where the vigilantes took justice into their own hands. Mega-cities like Wonder City were too big for their own good, and the police force was overmatched by a growing population of supers looking to make a name for themselves.

Really, though, what was so wonderful about this city?

In fact, the wonder in Wonder City hadn't been so wonderful in quite some time. The city was a mess. The once shiny veneer that gave the city its luster had long since been scraped away after heavy abuse, not to mention the night-after-night battle between *good* and *evil*.

Tori remembered what it was like in the beginning. She was just a little girl when her mom took her to see the big city sights. They marveled at the skyscrapers, ate delicious food, and even cast wishes in wishing wells. She saw Mayor Haines give an important speech that day, long before he became president—her mother wanted to meet the man in person.

"See that man?" her mother said. "He's going to do great things for our country one day."

Sometimes *great* didn't mean *good* either.

It was a special day. She even went home with a t-shirt.

"Wonder City," Tori read aloud. "The Eastern Beacon of Hope."

Funny how the memories came when they wanted, bubbling up after the slightest reminders, but never when she wanted them.

"Need any help, ma'am?" asked the merchant with a belt buckle the size and shape of Texas.

"No," said Tori, admiring the t-shirt on the rack next to a *Crimson is Justice* t-shirt. "I had one just like it as a kid."

Tori didn't have any cash. Nobody said admission was going to gobble up her last twenty bucks. She may have bought the t-shirt, if for nothing more than the memory…

The merchant glared at her suspiciously, appraising her costume like he was trying to grasp a joke that had soared over the yawning bald spot on his head. The face paint, the hair, the denim vest and pins, the torn jeans and boots—she almost forgot she was wearing them.

"Maybe I'll come back," she said, then slunk away into the crowd.

Supes-Con was a wonder to behold, but just like its host city, that wonder didn't mean it was any good. Tori felt these cons attracted the wrong kinds of people. Supe fascination was entirely expected, but the obsession made her uncomfortable.

The convention was a giant indoor festival. Amidst all the comics, autograph booths, the replicas, t-shirts, and other memorabilia were items of a more heinous nature. There were vendors selling Blu-ray collections of the greatest supe eviscerations caught on cam. Crimson Justice had his own three Blu-ray set. But the depravity didn't end with explicit violence—there were nude photos of Saturna the Alien Princess and Robo-Lad; there were bloody costumes worn by supes—the price of the garment determined by the blood's owner; and items far worse. If one was determined to be disgusted, all one had to do was browse long enough.

However, every now and then something stood out. Like books, old-timey steampunk costumes, and a fuzzy monster purse with googly eyes and fangs. Amanda would have loved it. Tori was a grown woman, but she would've bought and used and loved that purse until the eyes fell off.

She was admiring the fuzzy green one and purposely attempting to avoid the price tag when someone yanked on her denim vest.

"Hi," whispered a little girl. She had curly hair and a dark complexion that made her bright green eyes pop like jade, and she was dressed in an unfamiliar costume. She had black and gold pants, a black jacket, and bright star-shaped earrings.

"Hi sweetie," said Tori, kneeling beside her. "What's your name?"

"Sally," she said.

"Hi Sally, I'm Tori. Where's your parents?"

"Daddy's over there." She pointed to a man haggling for a Crimson Justice cape replica and howling over the price. "Are you the real Crystal Beth?"

"Do I look like the real Crystal Beth?" replied Tori.

"No, she's scary. My daddy says she's the worst."

"Well, your daddy's right about that," said Tori.

"My daddy says Crimson Justice is our savior."

"Well, daddies can't be right about everything, now can they?"

The girl smiled—her two front teeth were missing. It was the kind of friendly smile that Tori needed, and she gave one back in return. It had been way too long since she last smiled. Not since shooting star number six.

"I like your tattoos," said Sally, and Tori angled her arm so she could see the whole sleeve.

"I like your eyes," said Tori, making Sally blush. "Love the costume. Who are you cosplaying?"

"My own super," she said and balled her fists, striking a pose. "I want to fight for people like me."

It was sweet. It was honest and innocent, but there was something about what she said that scared Tori right down to the bone.

"Fight is an interesting word," said Tori. "Remember, you don't need your fists to fight." She took the girl's hands and unballed her fists. "You can fight just by being you and standing up for what you believe in."

"What do you believe in?" asked Sally.

Tori opened her mouth to speak, but nothing came out. She knew the answer, didn't she? Or had she lost it along the way?

"Hey! Get away from her!" It was Sally's father, and he was charging in with a finger angled directly into Tori's face. "How dare you talk to my daughter dressed like that!"

"Hey," said Tori, backing away with her hands up. She wanted to curse, but Sally was still watching—the girl's eyes wide and frightened. "Hey, it's just a costume. Chill out."

She should have stayed with the others. There was safety in numbers. Especially when dressed as the most notorious supervillains since the Syndicate went underground.

"You chill out! Infecting my girl with that-that-that nonsense!"

He was pointing at her t-shirt.

Tori quickly covered herself with her denim vest and spun to move away. She didn't want to make a scene. Not here. Not with Sally watching— her eyes watering as her father raged. She swam through the crowd, past a congregation wearing...*bedsheets?* Then she slipped into the hallway and jogged to the escalators.

This may have been Amanda's day, but the way things ended with Jordan last night, she wasn't sure how much more she could withstand.

She felt broken inside. She wanted to get far away from everything, including herself.

Tori stepped off the escalator and caught her reflection in the glass pane of a directional kiosk. This was the face of someone who didn't like who she was. This was the face and costume of a killer, and Tori didn't know why she was doing this.

All she wanted, all she needed, was some shred of something good to hold onto, so she didn't fall away into the black void below.

12:20

"You're an addict, Deano," said Rudy. "Brie is your drug of choice. If you're not chasing her, you hope she's chasing you, and that's not hope, that's poison! Remember, I'm not just your best friend, or your peer, or your business partner, but I'm also your sponsor." Then he held out his hand and waited.

"Are you looking for a low-five," asked Dean, "because I have to tell you, that went out of practice long before the high-five."

"Your phone," demanded Rudy. "Give it to me, Dean."

"You're crazy."

"Am I?" said Rudy. "Trust me, as your best friend, I know what's good for you. When Franklin ripped out my heart and Hammer-danced all over it, the only thing that got me through was to take away the crutch. You may be hanging on *only* by a thread, but it's still a thread. And if you don't sever that tie fully, you'll never notice the gals right in front of you."

"Hi!" said a female voice.

Rudy slid his fancy shades down the bridge of his nose so Dean could see his eyes. They were wild and serious. He made a slight twitching gesture, indicating that Dean should fork over his phone and help the young lady who had approached his table unsolicited.

It took a beat or two, maybe even three, but Dean eventually relented, handed over his phone, then turned to the woman with a delightful, "Hi! How are you? Enjoying Supes-Con?"

She was dressed as a gender-bent Crimson Justice with a bare midriff and thigh-high boots. She had cute freckles, and Dean found her attractive even though she had chosen the supe he despised the most to cosplay.

"It's okay," she said. "I'm actually not much of a supes fan."

"Oh, really?" said Dean, perking up. Common ground was good. He peeked over at Rudy, who was sitting back and smirking like a raging lunatic. "I'm Dean."

"I'm Kristy," she said. "Did you write these? *The Knightmares*?" She read the title in a way that made his chest pitter-patter.

"I did," said Dean.

"Is it part of a series?"

"It will be," he replied.

"Who did the cover art?" she asked. "It's rad."

"Hello," said Rudy, sliding into the conversation and placing a hand on Dean's shoulder. "I'm Dean's best friend and cover artist. I'm also his hype-man, and I'm here to say he's a gifted individual with a talent for storytelling..." During Rudy's brief pause, Dean thought Rudy might actually be the best wingman he'd ever had. Rudy put Pete to shame—Pete couldn't put five words together in front of a pretty girl until he met Tammy. The fact that Dean had doubted Rudy made him feel guilty—until Rudy added one final thought. "…and single."

"Oh," said Kristy.

It was the kind of "oh" that wasn't good. It wasn't quite a startle, but it also wasn't labored or exasperated either. It was a caught-off-guard "oh" that left Dean with a pit forming in his stomach.

There was a crowd of people behind her he hadn't noticed. A crowd of people that appeared to be fighting for position, as if someone important were amongst them signing autographs and taking pictures. As Kristy looked back at the crowd, it parted on cue, and out walked a glowing Greek god made of tanned abs, pecs, and biceps wrapped in a brilliant white toga.

"Hey babe," said the man—his skin was so taut and toned, it was like he was made of pure rebar. "What've you found here?"

"Some cool books." Kristy gestured to the man. "This is my boyfriend, Apollo."

The crowd had followed him over, and for the first time ever there was a swarm of people looking at Dean's books. Most of them were in awe of the newest supe in Wonder City, but Dean suddenly felt exposed, and he had the sweaty brow to prove it. Apollo had been in town for a few weeks and was already making headlines. According to reports, he had the strength of a hundred men, was bulletproof and impervious to pain, and was a self-described hedonist who bragged often about his ability to glow when aroused.

"*The* Apollo?" Rudy gasped.

"The only," said Apollo.

His smirk looked like it was engineered in a lab. Every single hair on the top of his sandy blonde head was in precision with the others, like his coif was crafted out of the finest marble. His skin was a flawless sheath of perfectly tanned leather, his bare chest as smooth as a baby's bottom after being dipped in Nair. His hands were huge, his eyes were ocean blue, and he smelled like clean sheets—which was probably just the toga but intoxicating all the same. The man was flawless down to a molecular level, and it took only a single moment for Dean to dislike him.

Dean loathed him, not because Apollo was good-looking and a supe. Not because of the awful gossip surrounding his championship win on *American Supe*. Not even because most supes were no-good, even the ones who were supposed to be all-good. Dean disliked everything about him because of the way he walked, talked, looked, smiled, and stood. He was a pompous ass, and it took Dean all of ten seconds to identify the arrogance. Sometimes, Dean couldn't hide his disdain, despite all the well-documented instances of his brutal honesty getting him into trouble.

"I thought I'd show up to brighten everyone's day," said Apollo, speaking to Dean and Rudy like they weren't even there. "Meet all my brilliant people. I call them my Sunnies. You know, like the fish."

"Like the fish?" questioned Dean. "What does that have to do with you?"

"Psshhh, nothing," said Apollo, apparently flabbergasted. "Apollo was a sun-god."

"Are you a god?" asked Rudy, almost gushing.

"You tell me. These muscles," said Apollo, flexing, "*are* heavenly."

"Why not call your Sunnies a cult?" offered Dean. "The Greek god, Apollo, had cult worshippers."

Apollo's face darkened, and oddly, so did the room.

"Dean," whispered Rudy into his ear, "now's not the time to prove how smart you are."

"Did you just call my Sunnies a cult?" asked Apollo, and the swarm went quiet. The crowd hung on every word.

Kristy said, "C'mon, babe, I don't think that's what he meant."

Apollo put his hand in her face and said, "Shush now, men are talking." She immediately stopped.

"Oh no," groaned Rudy—he knew what was coming. Some things were inevitable.

The second Dean-Brie-Intervention had transpired last month at a swanky bar uptown, when Rudy and Arthur attempted to illuminate Dean on his unfortunate paraphilia.

"You have a hero complex, Dean," said Arthur while sipping on a mojito. "Some men prefer brunettes—"

"—Others like feet," added Rudy while obsessively stirring his blueberry martini.

"Yes, some do," said Arthur, embarrassed at the suggestion. "Dean, you prefer damsels in distress."

"I think you're making this up," groaned Dean.

"Honey," said Rudy, "take a look around this bar. Tell us, which of these fine ladies stirs *your* martini?"

Dean had to play along. They wouldn't leave him alone until he had spotted someone that fit the bill. And it had to be an honest selection, because whether he liked it or not, Rudy and Arthur knew when he was lying.

"Okay," said Dean, "Her. The brunette drinking Scotch at the end of the bar."

Rudy and Arthur spun in their chairs, looked at the woman briefly, then turned back to each other and cackled. Their hilarity made Dean uncomfortable.

"What?" asked Dean. "What's so funny?"

"Dean," said Arthur. "That woman exhibits a multitude of problems. Many more than you, which is troubling."

"How do you know that by looking at her?"

"Deano," said Rudy, "I'm a gay black man. I know oppressed when I see it."

"Out of all the women here," added Arthur, "you chose the one who's obviously taken."

"What? How do you even know?" asked Dean, smacking his beer against the table in frustration.

"She's wearing a ring," said Arthur, wiggling the appropriate finger.

"And she's drinking a Scotch. That girl's here to forget something," added Rudy.

He had no sooner finished talking when a man entered the bar and approached the girl like a heat-seeking rocket. At the sight of him, the two started bickering—which quickly ended with her drink being flung into his face. She stormed out a second later, stomping past Dean on the way.

As she passed them by, Dean felt something. A twinge. A tug. A gravitational pull. A need to grab a napkin to dry her tears. Then he took a gulp of beer, looked at his friends, and said, "I hate you. Both of you."

Rudy and Arthur snickered, but they were right. They were almost always right. Dean had a hero complex, and in a world full of supes, that was a dangerous thing to be.

"Do you think that's manly?" scolded Dean, erupting from his chair to look Apollo eye to...*nipple?* "Putting your hand in a woman's face like that?"

To say Dean had a deep-seated problem with men abusing women was like saying clowns could be creepy. As a man, Dean couldn't really understand how women felt. Yet seeing such behavior made his blood boil.

Dean was not a hot-head. Dean wasn't even confrontational. But like all people, he had his buttons, and this supe jammed a meaty finger onto the one button Dean couldn't ignore.

Apollo looked stunned—how often did a normie have the balls to stand up to a supe?

Rudy slowly backed away, took out his phone, and began recording the confrontation.

"Hey everybody," said Rudy nervously. "We're live on FriendSpace!"

Apollo brightened. Everything about him—his hair, his eyes, his teeth—all started glowing. He looked bigger and stronger too, like someone had said "lights, camera, action!"

"Dean, huh?" said Apollo, playing nice for the camera. "Nice shirt. Is that like science or something?"

Dean reflexively looked down at his t-shirt. It was a novelty tee lil' Pete had bought him on a field trip. It was a periodic table square for the element "UM" and a caption stating "The Element of Confusion."

"Oh, yeah," said Dean. "I'm sure the science flew right over your head."

Rudy stifled a gasp. Dean was going all-in like he had a death wish.

"Hah, funny guy," said Apollo with a humorless chuckle. "So, you're a horror writer, huh? At a Supes-Convention?" The crowd around them giggled. "That's so dim. I think you're in the wrong place at the wrong time, dimwit Dean."

"Yeah!" shouted one of Apollo's Sunnies.

"Story of my life," quipped Dean. "Getting kinda bright in here, big guy. Are you getting a glow-boner?"

"Oh, heavenly father," whined Rudy, both at the boner and the impending murder.

"Tell you what," said Apollo, aggressively poking Dean in the chest with a meaty forefinger. "I'll buy your book."

"Which one?" asked Dean. He had written three.

"I don't fucking care," said Apollo. "Sell me one of your books."

"What if I don't want to sell you a book?"

"I want to buy a book," said Apollo, glowing brighter than before. "Sell me a damn book. Now."

Dean may have been stupidly brave, but he wasn't plain stupid. He grabbed a book without looking, jammed it into a bag and handed it to Apollo.

"That's twenty bucks," said Dean.

"That's all?" scoffed Apollo. "How dull."

"Well, you know," mumbled Dean, "cover price."

Apollo reached down into his toga, somewhere between his massive pecs, and removed a roll of cash as fat as his own massive thumb. "Got change for a hundred?"

"No," said Dean.

Apollo slashed a mirthless smile and leaned forward, putting his face into Dean's personal space. Rudy moved in, his live feed blowing up to a few thousand viewers. Apollo smiled at the camera, then back to Dean.

"There's a bank. Across the street," said Apollo. "Go get change for my hundo."

"But that—" started Dean. He wasn't even sure what excuse he was going to use, just that he didn't want to go across the street to get change for a hundred-dollar bill.

"Go, or I'll rip off your nipples, then choke your lights out, live on FriendSpace." Apollo gestured to Rudy and his phone.

Dean left the convention hall, dodged a few cosplayers taking dramatic photos in the hallway, and scooted down the escalator before his anxiety caught up to him. Outside the convention center, he doubled over at the corner as Supes-Con ticketholders passed him by, wondering if they might need to call an ambulance for the guy having a breakdown.

Someone dressed as Karma Chameleon, the Supe from Portland, stopped to see if he was okay, then proceeded away after Dean caught his breath. Apollo had given Dean fifteen minutes, and five of those minutes had already passed.

The bank, Wonder City First National, was on the opposite corner. It was a huge structure reminiscent of a mini-fortress. With so many supervillains and attempted robberies, banks had been fitted with top-of-the-line technology and security. It was like entering North Korea…before the Supe invasion.

Once through the revolving door and past security, Dean stumbled headfirst into the queue. He had never seen a bank this full, not even after the Cash Vanishing—when Doctor Insane-O made all the money in the world disappear. There were no less than sixty people inside the bank, and each of them were dressed in cosplay of their favorite Supes or wearing Supe gear, as if the convention center had overflowed directly into the bank and surrounding businesses. The line weaved itself through the cordoned maze, then extended toward the offices at the back, where it made a zig-zag before wrapping around a pillar. A second line queuing into an overwhelmed ATM was intermixing to the point that Dean didn't know where one or the other line ended.

He checked his watch. Seven minutes left. He had to call Rudy and beg Apollo for an extension. Dean reached into his pocket and retracted his hand with the same kind of terror reserved for almost touching tarantulas and scorpions—

—Rudy still had his phone.

"Hey buddy," said some guy dressed like Green Falcon—Defender of the Skies. "The line ends back there."

Dean paced over to the end of the line, passed angry patrons who thought he was butting ahead, and stood there while counting every second.

There was no way he'd meet Apollo's demand and began to rationalize which option was best to prevent the removal of his nipples at the hands of a sociopathic supe. Return Apollo's un-cashed one-hundred dollar bill? Or wait it out, and explain the overloaded bank situation?

It was a valid excuse, right?

Dean was so caught up in his own troubles he hardly noticed the random assortment of cosplayers around him. The twenty-or-so Crimson Justice costumes, the Dope Gang—including a spot-on Crystal Beth and Dust cosplay—even a Rhea Ramsey look-a-like. Dean was so caught up in his own worries that he never heard the mechanical click or the scream. He barely saw the commotion—and the woman shouting, "No! What are you doing?"— before someone spun him around and hit him like a bulldozer.

Dean was out cold before he hit the floor.

CHAPTER 4

12:40 PM

CRIMSON JUSTICE ARRIVED ON THE SCENE IN A CLOUD OF DUST and debris. He landed at the center of the police barricade, cracked the pavement, and upended one of the cruisers—he even set off security systems on nearby cars and stores. A few bystanders had to be taken away for medical attention after being struck by flying junk.

Commissioner Dudley groaned. The mayor was sure to bill *him* for the damages.

The standoff had started only moments ago, and there were already tens of thousands of dollars in damages, caused solely by the super who had arrived in dramatic fashion as always.

Out of the dust cloud stalked a beast of a man—his shoulders as wide as a padded football player and covered in red and black leather. He wore a red hooded cowl and a black mask that allowed his wide jaw to protrude into the light—the only part of his face not obscured in shadow. The knuckles on his gloves were carbon fiber and stained with blood—they did not appear to have ever been cleaned, as if the stains themselves were trophies.

"Commissioner," growled Crimson Justice in greeting.

His voice was ridiculous, like he was gargling on a mouthful of thumbtacks.

"Crimson Justice," said Dudley, greeting the behemoth with a respectful nod.

Crimson Justice had appeared six years ago, and despite the collateral damage, he got things done…*mostly*. Commissioner Dudley often wondered why this lunatic was adored by so many. If they had half the interactions Dudley had with the masked man, they'd have called him a monster. Or an idiot.

Christopher Dudley was sixty-eight years old and had been dealing with supes for the last decade as Commissioner. He'd pleaded with Mayor Cromwell to let him retire, but Cromwell kept dangling the carrot of a full pension if he stuck around two more years. Dudley's wife agreed that a retirement on a supe-less island off the coast of Spain was well worth a two-year wait—if he survived. However, with the way things were going, the pension plan would be bankrupt, with all the damages being paid directly out of their retirement.

Dudley started his career twenty-eight years ago as a beat cop, before supers appeared everywhere across the globe. Those were simpler times. Petty theft, burglary, and the occasional murder were part of the day-to-day, as were the friendly services of attending school assemblies, rescuing cats from trees, and helping old ladies cross the street.

The world was a much different place with supes, and more of them were popping up every day with god-like abilities. It seemed like the more of them there were, the more *flawed* they became. Some had big, angry chips on their shoulders, but most were just awful human beings, and that included the *"good"* ones. Supes could do anything, and there was nobody there to stop them. Maybe that was why so many of them were awful. No accountability. No repercussions. Just money, fame, and power.

The rise of the supervillain had been steadily climbing the last eight years. The line between hero and villain had blurred. Just blocks away was an anti-supe protest, and the attending crowds had grown every year. These weren't your normal everyday "Sympies" either—and Dudley loathed that term. They called themselves Tin Men, and more and more "villains" joined their ranks every day. But these weren't the usual villains, like the Syndicate and their organized crime, or terrorists like Doctor Insane-O or the morally askew Killjoys. This was a new breed, battling vigilantes in the streets who felt the need to defend supe honor, even though supes could easily defend their own. It seemed like these vigilantes—these V-Boys and Khaki Klan—just wanted someone to fight, someone to bully, someone to murder. It was hard to understand who was good, who was bad, and who was manipulating the story.

The tension was broiling, and a spark could set the whole city ablaze.

"I heard the innocent cries of the meek calling out for Justice," said the supe. "It—has—come."

The commissioner had grown used to the melodrama—but it always impressed him how dedicated Crimson Justice was to speaking like a total dumbass.

"The Dope Gang tried to rob the Wonder City First National," said the commissioner. "Our negotiator gave them four hours in exchange for thirty hostages, and they immediately complied. But there are still an unknown number of hostages inside. We may not need you for this one—"

"The law never negotiates with felons and murderers," said Crimson Justice, moving at once toward the bank, his words chilling Dudley to the bone.

"Now now, hold on," said the commissioner. When Crimson Justice turned back toward Dudley, there was something about his stare that nauseated the commissioner. "I understand your interest in taking down the Dope Gang once and for all. Please take considerations. There are innocent people in there."

Crimson Justice leered at him, like the old man was confused about his place in all this.

"Law and order are my only considerations. The President has blessed me with impunity to reap justice," he said, pointing to the supe-license badge on his belt, "and the authority to uphold the law. Let villainry everywhere be warned. Crimson Justice has come."

"Did you say *villainry*?" asked Dudley.

"We love you, Crimson Justice!" screeched a gaggle of fans from behind the barricade.

"I wanna have your Crimson baby!" shouted another.

"Listen," said the commissioner, "destroying public and private property, wrecking police vehicles—they cost us a lot of money, but they can be replaced. Lives cannot be replaced. There is a line that cannot be crossed. A lot of people are growing increasingly agitated over the reckless endangerment of innocents. This sentiment is starting to make our jobs harder to perform, and the President's protections only extend so far." He scrutinized Crimson Justice, searching for a sign that the giant man understood him. "Do you grasp what I'm trying to say?"

"When the dawn of a new day sires the coming tide of order, I will rest," said Crimson Justice. "Till then, stay out of my way."

12:42 PM

"Hello FriendSpacers! Fans! Beloved followers!" said Rudy, holding his phone up to hit one of his many *angles*—the right side, three-quarter profile was his breadwinner. "Welcome to Moody Rudy's vlog! Those of you who are just tuning in, say hello to the new supe in town, the bright spot at an otherwise gloomy Supes-Con. Everybody, welcome Apollo to the broadcast!" In the background of Rudy's live stream was Apollo, his head resting in the palm of his hand, looking bored. He had dulled out to the equivalent of a daytime night-light and was sitting on Dean's table. His supe-butt was smashed on top of Dean's books with Rudy's cover art, but Rudy didn't care as he moved Apollo into the shot. "Say hello to the audience!"

"What is this?" groaned Apollo, as Kristy posed for the camera behind him like an Insta-model.

"It's a live stream to all my followers," said Rudy, smiling nervously for the camera.

"Oh yeah, all ten of them?" grumbled Apollo.

Rudy noted the steadily rising number next to the viewers icon—what he hadn't noticed was the ominous letter next to the number, only because he never saw it before. It must be a mistake, thought Rudy, because that would mean—

"Fifty-seven thousand," he gasped.

"Fifty-seven thousand?" perked Apollo. "Viewers?"

"Fifty-eight! Fifty-eight thousand viewers! Fifty-nine! Sixty!" shouted Rudy as he started screaming. This had never happened before. He had told Dean this was going to be an epic day, and he was right! He thought they were going to sell a lot of books, but this? This was something else! He was famous…to at least sixty thousand people.

Apollo started to glow as he leaned into the shot. His sudden radiance quickly gathered an audience as they "ohh-ed" and "ahh-ed" over his sparkle.

"Lights up, Sunnies!" said Apollo as he flexed his pecs and biceps while exhibiting a stupendous duck-face.

"Well," said Rudy, fanning himself with his free hand, "this is overwhelming!

Sixty thousand people!" Then it hit him. All of it. At once. Sixty—no, sixty-five thousand and growing—people were watching him, *right now*. In the camera view he suddenly became conscious of the blemish on his forehead and the ashy color of his skin. He needed moisturizer. He needed an eyebrow wax and trim. And what was that white thing? Oh, Lord have mercy, that white thing hanging from his left nostril was merely a glare, right? Please, let it be a glare. He wasn't prepared for this. Not now. He was working up to his first thousand followers, working out the kinks until his broadcasts were perfection. This was too much too soon. The enormity of the moment made Rudy feel sick.

"Sixty-five thousand people," said Apollo, "my Sunnies are shining!"

"Well," said Rudy, "it is my vlog. I mean, they're my fans too."

"Are you joking?" spat Apollo. "They're here to gleam me, not you!"

"I'm sure they're enjoying you on my channel, @MoodyRudy, but let's be clear," Rudy stated. "They're here for me."

Apollo eyed Rudy up and down. "You can have them. They're probably all fatties and uggos anyway."

"What did you say?" squealed Rudy.

"My Sunnies can't be fatties and uggos." As Rudy scowled, wishing Dean were there with a snappy retort, Apollo added, "Speaking of uggos, where's your friend? It's been a half hour."

"Maybe he got caught up at the bank?" suggested Kristy, but Apollo ignored her and started pounding his fist into his hand.

"Nah, he's just a pussy," said Apollo. "Probably stole my hundo."

Rudy didn't like the insinuation that Dean was a coward, nor did he appreciate the association with female genitalia. Women gave birth, which was more than just a kick in the balls, and that was exactly what he wanted to do—to swan-kick this arrogant dick of a supe right in the beans. Though, it didn't invalidate the question—what *was* keeping Dean?

"Why would he do that?" argued Rudy. "There's more than a hundred dollars of our books right here. Why would he leave all that behind to take your money?"

"Fuck if I know," said Apollo as he stood on the table and scanned the room for Dean—his sandals destroying a book or two in the process. "Wimps like to wimp out. That's why we call them wimps. If he's not back with my change in ten minutes, I'm going out there to find him. And trust me, he won't like it when that happens." Then he started pounding his fist into his hand again. Each time, the clapping noise got louder. "What's the dimwit's name again?"

Rudy ducked away and tried dialing Dean. It was double the fifteen-minute deadline Apollo gave him, and Rudy was struck with another psychic feeling—this one, however, was as if Dean had blipped out of existence all together. Where in the heck was he? And why wasn't he answering his phone? When Rudy's pocket buzzed followed by an "Answer me!" he was instantly filled with buttloads of dread, enough to necessitate the removal of his sunglasses as a sign of contrition.

"Mr. Apollo, sir," said Rudy nervously, cradling Dean's phone in his hand while maintaining the live video in the other.

"Now what do you want?" growled Apollo.

"It would seem that my business partner left his phone with me," said Rudy, purposely omitting Dean's name from the conversation. How would Apollo find him if he didn't know his name? Even if it was plastered all over his books, the postcards, the business cards, and the giant banner five feet away—but was Apollo smart enough to make that connection?

"Did that dim-shit steal my money?" roared Apollo. His Sunnies gulped and gossiped with conniving whispers of damnation.

"No," said Rudy, waving his hands back and forth. "I've known Dean for a long time, and he's no thief."

"Dean! That's his name! I totally forgot," said Apollo.

Damn, Rudy done messed up.

Kristy said, "Baby, it's just a hundred. So what?"

Rudy would've kissed a stranger's feet for a hundred dollars. He had licked a toilet seat once for a bag of Goldfish back in high school. Growing up poor would do that to you. Dating Arthur, a successful scientist, put Rudy into a situation he had never been in before. He had stability, trust, and comfort: all the things he never had with Franklin.

Still, a hundred bucks was a hundred bucks, and if this supe and his arm-piece wanted to waste it on Dean, then fine by him. Rudy would get a twenty percent cut of it anyway.

"It's not the money," growled Apollo, "it's the—the—"

"Principle?" offered Rudy.

"No," said Apollo.

"Situation?" offered Kristy.

"No, fuck!"

"Principle?" re-offered Rudy with a questioning tone.

"Yes! The principle! Exactly," said Apollo.

Rudy rolled his eyes, then remembered he wasn't wearing shades. Apollo may have been gorgeous, but he was as numbskull-empty as an upended bucket. And Dean—poor, sweet, pain-in-the-ass Dean—was going to pay for it. Rudy needed something—a distraction, a miracle, a gaggle of groupies—something to move this blonde dumbo off his missing hundred-dollar bill and onto something else...

"Crimson Justice!" roared a random guy in the crowd.

"It's Crimson Justice!"

"The Dope Gang just robbed the First National Bank!"

Eureka! A miracle! A distraction!

Oh...no.

"The First National Bank?" questioned Rudy. "But that's where Dean went."

"What?" said Apollo, perking up like a dog being bribed with a tasty treat.

Rudy's mind attempted to put "Dean" plus "The First National Bank" together to make "Danger," but it didn't compute straight away—and when it did, a chill ran up his back. If Dean could piss off Apollo in under five minutes, he could only imagine what his best friend could do with a whole gang of supes during a hostage situation.

"Babe!" shouted Kristy, clapping her hands together. "This is your chance!"

"I need to get my battle toga," whined Apollo, peering down at the linen draped across his body. He quickly flexed, bent over twice to touch his toes, then limbered up by twisting his abdomen back and forth. He looked at Kristy, gave her a peck on the cheek, and followed that with a firm slap across her bottom. "Wish me luck, babe." His glow went extra bright as he charged off, followed by his adoring Sunnies chanting his name.

The news spread from one end of the convention center to the other. People ran for the exits, excited for a glimpse of real supe action. Rudy, however, was still spinning on the First National Bank being robbed. His stomach roiled as he moved toward the window, but he couldn't see anything through the crowd.

Then he retrieved his cell phone and dialed Arthur.

Arthur would know what to do. He always did. And when it came to Dean, Rudy needed help.

Rudy wasn't the kind of person who had many friends. When he found someone worth his time, he often pushed them away with a variety of missteps. He was not what anyone would call personable. Rudy was a bit overwhelming—an artist, an entrepreneur, a provocateur, a vlogger with tens of thousands of followers—but for the longest time he didn't understand why people didn't like him. His mother said it was because he had a "strong personality," which wasn't exactly a bad thing, but he needed to be around people who were willing to see the good in him.

Then he met Dean one night when the poor guy accidentally wandered into Woody's—the gay bar on the east side. He was down on his luck, his job had gone up in flames, and he'd sleepwalked into a random bar for a drink. They spent the night talking about art, horror movies, and their favorite authors. It was the first time Rudy had met someone who wasn't trying to get into his pants. In fact, Dean was the first straight man who was willing to chat with him about everything and anything. Smart, witty, and interesting, he was a straight man who looked past sexual orientation and saw him as a fellow human being.

And through Dean, Rudy met Arthur—the smartest man he ever met— an astro-physo-bio-chemo-ist or some such sciency thing. Dean set them up because that's the kind of friend Dean was.

It had taken Rudy thirty-two years to meet a friend who had his back, and this wasn't the first time Dean was stuck in the middle of a supe problem. Messing with supes could get you killed.

"Arthur, honey," whined Rudy into his cell phone. "Deano's in trouble."

CHAPTER 5

DEAN REGAINED CONSCIOUSNESS FIVE MINUTES BEFORE HE opened his eyes. At first, he thought he was dead—the warmth, the color, the ringing. It was like he was floating through an endless sea of rainbows with humming angels that made his very soul vibrate like a tuning fork.

Then he relived the mechanical click, the commotion, followed by a sharp pain at the back of his head that sent bolts of electricity through his extremities. If he could feel pain, he probably wasn't dead.

When he decided it was time to move, he started small with just a finger. A successful endeavor—wiggling a pinky back and forth without pain. Since the pinky swiveled so well, he made a brash decision and sat up all at once.

Every. Single. Body part. Screamed. Fuck. You. Asshole!

"Owwwwww," he groaned after the pain subsided.

"Oh fantastic," said a female voice. "You're not dead."

She sounded sarcastic. Dean thought it was odd—if not flat-out rude—to be sarcastic about his death, even for a stranger, but his head hurt too much to unpack the situation.

The room was dusty. There was a serious structural problem punctuated by a flickering light in the corner. Ceiling tiles swung from still-attached glued sections, and electrical wires cascaded out from underneath. The foundation was cracked, and a wall of safety deposit boxes were so crushed that many of them had busted wide open, their contents belching onto the floor.

Dean was having a hard time processing where he was until he saw the bags of cash and a massive wall of mashed metal that looked like the inside of a bank vault door.

The pain in his head was starting to focus into one section at the back instead of the all-consuming thumping pain he felt upon sitting up. He had a big lump, and there was blood, enough to mat a portion at the back of his head into a gooey congealing mess.

"These taste wrong. Not bad, just wrong," she said. "I thought it was cherry, maybe strawberry, but it might be apple. Who puts lollipops in a safety deposit box, anyway?"

There was so much wreckage in the room that Dean overlooked her on first glance. She was lying on a mound of cash in the corner and staring at the sparking wires hanging from the ceiling. She looked to be in cosplay. The face paint, the fingerless gloves, the denim vest, and the spray-painted t-shirt—the curly blonde wave of hair with streaks dyed electric blue—it was a solid Crystal Beth costume. One of the best Dean had ever seen, and he had been traveling the Supes-Convention circuit for the last year attempting to sell books.

"Suckers," said Dean.

"What?" she groaned, as if on the verge of being offended.

"Who puts lollipops in a safety deposit box?" asked Dean. "Suckers. Suckers do. It was a joke."

The girl—nay, woman—yanked the red lollipop from her mouth and said, "Oh." She sounded unamused. "That was a terrific dad joke."

"Thanks," said Dean.

"It wasn't a compliment," she said, replacing the lollipop into her mouth and lying back down to stare up at the sparking wires.

Dean nodded. Tough crowd.

"Anyone else in here?" he asked as he sat up against the opposite wall.

"No, just us," she replied with an irritated tone.

"What happened?"

"A bunch of knobjockey supervillains robbed the bank. Tossed us in here and crushed the door." She pointed to the vault door without sitting up. "You didn't have to be conscious throughout the ordeal to figure that one out."

"Did I do something to piss you off?" he asked.

She flipped him the bird.

Moments passed, and Dean tried to remember what had happened. But the harder he tried, the worse his recollection became. Eventually, all he could recall was the mechanical clink, followed by the pain. Perhaps he had a concussion? He thought about asking her to check the wound at the back of his head but figured if he wasn't already concussed, he'd just be cussed for asking.

"Crystal Beth, huh?" asked Dean, noting her costume.

She sat up and glared at him. "Yeah, so?"

"Big fan?"

"No," she grumbled. "Not exactly."

"Isn't she an anarchist?" he asked. There was a gray Tin Men symbol on her t-shirt. Every news broadcast he'd ever seen of Crystal Beth touted her maniacal smile and her costume adorned with anarchy symbols.

"Sure," she said, "if you believe the news."

"Isn't she dead?" asked Dean. He was pretty sure she'd died, maybe a month ago. Could have been two months the way he was perceiving time lately. It made headlines, even if Dean didn't read the articles.

"No," she spat, like it was an insult. "That was Annie Phetamine. Jesus…"

Oh joy, he was locked in a bank vault for an indeterminate amount of time with a supe-loving—*nay*—supe-*villain*-loving grouch.

"Oh," he replied as she grumbled to herself. "How long was I out?"

"Not long enough," she mumbled.

"What?" he asked, even though he had heard.

"I don't know," she replied. "Twenty minutes?"

"Do you have a cell phone?"

"No. You?"

"No, my best friend—"

"—don't care," she sang, cutting him off.

"Dean."

"Bless you."

"No, my name's Dean."

"Oh, that wasn't a sneeze?" She was being difficult on purpose.

"I was just being nice."

"Yeah, every man thinks he's nice. All men believe they're *nice guys*." She rolled her eyes and added, "Especially the assholes."

Dean formed a response in his head—a real zinger—but thought better of saying it. Considering the state of the vault door, they were going to be stuck together for hours. Maybe days, unless someone could get Crimson Justice to free them. Or maybe Apollo—after all, Dean still had his money, *and* his change by the looks of all the bills in the room.

"Tori," she finally said.

"Bless you," said Dean. She scowled at him. A real evil scowl like he had just stunk up the place with a fart worthy of Peter's day-after-hot-sauce gas. "Kidding. Nice to meet you, Tori."

"We're stuck in a bank vault and it's nice to meet me?"

"Turn of phrase," said Dean, as he purposely hit his head against the wall. Shocks of pain shot all the way down to his toes—he'd forgotten all about his head wound. He was frustrated. She was frustrating, and he'd known her for all of five minutes.

This was what he got for moving to a Supe-City. When he received the call five years ago, he accepted the job straight away. It was a new beginning. He didn't care where he was going so long as he was away from Brie and the heartbreak. He should've held out—maybe a better opportunity would've come along in another place, at a better time. Instead, he moved to Wonder City, and two short years later the whole business went up in smoke.

Actual smoke.

Crimson Justice had tracked down a D-rated supervillain named Craze to the office building where Dean worked, and all six stories burned to the ground. Dean survived, but not everyone was as lucky. He was able to lead a group of co-workers to safety, and that got his face on the evening news, followed by 15 minutes of fame—and subsequent infamy on 5DUD—which he never wanted. He spent some time looking for work and found another gig that didn't make him happy—or sad. It was a job, but it gave him ample time to write and explore his other talents.

Three years later and he was still at the same complacent job. Still struggling. Still attempting to make ends meet and praying to get noticed. Now he was stuck in a bank vault with a woman who'd probably attempt to murder him before they could be rescued.

"I'm having a really bad day," admitted Dean. "I know we're both stuck in here, but please, cut me a little slack."

She groaned. "Yeah, *you're* having a bad day. I'm in here too, asshole."

"How *did* you get in here?"

"Same way as you, dummy."

Dean glared at her for a moment before closing his eyes and stuffing away his frustrations. But why? He felt like a tightly wound jack-in-the-box that was bursting at the seams, full of disappointment, grievances, and resentment. What did it matter if this woman liked him or not?

He pointed to his face. "Do I have a sign on my forehead that gives every woman I meet the permission to treat me like shit?"

"I don't know. You do have one of those faces."

Dean was shocked at her callousness, but when the jack-in-the-box blew, he saw the humor. Maybe it wasn't all that funny, but the more he thought about it, the funnier it became. He even started laughing out loud. "That explains a lot."

She smirked. "I'm not this bitchy, you know. I'm upset and I'm taking it out on you."

"It's okay," replied Dean. "I tend to bring that on myself."

There was a long pause.

"Why do you think every woman treats you like shit?" she asked.

"I don't know." He shrugged. "I thought we established it has something to do with my face?"

She laughed. "Oh, it does. But why do *you* think so?"

Dean laughed back. "I don't know. Maybe I'm too nice? Maybe I try too hard? Maybe I'm too picky? Why do you ask?"

"Because every guy treats me like shit, and I thought maybe there was a connection."

"I doubt that," said Dean.

"Why?" asked Tori.

"Because you're not very nice," he said with a smile—he was only partially joking.

It got so quiet, Dean could hear the throbbing thump as the blood rushed through the bump on the back of his head. He closed his eyes and tried not to think about how much he'd kill for a couple of Supe-Strength Tylenol. When he attempted to focus on something other than the pain, he started thinking of worrisome things, like what if they ran out of oxygen inside the vault, or what might happen if nobody came looking for them.

"My boyfriend," declared Tori, then clarified, *"ex-boyfriend*…he's a real piece of work."

"Why's that?" asked Dean. Did he really want to know? Why was she telling him any of this? It felt like the equivalent of enabling a bully, prodding her along despite his fluctuating interest in what she had to say.

"He makes me feel empty," she said. Her tone was contrite and drew Dean's attention. "He has anger issues, and when he wasn't gaslighting me or putting me down—sometimes getting violent—he was apathetic. If I wasn't pleasing him or going along with his plans, I was a skank, a bitch, or worse."

"Sounds like a real asshole," stated Dean.

"Yeah."

"I always felt that the right woman would bring out the best in me, and I in her." Dean imagined what could've happened if Brie had given him the chance—those old fantasies booted up like a bad habit. "I believe that with the right person, you could look into their eyes from across a crowded room and just know what they're thinking. That our smiles, our dreams, were shared. We would be each other's biggest fans."

"That's bullshit. That's a fantasy," said Tori. "Relationships aren't like that. They're hard. Sometimes awful, and sometimes you're in so deep you don't even know why you stay."

"It doesn't have to be like that," said Dean. "I mean, yeah, it's work, but most of the time it should be enjoyable work, right? I would give anything to make someone laugh, to make them smile because I made them breakfast or told them they looked beautiful. If that's hard, then maybe the problem is that people don't even want to try."

"You're a real odd fucking duck, aren't you?"

"Being a hopeless romantic shouldn't make me odd," said Dean, then he clarified his own statement. "More like hapless romantic these days."

There was another long pause. Dean was trying to clear his mind, but it was obvious she was thinking. It was almost as if he could smell it in the room, her thoughts eating her up inside. Dean knew that all too well. He was a victim too.

"Tell me," she demanded.

"About what?"

"About the girl who broke you."

"Why?"

"I don't know." She shrugged. "It'll be therapeutic?"

Then she stood up and dusted herself off, and for the first time Dean saw all of her. She was beautiful, in a deranged badass punk sort of way, which he realized was oddly, but effectively, appealing. Maybe it was the makeup—the face paint surrounding her eyes like a starry galaxy, making her blue irises pop as if they were twice the normal size. She was a knockout, and Dean consciously checked to make sure his jaw hadn't gone slack.

She wore Doc Martens and a pair of tight, torn black jeans that frayed from the knees to the top of her thighs. She had a bouquet of roses tattooed onto her leg, peeking through the strands of fabric, and another on her stomach below her shirt—musical notes. On her white t-shirt was a spray-painted symbol—like the number 2 and 4 had combined—a symbol that Dean had already recognized. It was the symbol for the Tin Men—made popular in the Second and Third World War, it had since vanished into obscurity...until now. His own Tin Men pin was fastened onto his jacket collar, which was still inside the convention center with Rudy.

Over her t-shirt was a denim vest covered in spikes, patches, and pins—one of which said "Resist" next to another that said "Badass Bitch"—both in all caps. She wore a pair of fingerless gloves, and her left arm was tattooed with the faces of classic horror movie monsters—from Dracula to Creature to Frankenstein and many in between.

If this woman wasn't already punk enough, it was her hair that really caught his attention. It was a natural wavy blonde. The left side was pulled back and braided tight, while the rest of it cascaded over the right like a waterfall—long tresses with stripes of electric blue threaded into the wave.

In any other situation, under any other circumstance, he may have been mesmerized—but a subconscious part of him begged for restraint. And he had questions—so many questions. Like, why was she was wearing a supervillain costume? Did she like Crystal Beth? Did she like supes? He was positive Crystal Beth was an anarchist. Wasn't she a murderer? What was this woman's deal?

Why did he care?

She paced toward him and sat down against the opposite wall. It looked like she had been crying—wet streaks ran down her cheeks, dragging the makeup with them—and there were bruises on her arms.

"Tell me yours," she said, "and I'll tell you mine. Maybe we'll learn a thing or two."

"No."

"Why not?"

"Because," said Dean. She was imploring him with a Bambi stare—her eyes big and wide, her bottom lip protruding with the slightest frown. It was like she knew what would work on him—like they had known each other for years…

…like Brie. Brie knew all the buttons to push, as if she had her own private Dean-Entertainment Center Console, along with all the cheat codes.

"C'mon!"

"I don't know," he grumbled. "I don't typically pour my heart out to strangers."

She leaned forward, half crawled in his direction, and held her hand out to him. "I'm Tori," she said.

He shook her hand and said, "Dean. Haven't already we met?"

She crawled back to her side of the room, sat cross-legged, then said, "Now it's official. We shook hands. We're not strangers anymore."

Dean stared at her. He felt compelled to talk to Tori. He felt compelled to connect. But make no mistake, it was a bad idea. What good could come from telling his sob story? It seemed like the antithesis of getting to know someone—to show them how vulnerable he was, a mushy marshmallow center that some preferred to feast on rather than savor. And yet, why not? He was used to baring his soul and being disappointed.

"What have you got to lose?" asked Tori, "We're going to be in here a while. What was her name?"

"Brie."

"Okay," said Tori, "tell me all about Brie."

76

CHAPTER 6

DEAN DID NOT HAVE A GREAT CHILDHOOD EXPERIENCE.

Family life was just fine, if not completely normal, but high school was a daily suffering. Yet he was sure it would get better once he was away from his peers. He was looking forward to life on his own, with the ability to create his own image, free from the perceptions that followed him no matter where he went or what he decided to do. He was a small-town kid at a university that enrolled a hundred thousand students every year. Classes were held in full amphitheaters, and lectures were just that—a teacher talking. Textbook reading was mandatory, and Dean was so used to being able to pass his high school curriculum without studying that the sudden change in difficulty was harder than it should've been. With time, however, he was able to adjust—but not everything about his new life came so easy.

The thing Dean had looked forward to the most about college was the chance to reinvent himself, and to socialize without his past following him around. But after a few weeks on campus it became clear that Dean was woefully behind—especially when it came to dating.

Within weeks, Dean had a date with a girl from his humanities class. She invited him into her dorm room after grabbing coffee at the quad. He was not aware of her intentions and blew every opportunity to kiss her. By the time he worked up the courage, she yawned, asked him to leave, and never talked to him again.

By the second month, Dean had experienced his first college makeout session, but with a similar outcome. The girl avoided him afterward without explanation. Did he do something wrong? Was he bad at kissing?

Dean had heard all the sayings about the birds and the bees, but he felt like he was getting stung an inordinate number of times.

"Dating should come with a debrief," stated Dean after a crash of dishes momentarily shattered the good vibes in the pizzeria. It was the crash that inspired him, since every attempted relationship had ended with a similar smash.

"A debrief?" asked Peter.

"Yeah," said Dean as he took another sip of his iced tea from the whiskey glass he specifically requested—he thought it made him look older. "You know, like a detailed explanation of what happened. That way we both can adjust to the things we did wrong."

"But," said Peter as he wiped his face clean of buffalo sauce, "what if you didn't do anything wrong? What if the things you did wrong are right for someone else?"

At the time, Dean had never heard something so dumb—and yet, Peter was magnificently naïve and wise beyond his years. If only Dean had listened to his armchair logic more often…

Peter, Dean's roommate, was the kind of kid that given the opportunity, would sit alone in a room playing video games all day—leave him some Mountain Dew and an empty jar and the guy might not even leave the couch. If Dean didn't tear him away from the controller and get him out into the world, their lives would've been very different. Dean wanted a wingman, and Peter, though horrible at it, still qualified—despite his confusion over the term.

"Thanks for the wings," said Peter. "I like being a wingman."

Peter had already polished off a whole order of wings and seemed to be eyeing up the menu for more. The restaurant was a typical pizza joint that served alcohol, and it was one of the few places students under twenty-one could go for some socializing off campus. It had big booths for large gatherings, a bar with stools, checkered tablecloths, pool tables in the back. And they played decent music. It was the place to be, especially since there were already a few inches of snow on the ground, and it was warm and cozy.

"You do realize that being a wingman means we work together to meet girls, right?" said Dean. He didn't have the heart to tell Peter that he was mistaken until it stood to reason that Peter's wing obsession might just ruin their chance at meeting anyone—what with all the hot sauce smeared across Peter's cheeks. And Dean was pretty sure the girls in the booth across the way were laughing at him.

"Oh," said Peter, wiping away the hot sauce with his sleeve. "I don't think I knew that."

"That much was clear," said Dean.

"Wait," said Tori. "Your friend didn't know what a wingman was?"

"Peter was a good kid, but he wasn't very…aware."

"Okay," said Tori, shaking her head. "Go on."

After two full orders of wings, Peter finally appeared gassed.

"I think I ate too much," said Peter.

"Ya think?" said Dean. "I think I need a new wingman."

"Sorry," said Peter. "Why do you need a wingman anyway?"

"Because of that," said Dean, pointing across the way.

There was a full booth of girls, laughing, jeering, and being rowdy freshmen.

"Yeah, so?" asked Peter.

"Tell me, Pete," said Dean, growing serious. "How do you propose a man, alone, goes over there to talk to them?"

"Well, I imagine it involves walking," he said sincerely, "and talking."

"Why are you making this so difficult?" asked Dean.

"I don't know." Peter shrugged. "My parents ask me the same thing."

And that's when it happened.

"Hi! I'm Brie," said a blonde approaching their table. "Johnny's on break, so I'll be covering his tables until he returns."

She was beautiful. Blue eyes and a smile that made Dean nervous. Her bangs were tucked behind her ears, and a strand of hair had sprung loose and bounced around playfully in front of her forehead.

Dean was staring. Dean was starstruck. Dean was confused.

"Who's Johnny?" asked Dean.

"Your waiter?" replied Brie, almost questioning herself.

"Can I get another order of wings?" asked Peter, finding his third wind. "I'm his wingman tonight."

Brie gave Peter a befuddled glance, but quickly retrieved her notepad and jotted it down.

"Hot or mild?" she asked.

"Hot," deadpanned Dean, staring at her like a lovesick puppy.

Brie smiled. "Hot it is. Your order will be out in ten minutes."

Then she walked away.

"Was I a good wingman?" asked Peter with a big proud grin, but Dean never heard him. He was too busy watching the girl that stole his heart.

"What is this shit?" asked Tori.

"Huh?"

"What's this G-rated shit?" growled Tori. "Where's the trauma, Dean? I thought we were sharing stories of our broken hearts, not recounting some mopey love-sick rom-com."

"I'm getting to it," he said. "Do you want to hear the story or not? This was your idea."

"Ugh! You're right," said Tori. "You're right. Continue. Just quicken it up a bit."

Dean may have met Brie that night, but she didn't meet him for another two years. Dean went back into that restaurant fifteen times over the next month and never saw Brie again. When he worked up the courage to ask another waitress what happened to Brie, he was told nobody worked there with that name.

It was a cruel twist of fate—Dean met someone who entranced him, truly captured his mind after the briefest of introductions, and she disappeared. Gone. Without a trace.

What transpired after, over the course of the next two years with the "help" of his hot-sauce-smeared wingman, was nothing to brag about. Dean struggled to meet women, and when he did, there were always...*obstacles*.

There was Monica, the girl who didn't realize they were on a date.

Dean asked her out to a movie. She was the one who suggested his place instead of the theater in town.

"Wait, is this a date?" she asked, incredulous.

"Oh, I thought..." he started to explain after she caught him putting his arm around her. Wasn't that what one did on a movie date—be it at a theater or a couch?

She was snuggled up close to him and sharing a blanket. Pete had said that if she sits on his third of the couch, she was interested, and sure enough, there was a whole two-thirds of couch beside her. He thought he was reading the signs. Why were the signs so hard to read?

"I mean, I put out candles."

"Oh," said Monica. "I thought the electricity was out."

"But we were watching a movie," explained Dean. "On my TV?"

"I don't know!" growled Monica. "I don't know what kind of electrical situation you have going on over here!"

She left moments later, leaving him alone with a bowl full of popcorn and half a beer. They weren't compatible—but Dean wasn't ready for that point of view. He was still trying to understand what he had done wrong.

Then there was Angela, who seemed interested in anyone and everyone else but Dean.

"Oh my god, and Kevin," said Angela. "He's just too interested in sports for me, you know? Like, I love sports, don't get me wrong, but a woman needs more attention than that."

"That makes sense," said Dean, nodding along.

"Oh, and tomorrow I'm going out with David. He's the one with the premature balding. Cute guy, but I don't know if I can date a man who's bald before twenty-five, you know?"

"Uh, sure," said Dean.

"And let me tell you about Joe. Have I told you about Joe? He's the one with the six-pack I love, but he's got this toe thing."

"Joe, with the toe thing," repeated Dean.

"Yeah! Exactly," she said. "You're a really good listener."

"So, I didn't know we were seeing other people," said Dean.

"Oh, I'm not dating them," she said. "I mean, I'm not dating anyone."

"But what are we?" he asked.

"If you have to ask that, you must not be listening," she said.

Then there was Melissa, the girl who thought she was a secret supe.

"I don't tell anyone this, like, ever. But, like, since we're starting to date, like, I wanted to give you a warning," said Melissa. She spoke so fast that if it wasn't for all the *likes*, he'd never have the chance to catch up. "I have, like, for real superpowers."

"You do?" asked Dean. "What are they?"

Dean had immediately lost interest in Melissa the moment she said she was a supe, but it was a long stroll to the campus gardens and back, and they were only halfway there.

However, when she snapped her fingers and said, "Ta-da!" Dean stopped walking. "See?" She had a big proud smile on her face and struck a pose like she had just nailed an Olympic landing.

"What just happened?" asked Dean. It had to be a joke, right?

"Exactly. What *did* just happen," said Melissa, who then unleashed the creepiest mad-scientist giggle Dean had ever heard—followed by a cute snort that made her giggle all over again.

Then there was Tammy, the girl who eventually married Dean's roommate.

Dean and Tammy dated for six months. They met at a football game between quarters at the concession stand. Tammy was a marketing major and, at times, overwhelmed Dean with her intellect. He liked that. She was so smart and pretty, he found himself falling faster than he could've realized, until one day…

"I don't think this is going to work out."

That was not what he'd expected when she invited him to her room for a talk. Dean was expecting commitment talk, but was shocked when she answered the door looking grim.

"Why?" He was devastated. Though, he had to admit, dating Tammy felt like trying to catch up to a speeding train—which was why the truth was so much harder to hear.

"I think I like someone else," she said.

"Oh," said Dean. "Someone I know?"

"Yeah," she replied. "I'm sorry, I didn't mean for it to happen. I just know I can't pursue how I feel until I end things with you first."

"It's okay," said Dean, even though it wasn't. "Who is it?"

"I'd rather not say."

"If it ever comes up, can we say that I dumped you?" he asked.

"Why is that relevant?"

"Because, if you date someone I know, and they find out you dumped me, it could make it awkward. Like I'm not over you."

"I see."

"But if I dump you…"

"It'll clear the path between me and him."

"Exactly."

"Sure, Dean," she said, placing a comforting hand on his leg. "You know, you're going to be okay."

"Hmmm?" said Dean. He was focusing on one of her posters—a shirtless picture of Jeff Goldblum—and he had spaced out staring at the bronzed pecs, attempting to make himself feel numb. This conversation hurt more than he wanted to let on, and Tammy saw right through it.

"I don't want to hurt you," she said. "We're going to be friends. We're going to be close."

"You and Peter, huh?" asked Dean.

"How'd you know?" She sounded as stunned as she looked.

"Whenever something doesn't make sense," said Dean, heavily in thought, "it ends up being the truth. Relationships tend to only make sense when they're not making any sense."

"Yeah." Tammy nodded. "I couldn't agree more."

"Oh damn," said Tori.

"Yeah."

"All that? In two years?"

He nodded. "Dating sucks. It's this game that nobody knows how to play, and everyone wants it played their way."

"Yeah," she agreed. "But some of those women sounded bonkers. Not gonna lie, I have my own issues, but there's no way to navigate everyone's trauma."

"Bonkers," said Dean. "That's a great word for it."

"So how did Brie come back into the picture?"

"Accidentally."

After Tammy, Dean went into a depression. He felt like a cast-off. A loser. He watched as Tammy threw herself at an oblivious Peter, and even acted as Tammy's wingman, pushing Peter toward the woman who wanted him.

Peter was a genius. A truly brilliant guy, but it was insult to injury that

Dean had to pry the joystick out of Peter's hands before he saw Tammy's interest. When it finally happened, there were instant sparks.

As for Dean, he suffered in silence—opting for early bedtimes on days he would've normally dragged Peter out and about. He withdrew from himself, and from his schoolwork, and his grades started to plummet too.

It was by chance, when Dean was at his most self-loathing, that he came across Brie in a bookstore. The old bookstore across town was where Dean went when he wanted to get away from campus life. Some days he'd pick up a copy of a book he had been meaning to read and would skim through a chapter or two to see if it held his attention. Most days it was horror, or fantasy, but that day he wanted to read about supes.

Dean was feeling too much. He was struggling, and wanted to know what it was like to be an impervious supe. He was aware that bullets and emotional strife were different kinds of pain, but if one were impervious, if one had the strength and speed of a god, wouldn't they have everything they ever wanted? Money? Fame? Even love?

No supe that ever pulled up their tights and slipped on a mask was ever without the kind of fame and power that brought all the money and love they desired. Was it real love? That was to be debated, but it was more than what Dean had ever had.

Dean was particularly drawn to the autobiography of Collateral Damage, the vigilante who saved the village of Mapletown from the clutches of a madman. He had been meaning to read it. He wanted to know, in Collateral Damage's own words, what the supe thought of the Massacre at Shady Lake.

Dean located the biographies and quickly scanned until he found what he was looking for: *Collateral Damage: Life of the Human Wrecking Ball.* However, when he pulled the book from the shelf, he hadn't even gotten through the preface before he heard a sniffle and a whimper from the next aisle. Dean was doomed as his hero complex immediately engaged.

The high-pitched sniffle and the cute way she sobbed only made the urge stronger.

Pacing over to the mouth of the next aisle, Dean found her on the floor, between Self-Help and the Mystical Arts. Her head was buried into her knees, but her long blonde ponytail shifted his hero-complex-driven curiosity into a craving to know her identity.

Dean said, "Hey, are you okay?"

From the moment she looked up, Dean was entranced.

"No," she whimpered. "I'm not okay."

"Brie?" he asked.

It looked like her—or at least what he remembered from a two-year-old, blurry mental snapshot of their brief encounter.

"Do I know you?" she wheezed.

"You waited on me and my roommate once," he said.

"But I haven't been a waitress for at least two years."

"Yeah," he said. They stared at each other—a long pause that extended awkwardly into silence. That silence grew until it was clear that Dean needed to do something, anything. "I'll be right back."

Dean dashed away, and Brie began to sob once again, but he quickly returned with a wad of napkins from the café in the back—and offered to dry her tears.

"Thanks," she said while dabbing them over her eyes and cheeks, then gave a small, embarrassed laugh. "That was nice of you."

He sat beside her on the floor. "Is there anything I can do?"

She shrugged, her sad eyes twinkling with the tears that hung in her lashes like glitter.

Twenty-five minutes later, Dean was making out with Brie in the back of his car, culminating in her bed to the tune of Aerosmith's "Angel" on the radio.

"Classy," said Tori, but Dean ignored her.

The next morning, he awoke in her bed, thinking about the whiplash life had served him. When he was at his lowest, he'd found something remarkable. He found Brie, and he was intent on making her smile.

When Brie awoke an hour later, Dean was gone. But before she had the chance to rub the rust from her eyes and slip on the clothes that were strewn about the floor, there was a knock at her door. Dean had bought breakfast and swooped into the room with an energetic charm.

"I noticed the *Bagels-2-Go* bag on your desk," said Dean, "so I went and picked up a little of everything.”

“That’s so sweet of you,” said Brie with a beaming smile that lit Dean up like a bundle of matches. “You’re like the cutest puppy.”

Dean opened the bag and asked, “What kind do you like?”

“Sesame seed, please.” After smearing it with a healthy dose of cream cheese, she added, “I’d be the happiest girl alive with a sesame seed bagel every morning and a handsome man to bring me one.”

Dean smiled. “So you’re telling me I nailed it on the first try?”

“You did,” she said. “You nailed it.”

“Are you feeling better?” asked Dean.

“Yes.” She nodded and giggled. “I’m all aces.”

“Can I see you?” he asked. “A little later?”

“Sure,” she replied. “I have a lot of studying to do, and I promised to run errands with my roommate Madison, but maybe sometime this week?”

“You got it.” He gave her a long passionate kiss and left with her number. He was higher than cloud nine. He felt like a supe. He felt invincible.

He sent a text that evening, wishing her luck with her studies—something short and sweet. All was well, even if she didn’t reply. She did, after all, tell him she had things to do.

The next day came and went, and Dean was worried that if he sent another text, she might take it the wrong way. Girls didn’t like clingy guys, but Dean was excited. He liked her. Heck, he liked her so much, he hoped for just a *little* validation. Even a quick smiley emoji would’ve made all the difference.

Three days passed, and Dean was struggling to stay out of his own head. Bad thoughts preyed on him like an owl picking off field mice. Every time a positive thought surfaced, it was gobbled whole by a negative force, affirming that nothing good would ever happen to him.

Tammy and Peter tried to cheer him up—Dean was beginning to bring them all down. It was hard to play video games when Dean was sulking on the couch next to Peter. And Tammy couldn’t cozy in next to her boyfriend with Dean there wearing the same clothes from three days ago. So, they did what any caring friends would do—they invited him out for Taco Tuesday.

It was a busy night. The bar was full. The music was loud. And Dean was finally showered and shaved.

"You know," said Peter, "hygiene looks good on you, pal."

Dean groaned in response.

"Dean," said Tammy, "why don't we do a few shots? Maybe it'll loosen you up?"

Dean shrugged.

"Dean," said Peter with a mischievous grin, "Remember last night when you promised to do my theology homework for Dr. Celestine?"

Dean moved his head—but it wasn't exactly a nod or shake. It was somewhere in between.

"Yeah," said Peter. "My roommate's officially a brain-dead zombie."

"This is going to be so much fun," Tammy said sarcastically.

The night progressed with Peter and Tammy carrying the conversation while Dean groaned and grunted, but as Peter dove into his third order of hot wings, there was a commotion at the back of the bar by the pool tables.

"Light it! Light it! Light it! Light it!" people chanted.

Then Dean saw a burst of flames.

"What was that?" It took a blooming fireball to rip Peter's attention away from his wings. "Do they have hibachi in the back?"

Call it intuition, but Dean was already on the move. Before Tammy or Peter could ask where he was going, Dean had leapt from his chair and was weaving through the crowd. He was curious, if not disturbed. The bar's staff were visibly nervous, and a few had retreated toward the front of the restaurant.

Another burst of flames was followed by cheers, and Dean swore he heard a familiar voice.

As he slipped into the crowd and shimmied to the front, he spotted Brie leaning against a pool table. She was all dressed up and draped all over some dude with long hair. He was pouring himself a series of shots along the expensive felt surface, spilling alcohol everywhere.

"Do it again, fire-man!" someone shouted.

"It's Torcher, numb-nuts," the fire-man said, like he had just been properly insulted. His muscled arm wrapped around Brie's waist and pulled her tight.

Then, to please his fans, Torcher did it again—he took a full shot glass, dumped it down his throat, then spat a wad of flames that scorched the ceiling.

The crowd went nuts, cheering for more—and that's when Brie spotted Dean.

Her smile withered, then melted away as she retracted her hand from Torcher's bare chest.

They watched each other for a moment. Then Dean left.

He charged out of the bar, past Peter and Tammy and into the cold night air before either of them had any idea what had transpired. Dean chose a direction and stormed off like he was about to walk all the way home in the sub-zero temperatures. This was the kind of pain he wanted to cure. He wanted to be immune to it, because if he was doomed to live a lifetime of this, he had to find a way to dull the ache.

"Puppy, wait," yelled Brie, but Dean wasn't slowing down. His frustration was as hot as Torcher's fire, maybe hotter. Brie ran to him barefooted, her heels in her hand as she attempted to cover herself against the brisk cold wind. When she caught up, Dean stopped—but only because she stepped in front and placed a hand into his chest. "Can we talk?"

"About what?"

"I'm sorry," she said. "I didn't mean to hurt you."

"Is he your boyfriend?" growled Dean. "Was he the reason you were crying your eyes out on the bookstore floor?"

"Yes," she whimpered. "And yes. Torcher and I…"

"Torcher? Is that his real name?" asked Dean, being facetious.

"No," said Brie, "he doesn't go by his real name."

"Of course, he doesn't," groaned Dean. "That's the real *torture*…"

"I needed to escape," said Brie, visibly restraining her emotions. "Torcher cheated on me, and I just wanted to feel something…*else*."

"Did it work?" asked Dean. "Did you feel something else?"

"I did." Her eyes watered.

"But it wasn't good enough for you," said Dean. "Because I wasn't a supe?"

"I never said that." Brie looked like she wanted to cry. "You're aces, Puppy. I just…"

Dean couldn't hide how badly it hurt. He was shivering, but not because he was cold.

"I meant nothing to you," he said, before she could find her words.

"That's not true," she replied. "We'll always have that night. You and I. 'Angel' playing on the stereo."

Dean laughed even though it wasn't funny.

"You're a sweet guy," said Brie. "Can we start over, Puppy? I don't know what the future holds, but can we be friends?"

"Wait," said Tori, "She used you to get even with her boyfriend?"

"Yeah." Dean didn't like feeling vulnerable, and now he felt like his heart was dangling from a vein-like thread, out in the open, exposed, and indefensible to attack.

"What a wankfaced jerk! What did you do?" she asked, still sitting cross-legged on the floor. "Don't tell me you chased that girl around like a *puppy?*"

Wasn't that exactly what Dean had done? Chased Brie around like a puppy?

Dean changed the subject. "It's your turn."

"Fair," said Tori as she leaned back against the wall. "Where to begin…"

"At the beginning is best," smirked Dean.

"Yeah," she agreed, "but what beginning?" She thought about it for a moment, then took a deep breath—the kind of breath one takes before cliff diving or bungee jumping. "I met Amanda in the second grade."

CHAPTER 7

1:05 PM

ARTHUR MET RUDY BEHIND THE POLICE BARRIERS, ACROSS THE street from the First National Bank, twenty minutes after they hung up. He arrived in the usual navy tartan blazer suit with burgundy highlights and his trademark red suede shoes, bearing lattes and a blueberry scone—Rudy's favorite—as well as the leather case Rudy had requested from his apartment.

Between bites, Rudy gave Arthur a quick play-by-play.

"Deano's in trouble. *chomp chomp* He was depressed... *chomp chomp* like usual... *chomp chomp* and I all but forced him to flirt with some hot thing. *chomp chomp* But, turns out she's a supe-groupie... *chomp chomp chomp* and the supe, some a-hole named Apollo... *chomp chomp* got all alpha on Deano... *chomp chomp* and bullied Deano into getting change for a hundo... *chomp chomp* at the First National Bank... *chomp chomp* that's being robbed... *chomp chomp* by the Dope Gang... *chomp chomp* and there's... *chomp chomp* a hostage situation!"

"Remind me," said Arthur. "What's a *hundo* again?"

"Hundred dollar bill," said Rudy with his mouth full of scone.

"Ah, okay. And what is the deal with Dean and supes?" asked Arthur. "I thought August was bad, but this?"

"Oh, that's a therapy sesh for another day." Rudy stomped his feet as the emotion of the situation took over—and not even a blueberry scone could fix it. "How are we gonna get Deano out of there? We know he can't keep his mouth shut! That boy is a walking supe insult."

"Crimson Justice is here," said Arthur, spotting the Red Guardian speaking with police. "He'll make quick work of the situation. Dean won't have the chance to get himself in trouble."

Rudy slipped his sunglasses over his eyes before his irritated glare slapped the serene right off Arthur's handsome face. Rudy had O.E.Y.I.F.—Over Expressive You Idiot Face—and it often got him in trouble. He couldn't hide the disagreement written in his wild eyebrow scrunching and forehead creases. Before the O.E.Y.I.F. melted through his expensive sunglasses, Rudy turned away and looked toward the skies.

The heavens above were cluttered with ZepNews Balloons. The zeppelins spotting the city skyline were like large, bubbled video screens displaying the day's most pressing, breaking news. Each of the three balloons within view were broadcasting live sky-footage of the scene with subtitles detailing the developing situation at the First National Bank.

Rudy noted how many in the crowd were watching the broadcast with their Tints.

"Three dozen hostages, Arthur," said Rudy.

"I wonder what the Purples are seeing," said Arthur. Nearly every person in the crowd was watching ZepNews while wearing their Purple Tints.

Tints looked like fashionable versions of the old 3D glasses with blue and red plastic lenses, but these were colored with the party affiliation of the user's choice, filtering the broadcast with ideological spin. Purple was the predominant color in the crowd—for a bunch of Supies, Rudy expected no less. Purple represented the current President and the majority party—the Ministry. Green represented the Reformist Party.

"Those Ministry quacks must be enjoying this," growled Rudy. "Every time innocents are caught up in a supe standoff, those assholes start blathering on about false flags and paid actors. I'm sure they can't wait to stir up trouble. All this happening right outside Supes-Con? My sniffer detects an actual conspiracy, not one of their loony theories."

The Ministry had a stranglehold over their loyal viewers. Every news story and scandal was twisted into an abomination of the truth so they would appear sympathetic to their followers. Obfuscating the truth to their advantage was as sinister as it sounded. All accounts were framed to make it appear like their belief system was being oppressed. Even when there was proof of atrocities committed by supes, the Ministry and their news services quickly went to work spinning tales. Lost in the messaging wars were real people, not props.

"Viewing the news through tinted glasses feels Orwellian," said Arthur. "The news through somebody else's lens. Did you bring yours?"

Rudy absentmindedly checked his pockets as if on autopilot. "Nah, I stopped using them. Besides, they clash with my fashion sense. And my common sense, for that matter. You?"

"No," said Arthur, as he watched Crimson Justice argue with police.

"Why do people wear Tints anyway?" Rudy didn't care who heard his ranting. "The facts are right there, people! Unfiltered! Why would anyone throw on a pair of Tints just to see a bunch of spin and fake news?"

"I think people are addicted to rage," said Arthur. "Why else would you choose to watch someone shout at you through the screen?"

Tints had been around for years, but ever since President Samuel C. Haines was elected, there had been an increase in usage. He told his faithful every day to fear the "evil" Reformist Party, and that *only* he spoke the truth. And they believed him—he had successfully hijacked the truth away from fifty percent of registered voters—while the other fifty percent spent their time debunking the lunacy at the expense of covering more important issues.

At the end of the day, the lies won.

"Bullshit Asymmetry Principle," said Arthur.

"Hmmm?"

"Nothing." Arthur shrugged. "It's an adage. The amount of energy expended to refute lies is greater than what is needed to create them."

Rudy and Dean had waxed philosophical about current events many times, often after a few pints when their speech started slurring. One of their many discussions was weighing heavily on Rudy's mind—*why be a supervillain?*

Subtracting those who robbed banks—and likewise, those who gave stolen money back to the poor—were supervillains misunderstood? Some of them marched against the Ministry in peaceful protests, engaging with V-Boys when needed. Others sought out dangerous vigilantes, like The Vigil, and even sparred with legalized supes for reasons beyond the public perception. Other times, it seemed like they were just starting trouble—their motives as alien to normies as their powers. But were they bad? Perhaps a better question—were they evil?

"I don't understand supervillains," groaned Rudy. "Don't they get tired of robbing banks? Don't they realize they're gonna get caught?"

"I don't know," said Arthur, cleaning his glasses with the untucked bottom of his shirt. "Maybe there's something really important inside that bank."

Rudy pondered that for a moment. The only important thing inside that bank, as far as he was concerned, was Dean. There were no less than five hundred people beyond the police barricades watching the event, many of them attendees from Supes-Con. This was just another form of live entertainment. Supe-history in person.

If it wasn't for Dean, Rudy would've been as far away as possible. Last spring, a whole crowd of bystanders was crushed by falling rubble and burned by an errant fireball as they watched the Blue Anvil take on the villain known as Torcher. At the time, Dean mentioned he'd once crossed paths with Torcher.

"You've met that guy?" asked Rudy. "The one wearing the deep-v-neck unitard, like The Demon himself, Gene Simmons?" They were watching the breaking news from Dean's apartment while snacking on bacon-wrapped scallops. Rudy made the best snacks and catered all their get-togethers—especially when Dean was hosting friends from out of town.

"Yeah," said Dean. "Brie dated him."

"You don't say," said Rudy, pretending to sound shocked. He was walking from person to person with a serving platter, making double the stops beside Peter.

"I remember that guy," said Peter between bites. "These are amazing, by the way."

"Thank you, Peter," said Rudy. He directed a proud grin toward Arthur sitting on a turquoise accent chair, who volleyed a double thumbs-up to his sweetheart for a job well done. Rudy even passed out scorecards at the end of every event, big or small, to get feedback on his catering.

"Chew your food," scolded Tammy, eyes rolling. "I get a night without the kid, and I'm still mothering somebody."

"What was he like?" asked Arthur. "Was Torcher always pernicious?" Arthur had been acting strange for weeks. Back then, he and Rudy had only been dating six months, and anytime a conversation about supes came up, he got weird—always asking about good and evil. Was there such a thing? It seemed more likely to Rudy that there were threads of good and bad in everybody.

Dean laughed. "He was always a dick."

"Aren't they all?" added Tammy.

"No," said Peter, still chewing, "he was a total dick."

"One day," said Dean, "with all these supes running around, things are going to get bad—SHIT!"

"Oh! What the fuck!"

"Did you see that?!"

"Oh my god. Oh my god!"

They saw it live that day. Thirty people dead in the blink of an eye, caught live via ZepNews. Dean was right—things got bad. The average citizen with common sense could no longer stay silent or ignorant. They were all shown the horrors of supe violence on live television. The footage, though graphic, was played a thousand times over the next several hours, as reporters and pundits, political figures and talk-show hosts all took sides.

The Ministry blamed the Reformists for putting themselves in harm's way to make supes look bad—blaming all those that died for being politically misaligned—even though nearly all the victims were registered Ministry voters.

A false flag, they claimed.

Which was why Rudy had asked Arthur to grab the leather case sitting on the kitchen counter, freshly unboxed the night before.

"Well, we can't let the entire situation get away from us, now can we?" said Rudy as he unzipped the leather case and pulled out his newest, most prized possession.

"What is that?" asked Arthur. He was a scientist, a rather brilliant one, and the thing inside the leather case seemed to befuddle him as much as the final episode of *Battlestar*.

"Arthur, for a man with more degrees than Jesus and Gandhi combined, how in the twenty-first century do you not know what this is?"

"Firstly," replied Arthur, "I don't think you realize just how true that statement was. Secondly, I'm a geneticist, biochemist, and biophysicist specializing in theoretical phenomena and its interaction with the human body." He pointed at the thing in Rudy's case. "But I don't get gadgets. Even my watch is a windup."

Rudy took a moment to pretend his partner didn't just call his newest favorite thing a mere *gadget*. He reinvented a smile across his proud-of-himself-for-his-cool-new-toy face.

"This," beamed Rudy, "is my future. It is a professional, and stylish, live-streaming headset."

Arthur looked at the thing inside the case as Rudy removed it from the soft foam interior and slipped it onto his head. Arthur tried not to offend the man he loved, so he chose his words carefully. "It's a camera someone glued onto a black visor?"

"Sometimes, Arthur," said Rudy, "I don't know what I see in you."

"Then what is it?" he asked.

"It's a *Go-Pro*," said Rudy, then shyly added, "that someone *hot*-glued onto a black, *Gucci*, visor." Rudy then hit the red power button and the Go-Pro powered on. "All I have to do is tether it to my phone, and I can live-stream everything, hands-free."

"Why are you live-streaming this?"

"It's a hostage situation, Arthur!" groaned Rudy. "The people love drama! So I'm bringing the drama to the people." Rudy then sighed as he thought of Dean. "Besides, when we get Deano back, I want a full record of this. It's a life lesson."

"Keep your mouth shut and don't mess with supes?" Arthur suggested.

"Exactly."

"The Red-Shitbag is here," said the man. He was wearing the top half of a Tragedy mask. Right below the nose was a jagged edge, as if someone had broken the mask in two. He was sweating, anxious, and kept pulling the mask away from his face to cool down.

He was on his tiptoes, standing atop a swiveling office chair on wheels, peeking out of a window at angles that kept him hidden from view. The window, set high into the marble wall, was beside the golden turnstile in the lobby of the First National Bank, and the floor was littered with glass and personal belongings—broken cell phones, purses, even house keys.

Someone yanked on his trench coat to gather his attention. When the man turned, the other began flashing signs.

"Sorry, Perc," said the man on the chair. "The boss ain't listening to me. Go ask Moll-E."

Perc tied his frizzy hair into a ponytail and straightened his mask—the lower portion of the same broken Tragedy mask his partner wore—so that it rested over his mouth, then set off into the darkened halls of the First National Bank. The lights were off to keep their movements concealed, but there were enough flashing red and blue lights from all the cop cars to keep the whole place doused in color.

Perc wandered down the hall, peeking inside offices until he spotted her. He approached Moll-E carefully—she was lying on a desktop full of papers, eyes closed and massaging her temples. He gave her a nudge to gather her attention and startled her. She gave off an audible yelp.

"Sorry," signed Perc.

"What the fucking fuck!" growled Moll-E. "I almost clocked you." She was holding a baton and tossed it onto the desk.

Moll-E wore a bright red wig fashioned into a bob with bangs, and an exaggerated sugar skull smile extended from ear to ear was painted onto her face. It made her look happy, even though she was all butterflies wrapped in black latex that whined every time she moved.

"That's the thing about being mute," signed Perc, with Moll-E translating out loud. "Everyone always acts like I'm sneaking up on them on purpose."

She rolled her eyes and groaned. "Whatever." Her heart was still fluttering.

When she had caught her breath, Perc signed another message—even his hand movements appeared frustrated.

"Where's Oxy?" she asked.

Perc signed something back that took her an extra moment to comprehend, then gestured over his shoulder.

"I can't go to the door," she argued. "Who's going to watch all these assholes?"

Behind her were three dozen people on the dusty floor, tied up and gagged with black tape. Perc shrugged, then fled back down the hall to rejoin Oxy by the window.

He left Moll-E alone as she stared down at all seventy-two eyes imploring her to let them go. Seventy-two eyes—some green, some blue, some brown, others with glasses—and Moll-E looked away. They were people, innocents, but they were also protection—a human shield keeping the cops and the big Red-Buttwipe from barging through the door. Still, the boss was way off-script, and nobody had given her the lines for the next scene.

"What's the plan, boss?" She could hear his booted footsteps moving closer from around the corner. Big ominous footsteps, with a calm gait that made her nervous.

"Moll-E," said the boss—his own face hidden under a Japanese war mask with big mean teeth molded into the metal casting that covered his nose and mouth. He looked angry—or at least, angrier than usual. "Fill them up, then take Perc and Oxy and get into the hole."

The man towered over her by more than a foot, which was almost six inches more than his usual size. That was her hint to keep it cordial.

"Fill them up?" asked Moll-E. "Dust, don't be stupid."

Dust sidestepped her, then paced down the hall toward the revolving door in the lobby and walked right up to the glass. There was a sea of people behind police barricades, cameras from every major network, and two dozen police cars. He stood there unafraid, exposed, and watched the red-hooded behemoth speaking to the commissioner. It was only a matter of time before that lunatic came busting through the wall, fists flying. Dust had gone toe-to-toe with Crimson Justice before. They had a past. But the dynamic of their rivalry had changed.

When Moll-E rejoined them in the lobby, Dust asked, "Is it done?"

"Yeah," she said sadly.

"Go," said Dust. "Get in the hole. I'm going to leave a message for our friend."

"What are we gonna do about the stash?" asked Moll-E, but Dust once again ignored her.

"Shit," spat Oxy. He hopped off the chair in a hurry and sent it careening into the opposite wall. "Are we really doing this?"

Dust and Moll-E flinched with all the noise, prompting her to ask, "Doing what?" but nobody answered her.

"It's time to hit the red lunatic where it hurts most." Even with his face covered, they could sense Dust smiling.

Perc clapped his gloved hands one time, as if to agree, then fist bumped Oxy.

"Seriously?" growled Moll-E. "Are we leaving them like that?"

"Just c'mon," said Oxy, waving at her to follow. "We'll tell you all about it."

As Oxy, Perc, and Moll-E fled into a back office—Moll-E arguing the whole way—Dust retrieved a can of metallic gold spray paint from his leather duster. He casually shook the can, mixing its contents as he passed the room full of hostages. At the sound of his reappearance, a few twitched, barely acknowledging his presence. Moll-E had pumped every hostage full of so much Moll-Energy, most of them were strung out, lying around, and riding the highest of pleasure highs.

Dust, however, wasn't interested in them.

Each of the three dozen hostages had been filled to the brim, pumped full of Moll-E's pleasure powers, on his orders. That much energy encased in human flesh was like a charge, just strong enough to put a hole in their heads should a large disturbance set them off.

Nobody told Moll-E the plan because none of them could stomach all the yammering that'd follow from her righteous mouth-hole. The last thing Dust wanted was someone to make him second-guess himself. This was what needed to happen. He was the leader. He called the shots, not Moll-E and her activism.

Dust had learned a trick or two, and sometimes the only way to win was to change the narrative. A narrative that blanketed everything in terms of good and evil. If he was evil, Dust was going to show them how evil he could be, and the payoff would be exquisite.

When he turned the corner to the next hall, he popped the cap with his thumb, letting it bounce along the floor and settle before he left his message.

Once finished, he threw the can as hard as he could—his supe strength busted the pressurized can wide open with a loud pop, as if he was testing fate. The next bang would do it. Then he retraced his steps and followed the rest of his team into the office at the back, gritting his teeth the whole way. They didn't get what they came for, but it wasn't all for nothing.

Dust was determined to make this a very good day.

Crimson Justice was furious.

The Dope Gang were holding hostages not two hundred feet away, and the dopey commissioner wouldn't let him do what he did best—bruise, bust, and bash. Time was ticking, and the commissioner wanted to "negotiate" for a "peaceful resolution" to the standoff.

Where the hell did he think they were? Canada?

This was the United American States! Home of Clint Eastwood, football—the kind played with the hands, not the feet—Thanksgiving turkey, hot dogs and ketchup—not that commie mustard crap—and the teeny bikini—with modesty, of course. Americans didn't negotiate with terrorists!

Dudley was a weak, pathetic old man who didn't appreciate the kind of Law and Order Crimson Justice brought to the city. Just because the un-Tinted news said that violent crime was at an all-time high, a three-thousand percent increase, didn't mean they were right. It was sensationalist bullshit. Reformist lies. Anti-Purple Sympie deceit. Fake news. Crimson Justice was the savior of the city. Only he could make it safer. Only he was capable of that.

President Haines had signed an Executive Order last year giving Crimson Justice, and those like him, special permission to do whatever was necessary to clean the streets. There wasn't a person in all of Wonder City who would dare litter, not even a piece of lint, knowing that a crimson streak was headed their way. A cleaner city was good for all. Cleanliness was Godliness, and Godliness was patriotic.

"Are you listening?" asked the commissioner. "We have jurisdiction here. Remember, the law is the law."

"Do not lecture me on the law," said Crimson Justice. "I am the law!"

Through the crowds of spectators came a series of chants and cheers as a bronzed man in a toga leapt over the police barrier like he was hopping over a puddle. He bounced over to them in three quick strides.

"Aha! Commissioner! Crimson Justice!" said Apollo, puffing his chest out as if attempting to look as large as the hooded supe. "I was in the neighborhood and thought I'd offer some glowing assistance."

"Who are you?" asked the commissioner.

"Apollo, Champion of the Light!" he said, striking a pose straight out of the Mr. Universe contest. Several women in the front row behind the barriers swooned, and Apollo brightened.

"What do you want?" asked Crimson Justice. He checked his Crimson Watch beneath his Crimson Gloves, as if he was running late for an appointment.

"To share my glow!" said Apollo. When nobody spoke, he clarified. "To help you."

"Are you suggesting Crimson Justice needs a...*sidekick*?" asked Crimson Justice.

"Do I look like a dim sidekick?"

The commissioner and Crimson Justice exchanged a glance, though neither of them felt the obvious answer was necessary.

"C'mon, man! I'm burning for some action!" said Apollo.

The hooded monster put a gloved finger into Apollo's face and held it there until Apollo's eyes crossed. "I am the sole upholder of the law," said Crimson Justice.

"That's not true," said the commissioner.

"I am the last true bastion of peace," said Crimson Justice.

"That's not true either," said Dudley.

"I am the blood of the justice system," said Crimson Justice.

"From a certain point of view," added Dudley.

"I do not need a *hand* from a half-naked hedonist with bad puns," said Crimson Justice. "I can handle the law's business alone."

"Oh yeah," retorted Apollo. "Just like you've handled the Dope Gang?"

Crimson Justice seethed.

He had been battling the Dope Gang for the better part of the last three years, ever since they showed up in Wonder City. It was a game of cat and mouse—every few months they'd peek their rodent heads of their rodent holes, and he'd come pouncing in only for them to scoot away, back into hiding. Cowards. They were all cowards.

But he got his revenge. He had killed Annie Phetamine and maimed Crystal Beth. And today, their time was finally up. They were trapped inside the First National Bank, and there was no escape. Not this time.

"You've been battling them for years," said Apollo, "and they're still causing you problems. I know why you don't want my help—because if I out-supe you, then everyone will know just how much of a flaccid dick you really are."

The parts of Crimson Justice that weren't crimson grew apple red.

Apollo turned and spotted half a dozen Sunnies, including Rudy with his visor, live-streaming the whole ordeal. He smiled for the camera and waved at Kristy, who screamed like a supe-groupie.

"My gal, Kristy," winked Apollo, gesturing toward her. "She really shines in that Lady Crimson Justice cosplay, doesn't she?"

Then Apollo gestured for Crimson Justice to lean in, as if the toga-clad supe wanted to share something personal. Crimson Justice bent over as Apollo propped himself up onto his tiptoes to get as close as he could to Crimson Justice's massive granite chin.

Apollo whispered, "You see, you and Kristy are a lot alike."

"Hmmm," replied Crimson Justice.

"You're both my little b—"

Many people believed Crimson Justice was a sluggish oaf. Before he died, Optimum Overdrive was the fastest man alive. He was a small man with the physique of an Olympic long-distance runner and could move so fast, he once was in two places at the same time to hide his secret identity. Crimson Justice, however, was as beefy as a heavyweight professional wrestler, and as tall as men could grow without artificial limbs and implants like those of Robo-Lad. There was a misconception, however, that the bigger one was, the slower they were, as if size and girth made one into a lumbering buffoon incapable of reacting as swiftly as Optimum Overdrive did. After all, that truth was backed by science—bigger was often slower.

Yet before Apollo could finish speaking, Crimson Justice snagged him by the throat in half the blink of an eye—so fast that there was an audible snap. As fast as Apollo was, Crimson Justice was that much faster, and Apollo's shine dimmed with every pound of pressure crushing his throat.

Kristy gasped.

"I am nobody's bitch!" growled Crimson Justice as he turned to the commissioner. "The Dope Gang was in your custody. You returned them to the streets to terrorize the people of this city."

"The charges wouldn't stick," argued the commissioner.

"Why not?"

Apollo's face was turning blue.

"Because you beat one of them to death!" shouted Dudley. "You put another into a coma. You assaulted them. They were defending themselves. They were defending their home."

"Are you suggesting that I broke the law? I, that am law, thus broken?" asked Crimson Justice. "Are you going to arrest me for taking two more criminals off the streets?"

"There are a lot of people," said the commissioner, choosing his words carefully, "that believe you do more harm than good."

With that, Crimson Justice had enough. His body shook with rage, but his eyes seemed to burn through the gloom of his shaded face.

"Pathetic," he fumed. "The bell of Liberty has stopped tolling in this once great metropolis. Wonder City's clandestine commissioner has lost his nerve. If you cannot do what must be done, then I shall become judge, jury, and executioner." Dragging Apollo behind him, he took two steps toward the bank before turning back to Dudley. "I never thought I'd see the day when the commissioner of Wonder City would turn Sympie."

Commissioner Dudley watched on as the six-foot-eight monster regripped Apollo by the head and tossed him overhand like he was serving up a hail-Mary. The Supe was a comet, zipping through the air with a loud hiss that silenced once he struck the golden turnstile door and punctured a hole through concrete reinforced walls. The immediate impact masked the brief sound of screams within the building, followed by three dozen pops, like firecrackers.

Before the dust had cleared, Crimson Justice marched through the hole with fists clenched—behind him swept Wonder City S.W.A.T., keeping their distance, weapons drawn.

From a heap on the ground, covered in bits of brick, mortar, and sheetrock, Apollo stood up, slurring, "You hit like a girl," before stumbling backward and out for the count.

Particles of plaster and sheetrock stirred into the air like a well-shaken snow-globe, so thick it was hard to breathe without a mask. The bank was dark, the power cut hours ago, and a gloom settled into the lobby. With a quick scan, Crimson Justice marched inward, following the scent of crime while S.W.A.T. kept pace.

The hallway opened into a waiting room, then bent around a corner.

Crimson Justice didn't stop to take in the scene. He merely disappeared into the next hall, hunting for his nemeses. He saw the scene—he had to—but he did not care. Crime was crime, and the law only cared for reaping criminals. It did not stop to view crime, only to avenge it.

"Help me," whined a young man covered in blood. His smile was so big, his eyes fluttering with pleasure, that he could barely steer where his legs were moving. He wandered into Crimson Justice's path, and the big red supe pushed him aside.

The man exploded, and Crimson Justice kept moving, paying the victim no mind.

"Oh shit," said one of gun-toting members of S.W.A.T., and they stopped following the supe. Crimson Justice didn't need their help. He didn't want it either. They got in the way and made things complicated. That was the problem with police: they were easy targets for villains. He only needed them to clean up the mess.

"Sir," said another—Crimson Justice could hear the radio waves connecting. "We need ambulances. And the coroner."

And they'd be cleaning up this mess for a while, thought Crimson Justice. He walked until he saw the crushed bank vault at the end of the hall, but his attention turned to the glittering gold along the white marble wall. The paint smelled fresh.

On the wall was a message, thick runny drips streaking down to the floor.

"Nothing's over," growled Crimson Justice. "Nothing's over!"

The supe spun, his cape flailing, and stalked back toward the exit. Along the way he passed S.W.A.T., many of them down on one knee or huddled over. One of them was puking into a garbage pail while a specialist inspected the victims. The commissioner was prancing up the hall in protective gear—and when he arrived at the scene, his jaw dangled open at the sight.

There were more than thirty people in the room. They were all dead. All of them with gaping head wounds—blood spattered from floor to ceiling. Many of them were dressed in costume—Supes-Con attendees in the wrong place at the wrong time.

"What happened?" asked the commissioner as Crimson Justice blew past, marching with a purpose, paying the dead no mind.

"They exploded," said the specialist, glaring at Crimson Justice after inspecting what was left of the victims. "He didn't even care, he just let them explode."

"What set them off?" asked Dudley.

"They were pumped full of Moll-Energy," he said. "Walking bombs waiting to go off."

"What does that mean?"

"Something particularly loud or throttling would do it," the specialist replied. "Just took one big bang, and the rest went off."

The commissioner had seen some callous shit in his day, but nothing as callous as this. The city's protector was a menace. Sure, the criminals were responsible for loading the gun, but it was Crimson Justice who pulled the trigger, just as they knew he would. They knew he'd destroy anything in his way—which included using a smaller supe like a battering ram.

"Stop!" yelled the commissioner. "Crimson Justice, you're under arrest!"

The men raised their weapons halfheartedly. None of them wanted to fire on the supe, their bullets sure to bounce off and put them all in harm's way.

Crimson Justice turned, looked at the commissioner, and said, "Try and stop me."

Then he waltzed out of the bank into the daylight, and with one leap he disappeared into the sky.

CHAPTER 8

"I MET AMANDA IN THE SECOND GRADE," SAID TORI. DEAN smiled, and she immediately felt the need to clarify. "She was my best friend, pervert."

"Hmmm?"

"I saw the look on your face," she said. "I'm not gay."

"My best friend is gay. No judgment."

"Oh," said Tori. She wasn't used to that. Defending her relationship with her best friend was a constant battle. All men that crossed her path seemed to think that just because they were close and unrelated, they had to be lovers. "Sorry."

She had her guard up for so long and found it difficult to lower.

"It's okay." Dean shrugged. "Go on."

"I met Amanda in the second grade."

Amanda was once Tori's neighbor in their small Pennsylvania town, and they were the very best of friends. Inseparable. They played in the woods behind their houses and watched horror movies in the dark while eating popcorn in their sleeping bags when everyone else was asleep. They bounced around on the bed singing Patty Smyth's "The Warrior" at the tops of their lungs, as little girls do, imagining rock star dreams and fairy-tale endings. There was nothing more important than their friendship, and there was nothing more upsetting when they had a falling-out.

Boys come and go, but best friends are forever—and Rick was the man who nearly broke that promise between them.

The girls met Rick at college. He was rich, captain of the baseball, football, and rugby teams—and he had no idea either of them existed as they watched him from their perch in the back row of their Economics 101 lecture hall. He may not have known them yet, but he was often a topic of conversation late at night as they laid in their beds, waiting to fall asleep.

The dormitory was noisy, even during night hours. Amanda was a light sleeper, and it often took her twice as long to fall asleep.

"If you had a superpower, what would it be?" asked Amanda one night, well past lights-out, as they laid in their beds.

Tori groaned and stuffed her face into her pillow. "The ability to super sleep."

"No. Really."

"The ability to tune out annoying roommate questions."

"Jerk."

"Jerkoff."

"Jerkhole," said Amanda. "Supes are interesting. I mean, how do they get their powers? Do their powers choose them? Is there a reason why Warrior Princess can create sonic booms by clapping her hands? Or why the Reaping Raven can manifest her psychic scythe?"

Tori wasn't as fond of supes as Amanda. She had her reasons.

Amanda often pondered these things—and *everything*—out loud. Posing hypotheticals to Tori in rapid fire, barely receiving an answer before hurling another, equally mundane question. Tori pondered them too—she just didn't want to share her opinions after midnight when she had a quiz later that morning.

"What do you think it's like to kiss the Perfectionist?" asked Amanda. It was the question all the young ladies wondered back then—the supe was… *perfection*…and died years later while striking a pose for the paparazzi as a two-ton safe fell on his head.

"I don't know," said Tori. "Wet. Squishy. Lots of puckering?"

"Stop!" laughed Amanda. "Do you think he has a girlfriend?"

"I don't know," droned Tori. "Probably."

"Oh my god, Tor, why are you being so flaky?"

Perhaps she was just tired. Perhaps she was tired of this game—tired of the imaginary, the hypotheticals and speculation.

The girls had dated only two boys in high school—one of whom dated them both. When Tori dumped Trent, she caught Amanda making out with him outside the comics shop in town. Amanda denied it, despite dating Trent for six whole months afterward.

The girls nearly came to blows.

Amanda cried and cried until Tori forgave her, and they added an amendment to their friendship: **Amendment 3**—*Henceforth, neither party may date, hook up with, or marry the other's ex—nor can either party compete for the same man once one or the other has called dibs or made their intentions known.*

It was ironclad. Neither would dare to lose their friendship over a boy ever again.

But Tori was older now and tired of boys. She wanted a man, someone she could connect with intellectually. She wanted excitement. She wanted to feel exhilaration when he was near—the pitter-patter of her heart racing in time with his. And she had suitors, just like Amanda, but she was looking for something special. They both were.

And the guy from their Econ 101 class fit the bill just right—if only she could get his attention…if only she had a chance to say hi and melt into those big muscly arms…

"I don't know," said Tori, finally answering after her mind wandered back to reality. "I'm tired. Can we just go to sleep?"

"Yeah," said Amanda. Then she giggled. "Sweet Econ dreams, Tor."

Amanda knew her better than she knew herself.

Tori smiled as she drifted off to sleep.

"Sounds like a rivalry," said Dean.

"Oh, it was a rivalry alright," replied Tori. "As much as I loved Amanda, our teens were frustrating. I always felt like she was competing with me. When I got compliments on my combat boots from the thrift store, she went out and bought brand new Doc Martens. When I made the marching band, the next day she tried out for the cheer squad. I never wanted to compete, but I also never stopped to think about why she did the things she did back then. I think she was dealing with her own trauma the only way she knew how. The more I tried to be my own me, the more she tried to close that gap."

"That sounds…" Dean fought for the correct word. "difficult."

"It was," said Tori. "Especially when you love someone."

It was winter. Tori remembered because Amanda was wearing that stupid knit wool cap with the obnoxious pink pom-pom bobbing around every time she moved. Their econ class had just ended, and as they filed out of the lecture hall, Amanda dropped her pen. Whether Amanda dropped it on purpose, or if it was cosmic destiny, Tori never knew. Not only did that pen roll, clank, and bounce down all thirty steps to the bottom, it avoided contact with no less than ten pairs of legs before it landed at the feet of Rick Jansen—the nameless hunk of Tori's fantasies.

He picked it up and seemed to smolder when he saw the perky blonde bobbing her way down the stairs toward him, her pom-pom bouncing, bouncing, bouncing. Tori was halfway out the door when she realized Amanda wasn't right behind her and ducked back into the lecture hall just in time to see her bestie engage in conversation with *him*. A conversation that involved way too many smiles. But it wasn't until Amanda used her go-to move—putting her hand playfully onto his shoulder, then retracting the same hand to brush the hair from her face—that Tori realized she was gritting her teeth. She stalked away to her next class.

"What was that about?" asked Amanda. She found Tori sipping from a gigantic coffee in the quad hours later, jotting down notes like she was attempting to murder the page.

"What was what about?" asked Tori. It was dumb to play dumb with Amanda. Playing dumb only worked on people who couldn't read every facial expression ever committed to the flesh of one's face. Amanda was the world's expert on all things Tori and saw right through her bullshit.

"Why'd you ignore me?" Amanda was irritated. This fight had been brewing for months—a culmination of unlike events—waiting for just the right moment to explode.

"I wasn't," said Tori.

"We finally had a chance to meet Rick, and you ran away," said Amanda.

"Who's Rick?"

Amanda rolled her eyes.

"I told Rick I wanted him to meet my hot friend," said Amanda.

"Liar," groaned Tori, her tone stuck somewhere between joke and accusation.

"You just can't be okay with me dating the hot guy first."

There was something disturbing about what she said. Something that stuck like a pin prick into a flaring nerve.

"What does that even mean?" argued Tori. "Are we forever bound to date each other's sloppy seconds, or something?"

"No, I just…" The wind in Amanda's angry sails had blown itself out. "I thought life was about experiences, and if you can't share those experiences with your best friend, then what have you got in the end?"

It was a poetic slog of shit. Shit for sure, though still poetic, and heartfelt in a twisted way.

"Yeah, we don't have to do that," said Tori in the most sarcastic tone she could perform. "Date who you want to date."

"Okay," said Amanda. "Well, I want to date Rick, and we're going out on Friday."

"What ever happened to Amendment 3? You knew I was interested."

"Tor," growled Amanda, "sometimes you can be so self-centered." Then she stormed off and left Tori to stew.

For the next few days, the more they danced around the topic, the more irritated each of them became. Innocuous questions like, "Did you eat all the cereal?" suddenly became Chernobyl-level meltdown events hidden beneath the cold war between them.

Tori decided on principle alone that she didn't want Rick. The fact that he'd choose a girl with so many issues proved that he was undatable. Friday came and went, and Amanda made no mention of how her date had gone. And Tori refused to ask.

However, every other evening, Amanda would finish her homework and start a new ritual of bathing, shaving, perfuming, and dressing in her nicest clothes.

Tori decided it was just a phase—a week-long romance soon to implode. In fact, Tori started dating too, but she was too distracted and broke it off after two dates. When Amanda began sitting next to Rick in class—a class in which Tori retained zero information—she swore to herself that love was the last thing she wanted, right after a punch to the throat.

Five Things I Want More Than Love
#5 – Jury Duty on a Saturday
#4 – Sitting next to an unshowered bro on a crowded subway
#3 – A papercut soaking in lemon juice
#2 – A root canal without novocaine
#1 – A punch to the throat

The pit in Tori's stomach widened every time Amanda bounced out of their room to meet Rick for yet another date. She struggled to understand what she was feeling until one day she came to a horrible realization…

…she was jealous, and she immediately hated herself for it.

A few weeks later there was a knock on the door after Amanda left for yet another rendezvous with Rick. Frustrated and angry over the trajectory of her life, Tori's nights devolved into wearing a ratty old t-shirt and pajama bottoms while eating dry cereal directly out of the box. But that fateful knock brought her to the door.

"Did you forget your keys?" She swung the door wide open with a dried piece of Captain Crunch welded to her cheek.

"No," said Rick. "Hi, um, is Amanda home?"

Tori felt the stray morsel slowly detach itself from her cheek and fall to the floor—quite like the last shred of her pride. Rick looked like a golden god—tan, sandy blonde hair, steely blue eyes, and tall—oh man, was he tall up close. And his smile? His embarrassed smile, that she only later realized was embarrassed *for her*, set Tori aflame.

"No," she stammered. "Amanda—She's not home. Was—was she not out with you?"

"Unfortunately, no," said Rick. "I tried calling, but it goes to voicemail."

"Let me try," said Tori, as she grabbed her cell phone from her pajama pocket and quickly dialed the only number saved in her favorites. It never even attempted to connect.

"See?" he said.

Tori held a forefinger up as if to pause the conversation. "Wait right here." Then gently closed the door.

Once out of sight, she ran to the closet and retrieved her clothes from the hamper, then wrangled them onto her body along with a quick reapplication of deodorant, chased by a gulp of mouthwash she forced herself to swallow without a sink to spit in. When she reopened the door moments later, Rick was waiting patiently as she entered the hall with her coat and keys.

"What are you doing?" he asked as she locked the door behind her.

"Amanda's not answering her phone," said Tori. "So let's go look for her."

The conversation started slow. Not that Rick wasn't a confident guy capable of having conversations with any woman he chose, strictly because he could break the thickest ice with only a smoldering glance. Conversation was slow because Tori was waging an internal war, fighting back the compulsion to jump into that man's arms and make out with him on the spot.

She spent so much time denying her attraction that it was bubbling over like a boiling pot overfull with macaroni.

"Where do you think she is?" asked Rick as they entered the stairwell and started descending.

"Where did you agree to meet?"

"At the Warminster." It was the most expensive restaurant in town. The kind of restaurant where fancy people dined, not students.

"Well, did you check there?" she sneered as they exited the dorms and into the courtyard.

"I was just there fifteen minutes ago. We were supposed to meet over an hour before that," he explained through puffs of white vapor in the cold winter air.

"You waited for almost an hour?"

"Yeah." Rick shrugged bashfully, like he was receiving a compliment.

"And you didn't think something was immediately wrong?" she growled, wiping the grin off Rick's smug face. "That girl's never late for an appointment, let alone class, meals, homework assignments, *or her period*. She'd never, under any circumstances, show up late for a dinner date."

"I didn't know," said Rick.

"Yeah, how would you know? You don't fucking know her."

An uncomfortable silence passed between them, then Tori chose a direction and started walking. Rick jogged along to catch up to Tori's furious pace, over patches of icy, half melted snow that spotted the courtyard like slippery landmines.

"How long have you two been friends?"

"Forever. Since we were five."

"That's a long time. That's more than half your life."

"You can math!" she jeered. "Wow, can you read too? Or are you just a typical dumbfuck jock?"

"Whoa," scolded Rick, his eyes flaring. "What the hell is your problem?"

"My problem is that you lost my best friend." The truth was, she was taking her anger with Amanda out on this big hunk she'd fought so hard to hate. She didn't even understand why she liked him. He didn't seem smart. He didn't seem like the kind of guy who could even hold a conversation, let alone make her laugh. He was the Venus flytrap of men—all allure until the jaws slammed shut.

And yet, when she peered at him over her shoulder while storming toward the bus stop, tromping over icy hills of plowed snow, she felt an awful twinge in her gut. She wanted that boy to look at her. She wanted him to want her.

They stepped off the bus into town, right outside the Warminster. Amanda was nowhere to be found. Not inside—the hostess shrugging—nor outside in the parking lot.

Tori tried calling her again.

"Where now?" asked Rick as Tori leaned against the stucco siding of the restaurant.

Straight to voicemail.

"I don't know," said Tori, hanging up.

"Is there someplace she likes to go that maybe—"

"Fuck!" growled Tori. "I don't know, dipshit."

"You curse a lot more than women should," said Rick.

"Fuck you," she spat. "No wait, fuuuuuck youuuuuuu." As she finished, she gave him a double shot of middle fingers, wagging them around as if she were mocking him, and heard Patty Smith singing "bang bang" in her head.

Rick stepped closer to her. Too close. She looked up at him, he down at her, and seconds later she was pulling herself away from his lips. They had kissed, and Tori wasn't sure who initiated. It just happened.

But then he was back. Close to her again, and she couldn't say no. She gave in. She relented and was consumed in the passion—until a busboy opened the back door and tossed a full bag of trash into the dumpster. The noise startled them enough to break their connection.

Feet apart, they stared each other down, panting for air. When Rick motioned toward her again, Tori squirmed away.

"I can't," she said.

Rick ran a hand through his hair. He didn't seem upset or confused. He seemed eager. As much as Tori wanted it, she wanted to find Amanda more. She kept imagining all the horrible things that might've happened to her, and it was making her upset.

"What exactly were your plans for tonight?" asked Tori. It started off as an accusation, and as Tori heard the words leave her mouth, she adjusted. "Meet at the Warminster, six PM sharp?"

"Yeah," said Rick. "I texted her earlier today between classes."

There was something about the way he said it that gave Tori a hunch. Like a detective putting together various pieces of information, then making a logical leap.

"Rick," said Tori, "what exactly did the text say."

"Meet at the Warminster at six PM."

"No," she groaned. "Read it to me."

Rick retrieved his phone, carefully unlocked it, and swiped into his messages. Then he began reading it to himself. "Oh."

"Oh?"

"I may have told her to meet at the West Street."

"The West Street?"

"Damn fucking auto-correct," he scolded himself. "It says WestSmtrt."

"That's not auto-correct, you fuck-knob, that's fat-fingered carelessness," she growled. "What's West Street?"

"It's a dive bar," he said, then waved. "Come on."

After a quiet five-block walk down a small side street, they came across a pub that embodied everything one considers when affectionately calling someplace a "hole in the wall." Inside the pub was an actual hole in the wall. In fact, it had plenty. It was mostly empty, but the clientele were townies and older gentlemen, a few of them smoking cigars in the corner.

"How do you know about this place?" asked Tori.

"Me and the boys come here all the time," said Rick.

Tori nodded as she walked over to the bar and waved down the bartender—an older fellow with a thick mustache that looked like a scrubbing brush.

"Hi, we're looking for our friend," said Tori.

She had no sooner finished speaking when the bartender said, "Blonde lass named Amanda?"

"Yes! You've seen her?"

"I have. Left here about forty minutes ago. Told me all about the fella she was meeting here. Her phone died, and she was quite upset when he didn't show." He looked over at Rick. "You the fella?" Rick nodded. "She went on and on about you."

Tori felt about as low as she could possibly feel.

Amanda was probably back home crying her eyes out, thinking she was stood up. And while they were out looking for her, Tori had managed to stick her tongue into Rick's mouth.

"Thanks," said Tori.

"You betcha."

When they left the bar, Tori was too lost in thought to hear Rick. He was yammering on about something, but all she could think about was Amanda, and how devastated she must have been. Eventually Rick grabbed her shoulder and spun her around before she stopped walking away from him.

Tori shrugged it off aggressively, then glared at him for touching her.

"So, what do we do now?" asked Rick.

"What do you mean what do we do now?" she said. "I go home. You take Amanda on your date."

Rick ran another hand through his hair and grinned. "We're out. Why don't we grab a bite instead?"

"No," said Tori. She had started to walk away when Rick stepped into her path. His closeness was disarming, and she hated the way she felt around him. All weak and helpless—on the defensive.

"Why not?" he asked.

"I thought it was obvious," said Tori.

"Maybe I want something else."

"Amanda's my best friend."

"So?"

"So, what did you do?" asked Dean.

"I'm not proud of myself," said Tori. She winced just thinking of her impropriety.

"Oh," said Dean, "Shit. I wasn't expecting that."

Tori glared at him through narrowed eyes. "Fuck off. I didn't ask for your opinion on my life choices. What gives you and anyone else the right to judge me?"

"I wasn't judging."

"But you did." She got up and audibly groaned. "Right now, you're developing an opinion of me. There's a shitty word that's swimming around in your shitty head."

"What word?" asked Dean. He got up from the floor—it seemed weird to be debating someone while sitting on the ground below them.

"Oh, come on!" she shouted at the ceiling. "The word. The word guys use when they want to make a girl feel like slime."

"I have no idea what you're talking about."

Was he really that naïve?

"Just say it!" she shouted, pointing at his chest. "Say it! Tell me I'm a slut!" When Dean didn't answer, she took two steps toward the crushed vault door and wound up. "I don't want to be in here anymore!" Her fist connected against the five-foot-thick slab of crushed empyrean steel with a high-pitched plunk. "Owww! Fucking hell!"

"Are you okay?" shouted Dean, rushing over to her.

"That really fucking hurt," she said, cradling her wrist. "I'm fine."

"Are you sure? Let me see." He reached out and gently held her arm. "You wound up and bashed your hand pretty bad."

"Thanks for the play-by-play, wankface." She snatched her arm away.

Tori walked back to her original spot by the lockboxes on the other side of the room and plopped herself onto a thick bed of cash on the floor. From where she was, she couldn't see Dean over the debris. After a few moments of silence, she peeked up over the mound and caught Dean with his eyes closed and shaking his head. Was he scolding himself?

The poor guy was locked inside a bank vault with a lunatic, thought Tori. He didn't deserve that. Dean wasn't the man she wanted to punish. He was just the only person in the room.

She sat up and propped herself against the wall.

"Your turn," she said.

CHAPTER 9

1:15 PM

"HELLO FRIENDS! BOYFRIENDS! GIRLFRIENDS! BOY-GIRL AND girl-boy friends! MoodyRudy here with an update, live from the scene of Wonder City's latest supe throwdown!"

Rudy forced Arthur to wear the Go-Pro visor so he could speak to his audience, and though Arthur would do just about anything for his partner, this was coming close to the line.

"The Red Guardian himself," said Rudy, framed by the First National Bank and a series of police cars behind him. "Crimson Justice stormed into the Wonder City First National using the supe known as Apollo as a projectile weapon. The Wonder City S.W.A.T. followed them inside, guns drawn, ready to take down the Dope Gang once and for all.

"But" continued Rudy, "just a moment ago, Crimson Justice marched out and flew away." Rudy pointed to a big hole in the First National Bank outer wall, where Crimson Justice tossed Apollo through the plate glass turnstile. From the darkness inside the building emerged a steady stream of S.W.A.T., their guns and heads lowered as sirens blared in the distance.

"My man," said Rudy, waving down the nearest officer. "What happened inside the First National Bank?"

"They're gone," said the officer. He seemed distraught.

"Could you elaborate?" asked Rudy, a big smile still plastered all over his face.

"They're dead," he replied. "All of them." Then the officer looked straight into Rudy's eyes. "Crimson Justice killed them."

Rudy's smile melted. "Hold on, who did Crimson Justice kill?"

"The hostages."

"But," said Rudy, his mind not making the proper connection, "my best friend is in there." The officer shook his head and walked on as the surrounding crowd gasped. Rudy's reaction was immediate. He started hyperventilating, then began to cry. "Crimson Justice killed my best friend."

Arthur removed the visor, but the live stream kept broadcasting. He put his arms around Rudy, and as Rudy wept into Arthur's shoulder, the live feed rose to more than three million viewers.

EARLIER THAT DAY...

"Julian," said Joseph, peeking around his son's bedroom door. "Pal, let's go, it's time for practice." It was Joseph's week with his son, and every day had been a struggle to get Julian to school or Scouts or any of his extracurricular activities. This morning was piano, then soccer.

"Do I have to?" whined Julian, his head stuffed under his pillow with the illustrated hockey pucks on the pillowcase.

"No, you don't have to," deadpanned Joseph, and Julian's head erupted from where it was wedged beneath the pillow.

"Really?"

"No, not really," he said, "C'mon, you're going to be late, and I have to go into the office."

"On a Saturday?"

"I love it so much, I get to go on Saturday. That's sales for ya, pal."

The ride over to the middle school was an easy fifteen-minute drive through the Wonder City suburbs—and thank goodness for satellite radio. Joseph couldn't bear to listen to the local sports talk and their naïve fantasies of the Wonder City Soar taking the division title over Joseph's Metro City Sentinels. There were few things that got his blood boiling, and Sentinels hockey was one of them.

The host began the Metro City sports update with a note about the Ultramen football team before diving into hockey talk. "Sentinels forward Richie 'Rock' Atkinson has been activated from the IR and will return to practice today."

"Dad!" cried Julian. "Rock's back in the lineup!"

"I know." Joseph calmly merged into traffic. "I heard."

"When can we go to a game?"

"I don't know, pal." Joseph sighed. "Tickets are expensive."

"Yeah," Julian grumbled. His spirits had been crushed enough times to know not to pester Joseph about the things he couldn't afford.

"I guess it's a good thing your birthday is next month. The Sentinels play the Soar here in Wonder City that same weekend."

"Huh?"

"I got us two tickets," said Joseph with a smirk.

"Are you serious? Or are you joking?" asked Julian, his eyes narrowed suspiciously. "I don't think I could take it if you're joking."

"No jokes here, pal," said Joseph, amused with his son's sense of drama.

"Awesome!"

The last five minutes of their ride together consisted of Julian asking about all the things he wanted to eat and drink at the game—from hot dogs to popcorn, to cheese fries and chicken fingers. Once they pulled up to Mrs. Wilson's house, Joseph said, "Remember, the Bennetts will pick you up after piano and take you to soccer practice, then back to their house after. I'll pick you up this afternoon, okay, pal?"

"Yeah," groaned Julian.

"Alright, love ya," said Joseph.

"Love ya, dad," groaned Julian.

Before Joseph stopped at the next corner, he had already flipped the station over to WTIN.

"Professor Anders, can you speak to your experience with supers and the threat they pose to our society?" asked Al Moore, the host of Joseph's favorite program.

Joseph felt his blood pressure rise with the question. Sentinels hockey and politics were his two hot-button issues—but with the Sentinels in first place, there wasn't much rage in the tank for hockey these days.

"What we have here is a complete disregard for human life," said the professor, already agitated. "Supers are only part of the problem, and if nobody holds them accountable—if the government turns a blind eye to the threat supers pose to everyday people, all in the name of Ministerium power, then we will see a dramatic rise in casualties in direct correlation with the increase in supers. For every one super, on average, thirty-three innocent people die. And those are only the reported statistics."

"Wow, that's shocking," said Al Moore, though he didn't sound shocked.

"More and more people are going to die while the Ministry looks the other way."

"Why is that, Professor?"

"Look, there's misinformation everywhere. Bolstered by @NON conspiracy theorist nutjobs and domestic terrorist groups infiltrating the military and law enforcement agencies—we're fighting an uphill battle. But it is up to the people—the people like you and me—the normal everyday people who are tired of this *shit*—we need to show those in power that we're not going to accept it."

Joseph nodded throughout the entire conversation. He even thought about calling in, something he debated almost every day, but decided not to put himself on the Ministry watchlist—they were listening, after all.

He stopped off for a caramel macchiato, then continued to work, arriving only five minutes late. By the time he settled into his chair and called the first dozen numbers on his list, it was already ten AM.

Two meetings later and a trip to the water cooler, and suddenly the morning had whizzed by like a VHS tape on fast forward. At lunch, he walked to the pizza shop on the corner and grabbed himself a slice of Giordano's pepperoni heaven, then took a stroll around the block for fresh air.

Supes-Con was in town that weekend, and he was thankful Julian hadn't asked to go. His mother was a Supie, and he was worried her fanaticism would infect his son. Supers flying around, violently assaulting people, playing judge, jury, and sometimes executioner—it was terrifying. Joseph lived in a constant state of fear that at any time a fireball or a laser might cut through the sky and incinerate him, his job, or worst of all, his son.

Julian was growing up in the worst of times. When Joseph was a kid, he was lucky—too young to get drafted into the Third World War, and all the other American skirmishes throughout his life didn't need his service. There was a time in his life where he would've shipped out, if needed, and fought for democracy. To stand up to dictators and to defeat fascism, communism, totalitarianism, and every other form of government that oppressed its people in the name of power and lined their pockets with as much loot as possible before the next guy took over.

In a lot of ways, Joseph was still that person—only older, wiser, and jaded, having watched his own country slip away, down the same dark path they fought so hard against.

As Joseph rounded the next corner, he heard a commotion.

"Did you see that?"

"What just happened?"

"Oh my. Oh no."

There was a group gathered and staring up at the sky—ZepNews Balloons circled overhead, each displaying the same footage with closed captioning. Some of the people were wearing Tints.

"What happened?" asked Joseph. He adjusted his glasses absentmindedly, as if the angle with which they rested on his nose might aid his perception.

"Crimson Justice," said someone. "He murdered three dozen people."

"I don't know about murder," said another. "Negligent? Sure. But murder?"

"What a menace," growled someone else.

"Crimson Justice is the greatest human being that ever walked the face of this earth!" shouted some other guy.

"Keep dreaming."

"Wake up, sheeple! You Sympie cucks are going to get what's coming to you."

Joseph literally bit his tongue to avoid speaking and left at once. His leisurely stroll became a roaring engine of restraint as he powerwalked toward the parking garage.

"This is Joseph," he said into his cell phone after dialing his boss. "I got sick at lunch. I'm going home." He ended the call before his boss could respond and quickly dialed his ex. "Hey, can you pick Julian up from the Bennetts'? — — I'm going to be stuck at work. — — I don't know how long, I just know I won't be there to pick him up. — — I'm sorry it's inconvenient for you. — — Please, just do it!"

He arrived home thirty minutes later and went straight to the bedroom.

He tossed his work clothes into the hamper and removed the top drawer of his dresser, then retrieved a plastic bag that was taped to the back. Inside was a pair of gray canvas Converse high-tops, black jeans, and a gray hoodie. He quickly changed, pulled the hood over his head, tightened the drawstrings so nobody could see his face, and added a pair of sunglasses just in case. Then he removed the last item inside the bag and connected it to a long wooden pole he used to hang the clothes in his closet.

It was a black vinyl flag with a gray symbol—the symbol of the Tin Men.

He stashed his wallet by the front door, then locked up the house with the spare key, re-hiding it in the fake rock resting in his overgrown garden, and walked to the nearest rendezvous.

ELSEWHERE...

Lou was out back shooting when his phone went off. It buzzed in his pocket so intensely that he missed his shot. He ignored it and lined up another—this time he was aiming for Annie Phetamine's head—a cardboard and paper mâché cutout crafted to look like the recently deceased member of the Dope Gang. He'd seen her once on the streets of Metro City four years ago—before he joined up and started training at The Ranch. After the news that she had been brought to justice by the Red Guardian himself, Crimson Justice, Lou couldn't help but feel like he had missed an opportunity to make a name for himself.

If he had only squeezed the trigger when he saw her—jail time or not, he would've been called a hero.

Resetting, he placed the crosshairs over the fake target and squeezed the trigger—a hollow point smashed through her paper mâché head and smacked into the metal sheeting behind her. Lou didn't chicken out this time, even if it was only make-believe. He wouldn't make the same mistake twice. If one of The Dope Gang, or any other supervillain, crossed his path again, he wouldn't flinch.

The Ranch—that's what they called the training facility—though to call it a facility was probably giving it more credit than was due—was ten acres of obstacle courses made from old children's playground equipment and large, man-made mud puddles, located about thirty miles outside Wonder City. They had a shooting range, bunk beds, and a chow hall, and they lived like soldiers every weekend. Alvin had started The Ranch five years ago, and they all paid dues to become official members of the V-Boys. The Official V-Boy Starter KitTM included an armband with a red V, a special recipe to make homemade bear repellent—with the claim that it worked on Sympies and Supervillains alike—as well as discounts for firearms and body armor at supporting stores.

Lou had been training at The Ranch for the last ten months, shooting every day while listening to his favorite podcast—the Bro Experience, hosted by Alex Brones.

"Reformists are stealing our way of life!" shouted Brones, and Lou giggled at the mental image of the podcast host turning bright red while shouting into the microphone. "They are raping America! Bastardizing what our founding fathers had in mind when they wrote the Constitution. We are under attack! Supers are the only thing standing between radical Reformists and the complete obliteration of the American way! They are destroying masculinity. They're stealing your money. They're oppressing your religion. They're stealing who we are, and if we don't stand up and put bullets right between their beady, Sympie, rat-faced eyes, then we are as good as dead! Dead, I tell you!"

When Lou's phone buzzed again, he nearly lost it. Everyone knew to leave him alone while he was training. He swiped it from his back pocket and glared at the LED screen, half expecting Eddie to be texting him to pick up a six pack on his way home, when someone shouted, "Lou! Let's go!"

"What?" asked Lou. "Where?"

"Where?" repeated Suggs incredulously, running down the hill toward him. "Hoodaloo! Check your phone, dumbass!"

Lou checked the newsfeed on his phone and read the headline: "America is under attack! Crimson Justice framed! Reformist scum responsible."

"It's happening. It's finally happening," said Lou, with tears in his eyes. This is what they had been waiting for—Hoodaloo—the Civil War sequel nobody expected—a made-up word that Lou had never bothered to research or understand. It was childish gibberish they used to confuse people, and it worked. Nobody batted an eye when they said it, like a bunch of kids playing a foreign trading card game, the names of the cards so ridiculous that it made adult eyes glaze over.

"We're going to war," hooted Suggs. "Grab your gear."

"It's at home," whined Lou. "I'll go get it."

"No time. Alvin's waiting for us in the van."

Two dozen men in fatigues loaded up into three unmarked white vans, each carrying a semi-automatic rifle with a canister of bear-repellent tucked neatly into their camo vest with the red V stenciled onto the back.

Lou got goosebumps. Tonight was open season on Sympies.

3:15 PM

"It stinks down here," whined Oxy.

"It's a sewer, asshole," spat Moll-E as she hopped over the carcass of something that looked like a rat, but was the size of a Jack Russell Terrier.

The sewers of Wonder City weren't just grimy, smelly, unsanitary, and gross—they were the home to all kinds of...*things*.

Perc giggled silently and rubbed at the scar on his throat.

"Do you two always bicker this much?" asked Dust. "Or am I just now noticing?"

"Have to say, boss," said Oxy, "You were a bit distracted before."

"How much longer?" asked Moll-E.

Dust peeked around the next corner. There was a flickering light at the end of the next pass, and Dust didn't want to make the wrong turn.

"Another half mile," said Dust. "At least."

"What?" groaned Moll-E. "We've been down here all afternoon."

"We were told to escape through the sewers and lay low. It's part of the plan." Once he was sure the coast was clear, Dust stepped out and navigated them toward an adjacent pass. They had been following the path marked in gold spray paint that Dust had painstakingly mapped out for them the night before but had somehow made a wrong turn. It had been quite some time since he last saw one of his marks on the walls, and he wondered if someone had removed them.

"Since when does anyone tell you what to do?" sassed Moll-E. She knew to keep her voice down, but she didn't care.

"Since our benefactor approached us with a big payday, and I developed a plan to take care of our Crimson Justice problem."

"*You* developed a plan? And what happens after?" asked Moll-E. "What happens when he's out of the way?"

"We do what we always planned to do," said Oxy.

"Remind me again, what is that?" asked Moll-E. "It seems to change frequently."

Oxy groaned. "To rid the world of Supes. To rid the world of their duplicity. To oppose them wherever they are."

Dust wasn't paying attention to the conversation. He was too busy concentrating on the movement ahead in the shadows. It was known that the sewers were home to many things, including mutants. Mutants came in all varieties; hairy, phosphorescent, three-eyed, two-headed, tall, small, even monstrous—and what lurked in the shadows ahead could've been any one of those, or a combination thereof.

"Sounds noble," said Moll-E sarcastically. "But what about the part where we started robbing banks?"

"How else are we going to lure them out of their stinking holes?" argued Oxy. "To reveal themselves and who they truly are to the public? They didn't notice us until we started robbing the man of gluttonous mounds of money."

Perc nodded along.

"Lifting a few bucks here and there to pay the bills is one thing," said Moll-E. "Giving it back to those in need is another. Going after millions to line our own pockets? That is a whole different situation I'm not sure I want to be a part of.

"I want to get back to bashing supe heads," she continued. "I want to get back to the plan. Not all this cloak and dagger, cops and robbers bullshit." She stepped in front of Dust. "I'm all for retiring three decades early to a life of luxury in Cancun, but this isn't what I signed up for, bub."

Dust stared straight through her. Or, more accurately, was staring past her into the gloom beyond. Dust knew the danger that lurked in the sewers. He had heard all the stories, just like everyone else, but this was the third time he had ventured down into them. The darkness had a way of playing games with his head, and he was trying to determine if this was just another game or if what he sensed in his gut was real.

There was a flicker of movement followed by the immediate lashing of tentacles. One of them grappled Moll-E's ankle and snatched her away, screaming.

"Mutants!" yelled Oxy. He and Perc scattered after Moll-E. Dust, however, remained calm—or rather, he fumed in place and appeared to grow three inches in every direction, his body mass doubling within three heavy seethes of anger.

Perc dove and snagged Moll-E by the arms as Oxy fed off the creature's hunger—siphoning its aura into himself, like breathing it straight from the air. Oxy's body manipulated that energy and turned it into a blast that shook the very streets above. A concentrated blast that erupted from the ends of his outstretched hands.

The thing released Moll-E with a screech, but not before it launched itself into the sparse light filtering through a grated sewer drain above. It was all eyeballs and tentacles, with a giant gaping, slobbering mouth hole, looking to feed. Sharp teeth gnashed and spittle sprayed as it barreled forward, looking for a Moll-E snack.

Perc hit it with an energy blast equal to Oxy's, but the thing kept coming, like a runaway train—until Dust stepped forward and splattered the beast with one punch. Its guts shot out its back and painted the far wall.

"As I said," shouted Moll-E as she wiped the slime from her latex pants. "How much longer do we have to stay down here?"

"Would you rather get arrested by the pigs?" asked Dust, kicking a twitching tentacle.

"Of course not," said Moll-E. "Like they even could arrest any of us."

"Hear that?" said Dust, pausing after cleaning the goo from his fist.

"Hear what?" asked Oxy.

Perc signed something, but nobody was paying attention.

Dust jumped, grabbed hold of the grated drain above, and pulled himself up for a better look. The streets were full of protestors. Angry protestors. Anti-Supe protestors. He grinned beneath his mask.

His plan had worked. Why else would they be marching? Crimson Justice took the bait, because of course he did. He was a menace, and they wanted nothing more than to rid the world of him. However, for Dust it had become an obsession, and he didn't care how many people he had to hurt to make sure that happened.

"The fuse is lit," said Dust after he dropped to the dank floor.

"What?" beamed Oxy. "Really? It worked?"

"Did you have any doubt?" said Dust, fist-bumping Perc.

"To what end?" asked Moll-E. "If you're right, a whole bunch people died."

"Stop being a fucking buzzkill," said Oxy as Perc signed the same message. It was cold down in the sewers, but Oxy suddenly felt warm all over, like he wanted to lie down in the rotten water and drift off to sleep.

"Do you hear yourselves?" asked Moll-E, holding her hands out wide. Bands of rippling translucent waves ensnared them. "People fucking died! Their lives are on us!"

Moll-Energy, Moll-E's pleasure power, was overwhelming them. They were getting hot. Sweltering, like they were going to burn alive.

Falling to one knee, Perc hit Moll-E with a blast that sent her flying into the sewer wall. She rolled down the tube's incline and settled beside a stream of rancid water.

As Moll-E fed her will into Oxy and Perc, filling them up with feel-good pleasure, Perc and Oxy were also feeding off her, creating powerful blasts that could rupture organs and shatter bones.

As Moll-E crawled through the stinking mud, she whimpered, "You're all assholes." Dust grabbed her by the back of her neck like she was nothing but a toy doll. He shook her around, sharpening her unfocused eyes.

"You short-sighted pain in the ass," growled Dust.

"You made me a murderer," sobbed Moll-E as Dust squeezed. She pulled a knife and stuck him in the chest. The look in her eyes was all fear. Fear of what her own friends might do to her now that she disagreed with their methods.

When she retracted the blade, the tip had broken clean off. The knife never even penetrated his skin.

"Sometimes," said Dust, "you must crack a few skulls to make a mad world bleed."

4:05 PM

Harden Bishop had been Chief of Staff for only sixty days. The last chief had lasted seven whole months before disappearing into the dead of night along with half of the Reformist opposition. Harden wasn't sure why he was selected out of the group of highly touted politicians, but he knew for sure that he was the least qualified for the role. He had a squeaky-clean past—one that was bought with his parents' money—and was living a decent life as a lobbyist when he received the call from the President himself.

One does not turn down President Haines when asked for service, and Harden decided it was an honor to serve. After sixty days, Harden wished he had found a way to say no—he would've accepted Soviet poison applied directly onto his bare tongue just to be rid of the nightmare.

Every time he was summoned into the Oval Office, he arrived on the verge of a panic attack, praying to be tasked with some silly errand like choosing holiday decorations or research. Research was easy, and he would gladly have spent days and weeks locked away inside the national archives looking up precedents and constitutional law—anything to be as far away as possible from the elected madman. This evening, however, was not going to be one of those days.

When he entered the Oval Office, the Senate majority leader was already there, along with half the Caucus—the loyalists, who'd do anything in the name of absolute power—and a few self-proclaimed centrists who switched sides to back a winning horse. It was so startling to see all the smiling faces within the room that Harden almost immediately keeled over in panic.

"Harden," said President Haines from his seat behind the Resolute Desk. The high-backed office chair towered over his small frame, making him look ancient. "I have a very important task for you this evening."

"Of course, Mr. President," said Harden, who couldn't help but wonder how old the president was behind the cataract glasses he always wore. The president had a light sensitivity the White House physician explained was part of a strange disease Samuel Haines contracted when he was just a boy from the great state of Pennsylvania. When he was elected thirteen months ago, he was officially seventy-nine despite never surrendering his birth certificate, but he looked much older and rarely made public appearances. When he did, he always arrived looking twenty years younger than he currently appeared—a feat that the president assured was merely the power of a good makeup artist and the camera adding twenty pounds of health and vigor.

"President?" bemoaned Haines to the scowls of loyalists across the room.

"That title is so unbecoming of you," said one of the more sniveling senators from Texas.

"Indeed," said Haines. "I shall have to remedy this after the vote this evening."

"What vote?" asked Harden. As Chief of Staff, he knew all the comings and goings in Washington, but was unaware of any vote.

"That is exactly the reason I have summoned you this evening," said Haines. He stood up and smiled, then handed Harden a piece of paper that appeared to be an official Executive Order.

"What is this?" asked Harden, quickly scanning the document.

"I have signed an official proclamation to disband the Secret Service," said Haines, "effective immediately."

Harden sucked in a breath. "Sir, I don't think you can just—"

"Oh," said Haines, cutting him off. "But I already have. Not only have I disbanded the Secret Service, but with the help of my most loyal servants, I have created a new conscripted elite force known as the Ministerium Guard. They shall take their orders directly from me."

"But sir," said Harden, "this sounds like a private army. This is unconstitutional."

"Bah," said Haines playfully, followed by laughter from the surrounding lawmakers, most of them chewing on unlit cigars and drinking Scotch.

"This looks like a celebration," said Harden, feeling an overwhelming urge to flee.

"It is," said Haines.

"Haven't you been watching the news, son?" said the senator from Florida, a real smarmy lawyer who had broken more than enough laws to find himself on the other end of Crimson Justice's fists—but, like any politician, was above the law.

Harden shook his head.

"Recent events in Wonder City have changed our priorities." Haines clicked a button on his desk, and a television screen revealed itself in the wall opposite him. It immediately flickered on to live satellite footage of Wonder City in a split screen with various news broadcasts from varying political spectrums.

"This is happening?" asked Harden. "Right now?"

"You chose *him* for Chief of Staff?" groaned the porky Senator from South Carolina.

"Indeed, it is," said Haines. "Fate has given us opportunity."

"What opportunity?" asked Harden.

"In thirty minutes," said Haines, "the Senate will pass a unanimous bill giving me sole power over both the executive and legislative branches of government. A position that I shall have for the tenure of my life."

"What?" said Harden, unable to keep the shock out of his voice. "How will that even pass? A bill like that would need at least seven senators to cross party lines as well as ratifying a new constitutional amendment. And that's even if you have everyone from your own party voting in agreement."

"Indeed," said Haines, "but that will not be necessary."

"Why's that?" asked Harden.

"Because," said Haines with a snarky smile, "the only members of the Senate who are still alive are sitting in this room. Twenty minutes ago, the newly formed Ministerium Guard killed them, their aides, their security, their families—everyone who might oppose."

Harden felt the blood drain from his face. This was a power grab unlike any that had ever transpired in the history of the nation and the most heinous since the second Civil War. "Why?" he asked.

"Why!?" scoffed the senator from Indiana—an @NON *true-believer* who wholeheartedly believed that every Reformist was a devil-worshipping pedophile.

"How will you get away with this?" asked Harden.

"Easy," said the senator from New York. "We'll just say the Reformists did it. Our constituents will eat that hokum right up."

"Let me get this straight," said Harden. "You're going to tell the public that the Reformist senators shot themselves?"

"Well," whined the senator from the New York, "It sounded better in my head."

"Why would you do this?" asked Harden. "You already had the majority vote."

"Let me answer you, my boy," said Haines, "with another question. What do the citizens of this country want the most from their government?"

"I don't know," said Harden. A few of the Senators in the room snickered.

"Law and order, son," said Haines. "They want law and order."

"The Reformists were turning this country into an absolute Sympie shithole," said the senator from Florida.

"The lawlessness displayed on that television set," said Haines, pointing a bony finger at the screen, "is exactly the kind of chaos that gives me the ability to usurp power and declare martial law. This power is afforded to me by the Insurrection Act of 1807."

"But that was what I was investigating for you *last week*."

"A timely investigation, if there ever was one," said Haines with a smirk. It was as if the president had known—or worse, had planned for this.

"Sir," said Harden, feeling the bile rise within his gut, "this isn't right. I cannot aid and abet this kind of malfeasance. I took an oath."

The smile on Haines' face disappeared. The old man sighed, and then looked around the room at his loyal followers. "Senators, the Ministry thanks you for your service. Please, allow me some time to discuss the matters with my chief of staff...*privately*."

One by one, the senators stood and exited the room, and Harden had the terrible feeling he was about to disappear, just like the previous Chief of Staff. When the last senator left the room, President Haines smiled, exposing all his creepy yellow teeth.

"Harden," said Haines, "Do you understand why I hired you?"

"No, sir."

"It is simple, really." Haines then walked around to the front of the Resolute Desk. "Your family were donors to my campaign. They showed themselves to be loyal. That loyalty deserved to be rewarded, so I took their only son, their pride and joy, and made him a valuable tool of this administration."

"I appreciate that, sir."

"Loyalty is everything," said Haines. "Loyalty is power. Power is everything. Do you know what led to the last World War?"

Harden shook his head. "The history books said it was the assassination of JFK. The Russians invaded, along with the Chinese, and the country was destroyed. In its wake, new cities were built. Metro City over the ruins of New York City, Wonder City over the destruction of Philadelphia and Baltimore, and so on."

"I am disappointed," said Haines. "The real reason we went to war for the third time last century was for power. Weapons, Harden. Nuclear weapons. Approximately seventy years after those events, we are in another arms race. Supes, Harden. Supes are the new nukes. The country with the most supes has the power."

"I see, sir," said Harden.

"No," said Haines. "You don't see. Not yet." Haines removed the cataract glasses, and Harden knew things would never be the same.

CHAPTER 10

"Your turn," said Tori.

Her sudden change in attitude surprised Dean. After the way she'd reacted to him just moments ago, the way she put words into his mouth, he thought she'd refuse talk to him for the remainder of their time stuck inside the vault.

Screw this—if that's the way she wanted to be, he'd ignore her. He didn't need the frustration, and he couldn't wait to get out of there and chew Rudy out for proclaiming that this day was going to be something special. He should've stayed in bed.

Dean's butt stung from sitting on the hard floor. He stood up before he lost all feeling in his toes and opted to lean against the wall instead. From the floor, he could only view the top of Tori's curls behind the mound of debris, but once standing, he took an innocent glance. Their eyes snagged, and Dean defiantly crossed his arms and looked away. He wanted to be angry at her but couldn't, and his frustrations evaporated as quickly as they mounted.

He caved immediately and hated himself for being so easy.

Ugh, why was he always so weak when it came to a pretty face?

"Are you sure?" he eventually asked.

"What else are we gonna do?" she said as she unwrapped another lollipop and popped it into her mouth. Her tone wasn't mean or even kind. It was indifferent, which in a way made Dean feel worse about himself.

"Where was I?" he asked.

"You fell for Brie," said Tori, "and discovered she was dating a supe."

"I hate supes," groaned Dean.

"Because Brie was banging one?" she asked with a mirthless giggle. She was still staring at the ceiling, and Dean wondered if she even cared about his story.

"No," said Dean.

"Then why?"

"I have my reasons." He didn't feel like exposing his entire history of trauma to this random girl who was probably getting off on his story—his pain was her entertainment.

"Give me something?" she asked. "Why do you hate supes?"

"Because they're dangerous," said Dean, a little angrier than he intended. His anger made Tori sit up to inspect him. She was probably judging him too. "They can do whatever the hell they want, and nobody can do a damn thing about it." Then he paced back and forth nervously like a dog with a case of the zoomies.

"So, what's that to you? Are you jealous or something?"

"Fuck off," said Dean.

Her eyes lit up. She seemed excited, like she wanted to push the button again and see what would happen.

"Now you have to tell me."

"No way."

"You can't tell me to fuck off and then act like it didn't happen," she replied as she twirled a blue lollipop in her mouth.

"What's it to you?" said Dean. "You think this is funny?"

"Just fucking tell me, you wimp!"

"She died!" growled Dean.

"What? Who? Brie?"

Dean stopped pacing, then refolded his arms over his chest and sighed. He gave her a sideways glance and realized he had to tell her.

"I was twelve. Supes were just becoming a big deal. Showing up everywhere on the news. I thought it was the coolest thing ever. I wanted to be struck by lightning or hit by radioactive waves, like the classics." He took a deep breath and continued. "One day, out of nowhere—Dad was out in his shop and Mom was making lunch—something hit the house. I didn't know what it was. A plane? Meteor? Mom screamed, and I rushed down what was left of the stairs, surrounded by flames. Two men were fighting inside my house, punching, kicking, hurling balls of fire at each other—and as quickly as it happened, they were gone, followed by a bigger, much louder explosion. Dad burst through the door, grabbed me and Mom, and we made it outside just before the house collapsed."

"That's awful," said Tori.

"I'm not done," said Dean. "You see, most people react that way. They say that's awful. They say it like they don't really understand how I can feel so strongly against supes based on that one day, when my family and I survived with hardly a scratch."

"I didn't—"

"The thing is, it wasn't about me. As Mom and Dad protected me from the flames, we saw what was left of the neighborhood. It was like matchsticks. Pieces of lumber and fire scattered as far as the eye could see. And there, just across the street was my neighbor. Patricia was my age. In my class. Hell, I crushed on her in the second grade. But there she was, on the ground, dead, neck bent at the wrong angle—her eyes wide open." When Dean paused, he looked over at Tori. Her expression appeared sympathetic, though he was unsure she was capable of that kind of emotional empathy. "I'll never forget it. I still have nightmares about it. The Massacre at Shady Lake. I grew up in Mapletown."

"That's awful," said Tori. Then, as if she was reading Dean's mind, she clarified. "I remember that happening on TV. I'm so sorry you went through that. Nobody should have to endure that kind of trauma."

"Yeah," said Dean. He took a deep breath, walked over to the wall, and sat down beside it. "I'm sorry."

"What for?"

"For telling you to fuck off," he said.

"It's okay. I've been told worse."

"Yeah, well, that's not okay either."

"What do you mean?"

Dean laughed to himself. "My best friend, Rudy, and his partner, Arthur— they seem to think I have a 'hero complex.'"

"What's that?" she asked with a befuddled smirk.

"I tend to be attracted to women who I subconsciously believe need saving. And I tend to get upset when they're mistreated."

"Interesting," said Tori.

"Not really," said Dean. "I mean, that's what ruined my life. I chased after Brie because I subconsciously thought she needed me to rescue her. And I did it until there was nothing left."

Dean hated when Brie cried. It seemed like every time he saw her, she was mopping his shoulder in tears. Their entire relationship was based on Dean lending her a friendly ear. She whined, complained, and cried about Torcher. And when she was done, Dean dried her tears, made her laugh, then sent her right back to the man who kept breaking her heart.

Torcher *was* torture.

Some days he wondered if she understood what she was doing to him. The way she kept him at arm's length, only answering every other text or call—then she'd suddenly show interest and ask to grab a bite at a local pub. She'd charm her way into his heart—smiling, giving big body hugs, and laughing at all his bad jokes—only to break apart into another sob story when his defenses were down.

It happened countless times. A cycle of madness that drove Dean to dark places.

"Brie and Torcher had another fight," said Dean.

"Then, maybe you *should* do something for Valentine's Day," suggested Peter from the couch, his game paused mid-battle. "You know, go all John Cusack on her ass."

Tammy shot her boyfriend a sidelong glance from beside him. "You never went all John Cusack on my ass."

Peter shrugged. "I never had to win you over, did I?"

"True," sighed Tammy.

"So you're saying I should show up outside her bedroom window with a boombox?" The suggestion sounded ludicrous—and cold. It was winter, and the snow was falling in fresh sheets every other day.

"No, man," said Peter. "That's been done. Do something only you would do. An original Dean-Romantic-Moment."

"Is that like a Hallmark Moment?" asked Dean, heavy on the sarcasm.

What did Dean need with a girlfriend when he had Peter's undying man-crush?

"I think you're missing the point," said Peter. "If you really feel something for Brie, then show her. Do something only you would do."

Tammy nodded in agreement, so Dean spent that night concocting something sweet, but not too sweet, and thoughtful, just not overly thoughtful. He spent so much time trying to hit the perfect bullseye that he never stopped to evaluate what he had created.

When he was done, he put the plan in action.

It was a three-phase plan.

PHASE 1: REMOVE THE BUZZKILL

Brie's roommate, Madison, was a buzzkill. She couldn't stand Dean and often reinforced all of Brie's poor choices, raving about Torcher as if she were living vicariously through Brie. With Brie and Torcher on a break, Madison was all that stood in the way of Dean enacting his plan. At four PM, Dean paid Jake, the guy down the hall that hooked them up with beers, to show up at their door and tell Madison she had a secret admirer waiting for her on the quad.

PHASE 2: BAIT THE FISH

Brie would not be returning from class until four-thirty, giving Jake thirty minutes to leave the bait—a scavenger hunt that would lead her around town—to the restaurant they first met, the bookstore, Bagels-2-Go, and more—finishing at the China King, Brie's favorite. Dean had reserved a corner booth for two, complete with a bouquet of flowers and a poem he'd written for her. Jake would leave the first clue on her keyboard, with a trail of rose petals leading from the door to her laptop.

PHASE 3: UNLEASH THE BEAST

When she arrived, Dean wouldn't hold back. He'd make it known, once and for all, that this was where Brie's heart belonged. He'd pull out all the stops—

—except he never even got the green light.

Dean waited for her at the China King for hours. He wondered if maybe his instructions hadn't been clear, or maybe the scavenger hunt had taken her off course, or maybe it was taking longer to complete than he expected.

At six-thirty that evening, his phone chimed. She had updated her FriendSpace status.

"Homework, am I right?" it said. "Tasty snacks delivered straight to my door? I'm in!"

Something was wrong. *Tasty snacks?* Had someone beaten him to the punch?

A minute later he received a text from a BLOCKED NUMBER.

"I found someone more…palatable? Sorry, Dean."

He tried texting her back, but his text kept returning undelivered. Then he went to check her FriendSpace again—he was blocked.

She had deleted him from her life. Severed all their connections. Nothing could have made him feel lower than he did that day…or so he thought.

"Whoa, what the fuck?" said Tori. "She blocked you? Like, erased you from her life?"

"Yeah," said Dean.

"That's harsh." Then she shrugged. "I mean, she clearly led you on. She used you. And yeah, you went a little over the top, but her reaction was ice cold."

"Looking back, I fucked up. I went too far. But I learned something that day," said Dean. "Women like the idea of a romantic gesture, but only from the men they wish to receive them. A guy who goes out of his way to do something special, some crazy John Cusack boombox bullshit, means absolutely nothing to a woman who has no interest. In fact, they'll find it creepy. Disturbing even. Like you dropped your pants and wiped your ass all over the floor."

"Heh," laughed Tori. "You might've gotten a better reaction if you had wiped your ass all over her floor."

Dean chuckled. "Probably."

When you're depressed, sometimes you do stupid things. When you're depressed and drunk, you're guaranteed to do stupid things.

The first night of spring break started innocently. Peter and Tammy took Dean out on the town to cheer him up. Junior year was almost over, and they all needed a break.

In typical Peter fashion, he retired early after inhaling three orders of the hottest hot wings in town, much to Tammy's dismay. As the night dragged on, mistakes were made, and Dean woke up in Tammy's bed.

"Oh my god," said Tori. She was genuinely shocked.

"You want to know why I wouldn't call you a slut?" said Dean, "Because I've done things I'm not proud of either. We're human. And nobody deserves to be shamed for that. I'm sure we've beaten ourselves up over our mistakes more than enough already."

Tori nodded. "Sorry I put words into your mouth."

"It's okay," said Dean.

"What are we going to do?" worried Tammy. She was teary-eyed and wrapped in sheets, backed into the corner of the bed as far from Dean as possible.

"It was a mistake," said Dean. "We both know it was. And because we both know it was, it never happened."

"I love him," she cried. "Why would I do this?"

"I don't know," said Dean.

"I was so drunk," she admitted, which only made Dean feel worse.

"Neither of us would do something like this," he said. "So, let's forget it."

For the next few weeks, Dean avoided Peter and Tammy wherever possible. Peter spent more time with his video games and didn't appear to notice. The school year ended, and Dean went home for the summer. They parted ways on good, but somber terms, and if Peter knew, he never let on that he did. When the guilt and the sadness had numbed over, Dean tried to make the best of it, and re-entered the dating pool with high hopes…

…and met Lauren, the woman who communed with the dead.

Dean dated her for the entire summer break, and things had gone well. So well, in fact, that he invited her over to dinner with his family. It was strange, he thought, how normal she seemed while mini golfing, grabbing drinks, and taking long walks. But now, she was suddenly saying odd things at the dinner table while sampling his mother's lasagna.

"This house has history," said Lauren.

"What do you mean?" asked Dean's father.

"Lots of ghosts here."

"This house was built ten years ago," said his mother. "We had it built."

"I see them. They tell me something very different." She shoveled a mouthful of lasagna into her mouth and began chewing like she was her own personal internet meme.

Dean, searching for a transition—one that might lead them as far away from her imaginary ghosts as possible—made a regrettable pivot. "Why don't you tell my parents about the thing you did last summer?"

She glared at him, and Dean thought two people could not be more out-of-sync, when she suddenly smiled and said, "Oh yeah!"

Dean settled back into his chair, excited for the next exchange about how she had gone to Italy and traveled down the Amalfi Coast. However, once she started, he realized he should've clarified.

"So, last year," she bubbled, lovingly glancing at Dean before turning back to his parents. "I saved up a bunch of money and finally got breast implants." It took a few moments before Dean's brain caught up to the deviated path this conversation had taken from the one he had imagined. "My tits have never been so perky. Seriously, feel them." Lauren thrusted her enhancements toward Dean's father, who scowled at his son with extreme disapproval.

"What!?" cackled Tori, enjoying herself at his expense. "You're making this up!"

"I wish I was."

"Where do you find these women?"

"I've been asking myself that same question," he replied. "Lauren seemed nice at first, but that was an onion I wish I had never peeled."

"Can't put that toothpaste back in that tube," she said, and laughed even harder.

Tori had an infectious laugh that made Dean want to laugh with her, and the weight of his past suddenly seemed as light as a feather.

"So, what happened with Brie?" she asked. "That can't be the end of the story."

"It's not," said Dean. "When classes started that fall, we ran into each other the first day."

Senior year started like an old sock—form-fitted to the foot and gliding comfortably into place. Until finding a hole that had developed somewhere between the last wearing and the wash.

They arrived on campus to find new neighbors and fresh faces. Jake, their beer runner from down the hall never came back to finish his degree, and the new guy, Lawrence, moved into his room. Everything about returning to class that year felt like they were on a collision course to nowhere—a rush to a finish line nobody wanted.

Dean had spent three long years on campus and never saw Brie wandering around. He never saw her on the quad, in a classroom, or walking with friends. In fact, at one time, he questioned whether she went to school with him at all.

When Dean spotted Brie ahead of him as he yawned his way to his Tuesday morning class, it was like he had radar attuned to her exact signal. Her long, straight blonde hair gently swayed as she swept through the hallway ahead and into a lecture hall—the same room Dean was assigned.

He almost turned back, went straight to the scheduling office and dropped the class—which would've been a decent idea if he didn't need that class to graduate.

The lecture hall was built for a class of five hundred. Brie was sitting by herself on the far right, so Dean went to the far left, scooting into a spot behind a group of students. He sat down, grabbed his notepad and textbook, then sighed.

"Hey," said Brie, sitting down beside him. "How was your summer?"

"Okay," he mumbled. "Long. Yours?"

"I dumped Torcher. For good."

In the milliseconds between her proclamation and his inevitable answer, Dean's mind went through all the potential responses.

Should he…give her a round of applause?

Should he…scream out celebratory phrases like "Fuck yeah!"

Or, should he…play it cool with an "About time."

Instead, Dean's mind went blank, and he ended up using a non-committal "Oh."

By the end of the week, they were hanging out every day. They went to the movies together, to the park for long walks, to lunch and dinner, and eventually Dean was spending nights at Brie's place.

"Whoa, plot twist," said Tori.

"Yeah," said Dean. "My happiest moments seem to be the most fleeting."

Tori nodded like she knew that too well. "What happened next?"

Dean shook his head. "Your turn," he said as he hopped up onto the counter next to the broken lock boxes. There were wads of cash and odd trinkets everywhere. Value and sentimentality were different to all kinds of people. Knickknacks and paperwork, photos and stashes of cash were some of the more common items spread across the room. But there were odd things, like a box of crystals—big green and red stones that caught his attention.

"Okay," said Tori. She jumped up off the floor and paced around. "What I'm about to tell you, I've never told anyone." She stopped pacing and took a deep, soulful breath. Through the galaxy makeup, Dean could tell she was preparing to unload something important. She looked vulnerable, and somehow appeared smaller, as if she had shrunk several inches. "Please don't judge me."

CHAPTER 11

4:30 PM

DUST CLIMBED THE GRIMY LADDER AND SLID THE MANHOLE cover aside. It was quiet, as expected, and he exited into an alley under a darkening overcast sky. It would be night soon, but the city was on the verge of igniting.

"Is this the place?" asked Oxy.

Dust nodded, and Perc grabbed Oxy to gather his attention. He made a few exaggerated hand signals, and Oxy replied equally.

"What's he saying?" asked Dust.

"He wants out," said Oxy.

"Why?" asked Dust. His expression didn't change. There was no way to know what he was thinking behind the war mask.

"Moll-E," said Oxy. "She may have been Perc's ex, but she was still one of us."

"Did you remind him of the money?" said Dust. "A third of the loot sounds much better than a quarter." Dust gestured for Oxy to relay his message.

Perc signed, and Oxy sighed.

"He's mute, not deaf," said Oxy. "But yeah, a third does sound better."

Dust smiled, then started counting on his fingers. "Of course it does. That's a 9% increase!"

Perc rolled his eyes and shrugged.

"Yeah." Oxy sighed. "That's not how percentages work, but great. We're with you."

Perc shook his head and Oxy patted him on the back.

"It's just us now, boys, like old times," said Dust, placing a hand on their shoulders before giving them both a playful slap. "Come on, we're running late."

Money solved everything—at least that's what Dust's old man used to say.

They exited the alley in the bad part of town. The north side of the city was nicknamed the Dire District, and it was nothing but run-down warehouses, abandoned factories, Cash for Gold stores and Supe-Burger fast-food joints with enough bulletproof glass to create a whole prison.

That's what the Dire District was—a prison.

Crime was down, but the people who lived within the Dire District suffered in silence—too afraid to leave their houses, too afraid to show their frustration. They were forgotten, left to rot in their neighborhoods. There was exactly one job for every five people, and if one of those jobless four were to sell pot, a supe gifted with a super-smell would come barreling toward them at a few hundred miles per hour. No arrest. No judge. No jury. The people here were lucky to be hospitalized with only a beating—broken bones, ruptured organs. Many didn't survive the night. Those who did were left with crippling hospital debt.

As the remaining members of the Dope Gang walked the block through the wreckage—the destroyed row homes and the burned-out buildings—Dust remembered why he'd formed the Dope Gang and what they had suffered through together.

All that death, all that pain, felt so far out of reach. It was in the past now. For much of his life, the past loomed over him, controlling every decision like it had a game controller plugged into the back of his head. Now he felt free—powerful and in control. He could do anything he wanted. He no longer had to manipulate people; he could now intimidate them. And there were few supes who could stand in his way—the most prominent of which, Crimson Justice, was being broadcasted across every television set around the world, his reputation crumbling.

Crimson Justice was going to pay for what he did to them. Revenge would be sweeter than Dust had anticipated—not only would the big red asshole take a fall, but Dust was going to get rich doing it.

The warehouse was scorched, but its structural integrity was intact. Whole sections of walls and floors were missing, but the support held firm. It made for an interesting rendezvous, where every step was a potential death trap—well, not for Dust. He was nearly indestructible and impervious to pain, and he'd never forget the last time he felt it. It was burned into his memory—the knife gliding across his skin.

Oxy said, "This is the drop spot? This shithole?"

Perc signed something, and Oxy removed his mask to see Perc's message in the failing light.

"That's what I just said," groaned Oxy. "We could've met at the Supe-Burger across the street. I'm hungry."

"Shut up," said Dust.

"Seriously, bro," whined Oxy. "Sneaking around in these kinds of places, it's no wonder people think we're villains. And what do we do when they ask for the package?"

Dust stopped moving. He sighed, though it looked and sounded like a seethe. "Package or not, the outcome is the same. Besides, the package is going to come to us."

Perc shrugged, and Oxy glared at him.

It was inevitable.

It had been six years of consistency—and like clockwork, everything would come back together—things always went back to the way they were, and this time would be no different.

"You know, we don't have to split the cash three ways," said Dust, eyeing Oxy. "If you want out, Perc and I will split the dough."

"Bro," groaned Oxy. "They hired us to grab the package. A package we don't have."

"*Yet*," said Dust. "A package we don't have *yet*."

Oxy said, "Dude—"

Then Dust had him by the throat before he could protest any further.

"Do you need help shutting that big fucking mouth of yours?" said Dust. Without realizing it, he had lifted Oxy off his feet with one hand and could pop his head clean off with a simple squeeze and twist.

"We're in this together," croaked Oxy as he slammed his fist into Dust's arm to loosen the behemoth's grip. When Dust didn't ease up, Oxy blasted him with what should have been enough leeched power to blow Dust clean into the next county. Dust dropped Oxy and staggered backward. "You're my best friend, bro."

Perc signed something. Without a translator, it looked like solidarity.

Dust took a moment to breathe. Then he turned back to the hallway and started walking.

"Are you two coming?"

Oxy and Perc exchanged looks, then swept in behind him. They continued together down the hall.

Dust had grown up with Oxy and Perc before they erased their real names from all public databases and took on new personas. Six years ago, a whole lifetime. Six years of planning, plotting revenge, and creating the perfect conditions. This arrangement with their benefactor was their last remaining option to salvage something of their efforts. Losing Annie was tough, and Beth was out of commission—still, Dust didn't think collecting a payday was selling out, especially when he'd be sipping Mojitos on a beach in Guam.

They were waiting for them when Dust arrived at the top floor. The roof was a canopy of rust and crumbling concrete, the walls just panels of flapping plastic. The area was lit with a half dozen oil drums burning trash, and a cool breeze swept through the floor. It was dusty, and the whole place smelled like mildew and animal piss.

There were three figures in the room. Two of which were as big as Dust— the left in white, the right in black. The figure at the center, however, was much smaller and shrouded in shadow, wearing a red overcoat and hat.

"Are you the Benefactor?" asked Dust.

The Benefactor nodded.

The guard on the left said, "The Benefactor wants to know if you have what you were asked to retrieve?"

"No," said Dust. "We ran into a problem."

The Benefactor turned and silently whispered something to its guards. The guard on the right said, "The Benefactor would like to know what happened to your gang. Was not the Dope Gang five members strong when the deal was struck?"

"That's part of the problem," replied Dust.

There was a long pause. The sound of fire popping echoed throughout the empty room. Eventually The Benefactor turned and whispered to its guards.

The guard on the left said, "The city is erupting into chaos. Crimson Justice killed the hostages, and a manhunt is underway for his arrest."

"I knew that idiot would walk right into it," said Dust, brandishing a smirk beneath his mask.

"The red asshole can't go anywhere without destroying whole city blocks," added Oxy.

The guard on the right said, "This was not part of the deal."

"It was his idea," said Oxy. Both he and Perc pointed at Dust, quick to shovel blame.

"You asked us to get the package," said Dust. "You said nothing about Crimson Justice. I saw an opportunity and I took it."

The guard on the right said, "The city is on the brink, and you do not have the package."

Through a crumbled wall in the warehouse's exterior, the darkening skies over the city made it easy to see the ZepNews Balloons drifting past skyscrapers, replaying Crimson Justice footage from earlier that day. Dust couldn't help but feel proud.

"When are we getting paid?" asked Dust.

"You have not secured the package," said the guard on the left.

"We'll get you the package."

"The Benefactor will only pay when the job is complete."

Dust started to seethe. He could feel himself growing—shoulders widening, muscles adding density. He could span the distance between them and rip out the guards' spines before they could even pull their weapons. Then he would pinch The Benefactor's head right off and take its money.

The Benefactor stepped forward and placed something next to its throat. "If you take another step, we will release your records," said The Benefactor, its voice garbled by an electronic device. There was no way to tell if it was a man or woman.

"What records?" asked Oxy. Perc signed the same question.

"Leverage," said The Benefactor. He tossed a folder in their direction. Oxy quickly retrieved it folder and fingered through its contents. "We know your true identities, and more. Fingerprints do not change over time."

"They know," said Oxy. "They know who we are."

"The only reason you are still alive is because your idiot plan has provided us with an unforeseen outcome. An outcome that has sped up our efforts," said The Benefactor. "Get the package to us by midnight, or we will release this information to the press. The stakes have never been higher, gentlemen."

Dust envisioned all the gory things he would do to The Benefactor if given the chance. He was almost entranced in his rage, consumed by his anger, and he felt the hem of his pants pop as he started to grow again.

He wasn't always like this. Sure, he had his moments. Yeah, he would often lose his temper. But this wasn't the man he's been for most his life—things had changed since the "incident."

"C'mon man," said Oxy, placing a hand on Dust's shoulder. "Let's go get the package."

The Benefactor was gone. So were the guards. Dust never saw them leave.

4:40 PM

Alex Brones shouted over the car stereo.

"What you're seeing right now on the streets of Wonder City is a travesty! Rioters marching through the street, protesting the very core of our values! Truth! Justice! The American Way! Isn't that what supers represent? In all my years, I never saw more loathsome bottom feeders attempting to tear down society because their feelings are hurt. I bet those 'hostages' were working with the Dope Gang. They were probably receiving a cut of the loot! They got what they deserved when they broke the law!"

"Okay, V-Boys!" shouted Alvin after turning the volume down on the stereo. The whole van was full of men in camo and body armor, except the one guy with the biggest beer belly sitting all the way at the rear. Alvin slipped from the passenger seat into the back to address them. Each V-Boy shouted some form of "hoorah"—a few of them even saluted Alvin. "Hoodaloo! This is what we've trained for! This is what we were born for!" Then he grabbed his clipboard from the front seat as the driver started ascending the Old Philadelphia Memorial Bridge into Wonder City. "At approximately 1300 hours, Crimson Justice was framed for the murder of three dozen innocents."

"False flag!" someone shouted.

"Damn straight," agreed Alvin. "Crisis actors, every one of them. @NON already broke the story."

Several of them loaded their phones to read the word of their insider prophet, @NON, and his message board exposing Reformist plots to distract and upend the Ministry.

"Why can't these Sympies wake up?!" shouted Suggs.

"We'll just have to wake them up!" shouted Lou, to a chorus of "Hoodaloo!"

Alvin waited for his men to settle before he continued, tonguing absentmindedly on the wad of tobacco under his lip. "The BIG GUY himself called me on his personal phone and demanded every V-Boy Chapter rally to his cause. This is what we've all been waiting for."

"At 1800 hours," he continued, "we will rendezvous at the scene of the crime—the Wonder City First National Bank—with our V-Boy brothers and sisters, the Khaki Klan, and all the Supies we can rally to our cause. From there, we march on City Hall."

"What are the rules of engagement, sir?" asked Suggs.

"Let them make the first move, then shoot every Sympie cuck you can." Alvin sneered. "Self-defense. Every step forward is our territory. If they come at us, we're just standing our ground."

"What about the Wonder City Police?" asked Suggs.

"They won't help us," moped Alvin. "Ever since Crimson Justice showed up, they've gotten fat and lazy. He does all their work! In fact, they're probably against us."

"What about the military?" asked Lou. "What if they call in the reserves?"

"See this right here?" growled Alvin, pointing to a patch sewn onto the shoulder of his camo. "Two tours in Venezuela. The military is ours. They'll never draw weapons on us. And anyone who does? Well, friendly fire has a way of not being too friendly, ya know?"

Alvin looked like a madman, and Lou loved it. It was easier to do what needed to be done when their leader was so convincing.

"What are you wearing, Lou?" Alvin spit tobacco juice into a soda can.

"It's a Metro City Sentinels t-shirt," stammered Lou. In fairness, it wasn't the only thing he was wearing. He wore his V-Boys vest and the black armband with the red V.

"When we hit those streets," said Alvin, "there will be thousands of people on our side, but only those in V-Boy camo are the true patriots. Without that camo, how will we know who's who?"

Lou wasn't what one might call intelligent, but from time to time he surprised himself with profound logic. Though militia groups weren't exactly praised for their IQ, nor for questioning their leaders, Lou replied with an honest perception.

"I know we're gonna be in the city and all," said Lou, "but wasn't camouflage supposed to make soldiers blend in? Now we're using it to identify our brothers?"

Suggs looked like he had hurt himself thinking—the others too.

"When we took you in, I knew you were gonna be trouble," accused Alvin. "When we gave you a home at the Ranch, trained you, gave you a purpose, I knew that decision would come back to bite me in the ass." He pulled his knife, then grabbed Lou by the throat. Everyone froze. "Tell me, Lou, why shouldn't I cut you right now? You'll only get in my way if I don't. Give me a reason."

Lou was shaking. Every set of words that popped into his brain seemed to melt away in his throat where the sharp metal edge gently cut his skin.

"B-b-b-because…" stammered Lou, his eyes wandering around the van—glancing over the semi-automatic rifles, the body armor, the bear repellent, and the baseball bats wrapped in razor wire—when a series of words finally caught traction. "…every hooda needs a Lou?"

"Every hooda needs a Lou," repeated Alvin. Like a Christmas Grinch, his mouth slowly curled at the edges before developing into a smile. Then Alvin laughed and removed the knife from Lou's throat.

"Hoodaloo!" shouted Suggs.

The others laughed along with him, breaking the tension.

"Comic relief," said Alvin. "Boy, if you weren't on our side…"

Alvin never finished that sentence.

4:42 PM

Joseph met up with other Tin Men after receiving an anonymous text from a FriendSpace user who relayed information. Every member of the group was anonymous. There was no leader, no direct communication channel, website, or club, other than a single relay contact per city. They wore hoodies, face paint, sunglasses, and surgical masks—but all of them were dressed in gray—the color of tin.

They quietly marched like an army of mimes through Wonder City, starting at the train terminal and marching toward City Hall. Several members ran for cover when a streak of crimson soared overhead but rejoined the others when it was clear Crimson Justice had more important business to attend.

"Take one," whispered a fellow Tin Man. He was distributing a gray pill the size of a nickel.

"What is it?" whispered Joseph, as he watched others take them and swallow without speaking a word.

"A little something I cooked up," said the Tin Man behind a pair of darkened goggles. "Renders V-Boy repellent useless. Still stings the eyes though. Take these too." He handed Joseph an extra pair of tinted goggles.

"Thanks," said Joseph, taking the pill and goggles—a tremor in his hands.

"Hey, relax," said the Tin Man. "You're marching with all of us. We outnumber those assholes, and most of them are too chickenshit to do anything."

"How many chickenshits do we have on our side?"

"A few," said the Tin Man. "Usually we have a super or two marching with us for protection. I marched a few times with The Monocle and The Reaping Raven. Even had The Dope Gang show up once in the 'Burgh." He gave Joseph a once-over. "Is this your first?"

"No," said Joseph. "But the first in a long time."

"Ah, I see. Well, all-timer," said the Tin Man, "be warned. This one could get ugly."

4:45 PM

"Do you know who I am?" growled Apollo.

The security guard gave him a sideways glance. "Did you win *American Idol* last year?"

Apollo looked incredulous. "Almost. I won *American Supe*." It was meant to be a threat, but the security guard wasn't impressed. This wasn't the first supe who'd tried to get inside the morgue. They all fancied themselves as detectives, but in truth, most were as dumb as bricks. Even Detective Shade, the Super Sleuth of Detroit, was more about busting heads than he was about busting cases.

"What do you need to do in there?" asked the guard.

"I need to identify someone," said Apollo. Kristy looked bored, and the Sunnies, wrapped in bedsheets over their clothing like a traveling toga party, were fuming.

"Just let us in!" shouted one of the Sunnies.

"I can't let all of you in there," said the guard.

"I'm not asking you to let us *all* in," said Apollo. "Just me."

"Hey," said the guard, his face suddenly alight. "I do know you."

Apollo smiled.

"You're that asshole Crimson Justice threw around like he was flicking a booger."

The Sunnies gasped. "What did you say?" growled Apollo.

"Look, son," said the security guard, "you can't go in there. It's the law."

In order to win *American Supe*, Apollo had beaten fifteen other supes on his way to the championship. The first match that season was a Free-For-All—five supes in the ring at once, anything goes. The Cannonball Cannibal eviscerated two of the challengers before Apollo ripped off his genitals and stuffed them into his mouth.

"How does that taste?" he said into the camera as the Cannibal choked to death.

The other challenger—Darkum Gloom—had a light sensitivity, and all the blood from the three previous deaths made Apollo as radiant as a star. Gloom was rushed to the hospital for severe sunburn. Apollo never even had to touch him.

The next five rounds of one-on-one combat were won by either knockout, submission, or death. In the first of five matches, Apollo knocked Latin Steve's teeth into his mouth and shook him around until he swallowed them all, calling him his "maraca bitch." He didn't just win but was awarded five out of five in all the major categories—the ever-elusive SHOVE5: Style, Humor, Originality, Violence, and Emotion.

It wasn't just about beating his opponents—it was about cool moves, blood, flair, storytelling, and humiliating them with banter. The more points he scored, the better placement he'd receive when he won the championship. If he played his cards right, he'd score high enough to land in Wonder City— and this was an expansion year. New Supe-Cities were signing up after the last election. Scoring low meant being placed in cities like Indianapolis or New Albuquerque.

In the following match, Apollo dismembered Venus Sundew's leg and beat her with it, proclaiming he "plucked her by the stem," no less than fifteen times before the television cameras picked up the audio.

The next two matches with Albatross and The Mighty Fist were too close for comfort. Apollo took a beating but managed to make them both submit through a combination of eye gouging and genital crushing—in The Mighty Fist's case, it was both at the same time.

The finals, however, was where Apollo shone. He was pitted against the Texas Temptress herself, Cowgal Jezebelle. She was a yee-hawing, finger-gun-shootin', tobacco-chewing, star-striped, braided pig-tailed, daisyduke-and-cowboy-boot-wearing sorceress. And she was obnoxious, scoring high marks for her antics—in the second round she rode Mustang around the ring before she choked him out with her steely thighs.

The South and Midwest crowds loved it. She was their darling. They even aired a fifteen-minute special highlighting her going into the match, about how she was an "all-American gal" just "living the American dream," with her love of "guns, capitalism, and country. Oh! And the Bible—in that order, uh huh."

By comparison, Apollo was given five minutes of airtime to discuss his new line of breathable toga material.

When it was over, audiences were stunned. It was the highest-rated episode of *Sunday Night: American Supe* ever played for a live audience. Social media exploded as the clip was downloaded and watched more than six hundred million times around the globe.

Apollo broke her in half.

Cowgal's family filed a lawsuit, listing no less than ten serious crimes. However, she'd signed a waiver before appearing on American Supe, and the suit was tossed by a judge before it ever made its way to court.

The law was always on Apollo's side. No parking tickets or traffic violations. Not even a citation after a drunken barfight in Metro City before he got his powers. He'd never even had a detention growing up, despite all the shit he'd done to deserve one.

Which made it that much more frustrating when the security guard refused to let him pass. Crimson Justice may have tossed Apollo aside like he was shooting baskets with wads of paper—but that would never happen again.

"What can I do to get inside?" asked Apollo nicely, pointing at the morgue door.

"Get approval," said the security guard.

Apollo left in a flash and returned moments later with the highest-ranking officer he could find from the attached precinct. The officer's hand was bent awkwardly behind his back.

"Please let him in," whined the officer.

The security guard turned to unlock the morgue. Apollo released the officer's hand and gave Kristy a kiss before he went inside.

He was gone for less than ten minutes. When he returned, he didn't look happy or sad, but confused.

"What is it, baby?" asked Kristy while the security guard locked up behind him. The Sunnies fell in line, following Apollo down the hallway toward the nearest exit. "Did you get your money back?"

Apollo looked at her and smiled. He smiled so big and bright, she thought she might go blind. "No. I didn't."

Then he laughed and ran off without them.

CHAPTER 12

"PLEASE DON'T JUDGE ME," SAID TORI.

Dean nodded. There was something about the way he was looking at her that made Tori feel at ease. She couldn't say that about many men in her life. She felt like she could trust him. How far, or to what length, remained to be seen.

When she didn't immediately launch into her story, the pause offering her reasons to abort the conversation, Dean kindly urged her to go on.

Tori said, "I had cheated on my best friend."

Amanda didn't know.

That night, when Tori came home after searching for Amanda—then hijacking her date with Rick and hooking up at his place—Amanda was there, dancing to a TV commercial jingle in her PJs while eating cereal out of the box that Tori had started earlier that evening.

"Hey!" said Amanda. "Where've you been?"

"Out," said Tori. Something wasn't right—Amanda hadn't been this happy in forever, and that didn't make any sense after she'd been stood up. "What's gotten into you?"

"Nothing." She beamed, unable to hide her smile. "Rick and I had the best date ever."

Amanda was putting on a show. She couldn't allow Tori to see how destroyed she was after being stood up. She couldn't allow Tori to see how her budding relationship with the man Tori wanted had blown up in Amanda's face. It was always a competition.

And Tori couldn't let on that she knew—because *she* was the one who was with Rick all night.

"Cool." Tori yawned.

"We met up at this dive bar because he was running late, but then we went dancing and…"

"Can we save it for tomorrow?" asked Tori. "I'm exhausted."

"Sure," said Amanda, almost moping. "I'll tell you about it tomorrow."

"Great," said Tori, as she fell into bed face-first. "Tell me tomorrow."

She was asleep moments later.

Tori and Rick kept their entanglement a secret, a secret she would've taken to her deathbed. There, Tori would admit to her lifelong friend that they'd both slept with her one-time college boyfriend, and the two would have a big laugh over it.

The thing was, Rick wouldn't leave Tori alone, even though he and Amanda were still dating—even after breaking her heart, which Amanda refused to admit. His wooing of Tori started small—a text, a wink after class, a random note given to her by a stranger dictating where and when to meet. But Tori didn't engage. Each refusal only made Rick try harder. Soon she was receiving gifts and flowers.

Rick was on her mind whether she wanted to think of him or not. He pursued her as if he had nothing else to do with his time. How could he still be dating Amanda when he was constantly chasing Tori?

Tori and Amanda were like family. She'd never purposely hurt Amanda, but there was one thing Tori was learning about Rick—he was like a drug, and she couldn't resist him forever.

"Do you ever think about the future?" asked Amanda one night. The lights had been out for an hour, yet Tori was still awake as if she knew Amanda was holding onto something she needed to discuss. "Do you ever think about where we'd be if *things* had never happened?"

Tori knew exactly what those things were. Their pasts were intertwined.

"Yeah," said Tori, then waited for the follow-up question. There was always a follow-up.

When Amanda didn't respond with the usual part two, Tori sat up and turned on the bedside lamp. Amanda was lying on her side, silently crying into her pillow.

Every so often, Amanda was known to get blindsided by a new round of grief, but Tori had always been numb to it. She often wondered why she was immune. Like Amanda, Tori's scars weren't healed—they were jagged and scabbed and sometimes split wide open. Maybe Tori was rotten on the inside, decayed so badly that she couldn't feel anything but emptiness.

Tori got out of bed and into Amanda's, then held her until she stopped crying. They were together, but they were alone. Alone together. It was no wonder that they'd both suffered abandonment issues and clung tightly onto the few connections they had. And with each passing year, it became more difficult to identify the worthy from the unworthy. Sometimes they held on to people who should've been let go as if their lives depended on it.

Rick was no different, and they grappled onto him like there was no tomorrow.

"You'll always have me," said Tori. "No matter what."

"Ditto. I'll always need my hero," said Amanda as she drifted off to sleep.

"What happened?" asked Dean. "You make it sound like the two of you survived something awful."

Tori knew that telling her story meant she was going to have to explain certain things in specific detail that would make her uncomfortable. And yet, when the moment came and she loaded up her courage to tell Dean her darkest secrets, she heard the voice inside her head and the black-hole eyes sucking the warmth from her body.

She chickened out. She hoped Dean wasn't paying attention, that she might get away without having to spill her guts completely—except Dean hung onto every word.

"Maybe later," said Tori, as she scolded herself with an aggressive mental chicken cluck. Her cowardice would catch up with her eventually.

Tori couldn't remember how many times she met up with Rick, but she hated herself every time, and she swore she wouldn't do it again—or at least, not until Amanda and Rick were through. After all, if Amanda could break Amendment 3, then so could she.

Two women, best friends crammed into a tiny dorm room—the secret was bound to get out, and it was a minor miracle it lasted as long as it had.

Then, one day…

Tori had been working at the café for only a month. She took the job to ensure her free time was limited, thus preventing her from meeting Rick. Plus, it paid—a total win-win.

After pouring coffee and mixing smoothies for weeks, she was ready to give up caffeine. What was once a pleasant smell was suddenly as foul as armpit musk.

It was late, and customer traffic was thinning out when Amanda stopped in. It wasn't the first time Amanda had dropped by during Tori's shift, but it was the first time she didn't buy anything.

"Hey, do you have a minute?" asked Amanda. She seemed nervous, but that wasn't odd. She had suffered with anxiety issues since they were kids.

"Sure," said Tori. "Can't pass up an opportunity to de-café." She laughed at her own joke, but Amanda did not. In fact, Amanda hardly reacted at all. "Sorry, it was funnier in my head."

"I appreciated it," said Dean.
"Somehow, I knew you would," said Tori, smiling.

"Tank!" yelled Tori.

"What up?" said the beefy guy behind the counter.

"Watch the register."

Tori and Amanda stepped outside. The quad was empty, giving them plenty of privacy. But when Amanda didn't immediately start talking, Tori felt compelled to get the ball rolling. "What's up?"

Amanda was dancing around like she had to pee. It was making Tori nervous.

"Do you remember the sixth-grade play?" asked Amanda.

Shit. This was going to be a doozy.

"Yeah," said Tori, playing along. "*The Wizard of Oz.*"

"We were both up for the Wicked Witch," said Amanda.

"Yeah, because neither of us were lame enough to play Dorothy."

"But you got the part."

"Yeah, so?"

"The thing is," said Amanda, as she looked up at the sky, "I went to Mrs. Bally and told her to withdraw my name."

"What?" said Tori. "Why would you do that?"

"Because you *always* win. I don't like competing with you. It's impossible."

"Why are we competing in the first place?"

"Because living in your shadow sucks. I never wanted to be your sidekick!"

"Wait a minute," said Tori, "your audition was better than mine. You nailed it. I always said it should've been you up there in the green paint. That's why we wrote and recorded our own play."

The week before opening night, Tori and Amanda had camped out in the backyard and recorded an entire play they wrote themselves on cassette tape, called *The Witches of Grace Falls*.

"Wait," said Dean. "Grace Falls? Pennsylvania?"

"Yeah," said Tori. "Do you know it?"

"Know it? I went to Milton State University."

"No shit? Me too. I grew up there."

"Strange." Dean shook his head. "And Tank? Tall, chubby guy? Frizzy hair? I don't even know the guy's last name. We just called him Teddy the Tank."

"I think that was his last name," Tori said thoughtfully. "Theodore Tank."

"Really?" asked Dean, his face contorted like he had swallowed something bitter.

"No. I'm fucking with you."

"Jerk." He chuckled, and she laughed harder in response. "Sorry, go on. Small world."

"Do you think making silly voices on a cassette tape in my backyard makes up for the fact that you always get what you want?" asked Amanda. "You're better than me at everything."

"No, I'm not."

"Yes, you are," said Amanda firmly.

"No, seriously, I'm really not—"

"—Stop arguing with me!" shouted Amanda. Her whole body had gone rigid, and her hands were balled into fists.

Tori got quiet. Amanda never yelled. Tori was the loud one, the one who popped off and got angry.

"I just wanted one thing that was mine."

It was clear what she was talking about.

"What happened to experiencing the same opportunities?" asked Tori.

Amanda looked as if Tori had rubbed her face in dog piss. "Things change."

A handful of students went into the café, laughing, and the bell rang as they entered. This seemed too happy a place to be having this conversation. It was like attending a wake at a comedy club.

"What do you want?" Tori's voice was barely above a whisper.

"Nothing. I want you to be happy." Then Amanda backed away from Tori and said one last thing before storming off into the warm night air. "You can have him."

Amanda dropped a small piece of paper onto the ground as she left. It was a note—the kind that comes attached to a bouquet of flowers.

Tori,

Thinking of you.

-R

After Tori finished her shift—the longest shift in the history of shitty college jobs—so shitty that Tori butchered an order by using coffee instead of milk in a professor's smoothie—she arrived home to find an empty room with a bouquet of flowers resting on her bed.

However, their room wasn't just empty, it was missing things.

The television. The toaster. Even the Pop-Tarts were gone.

"What the hell?" she growled. "Amanda? Were we robbed?"

Only Amanda didn't answer. She wasn't in the room or down the hall. She wasn't anywhere.

On the dry-erase board by the door was a message Tori had missed when she first walked in, because she wasn't looking for one. There, in red marker, was Amanda's final bequeathal—

"You can have the room too. Moved back home. See you in class."

"Amanda was better than me in every way," said Tori. "She had her flaws, but she was always the good one. So innocent, so honest, so pure. It broke my heart that I broke hers. I never meant for it to go that way. And yet, looking back on it now, how come I didn't see that we were on a collision course?"

Dean said, "Sometimes we're too close to the moment to see the path we're on."

Tori nodded. "I wish I could have swerved."

"Yeah, me too." After a moment, Dean asked, "What happened with Rick?"

"I dumped him."

"I don't think I can do this," said Tori. Rick was watching her closely, waiting for a punch line that never came, a stupid-ass confused grin on his face. She'd already berated him for sending her flowers to the dorm room she shared with Amanda—an "honest mistake," he claimed.

They were on his stupid couch in his off-campus apartment, and the movie hadn't even gotten past the stupid FBI warning when she stumbled into a stupid rant that went in stupid circles before it finally ended there. Besides, there were only so many stupid comedies she could stomach with stupid fart jokes and stupid penis humor. And they weren't going to finish watching it anyway. Why did such a stupid good-looking guy have such shit taste in everything, from music to movies—even stupid women…

"Do what?" asked Rick.

Where exactly had she lost him? She thought she was being clear.

It had been a whole month since Amanda dumped them both, but it was their first night together after Rick's apology for sending the flowers to her room and not the café—a dumb mistake from a dummy. Tori managed to come up with excuses—a few valid—for not seeing Rick. She needed time to think. She needed time to heal. She needed to do her nails, wash her hair, study, finish visiting Aunt Flo, forgot what time it was, had to run errands, was feeling ill, might have an ear infection, was suffering through seasonal allergies, and didn't see his text from six hours ago. When she finally relented—out of need, lust, distraction, and curiosity—she showed up at Rick's with the intent to see where things would go.

She identified two possible scenarios.

Scenario 1 – She'd show up at his place, take one look at him, and jump his bones before he had a chance to ruin it with dumb words.

Scenario 2 – She'd show up at his place, feeling awful, but suffer through it until she grew so numb that she forgot all about why she was feeling awful in the first place.

However, the scenario she never considered was the one that came true. When she arrived and he answered the door, it was as if the magic was gone. Sure, he was a good-looking guy—big, strong, athletic, wealthy—but he was boring! He didn't even have good taste! If he did, he would've chosen Amanda.

"I think we need to break up," she finally said.

"Why?" he asked. He never stopped grinning, like it was all a big joke.

"Because, Amanda—"

"But I was going to dump Amanda," he said.

"What?" she replied. "Why? Why would you do that?" Before he could respond, she continued. "Amanda's so smart. She's the sweetest. She's kind, and warm, and loving, and she's ridiculously funny, and she's way hotter than me—"

Rick put a finger to her lips to shush her. It was an awful move, slightly demeaning yet ridiculously effective. She fell for it. Like shooting up that old familiar friend one last time, a junkie in need of one last hit before quitting.

She woke up in his bed the next morning and bounded off to the kitchen with a spring in her step. She was craving French toast or scrambled eggs and checked the fridge. There was old takeout, a box of stale cereal, four jars of Miracle Whip, protein shake mix, and a bag of not-so-frozen peas. Left with no other option and a growly stomach, she threw on some clothes and hopped into the bathroom to brush her teeth. She'd jog down to the corner as soon as she was done. She envisioned freshly baked muffins or maybe a couple egg sandwiches from the Bagels-2-Go.

Tori grabbed her purple toothbrush, the one he'd given her for sleepovers at his place, and quickly started scrubbing when someone shoved a key into the front door.

"Rick," said Tori, peeking into the bedroom, "someone's here."

"What?" he groaned, his face buried into a pillow.

But when Tori paced into the living room and saw the front door swing open, she saw someone she didn't expect.

"Oh shit," groaned Rick as he dropped his keys onto the coffee table. He was wearing a mesh shirt and...*mascara*?

Was she dreaming? Why were there two Ricks?

"Baby, why's she using my toothbrush?" said a brunette covered in ink, still drunk from a night of clubbing. She was sucking on a ring pop and was wearing at least five glowsticks.

Tori looked down at the purple toothbrush in her hand with the freshly foamed bristles. Rick said he had put it into the toothbrush holder by the sink just for her. She had used it countless times and even noted how cute it was that she had her own toothbrush at his place. The wheels of her brain started turning, starting up like a mental motor without proper caffeination, questioning how *that* toothbrush could both be hers *and* this woman's at the same time.

"What's going on?" asked naked Rick, wiping the morning rust from his eyes and walking up behind Tori.

"Rick," said the brunette, "you never said you had a twin."

"You dumb asshole," growled naked Rick. "You weren't supposed to come home till noon!"

"I'm the asshole?" roared raver Rick. "She wasn't supposed to spend the night!"

"Wait," muttered Dean.

"Yeah," groaned Tori.

"Oh, that's foul," said Dean, his jaw dropped open in disgust. "Can't put that toothpaste back in the tube."

Tori laughed then sighed, "That was my joke! And yeah, Rick could multiply, and ring-pop girl and I shared a toothbrush."

"What a duplicitous asshole," groaned Dean, and Tori smirked at the pun. "What did you do?"

"Well, first I ran into the bathroom before I gagged," she said. Dean nodded, as if to say he would've too. "Then I locked the door, took his toothbrush, and made sure to clean all the hard-to-reach places in his toilet before putting it back into the holder when I was done."

"Awesome," said Dean.

"And then," said Tori, "I exploded."

"What the fuck!" she yelled as she stormed into the bedroom.

"What the fuck?" scoffed naked Rick. "What are you so mad about?"

"What do you mean, what am I so mad about?" she yelled. "Who was that woman?"

"What woman?" he asked.

Tori stepped into the next room and found the apartment empty.

"Ring-pop girl!" she growled as she threw the toothbrush at him so hard it broke the porcelain base of his bedside lamp.

"I don't know what you're talking about," he said. "Did you hit your head or something?"

"Rick," said Tori, stepping toward him calmly, "why are you wearing mascara?"

Rick reached up and wiped at his eye, smearing the oily substance across his cheek.

She slapped him, and something strange happened—for a moment he split, forming two identical heads before snapping back together.

"You tried gaslighting me, motherfucker," she growled. "You tried to make me think I was crazy!"

"Oh, come off it, Tori. You'd do it too if you could multiply."

"You're a cheating shitspitting asshole."

"No, I'm not," whined Rick.

Tori got into his face like they were professional fighters at a weigh-in. "Did you really just say that with a straight face?" she whispered. Then she roared. "As if I wasn't the girl you were cheating with on my best friend!"

"Stop," said Rick. "You cheated on your best friend. I was just dating you both."

It hurt. He was right. She was the asshole too.

"How many women are you dating, Rick?" she cried.

He groaned. "Why are we having this conversation?"

"How many?" she asked again.

"Only you." He was lying.

The way he said it turned Tori's stomach sour. "Fucking liar."

"Why are you being such a bitch?" he said. "We had a great night, and now you're making up some other woman? Do you want to be with me or not?"

Tori didn't know which part of the conversation she hated most: the part where the man she loved was obviously cheating, or the part about how she had been messing around with her best friend's boyfriend, or the part about her being "bitchy," or the fact that his ability to split apart and date other women was somehow all her fault.

"Amanda and I have been through a lot together," said Tori. "It's my fault, but you helped destroyed that."

"So why aren't the two of you together?" said Rick. "If you love her so much, go be with her." He smirked. "You're so broken, and you don't even know it."

Broken.

They all called her broken. Ever since she was a little girl—either in hushed tones behind her back or straight to her face. An innocent word that scratched its way so deep into her skin that the mere mention of it made her spirit bleed. Orphaned, poor, and difficult wasn't a popular combination, and if Tori could've chosen a better set of descriptors for herself, she would have. But that's what people saw when they looked at her. Orphaned, poor, and difficult—a broken little girl who became an even more broken woman.

Rick didn't know how she felt about that word, but either way, he was going to regret saying it.

She slugged him. In fact, she hit him so hard he toppled over the bed and split in two. The rage filled her emptiness, and for the first time in forever, with that glowing hot anger, she felt whole.

"Bang bang, I am the warrior," she sang to herself.

The epiphany that followed sent marching orders before she knew where she was going. Both Ricks were growling threats, but she was already down the hall, her strides lengthening into a jog that broadened into a run. By the time she was in the courtyard of the apartment complex, she was sprinting past couples and dogwalkers, all the way to the highway. She ran across the bypass bridge and onto campus. She grabbed what she needed from her room and flagged down a cab.

"Where to?" asked the cabbie. The backseat was greasy and smelled of egg rolls from the China King, but Tori hardly noticed. She was on a mission.

"414 Cross Road," she said.

They arrived twenty minutes later in front of the house; Tori knew it like it was her own. She knew every creaky floorboard, including how to sneak out at night without a sound. She was practically raised there.

"Can you wait here?" she asked the cabbie.

"Sure, for an extra twenty?"

She handed him the bill with a grimace and closed the door. The upstairs curtains moved when she looked. She'd already been spotted.

Moments after she knocked, an older woman answered with a beaming smile.

"What're you doing here, sweetie?" she said. "I haven't seen you since Labor Day!"

"Hi, Aunt Susan," said Tori. "Is Amanda home?"

"She is," said Susan. "And she's been miserable."

"Mind if I go up?"

"Sure!" Susan winked. "I'll stay out of your way."

"Thank you," said Tori as she lugged her guitar through the door.

The stairs up to the second floor were narrow and steep, too small compared to her memory. She remembered running up and down those stairs a hundred times, racing each other out into the backyard, adventuring into the woods. Being in that house was like journeying back through time, when she and Amanda were too busy to fret about boys. Instead, they were playing Slasher and Final Girl with a rubber knife and hockey mask.

Amanda's door loomed at the end of the hall. There was a chance this would end ugly, and Tori prepared herself. Her best friend was her soulmate— not romantically, though more dependent than they should have been. Their shared past made them survivors. One could even argue that they shouldn't have made it into adulthood.

And what's the one thing all survivors know?

They know that friendships are the only things in life to be treasured more than life itself.

Tori knocked.

No answer.

Tori knocked again. "Amanda, it's me. I'm sorry. I should have come sooner." She thought about what she had said and shook her head. "No, I should never have let you leave." She stepped back from the door and opened her guitar case. "What good is having anything, experiencing anything, if you can't share it with your best friend?"

There was no answer, however, Tori spotted a shadow moving underneath the door. Amanda was listening. She could never refuse a good apology. She was too curious to toss on a pair of headphones or turn up the television volume.

Tori threw the guitar strap over her head and cleared her throat.

"I ended it with Rick," she said. "Did you know he could multiply? Turns out he wasn't just messing around with you and me. Who knows how many women he was screwing.

"The toothbrush he put out just for me," she continued, "turns out to be the same toothbrush the other woman was using. I felt so stupid that I decked him. I punched him so hard he hit the floor. And do you know what went through my mind immediately after? *You should know*. It was running through my head the whole way here. I betrayed you and that's not okay. I'm so sorry for what I've done."

Then Tori started playing their song. Patty Smyth never had such huge fans, a whole generation after her music became popular. Tori strummed and sang "The Warrior," lost in a daydream of days gone by—two little girls singing along to the radio and jumping on Amanda's bed.

She was so lost in that daydream, strumming and singing, that she never saw Amanda open the door. It almost frightened Tori, and she stopped playing, seeing the impassive stare on her best friend's face. Was she still angry? Had Amanda forgiven her?

"Was it the purple toothbrush?" asked Amanda.

"Uh huh."

"That was my toothbrush too," she said. "You asshole."

"Yeah, you asshole," said Tori, and Amanda gave her the biggest Amanda-bear-hug ever.

"Awww," said Aunt Susan. She was folding laundry in the next room, door wide open. "Nice to see a couple of assholes getting back together."

"Shut up, Aunt Susan!" Amanda laughed.

"It took a while," explained Tori, "but Amanda eventually forgave me." She sighed. "I wish we had never met Rick Jansen. Things might've turned out differently if we had avoided him."

"Assholes like Rick are everywhere," said Dean.

"Yep," said Tori. "How do I know you're not one of them, Dean?"

"Dean?" said a tinny, muffled voice, echoing Tori. It caught them both off guard. If they hadn't both heard it, Tori would've thought she'd imagined it.

"Who said that?" asked Tori. "Is that coming from the door?"

"Dean, are you in there?"

"Yeah!" Dean jumped up. "We're in here!"

He pounded his fist against the crushed metal door and smiled at her. They had been locked away for hours, but the time they spent together wasn't so bad. Tori had to admit, talking to Dean made it tolerable. They were about to be rescued and would go their separate ways once freed. Part of her felt a little disappointed, knowing she wouldn't hear the rest of Dean's story—and that he wouldn't hear the rest of hers.

There was a thump—a thump so loud that Dean staggered backward from the crushed door, the metal tolling like a bell.

"You prick!" shouted the muffled voice, followed by another thump so explosive it shook the room. The dangling tiles broke from the ceiling, and dust rained like glitter at a pretty-princess birthday party. "I want my hundo back, you piece of shit!"

CHAPTER 13

5:00 PM

THIS MUST BE WHAT IT'S LIKE TO WALK DEATH ROW.

It was hyperbolic and dramatic, but it wouldn't be Rudy if it wasn't one or the other—or both. He and Arthur remained at the bank and watched as EMTs wrangled the bodies into black bags and loaded them into a van, shipping them off to the morgue. Arthur had suggested they should identify the body and begin the process of notifying Dean's family.

"Are all morgues this big?" asked Rudy, his voice echoing off the vaulted ceiling as they entered the cold sterile room. Thirty-six bodies were presented on cold metal slabs, rows of stainless-steel freezers and hanging lights hovering over each body bag.

"No," said Arthur. He removed his glasses and wiped them with his shirt. "But Supe-Cities began investing in larger morgues for obvious reasons. Body counts tend to be higher."

Body counts.

Rudy felt a tingling sensation and began sweating like in spin class—not that he ever went. How had he lived in Wonder City for ten years and never once experienced loss? It was something of a miracle.

He felt so guilty, so useless, so irresponsible—and yet responsible for everything. If he hadn't nudged Dean into believing the next pretty face could be *the one*, none of this would've happened. Dean would've never insulted Apollo, never needed to get change from the bank.

It was Rudy's fault.

"I can't do it," cried Rudy.

Arthur had already stepped up to the first set of tables to begin inspecting what was left of the victim's…*faces.* "What's wrong?" he asked, unzipping the first body bag for a better look.

Um, besides the obvious!? Sometimes Arthur's profession created a chasm between them. He could turn on and off the mechanisms inside his brain that were responsible for empathy and disgust to examine the harsh realities of life.

"I don't want to call his parents, Arthur."

It may have seemed like a small thing compared to identifying Dean's corpse, but truth be told, having to be the bearer of bad news would crush Rudy even further.

"You should do it," said Arthur. "Dean's parents love you."

"I know," Rudy grumbled. "I won them over with my chicken pot pie recipe. And the crockpot chili recipe. And the black-bean brownies—Oh, those are delicious. I should make some when we get home."

"You're stalling. Besides, there's a chance he's not in here."

"Where else would he be?" whined Rudy. "Oh, Arthur! I don't want to do this! What if I have to call his friends too? What if I have to call that *demon*?"

"What demon?" asked Arthur.

"What demon? What demon!?" scoffed Rudy. When Arthur didn't respond, he spoke the one and only word he ever enunciated like it was an actual, vicious curse. "Brie." On second thought, there were at least three other words Rudy pronounced similarly, like *bitch, chartreuse,* and *rhubarb.* If one knew Rudy, they'd understand why.

Rudy was still wearing the Go-Pro Visor. He'd forgotten he had it on, let alone whether it was still live streaming. He was sad and scared. Identifying a body should not be a thing one does for the people they care about.

When he'd first met Dean, it was clear the guy needed someone to talk to. What Rudy didn't realize was that he needed Dean as much as Dean needed him. Rudy had been stuck in a cycle of perpetual distrust, wallowing in a bad relationship. Dean helped Rudy see that there were people out there who would like Rudy for Rudy.

And that was why he stopped walking into the room filled with bodies. To go any further meant finding out the truth—not knowing meant Dean was still alive, if only just in his head.

Arthur said, "What was he wearing? I'll do it."

Rudy nodded appreciatively. "He was wearing that silly t-shirt with the periodic element of UM."

"Um?" asked Arthur.

"I don't know, it was a science joke." Rudy shrugged. He'd always thought the joke was dumb, but he suddenly felt the urge to chuckle, as if to honor Dean. Then he added the caption with a pair of air-quotes. "*The Element of Confusion*—It was an unfashionable novelty tee."

"Oh," said Arthur. "I get it. Hah."

Rudy rolled his eyes.

Arthur set off across the room, checking the body bags one by one with the coroner. Rudy watched as they moved table to table, unzipping enough to check the clothing, then zipping back up. Once or twice, Arthur unzipped the whole bag to further inspect the remains, but each time he rezipped the bag and moved on.

By the time Arthur arrived at the final row, Rudy anticipated the inevitable bad news and closed his eyes. He could recall the night they met like it had happened only yesterday.

Poor Dean was obviously straight and so distraught that he had wandered into the wrong bar on singles night. Woody's was a gay bar renowned for its aggressive clientele—and Dean was fair game. He was dressed in office-casual, a messenger bag slung over the back of his barstool. He was trying to ignore the men sitting next to him as they took turns making passes. It was brutal, the way they teased him…

"Fuck me if I'm wrong, but is your name Easy Bottom?"

"Do you work for UPS? Because I thought I saw you checking out my—"

"No," growled Rudy, cutting off the burly suitor. "Nobody's checking out your package." He was tired of watching from the other end of the bar and decided to give the poor guy a break. "Go buzz off!"

"Whatever," groaned burly-suitor before he and his friend found someone else to torment.

Dean tore his eyes away from the bottom of his beer glass and gave Rudy a sideways glance. He was racing toward the worst hangover of his life, and

Rudy felt compelled to make sure the guy made it home okay. But then he noticed something on Dean's messenger bag.

It was a Tin Men pin.

"Either twenty-four is your favorite number," said Rudy, "or you're no fan of supes."

"Fuck supes," slurred Dean.

"Indeed," said Rudy. "I don't get this town. People stay inside and lock their doors at night, cowering to avoid danger, but run outside and throw parades after people die and buildings burn." Dean huffed, and Rudy realized he'd hit a sore spot. "You worked there, huh?"

It was all over the news. An office building on the east side called The Incubator—full of startups renting space—had gone up in flames earlier that day. Crimson Justice duked it out with the supervillain Craze and set the whole building on fire. Hundreds of businesses burned. In the end, Crimson Justice emerged with a meaty skeleton of charred flesh wrapped in Craze's signature green chainmail.

Rudy had his theories, though…that skeleton could have been anybody.

"Order delivered, under thirty minutes," said Crimson Justice straight into the television cameras before he soared away into the sky.

Rudy had been glued to the coverage, watching the whole event unfold. He couldn't believe it when the people cheered. Craze wasn't even a classic villain—he never robbed banks or destroyed property. Heck, he never hurt anybody. Craze was a super-powered community organizer, sticking up for the little guy against the Ministry and big business.

And the casualties didn't end with Craze.

"Yeah, I worked there," groaned Dean as he attempted to take another gulp of his empty beer. "I moved here to start over. I hate supes, but it was a good job. A good opportunity. Now that's gone."

Rudy knew what that was like. He came to Wonder City from a small town that didn't appreciate people of darker complexions and liked LGBTQ people even less. He told everyone all the time that he moved to the city to be an artist, a mogul—an influencer! But really, Rudy had wanted to start over in a place where people might accept him for who he was.

"You saved a lot of people," said Rudy, suddenly recognizing him from the broadcast. This man had run back into the building to get people out. He was a hero.

"I saved five," slurred Dean. "Twenty people died."

"But not twenty-five." Then he held out his hand. "I'm Rudy."

"Dean." They shook.

"Well, Dean, you have two options," said Rudy. "You can come with me. We can get some food, sober up, and talk about our mutual distaste for supes. Or you can stay here and wallow by yourself in a gay bar."

"This is a gay bar?"

"You walked into a bar called Woody's," said Rudy. "What did you expect? A woodpecker?"

Dean blinked a few times before the urge to laugh hit him. "Wait, you mean they're not the same thing?"

Rudy snickered. "That's not what I meant, Deano." Then he laughed. "Though it is funny."

"Okay," said Dean, standing from his barstool and grabbing his messenger bag. "Let's go. I really could use a friend."

"Okay," said Arthur. His return from investigating the body bags startled Rudy away from the happy memory.

"Okay?" asked Rudy. His stomach clenched.

But Arthur only nodded calmly. "He's not here."

"How's that possible? Are they storing bodies somewhere else?"

Arthur turned to the coroner and waved him down.

"How may I help you?" the man boomed. He was a stern fellow who looked like the embodiment of Death. Tall and lanky, with a pallid complexion that looked almost waxy under the fluorescent lighting and sounded like a tuba if a tuba could speak.

"We're looking for a guy wearing a silly t-shirt," said Arthur.

"Element of Confusion?" asked the coroner.

If Rudy's jaw could've dropped any lower, it would've fallen right off his face.

"How'd you know?" Rudy's heart thumped wildly in his chest. Was this man actually Death? How else would he have known something so specific?

"We don't have anyone here fitting that description. But there was a super down here looking for someone with that exact t-shirt."

"Who?" asked Rudy and Arthur in unison.

"I don't know," said the coroner. "But he wore a bedsheet and glowed the whole time. He asked if I was a Sunny."

"Apollo," whimpered Dean.

SLAM!

"Who?" Tori looked almost amused.

In times of chaos, Dean always managed to stay calm. When The Incubator was on fire, he'd grabbed his coworker by the arm and led her to safety through the shattering glass, the falling steel and concrete. When shit hit the fan, he never got soiled. Dean was a cool cucumber in a world of uncool customers.

Until now.

Dean's knees buckled. It was one thing to face an imploding building, racing for his life to find an exit. It was another to face a supe who could snare a nipple and rip the entirety of his skin right off with a simple tug.

"Apollo," repeated Dean as a ceiling tile broke free and smacked him on the head.

"What does he want?" Tori asked. Urgency crept into her voice.

"You stole my money!" shouted Apollo on cue. "You stole my hundo, you thieving dick!" They could hear his muffled threats before every room-shaking bash. He was either going to punch his way through or bring the vault down on top of them. "Now I'm gonna take both your nipples, you slimy shit!"

"Nipples?" Tori raised an eyebrow.

Dean shrugged. "It's a long story."

"But did you steal his money?"

"No. I mean, I have his money, but I didn't steal it."

"Oh," said Tori, looking disappointed. "For a moment, I was actually impressed."

"Look," said Dean. "I'm an honest guy, I really am. But I'm also an honest guy who may have insulted an asshole supe, who then threatened to hurt me, my reputation, and my best friend if I didn't get him change for a hundred-dollar bill! *gasp* That's why I was here in the first place!"

"Okay." She nodded. "Honest, but I'm still not impressed."

"Gee, thanks," he grunted. Before Tori could respond, Dean was struck with inspiration. He stepped over to the crushed vault door and decided to negotiate. "I have your money and I'll give it back plus interest if you get us out of here!"

There was a halt in the slamming.

"How much?" asked Apollo.

"How much do you want?" asked Dean. He was surrounded by enough cash to buy the Hope Diamond or a Saudi oil rig.

"How much have you got?"

"I'm in a fucking bank vault, you moronic fuckwit," shouted Dean.

There was a long pause. Tori started laughing.

"Did you just call me a moronic fuckwit?" asked Apollo.

"Back to being impressed," sang Tori.

Apollo said something that Dean couldn't make out. "What?" he asked as he leaned in and put his ear next to the vault door. "What did you say?"

SLAM!

The door popped and creased as Dean lost his balance and spun away.

"Oh shit," said Tori. "He might actually get in here."

"Dimwit Dean!" shouted Apollo. "I'm going to kill you, motherfucker!"

SLAM! SLAM! SLAM!

"Dude," said Tori, "you must have done more than just take his money." She paced the room like she was finally recognizing the seriousness of the situation. "He's got a total rampage boner for you."

SLAM!

Dean danced around the room looking for a way out—a weapon—a bribe—a hole into another universe—even magic beans. He didn't care as long as he was leaving that vault with both nipples intact.

SLAM! SLAM! BAM!

Dean was freaking out. The room shook, and a support beam overhead jarred loose with a jagged crack that seemed to yawn wider with every punch.

Dean was sweating bullets, Tori was the cool one, and he couldn't help but feel like he was failing her. Way to go, Hero Complex! Making him feel like a putz when his life was on the line. He hardly knew Tori, but he felt compelled to protect her.

"Get back," said Dean. "Stay behind me." He placed himself between her and the vault door and braced for impact.

"And now he's a chauvinist," she groaned.

SLAM! SLAM!

A sense of calm took over. If Dean was going to bow out now, he was going to do it with class—taking it on the chin for Tori. Apollo was his problem, not hers…

…wait, did she just call him a chauvinist?

SLAM! SLAM! SLAM!

There was so much dust in the air that he closed his eyes. He didn't need to see the end.

SLAM! SLAM! SLAM! BOOM!

"Dean!" Tori sounded far away, like she had been buried beneath the debris.

Dean opened his eyes and squinted through the dusty haze, searching for her. Where had she gone that fast? The room wasn't *that big*. She couldn't have gotten far, but the dust was falling so thick it was like a curtain obscuring every corner.

SLAM! SLAM!

He started coughing.

SLAM! SLAM!

"Over here!" she shouted.

Dean moved through the rain of dust and wires, ceiling tiles and fiberglass, using his hands to feel his way, and discovered something that wasn't there minutes ago—a giant hole in the wall. There was a whole foot of ruptured steel sandwiched between layers of plaster and wood, and the breach widened after each of Apollo's strikes. A metal beam broke apart and fell into the center of the room.

He couldn't find Tori. In a panic, Dean stuck his head into the hole searching for her, hoping she had fled the room, when two hands grabbed him by the shirt and yanked him from the vault.

SLAM! SLAM! SLAM!

He nearly hacked a whole lung up his throat as plumes of dust billowed into the hallway.

"Breathe," said Tori, patting him on the back.

"What? How?" Dean rubbed the dust from his eyes.

"I don't know," she whispered. "The wall fell apart right in front of me." Tori crept away to the end of the hall, listening to the thundering strikes hammering the vault door from just around the next corner. "C'mon, before that crazy douchecanoe figures out we're not inside the vault."

Dean didn't question it. Tori led them away from the dusty hall until he was able to see and breathe.

They could hear every punch rending metal, like two sledgehammers taking turns mangling the vault's foundation. However, even beyond the vault, there was structural damage forming—cracks in the plaster and clumps of falling dust from the ceiling. Apollo was so focused on Dean that he was going to bring the whole bank down.

"You little shit!" screamed Apollo. *SLAM!* "You think you can get away with this?" *SLAM!* "I want my hundo back!" *SLAM!*

He was right around the next bend.

They tiptoed to the end of the hall and past a giant splatter of metallic gold paint on the floor. It looked like someone had stomped on a leprechaun. As Dean wondered what it meant, he lost all track of Tori. She had maneuvered to the opposite side of the hallway, investigating something spray-painted on the wall.

And then, as if on cue, Dean performed his latest DDD.

"Deano," scolded Rudy, the angry voice of Dean's conscience. "You are not an ungraceful creature in any sense. Yet, time after time, you pull a DDD—a Dumb Dean Deed—and fuck everything up."

This particular DDD might have been his worst. While creeping backward, still examining the golden splatter, he accidentally kicked a discarded, golden cap from a can of spray paint. It made a hollow plastic tumbling sound as it slid across the floor—as loud and obnoxious as nails to a chalkboard inside an empty classroom.

Apollo stopped his assault just as the echoing plastic finished toppling, then rolled another insufferable five feet.

Tori's eyes went saucer-wide, and she scolded him with an angry shrug, then nabbed Dean's wrist, leading him away like a naughty child.

"Is someone there?" asked Apollo. The hallway lit up with a brilliant shaft of light as Tori and Dean slipped around the next corner.

"What the fuck," whispered Tori. She'd been so worried about getting caught that she never noticed the blood until Dean put his hand straight into a congealed sticky smear on the wall.

Along the floor were white chalk outlines of bodies, and a whole section of yellow police tape cut the room in half.

"Hello?" said Apollo. "Who's there?"

He sounded close.

Tori was frozen, rigid after seeing all the blood, evidence markers, and outlines.

She may have pulled him free of the collapsing bank vault, but it was Dean's turn to take over.

"Let's go." He took her hand, their fingers threading together naturally.

"All those people," she said, blinking away tears.

"C'mon," he whispered. "Or we're dead too."

Tori relented on the second tug and followed Dean down the hall as the light beyond the corner intensified. They ran into the lobby and through the vestibule with the missing revolving door—

—and stepped into a frying pan.

"Why's she dressed like Crystal Beth?" pointed someone in a Metro City Sentinels t-shirt.

A lot had changed since they were locked inside the vault.

For one, it was early evening, and the streetlamps were on.

Two, a crowd of people had gathered outside the First National Bank, and they were wearing cheap army surplus, some in khakis, and others with big red V's on their clothes and body armor.

The entire square surrounding the bank was lit up like Christmas—but instead of red and green bulbs and glowing signs of Crimson Justice in a big white beard and Santa hat, there were V-Boys and the Khaki Klan preparing to flood the city with tiki torches and Molotov cocktails.

"What the hell?" groaned Dean, noting the torches, pistols, swords, and semi-automatic rifles that were lowering in their direction. One of them, the bald guy up front with his face painted like he was going on safari, resembled the security guard he'd crossed that morning entering the convention center. The guy even blew him a kiss.

Then they started shouting.

"She's one of them!"

"Back to the scene of the crime!"

"Death to villains! Death to Sympies!"

"Hoodaloo!"

The crowd came to life. Some hurled insults, others hurled rocks, as they moved to surround and swallow Dean and Tori like a giant amoeba.

"Wait," said Dean, waving his hands as if to signal some sense into the crowd. "She's not Crystal Beth!"

"Oh shit," grumbled Tori.

A brick smacked into the wall beside them, and Tori yanked Dean back inside the bank.

"How are we getting out of here?" croaked Dean, as Apollo's shine lit the white stone hallway, stalking them like Michael Myers.

"I want my hundo!" shouted the supe.

Dean and Tori looked at each other, their fingers still threaded together as if superglued. They knew they could've gone their separate ways. Dean wasn't dressed like an infamous supervillain at the scene of a massacre perpetrated by The Dope Gang—and Tori wasn't the person with Apollo's money stashed in her pocket. It would've been easy to step away, to face the world apart…*alone.* They were used to it. They were lost souls who connected only briefly—just two inmates locked in a bank vault, passing the time.

But they didn't let go. They couldn't part even if they wanted to. Not yet. There was more to this story developing between them.

"This way," said Tori, and Dean nodded.

They ran together, hand in hand, to the back of the building and hid inside an open office with little more than a desk, a chair, and a window peering out into the lobby. The blinds were drawn, and as Tori peeked through them into the lobby, she witnessed the V-Boys coming face to face with the glowing supe, as attitudes flared like two alphas clashing for dominance.

"Who the fuck are you?" shouted one of the V-Boys.

"I'm a beacon of light," said Apollo, "not some vigilante wannabe. Shine off and get out of my way."

"You get out of ours!"

"No, you!"

"No! You!"

It was quite the standoff of mental giants.

"There has to be another exit," whispered Dean, nervously pacing the dark room.

"Probably. But I haven't seen one. Maybe we should—"

When she turned back to Dean, he was gone, followed by a thump.

"Ow!"

"Dean?"

Dean had stepped into a shadow behind the desk and fell. He fell a lot farther than the floor. In fact, he fell through it and landed on something semi-soft.

"Dean?" called Tori, staring down into the black hole.

"I'm okay."

Someone in the lobby shouted, "Why are you hiding them?"

Another shouted, "Hand them over." Then a gunshot.

Tori said, "I'm coming down," before the violence escalated.

"Okay." groaned Dean.

She fell through the hole and landed beside him on an old, stained mattress with springs sticking up through the fabric.

"Good job," said Tori.

"What for?" Dean ignored the spring that had poked him in the ass.

"You found the exit!" she beamed as a series of shouts followed a burst of gunfire.

5:30 PM

"That supe jerk won't stop till he gets his hundo," said Rudy as Arthur handed the coroner his business card—just in case Dean turned up. Rudy had been obsessing over Apollo's infatuation with Dean since finding out Dean was, *most likely*, alive, and that Apollo had visited the morgue looking for him.

"His what?" asked Arthur as they paced over to the security desk. "Oh,

I remember."

"Sorry," said Rudy, rolling his eyes. "His hundred bucks. Apollo calls it a hundo, so I naturally started calling it a hundo too—that way everyone's using the same terminology. It's like when you start a new job and everyone's using acronyms you don't understand, and you're like, wait-a-minute girlfriend, tell it to me in regular English, and then proceed to the next—"

There was a buzz in Rudy's pocket, cutting off his rant.

"Don't forget to sign out," said the security guard, pointing to a clipboard from behind a station of bulletproof glass.

Rudy went first, scribbling his name as another buzz went off in his pocket. As Arthur took the pen and began to sign his own name, Rudy said, "We need to find him, Arthur!"

"How're we supposed to do that?"

"I don't know, but we have to! Before that glowing creep rips off an extra nipple like a late payment fee."

His pocket buzzed again. This was a complete violation. Everyone knew not to blow Rudy's phone up, even in an emergency. Multiple messages made him irritable, and likely chuck his phone across the room.

Finally, he ripped the phone out of his pocket and answered in one sassy, fluid motion. "What!? What could possibly be so important?"

When the voice on the other end of the line responded, Rudy pulled the phone from his ear. This wasn't Rudy's phone with the designer case. It was Dean's.

"Oh. Hi, Brie."

CHAPTER 14

6:10 PM

CRIMSON JUSTICE WAS GIFTED WITH MANY SUPERPOWERS.

He had super-speed, though he wasn't as fast as the Bolted, who could run faster than sound. But that guy was dead. Crimson Justice had tripped the Bolted as he was chasing down a pair of supervillains in neighboring Metro City. He tumbled a few hundred times before impaling himself on the teeth of a backhoe.

"Oops," Crimson Justice had said, retracting his foot before anyone noticed.

Crimson Justice also had super-strength. He was tied with Blue Anvil for Mightiest Supe. Crimson Justice had tried enlisting Craze, the runner-up strongman, to assist in removing Blue Anvil from the equation so he could claim the top spot, unopposed. But the villain refused—and we all know how that ended.

Super-invulnerability was, at times, his most prized superpower. Though it also affected his pleasure centers. There were days when he didn't feel a thing, and often that was just fine by him. But it made his secret identity difficult to balance, and like all supes, he did have his weaknesses—albeit a singular weakness—and nobody was clever enough to put those pieces together.

Then there was the Red Death—a red, mist-like tear-gas he could eject into the air, but only after eating at Hot Tamales on 25th and Kent Street. Their tamales went straight through him…

And one could never forget the Justice Beams—great, angry power blasts that erupted from his mouth, typically when he prowled the streets post-couples therapy sessions with the wife. But the more he used it, the weaker he became until fully recharged. A cautionary tale after he almost lost his last tussle with the Dope Gang. *Almost.* After all, he did bring Annie Phetamine to justice, even if she wasn't breathing. And Crystal Beth was nothing but a bloody smear when he was done with her.

The Crimson-Poke, however, was his most fascinating power. Given the right circumstances, he could stare down his opponent and force them to offer up their darkest secrets. It worked like a charm—he even used it once to embarrass a rival.

And super-flight. Oh, he loved the ability to fly. He could soar into the heavens and watch the city below, scanning for wrongdoing at ten thousand feet with his complementary powers of super-sight and super-hearing. He could soar from one end of the city to the other in moments and snatch would-be wrongdoers right out of their shoes.

After storming out of the First National Bank, Crimson Justice took to the skies, scanning the city for the Dope Gang. They'd made him look like a fool, and he was going to make them pay.

He wanted the Dope Gang and their heads on pikes.

Typically, Crimson Justice had to wait for the bad guys to attack, or at least show they were going to attack. If they were holding a weapon—heck, even if it was just a pen, he could kill them and call it self-defense. He'd never be in any actual danger. After all, Crimson Justice was invulnerable.

But tonight, that didn't matter. At first sight of the Dope Gang, he'd strike like a viper. He'd rip their necks out with his teeth just because he could. Who'd stop him? Let the press write what they wish. All he had to do was give an exclusive to Rhea Ramsey and claim anything bad—written or said—about him was fake. So long as half the country supported him, he was golden. Nobody could touch him—not that they ever could. Even Blue Anvil couldn't take Crimson Justice down, at least not without an army of supes as backup.

The air above the city was choppy. He had been drifting from one side of the city to the other, waiting for the Dope Gang to rear their ugly, punk heads. He was so busy concentrating on the ground that he never noticed when the skies became a threat. A super-sonic threat that hit him like a bunker-buster. All he saw was a blue streak before he cascaded through the air, tumbling head over heels until he regained control.

"Crimson Justice!" shouted Blue Anvil. His girly gray tights with the silly blue anvil on the chest were super lame. He was a do-gooder—not a man of Law and Order. He didn't even wear a cape. Supes with super-flight should always wear capes. It was part of the appeal. "Surrender yourself to the Wonder City Police Department."

"Surrender?" growled Crimson Justice, hovering on a draft between skyscrapers. "There is no surrender when the world is burning under the infection of—"

"Shut up, asshole," whined Blue Anvil. "Seriously, give it a rest, bro."

"You give it a rest, loser."

"You're the loser!"

"Nuh uh! You are!"

"Bro," said Blue Anvil, shaking his head, "I hoped it wouldn't come to this."

Rising to either side of Blue Anvil were two black police helicopters. Each copter had gunners operating high-tech weaponry and spotlights shining 1200 blinding lumens directly into Crimson Justice's super-eyes. Even from a distance of seven hundred feet, he could read the label: Amycus Industries. Their headquarters were located nearby. The company held all kinds of government contracts, from security, defense, and weapons, to pharmaceuticals, aerospace, and theoretical experiments. They also built and operated The Cooler, the supe-prison located just beyond the city, over the bridge into Jersey—ugh, Crimson Justice hated Jersey.

His wife had made him move to be closer to one of her "clients." The only place worse than Jersey was Delaware, because really, what the hell was Delaware, anyway? It was shaped like a bottle opener and filled with strip malls and highways. The Diamond State? Who were they kidding?

Actually, Crimson Justice didn't appreciate a single state in the union. He tolerated other states more than he tolerated Jersey. And Delaware. There were too many Reformists in the northeast for his liking.

All Reformists were a pain in his big red ass. Every last one of them were Sympies. And right now, Blue Anvil and the Wonder City Police Department were brand new keister sores to pop.

Who knew when he woke up today and strapped on his utility belt that he'd be accumulating so many new enemies?

Once he was through with Blue Anvil, the Wonder City PD, and the Dope Gang, Amycus Industries was next. He was done playing Mr. Nice Guy—heck, he'd tossed Mr. Nice Guy into a volcano three years ago after a drug bust and took all the credit for himself. Crimson Justice did most of the work anyway. That goody-two-shoes didn't even kill a single one of those smack-traffickers. Crimson Justice cleaned out the whole nest of them. After all, the only good bad-guy was a dead good bad-guy—er, something like that...

Everyone who crossed him was going to get theirs—his Little League coach, the marriage therapist, old friends, and most definitely his wife's ex. He had years' worth of anger issues and an actual list tucked inside his wallet to prove it. He'd start with the most recent perpetrators and work backward. Like the box of frozen treats the wife kept at the back of the freezer—one sweet snack a week, or when she was having an extra "girly" kind of night—he'd savor every sadistic moment and not lose a single point in the polls.

This would be a new era for Law and Order. This would be the era of the Crimson Scare.

"C'mon, man." Blue Anvil floated closer, allowing them to talk without shouting over the helicopters and the whistling winds. "The wife's ovulating and it's date night, if you get what I'm saying?"

Crimson Justice didn't respond with words. He used his left hand in a reeling motion that slowly revealed the middle finger on his right. It was crass, but so was the President, and he got elected. Half the sitting members of Congress ran on platforms that spat in the face of decency—one of them poisoned their primary opponent the night of their first debate and blamed his own assistant. If they could do it, if they could be awful human beings, so could Crimson Justice.

"Seriously?" groaned Blue Anvil as he wiped the frustration from his face. Then he gestured back to the helicopters. "Those are experimental weapons. They hurt. I should know; they tested the lowest setting out on me." When

Crimson Justice didn't respond, he kept talking. "It's set to level three. Of four. Maybe that doesn't sound terrifying to you, but trust me, my man, it's like a normie getting hit by an electrified harpoon."

Crimson Justice was not amused. He had heard stories about Blue Anvil's behavior. He talked like a Sympie—all "bro" this and "my man" that. He was no more Law and Order than the Dope Gang. Death was the only possible fate for supes like him.

Crimson Justice made another crude gesture, wagging his first back and forth.

"Okay, big red dick," groaned Blue Anvil under his breath. He waved, and the gunner on the left opened fire with a single round. It glowed like a piece of red-hot rebar, moving faster than a bullet, a rocket, and The Bolted combined. Even Optimum Overdrive wouldn't have been able to catch it. The gunner had no sooner applied pressure to the trigger than the round struck Crimson Justice in the chest.

He tried to stifle the pain. He tried to hold it in. He closed his eyes, bit his lip, squeezed his fists, curled his toes, and his sphincter clasped so tight it could have cut a diamond in half. A rush of bile moved in opposite directions. He nearly soiled his pants and threw up in his mouth.

Crimson Justice felt it all the way down into his balls, like he'd been horse-kicked. He remembered how that felt—from before he got his powers—and doubled over.

"Owwwwwwwwww-weeeeeeeeeeeeeeeeeee!" he whined.

"Yeah," said Blue Anvil. "Want another?"

6:15 PM

"C'mon," said Arthur as he led the way to the shattered vestibule in front of the Wonder City First National Bank, stepping over rocks, bricks, and even a bag of soiled cat litter.

"Are you sure?" Rudy kicked aside a broken bottle. "It's a crime scene in there."

"Do you want to find Dean or not?"

"Yeah," sighed Rudy, "but we already checked his apartment, his favorite restaurant, the convention center, the parking garage, and the hospital. Why would he still be here?"

Arthur shrugged. "Let's find out."

Rudy thought it was odd how intent Arthur was to investigate the bank, offering to check multiple times during their Dean-centric scavenger hunt. He trusted him as much as he trusted Dean, so off Rudy went, unquestioning, following him into the building where more than thirty hostages lost their lives hours ago. He thought about the hostages with every step into the bank, which prompted a whole series of paranoid, creeping shivers.

"Arthur," said Rudy, "how long do you think it takes for a ghost to form?"

"What?" Arthur turned back to Rudy.

"I mean, thirty people died," Rudy explained. "Horrifically. How long do you think it takes for their ghosts to show up? Instantaneously? A few hours? Or is it like the next full moon or something?"

"That's werewolves," corrected Arthur.

"Are they real too?" squealed Rudy, shaking off another shiver. He wasn't thinking straight. He was twisted all around and not making any sense, even to himself.

"No."

Rudy ignored his partner's blatant disregard for the truth.

"Come on." Arthur took Rudy's hand and walked him through the bank. He asked Rudy to close his eyes as they passed the police tape and the blood. Once they were around the next bend, Arthur asked him to open his eyes.

"It's over," read Rudy, standing in front of a message in gold. "These protestors are in serious need of new messaging."

"Maybe that's what you and Dean should do," suggested Arthur. "Marketing. He can write the slogans and you design."

"Are you joking?" He should've given Arthur a piece of his mind for suggesting something so absurd. He and Dean were a team. They were going to put horror and fantasy fiction back on the map. Rudy wished he could articulate the way he felt reading a good book as a teen. Escaping reality into worlds both fantastical and scary was his only refuge against the real terror—being a gay teenager in a small town full of angry, bigoted, fearful, so-called Christians.

That's when Rudy realized Arthur was staring straight past him.

"Look at this," said Arthur, pointing to the end of the hall. The ceiling was falling apart, and the vault door was crushed open. When they climbed inside, up and over the jagged metal entry, Rudy stared while Arthur moved toward the lockboxes.

"It's like the president's piggy bank exploded all over the room," said Rudy. In some places, the mounds of money were so thick that they were as soft as yoga mats.

Arthur began rummaging through the lockboxes and spotted one on the floor that caught his eye. He picked it up, checked inside, wrinkled his nose, then discarded it.

While Arthur had his back turned, Rudy quietly pocketed a roll of hundreds that barely fit into his skinny jeans.

"No," scolded Arthur, without looking.

"Fiiiiine," groaned Rudy as he tossed the roll of hundos back to where he found it. "But just you know, I'm showing more restraint within this room than I've ever shown anything, anywhere, anywhen."

"Glad you know stealing is wrong."

"Is it stealing when it's just laying around like this? It's not even guarded!"

"Mmm hmmm."

"What—everrrr."

Rudy paced the room and discovered a hole in the wall behind a fallen support beam. Upon further investigation, he saw that the hole led into an adjacent hallway, but there was no sign of his best friend. Well, almost no sign.

Rudy stepped back into the center of the room. "Dean's been here."

"Are you psychic now?"

"No, but Mama Goudeau said I have a gift for intuition," boasted Rudy. "That and I can smell his cologne."

"Paco Rabanne?"

"SuperSteel. Only the good stuff for my boy." There was something else though, something sweet on the air that snagged Rudy's sensitive sniffer. He dug into the debris at his feet and retracted a lollipop wrapper from the floor. "And our boy wasn't alone."

"What?" asked Arthur. "How do you know?"

Rudy presented the crumpled plastic sleeve. "Deano doesn't eat candy without peanut butter."

Arthur stumbled over the rubble and snatched the wrapper from Rudy's hands. He sniffed it, dabbed at it with his forefinger, then held it up to the light, as if checking for something specific.

"What. Are. You. Doing?" Rudy asked.

"Do you see any more of them?" Arthur paced the room anxiously. He leaped over fallen debris, overturned pieces of ceiling tile, and finally found another wrapper mixed up in a heap of twenty-dollar bills.

"What's going on?" asked Rudy. When Arthur didn't stop his frantic antics, Rudy grabbed and shook his partner with extra verve. "Talk to me, Arthur!"

This was bizarre. Rudy had never seen Arthur so unhinged. The man had neurotic tendencies when it came to science and geeky stuff, but this was obsession. This was madness!

"Rudy." Arthur took a deep, calming breath. He didn't look like he had lost his marbles—in fact, Rudy thought he looked scared. He was sweating, and Arthur never sweated—not even at the gym. "We need to talk."

It was the phrase Rudy feared the most. He always knew Arthur was too good for him. Arthur was going wake up one day and feel the need to end their relationship. Though Rudy never expected that talk to take place today, nor within a bank vault surrounded by enough cash for Rudy to find himself a sugar baby and buy a small island somewhere in the Pacific.

When Arthur looked up at the ceiling and sighed, like he was carrying a larger regret than Rudy's own remorse over his hip tattoo, Rudy braced for impact.

"I think," lamented Arthur, "I might be responsible for everything that transpired today."

"Do tell," said a man standing by the crushed vault door. He looked like a body builder, his muscles popping from beneath his unbuttoned black shirt. He was wearing a mask over the bottom half of his face that was as infamous as he was.

Rudy recognized him immediately from all the news programs and F.B.S.I. Most Wanted bulletins. It was Dust—leader of the notorious Dope Gang.

Rudy grabbed Arthur and moved toward the hole in the wall, but Oxy and Perc stepped through, cutting off their escape.

"Nuh uh," said Oxy. "There's no way out, my friend."

"What do you want?" asked Arthur.

"I'd like to continue your conversation," said Dust, grabbing a piece of debris and crushing it with one hand. Dust grew three inches right before their eyes, his shoulders widening like someone was behind him with an air pump. "That part about being responsible for everything."

6:20 PM

Commissioner Dudley was sitting alone in his office. His eyes were closed, and he swiveled his chair away from the door. When Captain Glenn knocked, his stomach tightened.

"Are you ready, sir?"

"I'll be right there," said Dudley without opening his eyes.

Captain Glenn left the door open, leaving Dudley a final few moments before he had to be outside. They were hosting a press conference to update the public on the afternoon's events.

Dudley's office was full of case files jammed into boxes stacked higher than he could reach without a step stool. His desk was covered in reports he had yet to file, and his assistant had fled the city last month after The Vigil had crashed through her living room window during a shootout with the Cartel. Finding her replacement was the last thing on his mind.

Old, framed photos lined the walls, going back decades—he and his first partner, a yellowed clipping from his first major bust, the medal he received after rescuing the mayor, and the front page of the Wonder City Gazette from that time he saved the city from a deranged serial killer. Commissioner Dudley had done it all. Many in the precinct considered him a real hero—and he hadn't needed any superpowers to protect his city.

The commissioner knew this day would come; however, he was hoping it would occur on someone else's watch.

Could life ever go back to normal after the age of supes?

He got out of his chair, straightened his tie, and walked to the podium.

Dudley loathed press conferences. Not because of the microphones, camera flashes, television crews, or even the reporters—but because all eyes would be on him. It was his responsibility, even though he had no control over what transpired in his own city.

When he stepped up to the microphone on the front steps of the WCPD Headquarters, he was surrounded by the media, V-Boys, Khaki Klan, Supies, Anti-Supe protestors, and Tin Men dressed in gray. Both sides were separated by wooden barricades and a line of port-a-potties—a brilliant idea that kept them apart by stench alone.

"Hello," Dudley said into the microphone, adjusting its height with a crackle of feedback over the speaker system. "Earlier this afternoon, the Dope Gang attempted to rob the First National Bank. They were unsuccessful and remain at large."

The crowd was hanging on his every word.

"Sixty-six hostages were taken by the Dope Gang. Thirty of them were released in coordination with our negotiator when Crimson Justice arrived." There were scattered cheers at his name. "Crimson Justice disobeyed direct orders and entered the bank where the remaining hostages were left abandoned. The resulting aggressive entry triggered a chain reaction, killing all thirty-six. As of thirty minutes ago, we have procured a warrant for Crimson Justice's arrest for second-degree murder, assault and battery, destruction of property, and criminal mischief."

Dudley had no sooner finished speaking when chaos erupted. Every local and national reporter shouted questions at once—from factual follow-ups to accusations masquerading as questions. V-Boys kicked over port-a-potties with weapons drawn, engaging with Tin Men, while the police pushed back against the angry mob.

Then gunshots went off.

The melee was out of control, and there was nobody there to stop it.

CHAPTER 15

TORI HATED THE SEWERS.

Not that there were people who liked the sewers, but Tori had actual experience. She had been down in those dark, disgusting tunnels before, and she hated every moment of it.

Besides the obvious—the smell, the gunk, and the dampness—the ever-present chill permeating every dank corner troubled her. The chill, however, wasn't from the temperature but from the feeling of an impending threat hidden within every crevice and behind every shadow.

There were *things* down there lurking in the miles and miles of concrete tubes. Weird, unexplainable things. The whole labyrinth of tunnels puzzled her, and she had way too many unanswered questions. Why did traveling beneath the streets take twice as long as above? Who had strung up the endless series of construction lights that adorned every pass? And who was paying the electric bill?

"Do you know where you're going?" asked Dean, attempting to keep pace. "Because it kind of looks like you know where you're going. Have you been down here before?"

"Once," said Tori over her shoulder. "A while ago. I was homeless for a time."

"Oh," said Dean. "I've heard some strange things about the sewers."

She smiled at his pivot. "Don't believe everything you hear."

"I heard there were mutants down here."

She shrugged. "Well, that's true."

Dean stopped walking. "What?"

"Come on." She turned back to him with a devious grin. "Don't slow down. The mutants will get you." Dean's eyes widened, and Tori laughed. "I'm kidding. But seriously, don't slow down, the mutants will get you."

Tori was enjoying herself. She liked teasing him. She even liked it when he teased her back. She almost admitted to herself that she enjoyed being around him, but she shook off the thought like it was a tingle in her ear.

"Have you ever seen one?" asked Dean.

"One what?"

"A mutant."

"Eh. Once. Most of them are nice, but there are some bad ones out there. Like Nergal."

"Who's Nergal?"

"I don't know. I never saw him," she said. "Let's hope we don't find out."

When they passed another manhole cover leading up to the streets, Dean asked, "Why are we still down here? We could just leave."

"I wouldn't go up before we cross 15th Street," she replied, still leading the way.

"Why?"

Dean was falling behind. He didn't want to be there, she could tell. But it wasn't like she wanted to be down there either. "Safer than going up in the middle of a V-Boy parade."

"Oh, good point," he agreed. "How much further to 15th Street?"

"Few blocks," she said with a smile and stopped, allowing him to catch up.

He was spooked. She could sense it in the way he studied the ground before every step and slowed his pace into a creeping sneak. She probably shouldn't have affirmed his suspicions about mutants living in the sewers. There really wasn't much to worry about—at least not this far downtown. Uptown—that was where the weird things mingled.

When they were kids, Tori and Amanda would scour the horror section, squealing over gory covers and begging Amanda's aunt to let them rent something R-rated. She had so many great memories watching movies in Amanda's basement, half covered in blankets to hide under when the scary parts got too intense. For whatever reason, this reminded her of those simpler times, watching the idiots on screen as they crept ever closer to imminent doom…

"Are you a horror fan?" he asked.

"Totally," said Tori. She wondered how long he'd been holding on to that question. She'd caught him looking at her tattoo sleeve with the full lineup of classic horror movie monsters multiple times. "Amanda and I rented every horror movie we could on VHS."

"What's your favorite?" He sounded genuinely interested.

"Oh, that's too hard," she said, still smiling. "Too many to name. *The Thing* made Amanda and me scream the loudest. Her aunt Susan one time came running all the way downstairs to make sure we weren't being murdered by a cosmic alien monster." She paused, remembering how hard Amanda had laughed when Aunt Susan came barreling down the steps, her hair up in rollers. "I guess I like John Carpenter movies the most."

"For real?"

"Yeah." She nodded. "*Halloween, Big Trouble in Little China, They—*"

"*—Live?*" he finished, leaping forward with a newfound pep in his step, pacing next to her without giving a care to mutants… or Nergal. "John Carpenter is my absolute favorite director of all time."

"Really?" Tori asked. His entire aura went from puppy to geek in a freakin' blink, and Tori didn't know how she felt about it. She almost thought it was a joke until he started listing off favorites.

"*Big Trouble in Little China* is the greatest movie ever, but—oh man—*Prince of Darkness* and *The Thing* have a special place in my heart. And *They Live*! Hell, I love all his movies. They're such an inspiration to me…"

Full stop—what was he doing? One moment she had to invoke mutants just to get his feet moving, and now? He had transformed into a hyper, geeky, puppy-nerd.

Tori ignored him as he blathered on, continuing her pace. She skipped over a mound of goo that wiggled like a gelatin mold and pretended to listen. Dean's obsession over their common interests was a foreign concept to her. He looked as if he wanted to high-five and pal around, like they were a pair of best buds who played video games on a ratty couch with stained fleece and sticky Cheeto-fingers. But she already had a best bud. She already had that kind of connection with Amanda. She didn't need, or *want*, another.

Were women and men supposed to have these connections? The only reason she'd ever watched movies with a man was for a shortcut to the fun stuff; the men she dated had shit taste in movies, but it made surviving to the fun stuff more rewarding. Even if she had to suffer through another Charlie Sheen spoof, there was a prize at the end, like in a Cracker Jacks box. Would the two hours of subtle positioning, risky hand placements, and flirtatious gestures have been more enjoyable if they had similar tastes?

Debatable.

Was their random, but not-so-rare similarities supposed to mean something?

Doubtful.

Plenty of guys liked horror movies, and quite of few of those had to appreciate John Carpenter's genius. What exactly was the appeal? Dean's face looked like he had struck oil in a barren land.

And what exactly was she doing with him? Their engagement had ended the moment they fled Apollo and the V-Boys. Why did she care if he climbed that ladder in the middle of a V-Boy incursion?

And yet, she couldn't leave him. Look at the guy? He *was* a puppy.

Dean didn't dress or act like most of the guys she'd met. He wore Palladium boots, a black shirt with silver buttons, and a stupid novelty t-shirt that would have been amusing if it weren't so annoying. He looked like an artist—a creative type for sure, which was all very different for her. When she hung around creatures with Y chromosomes, they were often extra on the Y—total alpha male types who spat every ten feet like they were marking their territory.

But Dean? He wasn't exactly a grease monkey or a gym rat, but he wasn't out of shape or a loser. He was just…*different.* And she had to admit, he had a sharp sense of humor that didn't involve belittling others. Why was she always attracted to jerkoffs who put down everyone around them? She'd been trying to decode the part of herself that made bad decisions about men. Locked inside the vault, she thought she could pass the time by learning something new about the opposite sex—gathering crucial information from the male point of view. But she wasn't expecting someone so…*three-dimensional*?

How was she supposed to decode her love life with…*a puppy*? Wasn't that what Brie called him? Puppy?

"But yeah," Dean finished—whatever he had said over the last few minutes, she hadn't heard a thing—then smiled at her. "I like your sleeve."

Tori instinctively glanced down at the tattoo on her arm.

She and Amanda got their first tattoos together, right after they spotted shooting star number four. While Amanda got a tiny heart permanently etched onto her hip, Tori went with a Frankenstein's Monster on her shoulder—the start of a whole sleeve of classic movie monsters.

"Thanks," she said. "I've always loved monsters. Especially the ones who were misunderstood." She could tell Dean was concentrating, ransacking his brain for new questions to keep the conversation going. She decided to beat him to the punch and keep the *puppy* at bay. "So, you went to Milton State in Grace Falls. Ever visit the falls?"

"Yeah," said Dean. "A few times. I took Brie there once."

"Oh, really?" There was something about that name that bothered her, but she passed it off as general dislike for mean girls. "Do tell. Finish your story."

"Okay," he nodded, and his mood immediately changed. The puppy disappeared, and an old soul took its place. "Remember when I said I was spending nights at Brie's place?"

"Yeah."

"Well, that was misleading," he admitted. "I was sleeping in her bed, but nothing ever happened between us."

"What? So, you weren't together?"

"I don't know what we were."

Dean and Brie went everywhere together. They slept in each other's beds, were on a first- name basis with each other's parents, and took road trips together. Dean cooked for her, ran errands for her—heck, he knew her ATM pin. They even took loads of selfies together during their adventures. Though that was only after Dean took dozens of solo pics for her to post to the 'Gram: preset poses to capture all of Brie's best "angles."

They even double-dated with Tammy and Peter.

They were together, except Dean knew they *weren't* together.

To the outside observer, they seemed like a couple—or one of those disgusting inappropriate sibling pairs that seemed too comfortably close to have come from the same womb. But it was a mirage. A lie. A sham.

They hadn't kissed. They hadn't done anything intimate together. They hardly even spooned when sleeping in the same bed, always separated by two layers of blankets cocooning Brie like she was emerging into a new butterfly every morning.

They were a couple despite not being a couple at all. It was maddening. It was brain- scrambling.

How long was he supposed to stay writhing on her hook?

"Maybe you should date other girls?" suggested Peter while rapidly tapping the fire button on an alien shooter game at the local arcade. If Peter had one supreme talent, he was phenomenal at holding intelligent conversations while playing video games. He couldn't multitask while walking, but he could zap alien bugs and talk relationships—the guy could do long form division while avoiding barrels thrown from an enraged gorilla like nobody else.

"Yeah, bro," said Tank. "Right now, Brie's got a lockbox around your dong, and you need to pull out."

Dean and Peter glared at him over the bass-rattling booms and flashing lights. They would've laughed if the guy wasn't so serious all the time. How do you laugh at a guy who can't take a joke and doesn't know when he's being funny?

"You know what you need?" said Lawrence. "A good wingman."

Lawrence was the new guy down the hall who moved into Jake's old room at the start of senior year. He always found them as they were leaving—proclaiming to walk with them only as far as the library, then dramatically "deciding" to blow off his study session to hang, despite never being invited.

The guy still had his psych book in hand and was using it as a nacho tray for the awful radioactive, neon-orange arcade cheese that even Peter wouldn't eat. Maybe that was why he was a whole foot taller than Dean—Lawrence was nothing but a gangly doofus of wiry arms and legs, zits, and poofy hair— nourished by chemical *cheeze*.

"Hey," growled Peter while fighting with the controls, "he already has a wingman, bub."

"Riiight," scoffed Lawrence. "Let me talk to her, Dean. I'll have her tap dancing all over your dong in no time."

The proposal was a non-starter. Lawrence would never speak with Brie on his behalf. The guy was sure to disgust her with his awful eating habits—he was currently licking the leftover neon *cheeze* from his book cover.

"Tap dance? That sounds painful, bro," said Tank, who proceeded to argue for the next twenty minutes about why tap dancing was the wrong term.

"Would you rather I said tango?"

"Yes! That makes more sense, bro!"

Peter and Tank may have been worse than Dean when it came to dating, but their advice was sound. If Brie wasn't taking Dean seriously, he had every right to see what else was out there. But what if Brie finally concluded that Dean was the right guy for her?

The next day, Dean signed up with a dating app and began receiving matches. Despite the stigma of internet dating, Dean was excited about the possibilities.

First, there was Alex, the girl who showed Dean her toy collection on the first date.

Dean had never met a girl geekier than him, with action figures and collectibles, and his interest in her collection appeared to excite Alex.

"Wanna see them?" She beamed.

"Are you asking me back to your place?" They hadn't even finished the appetizer. Things were progressing faster than he could've expected.

"No, silly. I have pictures on my phone."

"Oh, cool," blubbered Dean, but Alex didn't seem to notice the awkward exchange and started swiping through pictures.

"This one right here," she said, almost glowing. "This is my favorite." She handed over the phone, and at first glance, Dean wasn't sure what he was seeing, until he zoomed in.

Dean felt faint. "You know, when you said toys, I thought something very *different*."

She giggled.

Alex proceeded to show Dean all thirty-two of her sex toys. A glamour shot of each progressively more massive than the previous—some even *inhuman*.

"You keep all these pictures…" said Dean, searching for the most judicious way to ask his question, "…on your phone?"

"Uh huh," she boasted.

Dean was sweating. "Why?"

"Why not?" she shrugged, followed by a flirty wink. "So, Dean, do you measure up? Oh! Want to see the porno I made?"

Tori was laughing so hard that she stopped walking. "What's wrong, Dean? Toy-girl wasn't up to your standards?"

"I prefer a little less plastic in my love interests."

"Good one." She laughed.

"Thanks." He smirked, but he was frustrated—she could tell.

"I don't get it though, Dean. How does one man attract so many oddballs?"

"I don't know." He sighed. "It's not like I purposely set out to meet them. If it wasn't them, it was me screwing up. Like Julia, the girl I accidentally texted during class thinking it was Peter."

"Oh no," said Tori. "What did you text?"

"I asked Peter if he wanted hemorrhoid cream for his face."

Tori laughed so hard she started coughing.

"You texted that *to Julia?*"

"Yeah, she did not appreciate it." He shrugged. "Then there was Anna-Nichole. On the first date she excused herself to the ladies' room only to return with a coke explosion under her left nostril."

"What?!"

"White stuff, everywhere. She told me the bathroom stall was too tight, so she had to do lines off the toilet seat. Out one chute and right up another," he deadpanned.

"What the actual fuck? Are you making this up?" She was laughing so hard, she almost forgot where she was, and that it smelled like ripe socks.

Dean crossed his fingers. "Scout's honor. Do you think I enjoy my dating history?"

For a moment, she pitied him. He seemed like a decent man, despite his puppy-like tendencies and the occasional screw-up—but who hadn't made mistakes like that? *Well, not like that,* but mistakes all the same? There had to be something wrong with him. Otherwise, why wouldn't Brie have snatched him up? He was throwing himself at that girl.

"What?" he asked. "Why are you staring at me?"

She was inspecting him, looking for things she may have missed. It was one part inquisition and two parts investigation. Why was this guy struggling so hard with love?

"Nothing," she said, leaping over a running stream of rancid water. "Go on."

"After that," said Dean, leaping beside her, "it seemed like every girl I met fell into one of two categories. There were those with promise, but I inevitably fucked up one way or another. Then, there were those who dated me like I was being evaluated against a series of checkboxes on their To-Marry list. Sometimes I was too short. Other times I didn't have blue eyes, six-pack abs, tattoos, money, blonde hair, shaved head, or even a man-bun. This one girl once dry-heaved at a restaurant because she saw a little chest hair peeking up from under my unbuttoned thermal."

Tori laughed, but Dean didn't. She quickly stifled her laughter. "Some women have to have exactly what they want," she said. "Be glad you're not with any of *them*."

"But I'm not glad," said Dean. "I'm not with *any* of them. I wasn't good enough to make it through any of their checkboxes. The only girls who found interest in me were the broken ones."

Tori wanted to respond, but his words hit harder than she expected. Did he forget that's what they called her? *Broken*?

Then, realization.

"I'm sorry," he said. He looked contrite, scared even, but it hurt her all the same. "I didn't mean to say that."

She nodded and folded her arms while he silently scolded himself for being so thoughtless.

"Go on," she said, cutting him slack.

"Then things fell apart with Brie."

"You've been dating?" Brie looked like a child after a parent took away the candy bar she had turned into a melty lump of tasty fingerpaint. "Other women?"

They were at the falls—three beautiful waterfalls that brought tourists to Grace Falls from all over the country. The larger two had observation bridges that spanned the Mkateewa River as it flowed south through the state. Dean could've spent hours there on that perch, watching the crashing water and listening to the rumble. It was a warm fall evening in mid-October, the leaves were changing colors to shades of yellows and oranges, and the sunset created the perfect mood for the perfect moment.

Dean was going to tell Brie *everything*, and "everything" started with an admission to a stint of dating app matches that had gone horribly awry.

"Yeah," he said, reacting quickly to her rigid posture. "I learned a lot, and I wanted to tell you—"

"I didn't think we were seeing other people."

It took a moment before Dean fully comprehended her statement. "Are we seeing each other?"

She glared at him like she was confronting a stranger. "The fact that you have to ask tells me all I need to know." As Dean contemplated jumping off the observation bridge, she added, "Some people are just better off being friends, I guess."

It felt like an excuse. Like he had given her an easy way out of the mess she had created by leading him on. She was using him.

And yet he still had hope.

That was the remarkable thing about Dean; he was a hopeless romantic who never gave up. A glutton for punishment, sure—but resilient. Even if it meant grasping at the flimsiest straws to stay afloat.

"Are you still coming to the Halloween party?" he asked. If she had said no, it was over...*forever*.

"Of course," she said with a faint smile. "You're my best friend, Puppy."

A week later was the annual Halloween floor party for the North Hall Dormitory. The entire third floor came together to buy food and drink, and costumes were required for admittance.

Dean prepared all week for Brie's arrival while working up the courage to make his move and finally tell her *everything*.

"I'm going for it," he said as he jammed a pair of plastic fangs into his mouth. Half the floor was dressed as supes, and Dean looked out of place among them. The floor was packed with hundreds of people, and it was standing room only, even inside their own room.

Tammy said, "Are you sure you want to do this?" She was wearing a Warrior Princess costume with leather pants, a whip, and a red wig.

"Yeah, are you sure?" Peter sauntered up beside her in a Robo-Lad costume with a homemade tinfoil helmet. "You're wearing that to bed tonight, right?" he said to Tammy.

"Shoosh, horny fool," she said in her best Warrior Princess voice. Then she tossed another pig-in-a-blanket into her mouth. She was eating so many, Dean thought she had made them for herself.

"Yeah, I'm sure." Dean swallowed.

"Remember the last time you tried something bold?" asked Peter. "You were so crushed, Tammy and I had to pick up the pieces."

Dean and Tammy's eyes snagged and immediately looked away. He remembered that mistake all too well. He still felt guilty about it. "That was before I knew Brie and I were dating."

"Were you, though?" asked Tammy before taking a swig from her Solo cup. The punch was incredibly strong and had already transformed the punch drinkers into party animals.

"Yeah, man," said Peter. "You weren't exactly dating so much as you were…*near*."

"Near?" Dean's eyes narrowed.

"Yeah," said Peter, holding a beer bottle in each hand and slowly putting them together until they were only a quarter inch apart. "Near."

"I know what *near* means," groaned Dean.

"We don't want to see you get hurt," added Tammy.

"You won't," growled Dean as his phone buzzed inside his pocket. He whipped it out and checked the message with the kind of excitement that could have also been absolute terror. "She's here!"

"Oh good," whined Peter sarcastically.

Dean made his way into the hall, through the crowds and over to the stairwell, waiting for Brie. He checked his watch—right on time. Everything was falling into place.

"Dean!" shouted Lawrence. "Trick or Treat, dude."

Lawrence's "costume" was a sweater vest with a name tag that read, "Hi, I am: The New Guy," which was exactly what he wore almost every day without the name tag—sometimes with shorts. He had exactly four different sweater vests he would pair with three different long-sleeved shirts, and two different t-shirts. His daily clothing combination depended on the weather and pant-length preference. Tonight's sweater vest was blue argyle with a streak of crumbs and grease from snacking without a napkin. He was lugging around a paper plate full of food that lost some of its payload every time he moved.

"Hey…*new guy.*" Dean pointed at the name tag.

Lawrence pulled something from his pocket, looked left and right, then tossed Dean a square wrapper and winked.

"What's this?" asked Dean before his eyes could focus on the label.

"Ultra-Bright Glow-in-the-Dark Condom, dude." Lawrence giggled like he had just snuck a peek inside a dirty magazine for the first time.

"Oh," said Dean flatly. "Cool."

"Yeah, I got a bunch of them. I am loaded up." Then Lawrence thought about what he had just said and clarified. "In more ways than one, am I right?"

"Right," noted Dean sarcastically.

"Great party, dude."

"Yeah." He gave Lawrence an awkward high-five, but only because the guy raised his hand and patiently waited for Dean to five him.

"Hey, have you tried the punch?" asked Lawrence.

Dean checked his phone. "No."

"Oh, you gotta try it. It's bangin'!"

"Right," he grumbled as he peeked into the stairwell.

When Lawrence shoved his paper plate into Dean's face and asked, "What's this stuff?" Dean almost lost it. There was a mound of pale goop in the center, right next to an unwrapped candy bar and a Rice Krispie treat with medicinal qualities.

"Hummus," said Dean.

"Hummus!?" snorted Lawrence. "Does it have any of that, uh, tahini in it? I'm allergic to that stuff." He was poking at it with a candy bar, and Dean seriously thought about lying. Lawrence was the kind of guy who couldn't read social cues—if he had, he would've scrammed by now.

"Most likely," said Dean.

"Where are we?" Lawrence asked, huffing around like he was preparing a joke. "Zimbabwe?"

The statement was so absurd—and racist—that it stole Dean's attention away from the stairs.

"Hummus," continued Lawrence. "They probably eat that in Zimbabwe, right?" When Dean didn't answer, Lawrence kept going, like he had to talk nonsense or face an awkward silence. "You know what else they eat in Zimbabwe. Brains, right? Your costume, it's a zombie? Right, my guy?"

Dean was wearing a leather jacket with a red shirt and fake plastic fangs in his mouth. He even had red makeup dribbling down his chin.

Dean was obviously a vampire. "Lawrence, are *you* a Zimbabwe Zombie victim?" The guy was often short on brains…

"Ha! So funny! Right! A vampire!" shouted Lawrence. "That was my third guess."

"What was your second?"

"Wolfman." Lawrence shrugged.

Dean ground his teeth. Brie was arriving at any moment, and everything had to be perfect. In haste, he said something terse. "Listen, Lawrence, can you buzz off? I'm waiting for a girl."

"Oh," mumbled Lawrence, his mood darkening. "Say no more, *neighbor*."

The crowd swallowed Lawrence up in the festivities. Dean could only endure him in small doses, and he would've had to ditch him at some point, even if Brie wasn't arriving in mere—

"Hey," she said, sneaking up beside him.

"Hey!" He gave her a big hug, which she half-heartedly accepted.

Brie was wearing a crown with a flowing red dress, clear stilettos, and a set of stubby little horns glued onto her forehead.

"You look gorgeous, but I have no idea who you're supposed to be."

"Really?" She winced. "I thought it was obvious. Cinderhella? The Princess Witch of Wichita?" C'mon, Dean, she's my favorite supe."

She was aggressive, like she was still mad at him. Dean had given her space while he came up with a plan to win back their *relationship*. He began to overanalyze her behavior and decided it was best she was still angry, because it meant she cared, right? Right?

Right.

"Oh, right!" he replied, despite not having the foggiest who Cinderhella was—and what the hell was a Princess Witch?

"You should really get on board with supes, Dean," she said. "They're the new gods, you know?" In all the time they had spent together, Brie never spoke of supes besides Torcher. He figured that a broken heart was enough to sour her taste on them. On second thought, maybe he only saw what he wanted to see?

Was he really that blind?

He never even saw the chaos coming until it was too late.

"Oh my god!" screamed Brie.

Dean turned just in time to see two costumed partiers fall to the floor, Solo cups in hand, then spring to their feet with glowing red eyes. Long tufts of hair sprouted from their face and arms—even the woman—and there was a ferocious howl.

One by one, everyone drinking from a Solo cup fell to the floor and repeated the same transformation. There was a sudden stampede for the exits. In the confusion, one of them jumped onto the R.A. from down the hall and chewed his throat out.

Brie was frozen in place as the rush blew past them like a hurricane. He grabbed her and shoved his way through, protecting her from the mob.

"Dean!" shouted Peter over the roar. "Dean! Help!"

Loyalty. Friendship. These things meant everything to Dean. He didn't have a lot of friends, but those he kept, he kept close. Peter needed him. Brie needed him to get her out of the building safely. He was torn between two people who meant more to him than he could ever profess. Like a puzzle, solving one quickly would help him solve the other.

Without thinking, Dean snagged Lawrence by the arm as he was rushing past and spun him around. He was shrieking, and Dean silenced him with a quick slap to the face.

"Get Brie out of here!" he shouted.

Lawrence dropped his plate full of un-eaten hummus and sugary treats, then nodded.

"Where are you going?" yelled Brie, clutching his arm with a death-grip. Her big doe eyes begged him to stay—to lead her to safety, like her own private hero—but he was needed elsewhere.

"To help Peter. I'll find you." He turned to Lawrence. "Don't let anything happen to her."

Lawrence escorted Brie away as Dean rushed back up the stairs against the current. He stormed onto the third floor, slammed one of the hairy infected into a wall, and jumped into his room. Peter was on the floor, fending a feral Tammy off with her own whip. She was on top of him, biting down on the whip like a chew toy.

"Don't hurt her!" shouted Peter as Dean locked them all inside the room.

Tammy snarled, then rolled off Peter and regrouped in a corner. She was growing more hair by the moment, and her teeth were sharpening into fangs.

Dean spat out his plastic teeth. "Let's lock her in your bedroom!"

"How?" Peter followed Dean's eyes across the room to the platter of pigs-in-a-blanket on his desk. There were only two remaining. "Yes! Yes, great idea!"

"I'll toss them in," barked Dean "You shut the door!"

"Why do I have to shut the door?" whined Peter. It was the more dangerous of the two jobs, as Tammy was swiping at them with a set of claws still painted Warrior Princess Red.

"Because she's your girlfriend!" shouted Dean.

"Good point!" shouted Peter.

Dean grabbed the last two pigs-in-a-blanket and tossed one at her hairy feet. Tammy instantly dropped to her knees and devoured it without chewing. Dean then waved the next around, gathering her full attention, and tossed it with an overhand throw toward the open bedroom door—

—great throw.

—good aim.

—only she soared through the air and snagged it in her mouth like she was snatching a Frisbee at the park.

"That was unexpected," blinked Dean.

"What do we do now?" whined Peter.

Dean grabbed the fleece blanket from the couch, tossed Peter the other half, and said, "Blanket burrito!"

"What!?"

"Go!"

They charged in and swaddled Tammy up within the blanket. She fought back and tore through part of the blanket with her claws, forcing Dean and Peter to use every blanket, sheet, towel, and pillow within the room to wrap her into a tightly wrapped un-edible burrito.

When the F.B.S.I. arrived—the Federal Bureau of Supe Investigation—they surrounded the building in HAZMAT suits and swarmed the infected. No suspects were apprehended. The transformation was traced back to a tainted batch of party punch. A bulletin was eventually released to the public: be on the lookout for a budding mad scientist supervillain enrolled in Milton State's science program.

"Oh my god," said Tori. "I remember that. You were there?"

"Yeah, right in the middle of it."

"What happened next? With Brie?"

When Dean was finally cleared by the doctors, he raced outside to find Brie. Facing off against an experiment gone wrong had made Dean feel more courageous than ever. He was going to do it, right now, and sweep Brie off her feet.

But Brie was gone, as was most of the crowd milling about the courtyard.

He gave her a call. No answer.

Then Peter handed him a wad of paper. He was gasping for air, having rushed inside to grab it. He had tears in his eyes—proud, happy, relieved tears. "People make mistakes, Dean. That's why I don't drink much. But you've always had my back, and I know you'd never hurt me on purpose."

All that time, Peter knew.

"You helped me with Tammy tonight, so I'm helping you with Brie. Go get her, and this time, leave no stone unturned."

Dean hugged Peter, grabbed the wad of paper, and ran. He ran all the way across campus to Brie's dormitory, dodging a variety emergency response vehicles. He tried opening the front door, but it was locked—the whole campus was on lockdown. Dean ran around the building, found her window, and was going to climb up if he had to. This time it was all going to work out.

Her light was on, but dim—a greenish glow, like a television or computer screen. Then it went off. Then it came back on again. Then off. Then on. Then off. Then on. It kept repeating like that until Dean realized the horrible truth.

"What horrible truth?" asked Tori. She had stopped walking. Dean's story had completely distracted her from their grimy surroundings.

"Ultra-bright glow-in-the-dark condom."

The look on Tori's face said it all. "She led you on for months, then hopped into bed the first night with doofy Lawrence?"

Dean nodded.

"What happened next?" She looked aghast.

"Nothing. She's still with him, eleven years later."

"Did you ever tell her how you really felt?"

"I did," said Dean. "Five years ago. On her wedding day."

"You tried to stop her wedding?" Tori was impressed with how ballsy Dean was. The guy may have waited eleven years too long to tell Brie how he felt, but he still did it, at the last, most-dramatic, second possible.

Dean sighed. "I told her at the reception, *after* the wedding. In front of everyone."

"Oh, shit. You loved her that much?"

"I did. Yes," said Dean. "Foolishly."

"Your capacity for love is…" she said, thinking of the right word, "…attractive."

Tori was jealous of Brie. That was why she hated hearing Brie's name—she couldn't stop wondering why she couldn't find a guy to love her like that.

Something yapped.

"What was that?" asked Dean.

"Run!" shrieked Tori.

CHAPTER 16

WHEN THE WALL OF PORT-A-POTTIES FELL, AND THE STREETS were awash with blue disinfectant and feces, Joseph suddenly found himself on the front lines. The police backed off, surrounding the press, and allowed the two angry mobs to come face to face. At first, they stared each other down, slinging insults—but soon the insults became a cloud of bear repellent. Then someone tossed a balloon filled with piss. A full-fledged riot erupted moments later, and the police began firing off tear gas canisters.

Joseph hit someone with his flagpole, then punched another guy in camo who fell over choking on his own bear repellent. It was chaos. There were popping sounds, like firecrackers, and fleeing footsteps in every direction. Someone screamed in pain, but the tear gas mixed with the bear repellent became so thick that even with his borrowed goggles, Joseph could hardly see who it was or where it came from. He was stumbling through the haze, swinging once or twice for protection, when someone collided with him. The impact knocked the wind from his lungs, and he laid on the ground, gasping through the mixing chemicals in the air.

When he opened his eyes, he was staring down the barrel of a gun.

"Eat shit, Sympie cuck!" shouted a baby-faced V-Boy.

Five minutes into battle and he was already dead. He thought of Julian, and his ex-wife. He thought of his dear mother and his father, who died last year after calling his son a "Sympie coward" for his Reformist views.

Pops sounded off in the distance as the tear gas and bear repellent swept by, drifting on a Wonder City breeze.

"I have a son," muttered Joseph, hands up, on his back, inches from a puddle of blue disinfectant and piles of cold feces.

"I don't care," said the gunman, but he still hadn't pulled the trigger. At one point the resolve on his face softened, and Joseph thought the gunman might just let him go, until he heard the mechanical click.

Then someone else had a gun at the gunman's head, and Joseph remained frozen in place.

"I knew you were a cuck, Lou, but I didn't think you were a Sympie too," said the other gunman. "You can't even shoot a heartless Tin Man."

"Alvin, I swear I'm gonna shoot 'im," said Lou. "Just give me a minute."

"You already had a minute, son. The Tin Men are on the run. They brought balloons filled with piss to a gun fight."

"I'm gonna do it." Lou's gun barrel shook.

"Be a man, son!" growled Alvin. "Either you pull the trigger and end this cuck Sympie, or I end you."

Joseph thought he was going to pee himself. Surely Lou would pull the trigger, but when he didn't, Joseph knew they both were about to die. Alvin looked like the kind of man Joseph had tried to avoid all his life—the toxic man's man who chewed tobacco and spat every few moments like he was attempting to coat the world in his own phlegm. And on cue, when Alvin angled his head to the side and squeezed out a black dribbling loogy, Joseph swung his wooden flagpole at Alvin's outstretched arm.

The gun went off, clipping Lou's arm, and Lou discharged his own weapon somewhere in the vicinity of Alvin's feet. The two separated, wildly firing in every direction as Joseph took off into a cloud of tear gas, running for his life.

6:45 PM

There were two valid reasons why Rudy had ended his last relationship. The first was that his ex enjoyed *American Supe* too much. The guy was obsessed with it—the more blood the better. Rudy felt oddly betrayed by this fascination. Rudy had experienced so much violence in his life already, and anyone who enjoyed watching arms being broken and veins sliced open in the name of entertainment probably didn't share many of his values.

Fiction was one thing. Reality was another.

The second and most important reason they broke up was because Rudy distrusted his ex with every fiber of his being. Franklin was a philanderer of both men and women, and Rudy couldn't trust him to keep his bits to himself—or strictly to Rudy. Every time Franklin touched his phone, it felt like there was something going on. And the late-night drunken phone calls, spouting poetry to people who didn't share his name, were the kinds of things that kept Rudy up at night.

Dean helped Rudy see that there were good men out there. In fact, it was Dean who introduced him to Arthur at an event to promote Dean's first novel, *The Knightmares.* Arthur was a member of Dean's book club, and he thought Arthur and Rudy would hit it off. Dean had good taste in friends—just not lovers.

That was why this whole situation was so awful. Rudy was beginning to realize that Arthur had kept a lot of information from him. His distrust was growing and spreading like an invasive plant species, taking root in the worst of places—right over his heart.

They were tossed into the back of an unmarked white van, and Rudy swore that this would be the last time anyone saw him alive. It was a ten-minute trip through the empty streets, and when the door slid open, Rudy was baffled to find himself in New Jersey.

"I always knew it would end in Jersey," he lamented.

"How could you tell?" asked Oxy as he and his silent compadre, Perc, removed Rudy and Arthur from the van and corralled them together.

"It's like stepping into a foreign land," said Rudy. "What is this place?"

He had no sooner asked when the details came together—the curvature of the architecture, the large slabs of concrete, the barbed wire. It was the perspective that threw him—the only times he'd ever seen this building were on ZepNews broadcasts from the skies. They were standing in a parking lot directly outside—

"The Cooler," said Oxy.

Arthur hung his head shamefully, and Rudy glared at him.

Not everyone was aware that Amycus Industries owned the supe-prison known as The Cooler, but Rudy was still spinning. His partner worked at a maximum security supe-prison!

Rudy had so many questions, his brain couldn't hold them all. They spun in a vortex around his mind, inevitably losing a few that sank down the drain to obscurity.

They entered The Cooler through a maintenance door. Arthur used a fob shaped like an actual key, which he kept on the ring next to his house and car keys. Rudy saw the irony—something that looked like something, that was something else, that still looked like something.

Oh, he saw it, alright. And thinking about it made him angrier.

"What else aren't you telling me, Arthur?" asked Rudy as they stepped through the maintenance door, bypassing security with Dust, Oxy, and Perc escorting them.

"Nothing I was able to tell you." Arthur pressed the call button on the center of three freight elevators. When it arrived, the door opened after a delightful ding, and they entered the cold mechanical box.

"What floor?" asked Dust.

"Six two," said Arthur.

"Uh, Arthur, honey? There are only ten floors." Rudy wasn't trying to help. He was pissed and would've criticized Arthur for giving too much information as well as too little.

Arthur sighed, then pressed the six and the two at the same time. Fingerprint scanners appeared on the buttons. After a double beep, the elevator started moving.

"Why are we going down?" asked Oxy. "We're on the ground floor?"

"Because floor Six Two is down six levels and over two," said Arthur, then clarified when Perc looked at him suspiciously. "Underground."

"So long as you aren't fucking us, Doc," said Dust, "I'm okay with that."

"But if you are fucking us," said Oxy, gesturing with a slash against his throat. Perc mimicked gesture, and the two halves of the Tragedy mask made them look like deranged twins.

"Right," said Rudy. "So long as you aren't *fucking them*." He groaned under his breath. "I'm the one getting fucked around here. Fuck fuck fuck."

"I'm sorry," said Arthur as the elevator slowed to a stop, then moved sideways until it made another happy ding, and the doors slid open.

Beyond the elevator doors was a wonderland of technology and science.

There was so much to see that Rudy had a hard time digesting it all. It was a marvel of sophisticated equipment, robotic arms, computerized dashboards, and oddities. The room was huge, with several branching hallways and rooms that split off from the main. There were computer terminals, flashing lights, test tubes, and sciency stuff that flew over Rudy's head. It reminded him of something he'd see on an alien spaceship, crossed with Doctor Moreau's lab. There were once-living things soaking in amber liquid, a plexiglass box that looked like a cell, and a stage with a giant ring of fancy metal—it was wired up to various appliances and terminals and looked equally complicated and horrifying. Along the wall were a series of empty glass vats, like swimming pools with attached hoses and nozzles—and Rudy imagined he could make a thousand-year supply of his famous sangria inside such a big bowl.

"What in the world is this place?" gasped Rudy. "Better question, what in the world do *you* do in this place, Arthur?"

"Yes, Arthur," said Dust, then cracked his knuckles. "Do tell."

Arthur took a deep breath and readied to unburden himself. "I wasn't keeping this from you," he said, looking into Rudy's eyes. "I wasn't able to tell you." Arthur stepped forward to one of the computer terminals and typed RUN SIMULATION into the prompt.

A series of readouts loaded, followed by detailed illustrations and animations—computer simulations of sciency stuff that, once again, flew right over Rudy's head.

"Mind giving us a little explanation, doc?" demanded Dust.

"Thank you!" said Rudy, "I thought I was the only one."

"We are not alone," said Arthur.

"Oh, honey." Rudy laughed. "Is this some alien bullshit? I may believe in ghosts, but aliens are a bridge too far."

"Shut him up," groaned Dust. Perc put a gloved hand over Rudy's mouth, nearly knocking Rudy's Go-Pro Visor from his head.

"I'm not talking about aliens," explained Arthur. "Thirty-three years ago, scientists at Amycus Industries made a landmark discovery." He hit a button on the keypad, and the simulation changed. It depicted a globe that split a dozen times, each of them a perfect copy of the other. "They discovered thirteen parallel earths existing in the same location, at the exact time and place, but out of phase with one another."

"Different dimensions?" asked Oxy, squinting from behind his portion of the Tragedy mask.

"Not exactly," said Arthur. "We all exist in the Third Dimension. We experience time, we perceive depth. This is something else. Imagine thirteen sheets of transparent paper on top of each other. Our Earth is one of those thirteen."

"Yeah, so?" said Dust.

"Each Earth, those exact copies of the other, exists in a parallel space. However, they are not exact. The matter is the same, but the outcomes are different. We were able to scan the next parallel world and discovered that Wonder City didn't exist there."

"What do you mean?" asked Dust.

"I mean it didn't exist," said Arthur. "It looked different. It was geographically altered. It was an entirely different city named Philadelphia, where our forefathers signed the Declaration of Independence. Their history did not include the events that destroyed Philadelphia and rebuilt as Wonder City, like ours. We attempted to go there, but those experiments sadly came up short." Arthur hit another button on the keypad, and the simulation changed once again. "Thirty years ago, however, something happened." The screen refreshed, and instead of thirteen orbs representing Earth, there were only twelve. "Twenty years ago." After a refresh, only ten. "Then eleven years ago." Only eight. "Four years ago." Five.

"What's happening?" asked Dust.

"Annihilation," said Arthur. "Something is happening to these other worlds. One could imagine that if these worlds are parallel with similar histories, they may end up experiencing similar political atmospheres. Perhaps they destroyed themselves? Nuclear war? Supe catastrophe? Some other threat?"

"How does this tie into your research?" asked Oxy. "We came here for a reason."

"Right," exclaimed Arthur, excitement in his eyes. "The First Law of Thermodynamics. Energy can be changed from one form to another, but it cannot be created nor destroyed." Arthur typed something new into the prompt and ran a different simulation. "Before my research began, there were studies conducted on low-level supes—those contained within this very supe-prison.

These were before my time, and the unethical nature of those studies has only recently been revealed to me." A video file loaded, depicting a screaming man constrained to a device that inserted a giant needle into the back of his neck, followed by a dozen more down his spine.

Perc's hand was still over his mouth, but Rudy closed his eyes and covered his ears. He didn't like seeing pain and torture.

"It was discovered that supes were entangled in a form of matter that exists, but until recently, we could not isolate," continued Arthur. "We call it the Deus Particle. Their organs, tissues, their very cells were bonded with it, resulting in a wide variety of outcomes and abilities. Thirty years ago, we saw a spike in new supes. And that frequency has exponentially increased."

Oxy scratched his head as if burning extra brain cells. "You're saying that the destruction of those worlds is what brought the increase of supes into ours? The Laws of Thermodynamics, like you said. Their energy transferred from one Earth to another?" Dust shot him a glare, and Oxy shrugged. "I took Intro to Physics in college."

"Exactly," praised Arthur. "The energy from those destroyed worlds still exists, as stated by the First Law of Thermodynamics. Right now, you and your friends are entangled in Deus Particles. The more powerful the supe, the more particles they're entangled with. I have built my entire career around that energy. Amycus Industries and their federal contracts tasked us to find a way to pull new energy from those ruined Earths into this one to create new supes." Arthur pointed at the huge metal ring with the attached gadgets on the stage. "We used the T.T.A., the Trans-Terrestrial Arch, to open a breach between worlds, but we ended up creating new uncontrolled breaches across our planet. The energy that poured through those breaches sought out hosts—people with specific genetic markers. And when we finally realized what that marker was, it was too late.

"That genetic marker," continued Arthur, "was directly tied to the kinds of powers the individual manifested, bonding with inherent traits of the host. We placed them into categories; Physical, Magic, Mutant, Mental, Cosmic, etc..., then provided them with a Greek numerical for how many power categories were present. We identified the number of Deus Particles per cell, from 1 part to 5 parts—five being the very most a human cell could entangle with these particles. A common classification might be Alpha 2, or Beta 3. Someone like the Blue Anvil is a Beta 4. He has great physical strength and can fly, but he can also absorb excessive amounts of physical pain—that equals two classifications, four particles each.

"But now," explained Arthur, "we can predict them, and we're working on a solution. A way to stop supes. A way to turn their powers on and off like a switch."

"How?" asked Oxy, translating Perc's question.

"With a glucose enzyme that saturates the cells through the blood or skin, like applying sunscreen," said Arthur. "It protects the cells from soaking up the Deus Particle energy."

"Start wrapping it up here, doc," said Dust, twirling his forefinger. "We came for the information you were storing inside that lockbox."

"Your lockbox?" asked Rudy, removing Perc's hand from his mouth.

"I was working with the F.B.S.I.," said Arthur.

"You were what!?" shouted Rudy. "Wait, are you a spy?" Despite his indignance, he was turned on at the thought.

"I was sneaking information out of this very lab to my informant through a lockbox at the First National Bank. However, my informant was just subpoenaed by the current Administration for High Crimes against the country. They disappeared."

"The president is a nutjob supe-lover," said Oxy.

"He's a fucking Supie," corrected Dust.

"Two months ago, I received an anonymous text message," said Arthur, "telling me that the president owns Amycus Industries through a shell company."

"Well," groaned Rudy, "this has become too convoluted for me."

"Just now?" whined Oxy. Rudy shrugged.

"What you're saying is that the president is running this operation? He owns The Cooler and Amycus Industries," said Dust. "So he can create loyalist supes and take powers away from others?"

Arthur nodded.

"It's whole new goddamn arms race," said Dust.

"With actual arms," added Rudy before Perc re-muzzled him.

"I wanted to make the world a better place," explained Arthur.

"You can," said Dust, "by handing over your research and the formula for that enzyme."

Arthur nodded again, then typed something into the prompt on the keypad.

"How long will it take to download?" asked Oxy.

"No time at all, because it doesn't exist."

"What?" scoffed Dust.

"I erased it," said Arthur.

"When?" growled Oxy.

"Just now," explained Arthur. "I typed Delete All, then hit enter."

"What the fuck, man!" growled Oxy as Perc dented a nearby metal panel with his fist. "We had a lot riding on that, you asshole."

"Un-delete it," growled Dust.

"I don't think you know how computers work," said Arthur.

"Arthur," whined Rudy, squirming away from Perc. "Let's not upset the dangerous supervillains who could easily kill us, please."

"The only copy of my research was in that vault," admitted Arthur. "It looked like the police picked that place clean."

"That's not possible," said Dust, looking to Oxy and Perc. They both shrugged, and Dust began to brood. When he turned, he backhanded Arthur across the room. Arthur hit the floor and slid all the way to the wall like a toy doll.

"Arthur!" Rudy darted to his side. Arthur had landed all wrong, his wrist awkwardly angled.

"I'm okay." Arthur grimaced. "I think my arm is broken."

"Oh Arthur!" said Rudy, "why did you have to go and be all heroic? Just give the bad men what they want."

"I can't," said Arthur.

"But they'll kill us."

"Listen to your boyfriend," said Oxy.

Dust sauntered toward them, seething, growing with each step. "You're going to cost us more than just a big payday, asshole."

"Rudy," said Arthur, "See that red button?"

"I do! I see it!" said Rudy.

"Push it."

"Oh no," said Rudy, shaking his head. "No no no, I've seen all the movies, and pushing the red button is always bad."

"Not this one," said Arthur, as Dust closed within ten feet, his fists the size of basketballs. "Hit it, Rudy. Right now!"

Rudy hit the button. Three times, just to be sure. A clear plexiglass panel cut Dust off just in time.

"You think that's going to save you?" Dust slammed his fist into it—then recoiled backward, glaring at his hand.

Arthur said, "I do. We made it. V.A.P. Glass. Vibration Absorbing Plexiglass. It's supe-proof."

"What about fire?" asked Rudy. "Lightning? Magic?"

Arthur groaned. "Let's not give them any suggestions."

Oxy and Perc stepped up, absorbing some of Dust's energy, and sent two blasts straight at the V.A.P. Glass without a single shake or shimmy. They hit it again in coordination with Dust's fist, but again, nothing happened. The recoil of the vibration torqued Dust's wrist.

Eventually Rudy took his Go-Pro Visor off his head and laughed.

"Hey fellas!" said Rudy, gathering their attention. "Welcome to the MoodyRudy vlog! We've been livestreaming the whole event."

"You've been livestreaming this whole time?" Arthur blinked.

"Not on purpose," said Rudy under his breath. "I forgot to turn it off."

Dust tossed a swiveling chair so hard at the V.A.P. Glass that it rebounded toward the heads of Oxy and Perc. They dived away just in time to prevent a beheading.

"This can't be happening," growled Dust. "We had everything planned out!"

Oxy looked at his watch and said, "We only have five hours, boss." Perc signed and Oxy translated. "Where are we going to get our hands on the research? It's gone."

"We know exactly where that research is," growled Dust. His eyes narrowed as he quickly swelled into another shirt size, his leather duster straining against his mass. "And I know just how to find it."

CHAPTER 17

"RUN!" SHRIEKED TORI, HER PITCH CURDLING MILK FOR MILES.

Dean couldn't stop laughing.

"What? Why?" he cackled. She was backed against the grimy wall, knees buckled as if she were cornered by a ferocious beast. It was the kind of reaction one had when faced with their worst fears.

The sewers didn't smell nearly as bad as Dean expected, even if he did have a shield of cologne protecting him from the stink. The tunnels were dark and gross, yet traveling through them wasn't the worst thing in the world, and not nearly as awful as he imagined. There were no signs of mutants, and things had just taken an interesting turn.

Yap! Yap!

A Dachshund barked at them. It was wearing a mini-dinosaur costume. The green T-Rex head was like a hood with googly eyes that boggled as the dog yapped.

"Are you okay?" asked Dean.

Tori was quivering, beads of sweat forming along her brow.

She shook her head between quaking shivers. Dean stopped laughing, but he couldn't wrangle the smirk from his face.

What was she so afraid of?

The girl who wasn't frightened by Apollo, who remained almost numb when surrounded by V-Boys, sank into a quivering mess when confronted by a tiny little dog in costume? It didn't add up.

"Hey," said Dean, stepping between her and the yapping mongrel. "It's okay. I don't understand what's happening, but everything's alright."

"You don't see it?" She trembled. The spikes and pins on her denim vest were rattling.

"See what? The tiny dog in a dinosaur costume?"

This was like the time Rudy caught a scene from *Grease* while channel surfing, mid- musical number. He crawled over the back of the couch to escape, dropping the remote in his scramble. If Rudy could be that frightened of John Travolta in pomade, Dean figured it was likely Tori could be afraid of tiny dogs in costume.

However, a strange thing happened when Dean looked over his shoulder.

The dog had multiplied.

Yap-Yap! Yap-Yap!

It was no longer a single Dachshund in a dinosaur costume, but two—the second wearing a mini tuxedo and top hat.

"They're not dogs," she whimpered.

Lots of things scared Dean. Used car salesmen, watching *Unsolved Mysteries* with the lights out, anything that slithered with no legs, anything that crawled with too many legs, and, of course, dying alone. But it was hard to relate to someone else's irrational fear—especially one so adorable.

"What do you mean they're not dogs?" asked Dean. "They're just two—"

Nope, not just two. Not anymore.

When Dean looked back once again, there was another. This one had a cone-shaped clown hat and a bright yellow coat with red pom-poms.

Yap-Yap-Yap! Yap-Yap-Yap!

Was it bizarre? Absolutely. But was it nefarious?

"Wait here," said Dean. He had an idea.

Tori shuddered. "Where are you going?"

"I'm not leaving you," said Dean as he gently removed the hand she had grappled around his forearm. "I'm...*investigating*."

"No." She clamped her eyes shut.

Dean leaped over the running water. The three dogs ignored him as he approached. They were solely focused on Tori, yapping in a one-two-three rhythm on repeat. They were so obsessed with her that Dean was able to get within five feet before all three turned to him and angled their heads the way cute dogs do.

They stopped yapping and tracked Dean's movements in sync—triplets in perfect unison.

"What are you doing?" asked Tori. She opened an eye when things got quiet. "Don't touch it!"

"Hey, boy," said Dean in a doggy voice, crouching down to give the nearest doxie, the one in the dinosaur costume, a nice scratching behind the ear. "There ya go, boy. Good boy."

"Oh my god, no!" yelled Tori, but Dean had already started giving the little guy some lovin'—and her reaction seemed over the top.

"See?" said Dean, turning back to Tori. "There's nothing to be afraid of."

She screamed.

It was one of those screams that made blood run cold. Freezing dread spread from the base of his skull down the back of his neck and shoulders, all the way into his ribs and legs and toes. As if everything were happening in slow motion, Dean turned toward the doxie trio and glimpsed something that shouldn't have been there—or at least, he wouldn't have believed if he hadn't seen it with his own two eyes.

The horror. The teeth. The shadow behind them.

The dino-doxie opened its frothing maw like a bear trap and snapped it shut, glancing across Dean's arm—if he hadn't already been running, the bite would have taken it clean off.

"Run!" yelled Dean.

"C'mon, man," insisted Blue Anvil. "Give it up already, bro!"

Crimson Justice had taken no less than ten direct hits from Amycus's experimental weaponry, and each one felt more excruciating than the last. The previous round had forced his Crimson Colon to pinch off a little Red Mist without fueling up on Hot Tamales. It drifted on the breeze, dragged along by the helicopter rotors, and Crimson Justice decided not to warn them.

He was immune to the Red Mist. All the sayings were true; whoever detected it ejected it—silent but deadly—but his favorite he saved for actual words. "Savor thy flavor, assholes."

When the Red Mist hit Blue Anvil, the supe lived up to his name and immediately dropped out of the sky. The helicopters, however, maneuvered away—their propellers blowing the mist into the streets below. It didn't take long for the humid red mass to drift down to street level, right into the middle of a standoff between V-Boys and Sympies.

The effects were instantaneous.

People fell to their knees, choking, while others ran blindly away from the stinging mist. Screams were followed by gunshots, followed by more screams.

Crimson Justice could've stifled it. He could've flown down there and caught every bullet, disarmed every provocateur, and put out every flame—but he decided not to. Let the city burn. Tomorrow, they'd ask why he didn't stop the unrest—and his answer would be simple. If they wanted his help, they should've shown him a little respect—and a lot more appreciation.

"Open fire!" shouted Gunner One—and a spray of experimental rounds were unleashed. The muzzle flash was so fast, Crimson Justice could barely anticipate the barrage as the bullets came screaming at him like flaming, screeching eagles. Out of the eighty rounds per second fired from two different gunners, only about a third of them hit Crimson Justice after a five-second burst. That was approximately two-hundred-sixty-four rounds of eight hundred possible screeching shots. One of them hit his pinky toe and another grazed his ear. Every shot felt like getting kicked in the balls.

Before he knew it, he blacked out and fell from the sky.

The sewers were a maze. Dean and Tori fled into the labyrinth with neither of them leading the way, zigging and zagging to put distance between them and the short-legged demons that were hot on their trail. By the time they had escaped the trio, they found themselves wandering through unknown passages without pattern.

The sewers on this side of town weren't gridded like the streets above. This was old sewer with twisting tunnels and strange sounds, dead ends, and random drops. The walls were made of cobblestone with thick, stinky mud slogging down the center. It was darker here, the old construction lights dimmed along the ceiling—humming as if struggling to stay lit against the will of the foul tunnels.

"Please tell me you know where we are," gasped Dean after catching his breath.

"Well, I did," growled Tori, "until some fucking didiot tried petting a sewer monster."

"What the hell is a didiot?" asked Dean.

"A dumb idiot."

"What is up with you and insults?" he asked. She kept throwing around mutated versions of swear words and taunts that bordered on the ridiculous.

"What's up with you and chauvinism?" she sneered.

"What do you mean?"

"You saw that I was scared," snapped Tori, "so you grabbed your nuts and said *let me show you why you're being a dumb broad*." She even acted it out, lewdly grabbing herself like she had a completely different set of plumbing.

Dean scowled at her. "You have no idea who I am."

"I have a pretty good idea. You're the kind of guy who plays the victim when you treat women just like they've treated you. You're so angry about being turned down by women because you didn't live up to some preconceived list of requirements, yet you do the same thing. Admit it, Dean, if a gal doesn't come along that looks and talks and walks and fucks like Brie, you're never going to be interested."

"You're wrong." He was steamed—piping hot—until she compared all the women from his past against Brie. That took the wind from his lungs like she had punched him in the gut.

"Yeah. Keep telling yourself that, pal."

He seethed. "That's rich coming from a gal who couldn't keep her hands off her best friend's boyfriend. How did you even fall for that? Dicks like Rick are a dime a dozen, always looking for another notch in their belts."

"And you're not?"

"No!" he shouted. "And if you haven't figured that out yet, then I don't know what to tell you. If you can't see the difference between me and someone like Rick, then there's no hope left for me out there."

"Stop it with the dramatic bullshit!" she growled. "The only thing stopping you is *you*!"

"Really?" He stomped toward her with a fire in his eyes. "Do you know why I put Brie on a pedestal?"

"No," stated Tori, crossing her arms defiantly. "I really don't."

They were uncomfortably close to each other.

"She's the only woman in my life who ever showed up. She at least pretended to be interested in who I was. She gave a damn, even if she didn't realize what she was doing to me. We hardly had anything in common, but at least she tried, even if she didn't know *how* to connect with me." Dean looked away for a moment. "The thing is, I've been looking for a girl like you my entire adult life. Smart. Funny. Sarcastic. Unique. And fucking beautiful! But we've been stuck together all day and you still don't see me."

"Wait," she whispered. "What?"

"From the moment you met me, you never gave me a second glance."

Her eyes were so wide, so beautiful, he could have gotten lost in them if he weren't so angry. Whether she was just another girl who never gave him a chance, or one he'd scared off after firmly planting both feet into his own mouth, it was probably a good thing—she appeared to have so much baggage, she was stuffing overflowed trauma into her carry-on.

Dean turned away. The longer he looked into her eyes, the more he imagined she was looking back. He was done with the fantasy and the nagging voice whispering, "what if?" at the back of his mind. He was done with hope.

"Besides," he said, "you may call it chauvinism, but I only meant to protect you. What good would I be if I did any less?"

"I can take care of myself," she said after a long pause.

"I fully believe you can. But you don't have to be tough all the time."

Tori shook her head. "I have to be tougher than everyone. All it ever took was one sign of weakness, one small hole in my defenses, and I was at a disadvantage. Being an orphan, being a woman, everyone saw me as weak— not because I was, but because of what happened to me. Nobody expects anything of me, and maybe I got used to living up to nothing. Living up to nothing is easy, since you can't even let *yourself* down."

He didn't know she was an orphan, even if the clues were there. "I understand," he said, and he meant it. Dean was fully aware that life wasn't fair. People were crappy to one another and often rushed to judgment.

Her frosty stance thawed with his empathy.

"My ex would've left me with the V-Boys and the hellhounds. But you didn't. You are different than him. You're different from most people I've met." She closed her eyes and let her arms drop to her sides. "Amanda would like you."

"Where to?" he asked.

Tori sighed. "I don't know." She walked past Dean, then turned around and walked past him again. "Which way did we come in?"

Dean wanted to be angry with her, but when he tried to remember which direction they came from, he couldn't remember either. Both directions looked the same. The construction lights strung from one end to the other seemed to lead into infinity. They both looked left, then right, and left again, searching for a difference, a landmark, anything to help them make a proper decision.

"We came from the left, right?" asked Tori.

"Right. But which way was left?"

"Right?" she agreed—or was she questioning him?

Then a lightbulb flickered.

"Did you see that?" she asked.

Dean saw it too, but by the time he started to speak, several lightbulbs had burned out in both directions. A sinister gloom settled in, followed by the patter of small feet from the right passage.

Yap-Yap-Yap!

"This way!" yelled Dean, moving left.

"No!" shouted Tori "Look!" She raised a shaky finger, pointing at something moving in the darkness, undulating like an ocean predator across the sea floor. It was creeping toward them, absorbing the light from each bulb before fading into the overwhelming dark.

"What is that?" Dean squinted through the failing light. He was mystified. The movements were hypnotic, freezing his feet in place and numbing his thoughts.

"Nergal."

"And what are those?" There was a skittering mass preceding...*Nergal*.

"Shit fucking bollocks." She shuddered.

A swarm of rats bounded toward them, fleeing the darkness as it approached like crashing ocean surf. They crawled up the walls and trampled each other, fleeing the terror. It was a tsunami of dirty fur, red eyes, and wormy tails, threatening to wash them both away.

"Shit," growled Tori. "Shit shitting shit-fuck!"

They were trapped. Dean knew it. Tori knew it.

Behind them, the trio of doxie hellhounds yapped and tracked them down—their true forms flitting in and out phase with reality—tethered by shadowy tendrils like leashes. In front of them was Nergal—a creature so terrifying that the light fled its very existence, the congregation of stampeding rats proceeding its arrival.

Both terrors were closing in—choking out their hope of survival.

It was over. The thirty-three years preceding to that moment were done. Dean's journey was complete. It wasn't all that bad. He made great friends. He attempted to live his dream. He even loved with all he had.

If this was his time to go, well, he wished it wasn't going to be so awful. He would've preferred an end that was more ordinary and less terrifying. But heck, maybe he'd write about it in the next world…

Tori didn't want to die.

This was a new revelation. She'd spent so much time hating herself that when the end was nigh, she'd expected to embrace it. Instead, she felt compelled to keep going. She had too many things to work out before she punched her ticket—and now she was stuck, evil closing in from both sides.

All she wanted, all she needed, was another direction. A way out. A new chance. A new opportunity to escape the dead end she had found herself in—and she wasn't just talking about the sewers. She was talking about the last several years and her highway to nowhere with Jordan.

"This way!" she yelled. Her story wasn't over—not yet.

"What way!?" argued Dean, but Tori was already yanking him toward an adjacent pass. An adjacent pass she swore wasn't there a moment ago. "Where did this come from!?"

"I don't know!" She didn't have answers, but she did have a theory…

While Dean closed his eyes and awaited death, Tori couldn't help but look back and forth between the dangers, as if bracing for the collision. She knew the sewers were a strange and terrifying place. She swore the tunnels rearranged themselves, because nothing looked alike when traveling through the same pass twice. She chalked that up to the fear that permeated every foot of stone and pipe running beneath the city—but after a whole new tunnel appeared right in front of them, just when she needed it most, she started to believe the tunnels were alive. *Rearranging* themselves.

"Why didn't we see it before?" Dean shouted as they fled.

"I don't know! Stop asking me stupid questions!"

The shadows behind them picked up speed and ground. They were running out of time.

As Tori and Dean dashed along banks of trash and grime, avoiding the slippery, stinky muck along the center, they couldn't stop to look back. Whatever form of creature it was, it didn't make the sound of footsteps as it moved, but a slither and slap—like undulating appendages rolling over the others for traction.

Tori knew fear—the world could be a terrible place when everything seemed to conspire against her—but otherworldly terror was different. This *evil* brought back memories of things she'd rather forget—like the old man with the black hole eyes.

They dodged a string of oddities—an old sofa, an arrangement of bowling pins, and even what may have been a severed arm. They passed anomalies, nonsensical peculiarities—like the service window of an ice-cream truck with a colorful Mr. Frozie painted onto the side. But stranger still, and odder yet, they passed an old wooden door that stood of its own accord—and Tori swore she heard three knocks as they passed.

"There!" shouted Tori, spotting a ladder to the surface. She had no idea what section of town awaited above, and as she climbed the old rusty ladder, she had visions of getting thumped like Whack-a-Mole the moment she peeked her head out of the hole. The cover peeled away easier than she expected, and she leapt out into the night, with Dean right behind her.

Once Dean was clear, they staggered away from the open hole a moment before a great tentacled arm sprung outward toward the sky. It flailed, then slapped at the pavement, grappling for an arm or a leg. It wasn't a squid or starfish, but like a combination thereof, with hooks, tubers, and suckers on the underside.

Tori ushered Dean back a safe distance—he appeared mesmerized by the creature. "What in the holy hell *is* that?" he squeaked between heaves.

"The biggest nastiest mutant of the underworld." She had her hands on her knees, gasping, and fought the urge to…laugh? Amanda would've died of laughter after an adventure like that.

And then *Dean* started laughing.

The giant slithering arm was still probing for a victim, and Dean was laughing like it was the craziest, most messed-up thing ever—and it was.

She stifled a giggle. "Why are you laughing?"

"My day," said Dean, shaking his head. "It started this morning selling books with Rudy at Supes-Con. By noon, I pissed off an asshole supe who forced me to make change for a hundred-dollar bill. However, instead of a quick run to the bank, I got knocked out and locked inside the vault with you. We narrowly escaped that same asshole supe and a crowd of V-Boys who thought you were the real Crystal Beth, then ran through the sewers and were almost eaten by a trio of doxies and a giant mutant."

"Sounds pretty awful." She felt sad and didn't know why—only that she didn't like the fact that Dean was having such an awful time. She wanted to believe that being with her was making it at least tolerable, but why did she care?

"Yeah," said Dean with one final laugh. "But it's actually been kinda fun."

"Oh." She turned away and allowed herself to smile, like it had to be a secret. "You and Rudy were selling books?"

"Yeah," said Dean as they walked away from the tentacle still slapping at the pavement. "I write horror and fantasy novels."

"Are you serious?" Sometimes Tori couldn't control her facial expressions. Women gripe over having Resting Bitch Face, but Tori's unfortunate face took it much further. She had what Amanda referred to as Automatic Bitch Face— it didn't matter what was said, she almost always looked angry or disgusted when she didn't want to be.

"Yeah," he said, noting her ABF. "Is that bad?"

"No! It's really cool. I'm impressed. I have a whole stack of horror and fantasy novels sitting on my bedside table."

"Wow," he replied. "I really misjudged you. When we first met, I took you for a typical supe-obsessed-fangirl.”

"Why?" she asked—her ABF acting up again.

"Because you're dressed like Crystal Beth."

"Oh, no, I hate supes, just like you," she confessed, shaking her head. "I'm dressed like this for Amanda." She decided to dodge the next obvious question by asking a question of her own. "Was that what you had for Brie? You said it was a wad of paper."

"Yeah," said Dean. "Brie always said I was good at telling stories. In my spare time, I wrote one and dedicated it to her. I wanted her to know she inspired me."

"Did she ever read it?"

"She hasn't read anything I've written, to my knowledge."

Tori thought for a moment before speaking. "Brie didn't deserve you."

He sighed, looking down at his feet.

Tori wanted to say that she would read his stories, but it felt like the wrong time and place. After all, she hadn't the foggiest where they were, and there was still a slimy tentacle feeling around the blacktop for them. The street was empty, and the building on the next block looked like the Wonder City Water Works. On second glance, the entire neighborhood was abandoned. There were no cars, parked or driven, nor lights inside any of the surrounding buildings—just the streetlamps and a cool breeze.

"I think we're down by the river," said Tori, noting the Water Works.

"We ran a whole mile?"

"Yeah," she said, pacing toward the following corner. "It didn't seem like it." Everything was quiet. Quieter than it should've been down by the river. It wasn't that late, was it? There were at least ten dance clubs on the next block, and she couldn't hear the thumping bass from any of them.

"Where to?" asked Dean.

She shrugged. "I guess I'm going home. It's been a crazy day."

"Which way is home?"

She pointed to the right. "You?"

He pointed straight and to the left.

"I guess this is where we part," he said, poorly hiding his disappointment.

"Yeah," she replied. "I guess."

Things were suddenly awkward. Tori became overly aware that she was still painted up and wearing a costume. Her arms and belly were bare, her curls a big moppy mess. She had to be a wreck—they were locked inside a dusty crumbling bank vault and then spent a few hours in the sewer. She managed to discreetly sniff herself without Dean noticing, and she was surprised by the results—shockingly all clear.

There was so much running through her mind that her ABF was likely out of control. For someone who always had something to say, typically snarky, she was suddenly as blank as a fresh sheet of snow.

"Are you going to be okay getting home?" he asked.

She nodded. "Yeah."

"Well." He nodded back, hands buried inside his pockets, and took a clumsy, half step backward. "It was nice to meet you, Tori. Thanks for the conversation."

"Yeah." She gave him a sheepish smile. "You're welcome."

Dean backed away, and Tori spun around, feeling like something was wrong. She took a step toward home and decided she was in a low-spot—a rut—and needed to keep moving forward. Not just toward home for the night, but toward the rest of her life. She started to imagine a hot shower, or better yet, a hotter bath. She started to think about slipping under the covers, going to bed, and sleeping off this awful day.

When Tori arrived at the corner, she spotted movement several blocks up the road. She wondered if the V-Boys were still prowling, and if she'd have to go around them. ZepNews Balloons circled the skyline in the distance, but too far away for her to read their headlines. She thought about waving down a cab, but there wasn't a single car on the road, let alone a city bus. It was eerie.

The more she thought about the eerie, empty city streets, the less awful she felt. She was getting her mind off *things*, and that was good for mental health. She didn't need to think about where Amanda was and if she was okay, what happened to her friends, or even if Dean was going to make it home without running into that crazy toga-wearing supe. But inevitably, those thoughts infected her mind all over again by the time she paced another half-block. She was left feeling exactly as she had the moment she spun away from Dean—

"Hey," said Dean.

Tori turned and he was there. She didn't hear him coming.

"I, umm," he mumbled. Paired with his t-shirt, the words made her smirk. "Can I walk you home? I want to make sure you get there safely."

"You don't have to," she said, her smirk growing into an actual smile. She surprised herself—she didn't say it like she hated the idea. She said it *almost* welcomingly.

"I get that," said Dean. "But I want to, and I'd hate myself if something happened to you on the way. It's the only way I know you'll get home safely."

"I could text you," she suggested. "I left my phone at home, but I could give you my number?"

"I don't have my phone. I think Rudy has it."

"Okay." She nodded and started walking.

"Besides," said Dean, catching up to her, "I want to hear the rest of your story."

"Ah, so there's a catch."

"No catch," said Dean. "It's business. This is transactional."

"Is it though?" she said. "I mean, what do I get out of it?"

"Good company?"

"Are you sure about that? I mean, average? I guess. Adequate? Sure. But good? Ehhhhhh."

"Alright, if not my company," he said, "what would you like?"

Tori thought about it for a moment. She dramatically placed a forefinger to her chin and looked up at the sky.

There was a flash, followed by a streak. A shooting star.

Tori almost lost it. Her eyes watered and her throat tightened. She took a deep breath and let the emotions sift through her. She had a wish—she had two of them, in fact. One could never come true, but the other? The other was possible. So, she made her wish—five-second rule intact.

"I want a signed copy of your book," she demanded.

Tori could be as socially daft as a sociopath. She wasn't one, but sometimes she missed obvious cues. She was hard on herself, alienating friends—even Amanda—more times than she'd like to admit. Eventually, she thought, things would have to work out because she couldn't possibly be that bad at human relationships. One day, she'd make the least amount of fuck-ups possible and meet someone who'd put up with her shit.

But look on Dean's face said the contrary.

"Oh, yeah, okay," muttered Dean, fidgeting with his shirt. It was almost sad.

He had just confessed that Brie never read any of his work, despite being one of the inspirations behind it. Perhaps Tori had overstepped? Perhaps she had misread the situation?

She backpedaled. "If you don't want to, that's fine."

"No," he said. "Don't take this the wrong way, but I've never known anyone interested in my work. Except Rudy and Arthur." Before she could respond, Dean clarified. "I'd like it if you read it."

She smiled, and they continued together down the empty street.

CHAPTER 18

7:35 PM

"EXACTLY HOW LONG ARE WE SUPPOSED TO STAY IN HERE?" whined Rudy.

Arthur checked his watch gingerly—the bone was definitely broken. "As long as it takes to be sure the Dope Gang's gone."

"*Exactly* how long will that be?" asked Rudy.

Arthur was sitting cross-legged in a corner, petting the suede of his red shoes, while Rudy did imaginary snow angels in the center of the confined space. They were still safely inside the V.A.P. Glass box, and Rudy was going above and beyond to ensure Arthur knew he wasn't happy. He childishly kicked his legs and made fart noises with his mouth.

"I don't know, *exactly*," said Arthur, cringing. "An hour?"

"*Exactly* how did you arrive at that calculation?"

"*Exactly* how long are you going to be mad at me?" asked Arthur.

"*Exactly* why haven't you told me about all the crazy stuff you do at work?"

"*Exactly* how am I supposed to explain top secret research to you?" Arthur crawled toward him. "I signed a non-disclosure agreement!"

"*Exactly* what's the point of being in a relationship if you're going to hide things from the person you love?" Rudy sat up and glared, his eyes boring holes into Arthur's conscience.

"I didn't want to drag you into this!" shouted Arthur. "If things go badly, I could end up in jail. I didn't want that for you!"

"That's the thing about relationships, Arthur," said Rudy. "When you're with someone, you're in it together."

Arthur sighed. "I didn't mean to hurt you."

"Well, you did, Arthur," said Rudy. "I understand non-disclosure agreements, *in theory*, but I deserve to know if you're risking your life."

Arthur took a deep breath and nodded. "Can you forgive me?"

"Get me out of here and treat me to a churro, and I'd forgive Madonna for everything after *Erotica*," said Rudy.

Arthur looked at his watch, then stood up, cradling his broken arm. He walked over to the red button, flipped it up to reveal a toggle switch beneath, and quickly snapped it upward. The clear panel lifted away, and Rudy popped up and danced out from underneath.

"There we go," said Arthur.

"Oh, thank heavens." Rudy shivered. "I felt like a specimen under glass."

"Unscientifically speaking," said Arthur, "you are a specimen."

"Stick a pin in me." Rudy fanned himself. "Please tell me what's going on next time, Arthur."

"Okay," he replied, pecking Rudy on the cheek before doubling back to the simulation monitor. He tapped away at the keypad one-handed.

Rudy crossed his arms and scowled. "Did you forget already?"

"Hmmm?" said Arthur, looking up from the monitor. "Oh, right." He waved Rudy over. "I noticed something." Three human-shaped silhouettes appeared on the monitor, with bar charts depicting Deus Particles for each subject.

"Who are they?" asked Rudy.

"The members of the Dope Gang that kidnapped us," explained Arthur. "While I was busy stalling by explaining my research, the sensors within the room were collecting data." Each of the three members of the Dope Gang were rated DANGEROUS by the computer, but only one of them was in the ninetieth percentile.

"Which one was that?" asked Rudy, noticing one silhouette shaded in red.

"That's Dust. According to this, he might be one of the most dangerous supes to ever exist. He's an Alpha-4."

Rudy gulped. "That big scary hunk of growl?"

"We've only ever recorded two supes with more power than an Alpha-4," said Arthur. "Crimson Justice is a Theta-4 and Blue Anvil a Beta-4."

"How much more powerful are they?"

"Well, considering the scale," said Arthur, staring at the monitor, "Blue Anvil is practically a god." He turned to Rudy with a fearful look that threatened to push him into another panic attack. "However, Crimson Justice is approximately twice as powerful."

"Are you kidding?"

"I wish I was. I began my research for this very reason. A supe like that cannot be controlled. I came up with a way to stop him, should we need it, and now that research is gone."

"I'm sorry," said Rudy. "Can you start over?" He was trying to be supportive, but when it came out of his mouth, he knew it sounded awful.

"I don't know. Science is often filled with happy accidents. I'm unsure I could replicate those circumstances again. However, I have no other choice." As Arthur finished speaking, the simulator flashed a warning. "That's odd."

"What is?" asked Rudy. He felt like he was in the presence of Willy Wonka, ambling around in a bizarre chocolate factory. He knew he scored a golden ticket when he met Arthur, only this wasn't what he had in mind. "I'm not a super-genius. Explain it to me like I'm five."

Arthur ran another simulation starting at the beginning, showing all thirteen different versions of the planet and running through the last thirty-three years—from thirteen Earths until it became just the remaining five, roughly four years ago. However, he let the simulation continue until it was dated three weeks ago.

They both gasped.

Even Rudy knew it shouldn't have gone up from five to six, then down to four in a matter of seconds—a total time of twenty-four simulated hours. Arthur looked faint. He attempted to sit in one of the swivel chairs but kicked it away on accident, then squatted instead.

"Something really strange is happening."

"Arthur," started Rudy, "which of those four Earths is our Earth?"

Arthur looked at him and blinked. "It could be any one of them."

"So, what would happen if our Earth was the next one to disappear?"

Arthur didn't respond. He shifted his glasses on the bridge of his nose and sighed. That was enough to ensure Rudy would have nightmares until something else came along that terrified him more—which was highly unlikely to happen in his lifetime.

Crimson Justice fell through the air at a whopping one hundred twenty-six miles per hour. When he regained consciousness, he had already plummeted through the roof and the top two floors of an apartment building. His size, mass, and invulnerability made him a near three-hundred-pound wrecking ball, crushing through layers of wood, plaster, fiberglass, and cement like it was wet paper. To stop his momentum, Crimson Justice reached out and snagged the first sturdy thing his hand could find—his fingers shredded sewage pipes, tile, electrical wires, and an unfortunate gas line.

The resulting explosion wasn't a Hollywood bloom of flames—it was a bright burst with debris flying in all directions. Crimson Justice found himself tossed aside, following an old tub through the sky.

He landed on his feet three blocks away, graceful as a cat gently coming to a trotting stop. His cape was singed, and a few holes had torn into his synthetic rubber uniform, but otherwise he was unscathed. He had made many supervillains blow up, but had never blown himself up. The experience was exhilarating.

"Oh my god!" someone shrieked—a woman walking a tiny, yapping dog. "Somebody call an ambulance!" She was in shock—he could hear her erratic pulse. There were screams everywhere, dogs barking, sirens blaring, gunshots popping—and Crimson Justice jammed two giant fingers into his sensitive ears.

"Shut up!" he screamed. "All of you just shut up!"

His therapist would consider this a meltdown. He thought about their last session and how he was supposed to handle stressful situations.

"The first thing," his therapist had said in her mousy voice, "is to remember that you can't be everywhere all the time. You're only human. Sometimes, you must let go and live for yourself. Be in the moment." She smiled, then told him to "just breathe."

Crimson Justice took a deep breath and smiled. When the anxiety passed, he realized that despite the many dying people within the rubble of that building, he couldn't be everywhere all the time. *Almost,* but not quite. He was only human, even though he was so much more than *only* human. He had to let go and live for himself. Weren't supes just humans in costumes? Was there a law that said they had to be heroes?

There was, in fact, a law that said anyone who was registered as a supe in a supe-city had to abide by the Supe Code—to protect and serve, like any other law enforcement officer. It was signed into law by that stupid Sympie President Armstrong, five years ago—a lame duck with an even lamer law.

The only difference between the police and Crimson Justice—according to that dumb, stupid, Sympie law—was that Crimson Justice wasn't getting paid. Well, not by the city. Supes received endorsement deals, from Nike to Arby's, from to Best Buy to the Waffle House. Crimson Justice's loyalty was to the people who signed his endorsement checks, not to the people of Wonder City.

"Crimson Justice!" A young man rushed past him toward the wreckage, carrying a first aid kit. "Let's go!"

"No."

"What?" He was confused. "C'mon, the people need you."

"Sorry. Law and Order are my only mistresses."

"You're not going to help them? Are you serious?"

"If you would like to help," said Crimson Justice, "be my guest." He tossed the young man three full blocks into the rubble. The man's screaming echoed off the buildings around them.

"What did you do?" asked the horrified woman with the barking mongrel.

"What I should've done all along," said Crimson Justice, then took off into the sky.

Tori could feel electricity in the air—like something was changing. Was it because of Dean? Or maybe because the city was empty? Something was afoot.

She felt relaxed. She felt at ease for the first time in what seemed like forever. And she was laughing. It felt so good to laugh. It felt even better to laugh and mean it.

"For real," said Dean as they paced along the empty sidewalk, "I don't get people who hate the Muppets."

"It's like they don't understand fun."

"Exactly."

"Who's your favorite?" she asked.

"Gonzo, hands down," said Dean, "closely followed by Sweetums."

"Sweetums?"

"I just find it fun to say."

"What about Fozzy?"

"Love Fozzy."

"You would," she teased.

"What's wrong with Fozzy?"

"His jokes are awful."

"I take offense to that."

"Why?" She couldn't stop smiling.

His face turned serious. "Because sometimes all we really need is someone to laugh at our bad jokes." He said it while looking her directly in the eyes. It was a meaningful look—a look Tori couldn't misinterpret. There was intent behind that look. There was vulnerability and yearning.

And before it made her uncomfortable, Tori said, "Do you want to know what happened next?" She said it playfully, and the changing subject disarmed him.

"Hmm?" he asked.

"My story," she clarified.

"Oh, yeah," he replied with a hint of disappointment. "What happened after the toothbrush caper?"

"Not much," she explained, "for a while." They approached an intersection, and Tori gestured for Dean to follow her to the right, toward the Dire District. It was a bad neighborhood, and she expected him to ask why they were going *there*. When he didn't say a thing—didn't even flinch—she continued. "I stayed mostly single for a long time. Dated a couple of guys, all trouble. When we graduated, Amanda and I got an apartment together. I was playing gigs—"

"Gigs?" asked Dean.

"Oh," said Tori, "yeah, I'm a musician—remember the song I sang for Amanda?"

"Yeah, but what kind of music do you play?" he clarified.

"I sing and play guitar. Some piano. A mix of singer-songwriter and heavier rock when the mood strikes." She blushed. It wasn't every day she met someone interested in her music. "I haven't found my sound yet, but I've always been drawn to rock and punk, some metal. Old pop-rock. I just want to make good music."

"Wow," said Dean. "That's awesome. I'd love to hear some."

"Yeah?" She felt so vulnerable speaking about her music. But tonight, that vulnerability didn't compel her to scream, then crawl into a fetal position—which surprised her. "It's my passion. I want to make people feel something. I want them to smile, to cry, to feel moved. If I do that, I'll feel like I did something right in the world."

"I hope you do," said Dean, and she could tell he meant every word of it.

"While I was waiting tables and pursuing my music," she continued, "Amanda got a job as a receptionist. We worked a lot of hours, and as time went on, we saw less and less of each other. Sometimes I wonder if we could've avoided the whole fiasco if I had paid closer attention to her."

"What happened?"

"What I'm about to tell you, I haven't told anyone besides those who already know." She got so suddenly serious that she scared herself. Was she really going to tell him her dark secrets? The ones she'd spent her whole life running away from? She'd avoided telling him earlier, but now seemed like the right time. "I need to trust you. Will you promise me you won't tell anybody? No matter what?"

Dean stopped walking when Tori did.

He placed a comforting hand on her shoulder. "We spent the whole day together locked in a bank vault. We're practically best friends."

She wanted to laugh but couldn't. "Please? I'm serious."

"You can trust me," said Dean. "I know you don't know me all that well, but I wouldn't do anything to betray you."

She nodded, then told him about the old man.

"When I was six years old, my mom and dad separated after a blowout fight. I haven't seen him since. I wasn't a problem child, but Mom often said I was *special,* in the way parents do when they know their kids will be outsiders their whole lives."

"It was summer," she continued, "and Grace Falls was so hot, some people thought it was the sign of something bad, like a higher power was holding a magnifying glass over the entire town, trying to boil us alive."

Dean nodded. He was listening closely, his dark eyes trained on Tori like she was the only thing in the entire world. His attention made her feel secure, like she could tell him anything.

"When it happened," she said, "it started small, as all evil things do. The murder of a young woman on the outskirts of town. The first murder in almost a hundred years. People gossiped, and before long, one body became two. Two became three. One body per day for a whole week straight, a string of missing women and girls that kept the whole town searching night and day.

"And nobody was there to stop it." Tears welled in her eyes. She scolded herself for crying, but that only made her cry harder. "Supes protected cities, not small towns. There was no end in sight."

"When was all this?" asked Dean.

"More than twenty-five years ago," she replied. "I was too young to remember it all, and the trauma fragmented my memory into out-of-order flashes and pieces, but only when triggered by certain sounds, or thoughts, sometimes even tastes."

"What happened to you?" he asked, in the most kind and polite way possible. All of Tori's apprehension melted away—the tone of his speech and the caring beneath the question calmed her.

"The bad man came for my mom and took us both." She looked away from Dean and gazed directly into the sidewalk ahead, watching the segmented sections drift by as she recounted her story. "He was an old man in a suit, wearing a strange hat and shaded glasses, escorted by two large men and a woman, all with long black hair and white masks. I remember screaming, and then nothing. The police found me and Amanda, covered in blood, on the observation bridge overlooking the falls near the old mill. The killers were supes—the first supe serial killers ever recorded. Three of them, manipulated by the bad old man to perform a cult-like ritual. And how they died is still a mystery."

"Holy shit," whispered Dean. "You were one of the Grace Falls Seven?"

It had been a national news story. Given their ages at the time, the media agreed to protect their identities. But that didn't mean she felt any safer. "Amanda and I, plus five other children, survived. All of us taken when the killers abducted and murdered our mothers. Amanda's Aunt Susan raised me.

She adopted us both." Before Dean could say anything, Tori shared one final thought—and if Dean ran away after she said this, she wouldn't have blamed him. "The old man haunts my dreams sometimes. I can hear him whispering, *Close your eyes, child. He who sleeps beneath the waves will need your eyes to wake and wander.*" A chill ran up her spine. "But the most frightening thing—the thing that really haunts me… he didn't have eyes. Just sockets of darkness, like two black holes that sucked the light out of the air."

Then she stopped talking. As the seconds ticked, she wondered if Dean was going to say anything.

"Tori," whispered Dean. "I'm so sorry."

He meant it. Tori could tell, and for whatever reason his compassion made her feel uncomfortable—like she had officially allowed herself to be *too* open, *too* exposed. She immediately regretted telling him any of her story.

"Whatever." She increased her walking speed and pulled away from him.

Dean jogged after her. "What happened with Amanda? You said there was a fiasco you wished you could've avoided."

She groaned. "Amanda joined a support group."

"Is that a bad thing?" he asked, and she shot him an angry glare.

"Nothing would've happened if I hadn't messed up," she fumed. "Amanda and I may be damaged, but we made it work. We had each other. Those dickweeds were a shitastrophe—a total shitty, catastrophic mess. They needed serious help, and they dragged Amanda down with them."

Trauma has a way of finding people on its own schedule. Like a heat-seeking missile. You can avoid it for a time, but the longer it takes to track you down, the bigger the explosion.

Tori had spent her whole life running from her past. She buried the trauma with sheer will and stubbornness, and although things in her life were going well, the emptiness inside finally escaped its cage and swallowed her whole.

It began with a commercial. Rhea Ramsey's first big break—an unauthorized twenty-year commemoration special covering the Mum Murders and the Grace Falls Seven. Amanda immediately flipped the channel, but the police sketch of the old man had already flashed on the screen. It left a dent in Tori's psyche, and a door inside her mind swung wide open.

Even though she was struggling with her demons, the choices she made thereafter were unforgivable.

A simple pick-me-up provided by a bartender before a gig was all it took. She was run ragged after a full shift waiting tables and jumped directly on stage a half hour later. That one moment of need—of weakness—led to another. Tori wasn't an addict, but she was vulnerable to escape, and before long her depression developed into a streak of self-destructive behavior that culminated one evening with a needle in her arm.

Tori had never attempted something so dumb before, and she never would again.

She stumbled home to their apartment and opened the door in a blurry haze. The world seemed to be moving a shade faster than she was, and she was so sweaty and hot that she started removing her shirt as soon as she tossed her guitar case onto the couch. The tank top caught around her neck as she ambled her way through the darkness toward the bathroom, but the refrigerator light caught her attention.

"Mannnda?" she slurred. "Why'zzz tha fridge opin?"

When she stepped into the kitchen, she didn't notice the crumpled figure on the floor at first—until the seizure started. Amanda began to convulse—the milk carton emptying all over the kitchen tile.

The chemicals in Tori's system burned off with the adrenaline. She was almost sober by the time the ambulance arrived, six and a half minutes later. She held Amanda's hand from the moment they loaded her onto the stretcher, until the moment she was forced to let go as they wheeled her into the E.R..

"I know what you're thinking," said Tori.

"Doubtful," said Dean, kindly.

"I've been sober ever since that night. Looking back, I should've done something, anything, but fall down that path."

"What happened to Amanda?"

"She had a panic attack. Passed out and hit her head on the floor," she explained. "She was okay, but it scared the blue piss out of me."

"Unlike the common yellow kind..."

"I had to be better," she said, ignoring him. "And if I had been better, I

would've arrived home fifteen minutes earlier, and we wouldn't have gotten into all the mess that followed."

"What kind of mess?"

She sighed. "If I hadn't spiraled, Amanda wouldn't have fainted and hit her head, and she wouldn't have ended up in the hospital, and she wouldn't have shared a room with an old friend."

Tori groaned. "I thought you said we were doing something special?"

They pulled up next to the local municipal building in Amanda's junky car with the loose muffler that scraped the pavement after every bump. The whole town heard them coming—it sounded like a tank, despite being a two-door four-cylinder with barely enough horsepower to travel up a twenty-degree incline.

"We are." The look on Amanda's face made Tori nervous. Amanda had been home from the hospital for only three days before she demanded that Tori dress up for a night out.

"Why?" Tori had asked from the couch. She was in sweatpants that needed a washing days ago, and her tank top had snack stains with a dribble of toothpaste. All of which she only noticed when Amanda shot her a disgusted glare.

"Because," said Amanda, "we're going out for the night. And eww, you're disgusting."

Tori shoveled a handful of kettle corn into her mouth. "Bite me."

The last time they'd gone out was a total bust. Some douchey-bro hit on Amanda, so Tori hit him back—literally. Busted his nose and started a bar fight that ended with the police. They weren't arrested, of course—what cop would believe that sweet little Tori and Amanda could start such a violent incident?

It was a fiasco that neither of them wanted to repeat. Though Tori wasn't exactly sure what kind of trouble she could stir up in a municipal parking lot.

The building was dark, and there were no other cars in the lot. The entire place appeared to be abandoned.

"What is this?" she asked.

"C'mon," said Amanda. "You'll see."

Amanda led them through a side door and into a large empty room with a ring of aluminum chairs at the center. There was a table of fresh Bagels-2-Go donuts and coffee sitting by the door, next to a pile of napkins and a leaning tower of Styrofoam cups.

"I guess we're early," said Amanda.

"Not really." A man wrapped his arms around Amanda from behind and pulled her into a loving embrace. He was tall, with dark hair and light eyes, and looked awfully familiar to Tori. "I see you brought the guest of honor."

"Hey, babe," said Amanda, leaning into his arms for a kiss.

"Do I know you?" Tori was creeped out. She didn't know Amanda was dating, let alone calling someone "babe."

"Oh, fun!" mocked another man as he entered the room. A tall, sandy-haired, broad-shouldered fella who looked even more familiar. He had a scar on his chin and a few days of facial scruff that made him look older than he was. "Look what the cat dragged in. Tori O'Neill, in the flesh."

"Who are you guys?" asked Tori, as two more entered the room—a guy and gal walking hand in hand. She had a short pixie cut, and his long hair was pulled back into a ponytail. All together, they looked like a bad co-ed boy band—as if someone had taken the Spice Girls and mangled them up with N-Sync.

Nobody answered her. They just smiled. Creepy, knowing smiles that felt like the beginning of something that ended in cyanide being added to the community Kool-Aid.

She had half a mind to grab one of the jugs of coffee and use it to waterboard these assholes for answers. This whole thing was freaking her the fuck out.

"You don't remember us, do you?" asked scar-guy.

"What?" said someone else, rummaging about behind her at the refreshments table. He was taller than the others, with a kind but dopey face and a curly mop of dark hair. He had just finished grabbing a couple donuts and licked his fingers clean of powdered sugar. "Tori O'Neill doesn't remember us?"

The room was spinning. This felt like a bad dream. In all her life, she'd never felt so out of place. She wanted to leave, but Amanda was walking toward her with outstretched arms.

"This is your family," said Amanda, wrapping Tori in a warm embrace. "Born in blood."

They stared at her with big, toothy smiles, like a dream sequence from a foreign horror film.

"Don't you remember us?" said Amanda's…*boyfriend*?

"No." Tori shook her head. She was shivering. She was about to pop.

Scar-guy laughed. "You're the reason we're all here."

7:40 PM

Lou dropped his gun when he ran out of ammo. He didn't remember firing that many times, but sure enough, when his gun started clicking after every trigger pull, he was tapped out. The gun slung over his shoulder was only slowing him down.

Alvin chased him through the tear gas haze, firing like a madman. Alvin was armed to the teeth and continued to fire long after Lou discarded his weapon. All Lou had left was a hunting knife.

Lou ran through the empty city streets, bullets whizzing overhead or shattering storefront windows. He stumbled into a group of Khaki Klan chanting "Hoodaloo!" and there was something about the way they scowled at him—like they knew he was a Sympie, a washout, a complete and total V-Boy disgrace. Before any of them could lift their weapons, he disappeared into a drunken parade of V-Boy wannabes—some of them carrying six-packs and lawn chairs as if it was the Fourth of July.

When he rounded the next corner, an explosion—a big one—went off somewhere deep in the city behind him. Lou tripped, skinning a knee on the pavement. He rolled around in pain, helplessly watching as a group of city children tossed a metal barricade through the glass storefront of a pharmacy before they began raiding and looting.

Lou yelled, "Hey! Hey! Stop that! Stop stealing!"

But the kids didn't stop.

More of them came, some leaving with whole cases of junk food, milk, eggs, even armfuls of toiletries. Any normal man might wonder why these kids were stealing food and soap, but Lou was just angry—as if they were stealing directly from him and his wallet.

Lou stood up, grabbed the laundry detergent from a young boy's arms, and shouted, "You dirty, looting pieces of—"

BLAM!

A gunshot.

BLAM! BLAM! BLAM!

The kids, as if professionally trained at how to evacuate from gunfire, scattered in every direction. Some dropped their payloads to flee as quick as possible, leaving dumbfounded Lou behind.

Alvin, Suggs, and a crew of heavily armed V-Boys stalked toward hobbled-Lou. His only option was to dive through the shattered storefront and hide behind a children's movie display. It was cardboard cartoon duck sitting on a wisecracking donkey, and Lou missed the punchline. He watched from the shadows as Alvin and Suggs approached, guns drawn.

"Suggs! What're you doing, man?" shouted Lou. "I thought we wuz pals!"

"Pals? We soldiers, Lou. All we have are brothers and enemies. You were my brother, now yer my enemy."

Lou wanted to cry, but he was too scared. He wanted to run, but his knee was bleeding all over the floor. He wished he was somewhere else, but he'd chosen this path. His ma had warned him not to get involved with Alvin, but he didn't listen to her. Now he was beginning to think he'd never see her again.

"C'mon out, Lou!" shouted Alvin. "We don't let turncoats walk. You know all our secrets—location of the training facility, our communication systems—"

"—how to make bear-repellent," added Suggs.

Alvin nodded. "How to make bear-repellent, our ammunition coupons. You're in too deep, Lou. We can't let you leave the city." Alvin aimed his gun into the darkness and stepped onto a bag of potato chips. The resulting pop became a flurry of gunfire.

Lou shook so bad that the entire duck display fell over, followed by a hailstorm of bullets. Lou crawled on his hands and knees to the back of the store, where the refrigerated items were kept behind tall, magnetic glass doors.

"Where you at, traitor!" shouted Suggs before spraying the pharmacy with bullets like he was hosing it down. The doors shattered, and Lou crawled through the glass and squeezed his tubby tummy into the refrigerated storage area behind the racks of caffeinated beverages. There he found an emergency exit and fled before Alvin and Suggs crashed through the refrigerated racks and volleyed a few dozen bullets into the door.

CHAPTER 19

8:10 PM

WHEN DUST DESIRED SOMETHING, HE HAD THE MEANS TO GET it. He wasn't just brute and brawn—he had years of experience honing his manipulation skills into a full set of talents to be deployed at will. The key was understanding what his victims needed, what they most desired, then controlling access to it. It was that easy.

There were few people in his life he didn't actively manipulate into doing the things he wanted. And even he would admit he'd been blessed with the kind of rugged good looks that turned heads. It was his original superpower, before the strength and rage. Without winning the genetic lottery, Dust was just another bro.

Bros…

Those were the days, right? Beers. The boys. Getting shitfaced, starting trouble, and picking up girls who seemed drawn to the trouble, like they couldn't get enough of it. He missed those days, especially on nights like this.

The shit had hit the fan, and he refused to get caught up in the spray. One way or another, he'd find someone to take the fall, even if it meant throwing one of the aforementioned boys under the bus—and he'd do it without throwing a single punch.

Sometimes, manipulation was easier than fisticuffs.

When he had started down this path, the future seemed wide open, like a Tom Petty music video. Every avenue was a chance to track down meaning and happiness or to erase the past. An end to his problems. The issue was that somewhere along the line, that wide open future had narrowed into a single path. A path toward blind revenge and money—in that order and never without the other.

Dust rarely felt remorse for the things he had done. Every step and every decision brought him closer to the end. A long six-year journey that seemed as close to fruition as ever. His revenge so near, he could almost taste it…

…or maybe that was the blood in his mouth.

He was biting his lip. Sometimes that was the only way he could control the rage. Ever since he acquired his powers, his moods swung uncontrollably. His body boiled at the mere thought of how he'd been wronged and what he needed to make it right. Rage reigned over every emotion—over love, relationships, even loyalty. With that rage came the pain—the rapidly expanding skeletal structure and muscle, the adrenaline, the numbness that dampened every sensory input except the internal agony, and the urge to hit something until the rage depleted. He once filled himself with so much rage that he tossed a two-ton ball of cement at the head of the Eviscerator—the supe from New Albuquerque they had tracked down for information—the information that led them to Wonder City and to revenge.

They were riding along inside Rusty, the roaming box of tetanus Dust affectionately called his van, cruising down the freeway toward the north side of Wonder City. Oxy and Crystal always gave him a hard time about the name, but he liked the way it rolled off the tongue—Dust and Rusty. He'd never owned a dog, but he imagined the companionship was something similar.

Time was ticking.

They had had five hours to find the missing research. Retracing their steps, they started at the First National Bank. When they arrived, they found it abandoned and covered in graffiti, the interior littered with beer bottles, broken glass, and dirt, like a whole parade of people had trampled over the scene. But what worried Dust was that someone had broken into the vault— and that someone was sure to have what they were looking for.

"You know, there's something I don't get," said Oxy as they zipped down the ramp and began merging onto the expressway. All traffic was in the opposite lane, leaving the city.

"What's that?" asked Dust absentmindedly as Perc signed a similar response.

"The doc said he was working with the F.B.S.I.," said Oxy. "He'd put the information in the lockbox, and the F.B.S.I. agent would collect the information."

"Yeah, what's your point?" grumbled Dust.

"How'd the Benefactor know about the lockbox?" asked Oxy. "I mean, you told us they contacted you, right? Is the Benefactor an F.B.S.I. agent too?"

Dust peeled his eyes off the road to stare Oxy down. "I don't know and I don't care. We're on the hook for a lot of money. Crimson Justice is going down, and we'll be off to paradise by morning." Visions of sun, sand, and bikinis danced in Dust's head, but Oxy was right to question the Benefactor. Sometimes the boys were too smart for their own good—but it didn't matter; they'd never learn the truth. Not now. The F.B.S.I. was beyond their concern.

"Yeah," said Oxy, sounding almost disappointed. "But it feels like we didn't do what we always set out to do."

Perc signed his agreement from the back seat.

"Crimson Justice is indestructible," said Dust. "All six of us couldn't beat him. But he's not infallible. He can be destroyed. His reputation is disappearing faster than our chances to make this deadline. If he can't be physically beaten, then we beat him where it matters."

"Where's that?" asked Oxy.

Dust groaned. "The court of public opinion, numbnuts! Get your head in the fucking game and start thinking."

"Start thinking about what?" whined Oxy.

"About where the rat got off with our cheese," growled Dust. "Where you at, little rat? Which hole are you in?"

8:15 PM

It was fall, and that meant warm days and cold nights. It was Dean's favorite time of the year. The spooky season. There was something about the buildup to Halloween that excited him, even though it reminded him of the disaster from eleven years ago when a budding mad-scientist's terrorist plot spoiled his chance with Brie. Yet there was still a kind of magic about it— like something extraordinary could happen. Like the entire world could come together to shape destiny.

Was it destiny that he found himself walking Tori home for the night? A sassy, gorgeous cosplayer whose nonstop witty banter left Dean feeling like he was walking with a forward lean, anticipating the chase. He hadn't felt this exhilarated, like his blood was electrified, since he first met Brie on campus all those years ago.

He didn't want the night to end. He only wanted to stay a while and see about the *what if*? What if Tori was the one? The storm clouds weren't just parting, it felt like they were lifting altogether.

This wasn't the first time he had thrown caution to the wind in the name of potential love. He had buried so many past attempts at fulfilling destiny. A landfill of the forgettable, yet unforgettable, disasters he had been trying to avoid for years.

Dean knew there was no such thing as perfect. Everyone had their flaws, and Dean surely had his own fair share. He had trust issues, a hero complex, and found a way to screw up every potential relationship. He didn't have movie-star symmetry or a fully formed ab, let alone six of them. Given fifteen minutes and a whole stack of paper, he'd come up with a master list of everything that was flawed about himself.

But Tori? He was still waiting for her flaws to reveal themselves. She could be a grouch, but then she thawed. She had her boundaries, and Dean was able to avoid those pitfalls once he discovered them. She had been through a lot in her life, but it didn't deter him from wanting to know more. Even if she was wearing a supervillain costume, she was still a dream.

So why was he so worried that this was going to blow up in his face?

The crescent moon was shining in a cloudless sky, and a cool breeze crept up behind them as they continued toward the Dire District. It was the city's oldest section, where the streets were darker, and the stores were...*boarded up*? Dean wasn't paying as much attention as he probably should have to his surroundings, but what should've thrown a red flag was just scenery, background noise, as he escorted Tori home.

Dean removed his button-up and slung it over Tori's shoulders. "What's this?" she asked.

"You were shivering," said Dean.

"Oh. Thanks." She smiled and looked away from him.

Was she so deprived of decency that she almost took a gentlemanly gesture as a nefarious plot? The longer Dean spent with her, the more he wanted to make her smile.

"You're welcome," said Dean.

A stillness lingered between them. After her story trailed off, Dean had begun to overanalyze everything. Eventually, his words caught up to his buzzing brain. "I'm sorry about what happened in the sewers. I said a lot of stupid stuff."

"It's okay," she said. "I'm sorry too."

"Don't be. I want you to understand," he elaborated. "My story, about Patricia, the girl who died? I hate supes. I mean, I really hate them. They have all this power, and no responsibility for the damage. I know there are good ones here and there—Wolfgang Stranger, Robo-Lad, maybe a few others. But I think what happened back then is why I am the way I am. I wish Patricia had someone there to protect her. A real hero. Someone who would've stood up for her. Maybe I overcompensate. If nobody is there to do or say anything, then I will, ya know?

"I was an outcast in grade school," he continued. "I took on every bully and received my fair share of beatings. I don't want you having the wrong opinion of me. My attempt to protect you—it comes from a good place."

Tori didn't react to what he said. Her expression and body language did not divulge her secret thoughts. They walked quietly, past a coffee shop and a restaurant that served "Supe Sized Salads," both of which were closed. Dean wasn't wearing his watch, and it could've been well after midnight. Still—it didn't seem that late.

Tori nuzzled her nose against the collar of Dean's shirt. "It smells good."

"I cannot claim credit there," said Dean. "Rudy picked out my cologne."

"You're really close with him, huh?" she asked, wrapping his shirt around her tightly.

"Rudy's a good man. He picked me up when I was down. We've only known each other for three years, but he's sort of like your Amanda."

Tori reacted with a wince. Dean wondered what piece of information he was still missing.

Then it hit him—he really could screw this up! He had to know everything about her before he ruined it—or before she realized he didn't check off all the boxes on her own list…

"Who were those people?" asked Dean, gently prodding her story along. "The support group. How did they know you?"

"They were the other kids. The other Grace Falls Seven." Her expression changed, like she had seen a ghost. She removed Dean's shirt and handed it back to him without looking.

He felt like a total putz.

"I can't tell if I'm reading this right or not," said Dean. "Was that a bad thing?"

"Of course, it was a bad thing," she hissed. "There was a reason Amanda and I didn't stay in contact with them."

"Which was?"

"When kids go through the kind of trauma we went through," she said with heartfelt sincerity, "you have two paths. You can push it aside and move on, living your best life like Amanda and I tried so hard to do."

When she didn't continue, Dean asked, "Or?"

"Or," she said, "you end up trouble."

Dean imagined how true that statement was. The trauma in his own life seemed minor compared to what she had gone through, and even that had affected him.

"A year later," Tori continued, "I started hooking up with one of them. Jordan—the guy with the scar. In the beginning it was fun. I thought he was hot—as did every woman who ever laid eyes on him—and he knew it. A total sociopath. Arrogant as fuck—even if that confidence was attractive at first, it quickly became irri-fucking-tating. Our *relationship*, if you could call it that, was lust—but we weren't together. It was just something to do. A distraction.

"Then I caught him flirting with other girls." She kicked an empty Captain Cola can lying in the street. "I lost it. I was so jealous, I did such *stupid* fucking things. Abandonment is a terrible thing to fear. It gets in your head and fucks you up."

"Yeah," Dean agreed.

"Yeah," she acknowledged. "I was stuck with him whether I wanted it or not. It was either date Jordan or be alone—because who else would accept me? He knew everything, saw all my dirty laundry, sometimes with the skeletons from my closet still wearing them. I chose to be with him, and he eventually proposed.

"The thing about Jordan is," she continued, "the way he loves is based entirely around his own needs. The more he took from me—my loyalty, my love, my body, my heart—the more he expected that those things would always be his. He took me for granted, but I was never enough. I was just a conquest, and when he had taken everything from me, I wasn't important anymore.

"He cheated. But a week later, he was begging me to take him back. And that's when things got interesting, because when I pulled away from Jordan, he came rushing back to patch things up. Like a dope, I fell for it, every time. I even started pulling away on purpose just to get the attention I wanted." She sniffled, either wracked with emotion or suffering in the cold night air. "I must be unlovable. Everyone leaves me. Even the man who put a ring on my finger." Then she looked at Dean like she wanted him to see the ugliness she saw in herself. "Why am I so unlovable that I have to trick someone into giving me the attention I need to feel...*loved*?"

Tori paced twice, then stopped at the edge of the intersection. Dean followed suit a second later, stepping off the curb, then turned back to look up at her. She glared at him with an air of defiance—the wind blowing a ringlet of hair into her face, her lower lip stiff. Her head was haloed by the streetlamp behind her.

Dean was trying so hard not to put her on a pedestal.

Tori was holding back a flood—of tears, of anger, of pride, of passion— Dean couldn't decide which. Her makeup was runny, streaking down her cheeks like a galaxy full of shooting stars. The blue and purple makeup surrounding those ferocious, crystal blue irises had the intensity of cold steel. She was a force of nature in pretty wrapping—a cyclone spinning within a glass bauble: transparent, stormy, and as beautiful as the following sunset.

And she was staring at Dean like she was daring him to run away. Daring him to flee lest he be crushed by her complicated mess of humanity.

Flee or fall.

There was a drumming in his chest. A dare—do it, and do it now, or never get another chance. *Pop, pop, pop,* in his chest—his mind resolute.

He stepped forward. Close. So close it might've been uncomfortable if he wasn't going to kiss her. So close he could feel her shallow breaths while her eyes still begged him to run away.

Pop, pop, pop in his chest—like someone beating a drum.

"Hey! It's Crystal Beth!"

Three drunk and angry men were glaring at her like she was vile.

"Crystal Beth!" sang another.

"She's not Crystal Beth!" shouted Dean.

The drunkest of the three, the one that was drooling all over himself, waved down the street. "It's Crystal Beth!" he shouted.

One of them carried a crowbar, and another hid something behind his back as they drifted toward Dean and Tori. They were wearing camo with big red Vs.

"She's not Crystal Beth!" Dean shouted once more.

"I don't think they're listening," said Tori.

"We have a bone to pick with you," slurred one of the men. "You and your *Dope Gang*."

"You framed Crimson Justice!"

From the side street came a flood of people, one of them banging away at a five-gallon bucket like a drum—like the thumping in Dean's chest.

Suddenly, they were surrounded from several directions at once—men and women, wearing khakis or red Vs, and carrying weapons. Some were dressed in tactical gear and loaded up with equipment, while others appeared as if they were there to drink beers. Dean even caught one carrying around a foldable lawn chair and cooler.

"This might be the worst case of mistaken identity ever," said Dean.

"Story of my life," groaned Tori.

"Get her!"

"Oh shit!" yelled Dean and Tori simultaneously as the mob advanced.

8:20 PM

Lou needed time to rest. He had been rumbling and stumbling all over Wonder City for the last hour. Alvin and Suggs were never more than a block away, following a trail of his blood. He was looking for refuge—a hole to crawl into before his lungs burned out and he dropped dead on the spot from too much beer and pizza.

Before his throat caught fire, Lou stumbled into an alley, diving into a pile of garbage bags as a series of footsteps clapped into the street behind him.

"Where'd he go!?" shouted Alvin.

"Shoot," groaned Suggs. "He can't be far."

With his back against the brick wall, Lou slid to the alley's edge for a sneak peek. Alvin's eyes were like a hawk's, sweeping the block—scanning back and forth between a consignment shop and bakery, his eyes shifting closer and closer to Lou's position in the alley beside the Muffin Top sign.

They were going to find him. They were going to fill him with so much lead, it'd take a forklift to move his body. He almost walked out of the alley to put an end to it when someone slapped a hand over his mouth and yanked. Lou swung his knife, ready to jab and stab, but the tall skinny Tin Man with the goggles backed down, shoving a forefinger to his mouth to hush Lou before he gave their position away.

Lou followed the Tin Man into the darkness, tiptoeing over wads of garbage, as Suggs and Alvin jogged past the alley, continuing their hunt.

"You have a death wish or something?" threatened Lou, waving his knife around.

"Do you, Lou?" asked the Tin Man.

"How do you know my name?" he spat.

"Alvin," said the Tin Man, gesturing toward the other V-Boys, "called you Lou."

It took another second for him to make the connection. This was the Tin Man who'd been under his crosshairs—but why would the man in gray help him? They were enemies. "Right. If you know my name, I wanna know yours."

"Call me...*Joseph*." He smiled and removed the goggles. Joseph's hood was tightened around his face, but Lou could tell the man was nearly twice his age.

"Is that your real name?"

"No," lied Joseph. "Why would I tell you my real name?"

"Good point. Lou is actually my codename."

"Riiight." Joseph grinned. "Great codename. Keeps us guessing."

"Exactly," he said, then peered over his shoulder. "Do you think they're gone?"

Joseph raised a cautionary finger, then crept to the dumpster and used his long frame to check for V-Boys. "Coast is clear." He waved and Lou followed, sneaking away in the opposite direction of their pursuers.

They avoided a group of V-Boy wannabes yelling "Crystal Beth!" and banging on plastic buckets, then ducked down another side street, swiftly moving away from the chaos. When they had gotten all the way to the highway, eighteen blocks north of Police Headquarters, Lou stopped and leaned against a mailbox to catch his breath.

"Where are we going?" asked Lou, inspecting his bleeding knee.

"We? I don't know about you, but I'm walking home."

"Shit, man! I thought you had a plan!"

"I do. I'm walking home."

While Joseph spied around the next corner, Lou closed his eyes. This was supposed to be his big day. Some people imagined their big day was getting married, or getting that big promotion at work, but to Lou it was Hoodaloo. When the frustration and the anger became too much for him to bear, he punched the mailbox with all his strength. The tolling noise matched the pain as he yelped and cursed and spat.

"That looked about as dumb as it hurt," whispered Joseph to himself.

"Why'd you do it?" asked Lou.

"Why'd I do what?" asked Joseph, walking away.

Lou power-limped to catch up and Joseph rolled his eyes.

"Why'd you save me?"

"I didn't save you. I saved myself. If he was going to shoot you, he was clearly willing to shoot me next. He was always going to kill me. You were fifty-fifty."

"Ah, playing the odds." Lou nodded. "I'm kind of an odds man myself. I bet on the Sentinels last night. Won twenty bucks."

"You're a Sentinels fan?"

"Yeah." Lou unzipped his vest. His Sentinels t-shirt had seen better days—specifically the days before the unfortunate mustard stain—but it was his favorite.

"Me too."

"Did you hear? Rocky Atkinson is back!"

"I heard." Joseph nodded.

"Weird, right?" said Lou. "Meeting another Metro City fan here in Wonder

City. That's rare, man."

"I suppose."

"I'm so tired of these Wonder City idiots always boasting about how they're going to win the cup. And I'm like, *yeah, ya gotta go through the Sentinels first.*"

"I know." Joseph was beginning to thaw. "The fans in this town are so rotten. They think they're going to win it every season, and they haven't won the cup in forty years."

"Right!"

"I think they like getting their hearts broken. The Sentinels have the best player in the league. Call me when you get a sixty-goal scorer."

"Amen!" shouted Lou with a fist pump. "Remember the OT winner against the Soar in the playoffs?"

"I was at the game!"

"No fucking way!"

"Yes fucking way!" shouted Joseph. "Atkinson to LaPrince back to Atkinson, backhander, top shelf. The crowd went nuts!"

"Did you go to the parade?"

"I did. Best day of my life." Joseph beamed, then shook his head. "Well, second best—after my son's birthday."

"Right on man, right on. I wish I could have gone," said Lou. "Think they'll win it all this year?"

"With Atkinson? The Soar don't stand a chance."

"Fuck these Wonder City Soar sympies!"

"Hmmm…uh, yeah..." Joseph trailed off.

8:30 PM

Crimson Justice was back in the skies, listening, when he heard something that piqued his interest. The sound of a name he could never forget.

"Hey! It's Crystal Beth!"

From the volume and refraction, Crimson Justice estimated the voice was six miles away, toward the Dire District. He smiled, imagining all the ways in which he was going to throttle her. Round two was going to make round one look like an episode of *Dancing With The Supes*—which he won two seasons ago.

"Really bro? It's gonna be like that?" said Blue Anvil, appearing like a ghost. He was accompanied by Robo-Lad, with blue flames erupting from his jetpack and five helicopters that immediately swarmed them, each with a gunner aiming one of Amycus's weapons. "I know you didn't just crop dust me back there."

It was one thing to battle two helicopters, but *five*?

Crimson Justice attempted the math—he could defeat Blue Anvil in under five seconds, Robo-Lad with an additional two. But how many of those experimental rounds would strike him before he could rip all five helicopters from the sky? Being shot by those experimental weapons was like being stung by a bee—he wasn't in any mortal danger, but that didn't mean he wanted to be swarmed upon.

"Your move," said Robo-Lad.

Crimson Justice smiled.

8:45 PM

"Fuck these Wonder City Soar sympies!"

"Hmmm…uh, yeah..." mumbled Joseph.

That word again. It was one of *their* favorites. There was no better reminder that Joseph was fraternizing with the enemy than when they threw around their cute, demeaning slang.

"What's wrong?" asked Lou.

"Nothing," said Joseph as he re-checked the following corner. He was still on high alert, even though there wasn't another person within five blocks… except Lou.

"Hey, who would've thought a fucking sympie Tin Man would be a Metro City Sentinels fan?"

"Why is that so hard to believe?" Joseph turned to the plump little man and took note of his age. He probably wasn't old enough to drink.

"Because." Lou shrugged. When Joseph didn't respond, Lou appeared nervous. "Fuck, man, you're a fucking Tin Man sympie."

"So, I can't be a fan of the same ice hockey team as you because I believe in democracy and the right to not be killed by supers and vigilante soldier wannabes?"

"Well, yeah!" scoffed Lou. "But I totally believe in democracy. Supies are the true patriots."

"Patriots? You don't know what that word means."

"Fuck you! Of course, I do!"

"You seem to be confusing fanaticism with patriotism."

"What's the difference?"

"A patriot does what's right for the country. But a fanatic is only interested in their side."

"I do want what's right for the country!" growled Lou. "And fuck you, sympie!"

"What is this?" said Joseph, gesturing to Lou's attire—the V-boy vest, trucker hat, armband, and utility belt. "You look like an asshole."

"You look like an asshole." Lou pulled his knife like he meant to use it.

"Why are you so offended?" Joseph noted the knife.

"Why am I offended? You guys get offended at everything! We call you sympies and cucks and you start crying."

"We're offended because you're trying to offend us," explained Joseph. "You're not saying that to be nice. You're trying to hurt, and then you get upset when people tell you they don't like what you've said."

"So?"

"Have some accountability for what you say. Have some accountability for what you do."

"What we do?" scoffed Lou. "You Tin Men assholes aligned yourselves with supervillains, hiding your faces behind your gray hoodies, throwing piss-balloons and punches. If I'm a fanatic, then so are you! We're exactly the same! Two sides of the same coin."

"No, we're not." Joseph ripped the hoodie from his head. "I dress like this and hide my face because I believe in something so much that I *must* hide my face. I have something to lose. My son. I do this for him. And let me make myself clear." Joseph took two long, lanky steps forward and put his finger in Lou's chubby face. "I may resort to violence because that's the only way people listen these days—but I use my fists. I use a wooden pole—"

"—Don't forget about piss-balloons."

Joseph nodded, although he hadn't participated in that specific activity. "Fine, some of us throw balloons filled with piss. But I don't want to kill you. I don't want to maim you. I want you to realize you're wrong. I want you to realize your violent fantasies are ridiculous and dangerous. I want you to understand that I am scared the next time Crimson Justice takes down a member of the Dope Gang, or the Syndicate, that he's going to kill my son in the process. I am scared out of my damn mind that I might lose my boy. So I put on my gray hoodie, and I cover my face, and I take to the streets, so I can punch you in the goddamn face, so that I might jog some sense into your thick supie skull."

Lou's face puckered like he'd just eaten a piece of sour candy. "How is punching me in the face and throwing piss-balloons going to prove you're right?"

Joseph smiled. "How is killing me going to prove that *you're* right?"

"Less of you to go around."

"I think you just proved my point."

Joseph flipped his hood over his head and jogged away into the night.

Lou began shouting. "What? Where are you going?! Tough guy! Running away! Get back here! Show me how tough you are, Tin Man! Show me you're right! Come back here and beat my head in and tell me how you're right!"

Joseph kept running. He ran all the way to the edge of city limits and all the way home.

He burned his gray hoodie that night. Violence, though headline-grabbing, wasn't the answer.

Unfortunately, there were no answers.

CHAPTER 20

8:30 PM

"I ASK MYSELF ALL THE TIME," SAID TORI, "WHY AM I SO unlovable that I have to trick someone into giving me the attention I need to feel…*loved*?"

Tori took two more steps, then stopped at the intersection next to the traffic light on the curb. It was an abrupt halt—an urgent need to stop and think.

She'd endured so much pain and emotional torment over the years, yet she swore to Amanda that she wasn't going to hurt anymore. She swore she would guard her feelings like she guarded Amanda's well-being—feverishly fighting for herself for once.

What the hell was she doing now?

Her heartbeat soared. She felt like she was falling—falling off that rusty metal ladder and down into the darkness below. She needed to slow down, to catch a rung and hold on. Slow down or face the inevitable hurt that would follow when this too blew up in her face.

Dean stepped off the curb a second later, then turned back. He looked up at her and she saw it—that look of a doomed man.

She stared at him with an air of defiance, the wind blowing a ringlet of hair into her face, and her lower lip went stiff. She knew how this would end.

"*You're so broken, you don't even know it,*" said Rick inside her head.

They all told her she was broken. Jordan. Bert. Danny. Ray. They all said it. They all knew her damage.

She didn't want to hurt Dean. She didn't want to be hurt by Dean.

He was so close, and yet she wanted him closer.

She could see it all, as if Dean was already a part of her…

"Hey! It's Crystal Beth!" someone slurred from down the street.

Tori had seen violent men before, and that guy wasn't the typical drunken douche with a teeny peen—this was a liquored-up loser, high on mob rage. And what was once a nice stroll with enjoyable company turned into a crowd—a crowd that filtered into the intersection from all directions…

…except south, back into the city.

When a V-Boy yelled, "Get her!" the crowd lunged forward, and Tori yanked Dean by the sleeve and ran. She sprinted across the street, then cut through an empty parking lot and around a shuttered strip mall.

Tori had experience with drunken angry mobs—she'd once worked retail on Black Friday. She was struck with terrible flashbacks before the end of the next block, of Door-Buster deals annihilated by swarms of stretchy-pant clad-mothers fist-fighting over the last box.

She pondered which was scarier: Karen and Mary duking it out over a 40-inch TV? Or Chet and Darren with a cattle prod and a six-pack?

"Where are we going?" shouted Dean just before a wave of Khaki Klan forced Tori down a gloomy side street.

"I don't fucken know!" yelled Tori as she picked up pace.

They were halfway to the end of the following block when Dean finally caught up. However, this wasn't Tori's first chase. She knew how to shake people she wanted to avoid. But she'd never run from a mob of hundreds—they cut through buildings, smashed through windows, and jumped over fences to close the angle on their escape. Bricks were tossed, a gunshot went off, and enough obscenities were hurled to rival Eddie Murphy's whole standup career. What they'd do to her and Dean if they got their hands on them was tough to say, but it was sure to end with pain and blood.

Tori funneled them through an alley, the mob filtering into the narrow space in a collision of drunken bodies shouting profanities. She sprinted around a dumpster and leapt over a fallen pallet wedged into the cramped space, all with Dean close behind. Once they emerged from the other side, Tori slid to a stop.

"Oh shit," she grumbled.

There was nowhere to go.

Tori found herself facing the entrance to Monaco Park across the street. The park was a wide-open grassy field with fountains and benches to sit and feed pigeons. They couldn't hide from the mob there—they'd be surrounded in moments.

She had only seconds to plan her next move—left toward the art museum, or right toward a string of shops—a laundromat, a Cash-4-Gold, a series of boarded-up buildings.

Time was ticking away when another option revealed itself like angels blowing trumpets.

BWAAAAP!

The subway entrance was only a few strides away.

Tori devised a plan as she observed the flashing yellow light on the digital sign—the 8:30 train was pulling into the station, horns blaring.

Tori flew down the stairs below street level, ignoring the ammonia stench, then leapt the final six steps and sprinted to the turnstiles—and Dean was right beside her. She smiled. It wasn't every day she met someone who could keep up.

BWAAAAP!

Over the turnstiles, they ran toward the tracks as the train entered the station with a roar of squealing brakes and grinding metal. As the doors flung open, Tori boarded the empty train and kept pace.

"Where are you going?" shouted Dean.

"This way!" she yelled, zipping down the narrow aisle to the back of the car, through the doors and into the next.

By the time Dean had slid the next door shut, a man carrying a length of chain entered the front and immediately gave chase. Tori sprinted through a dozen cars all the way to the rear, Dean never more than a half car behind. She hopped out through the back door as a warning tone chimed—the first of three beeps before the train left the station.

When the second beep sounded, Dean still had a half car to go.

"C'mon!" she yelled as third beep tolled, her outstretched hand awaiting him.

He wasn't going to make it. The doors were closing. Tori hotly debated re-boarding the train to face their fate together…

Why would she do a stupid thing like that!?

But how could she leave him behind with those lunatics?

The pneumatic doors released, methodically clamping shut like the jaws of a robotic shark—

—when Dean took her hand.

He wedged himself between the unforgiving metal doors as Tori pulled, his ankle catching before slipping through, the doors locking in place while the final car filled with V-Boys.

BWAAAP!

Tori flipped them the bird as the train began to move, one of them bashing a length of pipe against the plexiglass window while others made threatening gestures—their words muffled inside the car as it pulled away.

"Buh-bye, dickfuckers," she cackled.

But then Dean put a warning hand on her shoulder, drawing her attention to the commotion at the far end of the station.

"Where is she!?"

"Where the fuck is that bitch?!"

V-Boys were filing into the station like a giant snake, the line cut in half where the subway doors closed a dozen cars ahead.

"Where the fuck is Crystal Beth?"

As V-Boys continued to rumble down the far stairs, the hooligans found the back dozen subway cars stuffed to the brim with furious compatriots as it zoomed out of the station at top speed. While some continued to hunt for Crystal Beth like she may have developed new powers—incredible shrinking abilities to hide herself under an empty bag of pork rinds or within a nearby trash can—others moped, wondering if they had missed their chance to "rough them up something perty."

"Stay low," whispered Dean as they crouched and crawled their way from pillar to pillar, then dashed up the near stairs, exiting as silent as ghosts.

"Did it work?" she asked, as they climbed the stairs toward street level, moving like ninjas, ready to flee at a moment's notice.

Dean scaled the last few stairs, exiting the subway next to a Wonder Wash 'N Go laundromat with a big red neon "OPEN" sign hanging in the front window. He peeked over the railing toward the subway entrance a block away. The mob was still filtering down into the station, shouting angry taunts and banging on bucket drums. The mob had no idea Dean and Tori had escaped or that the train had already left the station—they were following the others like a horde of zombies, or—

"Lemmings," growled Tori, and a random thug with a baseball bat lifted his head in their direction.

Tori froze.

It wouldn't be the first time her big mouth had gotten her in trouble. It wasn't even the first time she had said something snarky a little too loud and got caught. It also didn't help that she was wearing a getup that had gotten her noticed at Supes-Con—where everyone was wearing something blatantly ridiculous.

However, before the thug could even lay eyes on her, Dean sprang into action. He performed two very remarkable things she never expected a guy like Dean to do…

1. He gently took her by the waist, then swooped her aside and into the doorway of the laundromat on the corner.
2. He shielded her from being seen, moving ever so closely to her, like a dancer gliding with her in unison—and right into…

…not a laundromat.

From the outside, the corner building said Wonder Wash 'N Go—with big dirty windows, horrible fluorescent lighting, rows of washers and dryers, red tiled floor coated in soap scum, and an old woman washing her knickers—but on the inside, beyond the threshold of the door, were two large projectors, projecting the scene to the outside public while keeping the secret interior hidden.

"What the…" muttered Tori, as every available curse word momentarily fled her vocabulary. They had stumbled into something they weren't meant to see, but they couldn't stop gawking all the same—like they'd just seen the results of bad plastic surgery, a public meltdown, or literally anyone picking their nose.

What was a laundromat on the *outside* was a bar on the *inside*. A big, old-timey pub with clientele as attractive as a blobfish in a bowler hat.

"Who're you?" grumbled the guy in a corner booth by the door. His tommy gun was his dinner date, and they were sharing a plate of cheese fries as he moped his way through a half empty pint.

"Where are we?" asked Dean.

"How would I know?" Tori gambled a few steps inside to absorb the full scene. It was a hole in the wall bar, just like the West Street Pub in Grace Falls—with crumbling plaster revealing the original brick beneath. Along the left wall was an old wooden bar with tables and booths on the right. At the back were pool tables, a dartboard with a barely recognizable picture of Crimson Justice tacked to the center, and a small hallway leading toward the kitchen and restrooms.

A TV hung over the bar recapping the day's breaking news. The headline "WONDER CITY BURNS" in big bold red letters sat above an anchor detailing the latest reports. The ticker below scrolled from right to left with various details: "fires rage out of control," "apartment complex explodes," and "V-Boys stir the pot, inciting rioters."

It was chaos.

Tori and Dean read the headlines, then turned to each other sporting the same dumbfounded look. What the hell was going on in their city? And what the hell was this place?

The bar was only half-full, but even being half-full provided a plentitude of characters—mostly mobsters in various shades of gray and checkered suits, some with fedoras. But there were a few supes too—supervillains, to be exact. Most of them were low-level creeps in loony costumes, but still, Tori and Dean were in a bar full of—

"Welcome to Mooks," said the bartender. "What'll ya have?"

Dean whispered, "Mooks?" with a chuckle, and Tori elbowed him.

"Rum and coke?" asked Tori.

The bartender shook his head, his jowls sliding from side to side. "You're Crystal Beth, aren't ya?"

Pros and cons soared through her head as she calculated the appropriate answer. Amanda once told her, "When in Old Vegas…" despite the fact that neither of them had ever been to Old Vegas.

"Yeah, so?" said Tori with the least amount of confidence possible.

The bartender shrugged. "I figured a high-profile villy like you had been here before."

Villy—it took a moment. In-slang for villain.

"Not for a while," she lied. They were being watched. She could feel a barfull of eyes grazing over them suspiciously.

"Who's this?" asked the bartender, eyeing up Dean's novelty tee like he was a real scumbag…in a bar that catered to scumbags.

"This is my—" she trailed off, then swallowed the lump in her throat before finishing with "sidekick."

"Sidekick?"

"Yeah, they call me, uh, Rusty Crank," Dean interjected. "You wanna make something of it, pal?"

Was he serious? He'd adopted a whole personality on cue, like a tough-guy, street-smart smack dealer. He was convincing, if not a tad over-the-top, and it took all her composure not to laugh.

"Never heard of ya," said the bartender, who placed both hands onto the bar and leaned in, as if interested in learning more about Rusty Crank.

"I tend to stick to the dark, dirty places, ya know?" prattled Dean. He was nodding as he spoke, using his hands to motion a kind of violent beating meets objectionable sex act.

An uncomfortable silence grew among them. "Yeah, right on," said the bartender after a suspicious pause. "Would ya's like a menu?"

The guy on the next barstool peeked over his shoulder as if gauging their interest in the menu. He was as big as a house in a gray pinstripe suit and black fedora.

"Sure." Tori nodded, and the bartender slid one across the bar top. It was a simple trifold piece of laminated paper with the Mooks logo at the top. She expected the usual appetizers, drink specials, and beers on tap—but the contents were much more odious.

It appeared to be a list of illegal services provided by the establishment. Everything from destroying evidence, to providing samples of prominent supe weaknesses, like silver bullets—the obvious and only weakness of Wolfgang Stranger, werewolf guardian of Oakland. There were other listings too, like getaway services and drivers, alibi actors and scripting, costume cleaning and restoration, hideout installation and setup, chemical cocktails for supe powers with a disclaimer to take at the user's own risk, and the most ominous item of all—a talk with The Boss.

"Actually," said Tori, after giving the menu a brief read, "I think we need to get going."

Some of the clientele stood up, like they smelled a rat.

"You sure about that?" asked the bartender, with the big guy on the next stool still watching over his shoulder. "There's a riot outside those doors. Supes and vigilantes are flooding into the city from all over. Word is, even Blue Anvil and Robo-Lad are in town. Best to lay low and let the whole thing blow over."

"Honestly," said Tori, "that's what we plan to do."

"Lay low?" scoffed Dean. "Till the whole thing blows over?"

Tori was stuck in place. It was like watching an accident unfold in slo-mo. She had no idea what Dean was going to say, and her anxiety bloomed. He was still a stranger she'd only just met, and he was about to say something dumb. Depending on the content, it might be dumb enough to get them both killed.

"What of it, kid?" said the big guy on the barstool. He swiveled toward them, and Tori fully gauged his colossal width. Beneath his light gray suit was a black shirt and yellow tie. He had a rotund belly, like an Italian buddha, and wore a fedora with a yellow feather stuck into the band.

Dean glared at him. He glared at the whole bar full of *Mooks*.

"Half of you sitting around drinking are supes. You have abilities to change this world for the good of civilization, but instead you plot and plan on how to get rich quick by robbing banks and scheming revenge on supes who get in your way." Dean balled his fists.

Oh holy shitballs—Tori was awed, alarmed, frightened, and afraid. Dean re-clutched, launching into the second act of his murderous rant—their murder, to be clear. "You have something any normie would kill for, figuratively speaking, and you trashed it. You could be out there doing good! Helping people! Instead, you're in here wallowing away while the city burns!"

He pointed at the TV, and not one of them looked up at the chaos broadcasted live from the skies over Wonder City. However, every Mook had a hand resting on a weapon—tommy guns, pea shooters, and even a few knives.

"Why?" mouthed Tori. She glared at Dean like he had taken a piss in her Lucky Charms. She was aghast. They'd escaped an angry mob of V-Boys only to stumble upon a mobster hideout, and now Dean was insulting these guys like they weren't a bunch of dangerous criminals. He really did have a problem with keeping his mouth shut around those who could shut it for him…

Then he answered her…

"Nobody's the villain of their own story. You all have good in you. It's time to do something about it." Dean lifted his chin, as if daring them to do what's right.

"Kid, what do you think you know about us?" The big guy had arms the size of barbells, and the circumference of his waist was longer than Tori was tall. "You think we give a damn about what happens out there? Because we're red-blooded Americans?"

"No," scoffed Dean. "Because you're red-blooded human."

The two men stared each other down. Fifteen minutes ago, Tori had stood on a curb and begged him to run away. He didn't back down from her. He wasn't even backing down from a guy who could have tied him up into a pretzel. In fact, she was starting to wonder if he had a death wish, or maybe he wasn't playing with a full 52. Was this a red flag? Or was he just a brave man with convictions after suffering through the awfulness of the world left behind by supes?

And then…

WHAM!

The whole bar shook, and something hit the glass projecting the woman still washing her dirty knickers. The glass cracked; the splintering pieces crept outward from the impact until the whole pane broke into a shower of tinkling bits. On the street beyond Mooks was the flaming wreckage of a helicopter— rotors bent and spinning.

Then came the sound of footsteps across broken glass, and all eyes focused on the front door.

When it opened, there was momentary blindness. The light emanating from a malfunctioning spotlight poured into the bar, silhouetting the shape in the door, while the mobster sitting there stood up and drew his tommy gun.

Crimson Justice strode into the bar like a twisted lawman entering a wild west saloon and dropped Robo-Lad by the coat rack. The hero landed with a lifeless thud, wires dangling from his chest. The bar full of villains and mobsters watched him enter, fingers resting on itchy triggers.

"I've come for her," declared Crimson Justice.

All eyes followed his outstretched finger until they found the target of Crimson Justice's jurisprudence…Tori.

Before she could formulate words—before she could even tabulate the circumstances—the enormous mobster with the yellow feather lumbered forward and put his gigantic frame in front of Tori and Dean.

"Crimson Justice," greeted the mobster, like they were old pals. "I'm gonna have to ask you to leave the premises."

Crimson Justice tilted his head to the side. "Do you oppose the law?"

The mobster turned to the bartender and nodded before glancing at Tori and Dean. "Get them the special," he said.

The bartender hopped over the bar and grabbed Tori and Dean by the arms. "This way."

"Where are we going?" she asked as he hustled them to the back and into a hallway. She was glad to be further away from Crimson Justice but didn't feel comfortable with anything called—

"The Special," replied the bartender.

"*Is what*?" demanded Dean as the man stuffed them all into a cramped restroom and locked the door.

The bartender said, "Didn't you read the menu?" as a gun popped off. There was a scream, followed by a flood of gunshots, commotion, breaking glass, and thumps. "Today's special…" A bullet ricocheted through the bathroom wall and careened overhead, making them duck. "…is the nachos."

"*The nachos*?" squealed Tori, as the bartender huddled them into the spare toilet stall with an out-of-order sign on the door. Inside was an explosion of feces and misogynistic notes left behind in sharpie on the walls. "Fuck! What the fuck is this?"

"It's a shitastrophe," offered Dean—quoting Tori from earlier that night.

Jokes at a time like this?

The bartender lifted a lanky leg and used his shoe to flush. "Yeah, the nachos. Nacho Problem!"

"What!?" they shouted.

When the toilet bowl cleared, the floor gave way like a trapdoor before the throne of an evil genius—albeit a throne made of porcelain—and they fell…

They fell for what seemed like forever…

…falling down down down into a chute of darkness.

Tori heard Dean cursing from somewhere in the darkness above. He was still there with her—dropping to their doom—but at least they were doomed together. Right when it seemed like there was no end to their descent, she plunged into something soft, like a plastic ball pit for kids. After an awkward mix of swimming and crawling, they surfaced. Tori hauled herself onto a platform as the lights flickered on.

Dean swam to the edge of the massive ball pit, and the bartender hobbled over and helped him out.

"Where are we?" asked Dean, his eyes flitting to every detail. They were back underground, but at least they weren't in the sewer.

They were in a cavern with huge metal bands reinforcing the rocky walls leading to the chute high above the pit. The plastic balls were metallic gray, and the platform surrounding it was blue. Everything within the cavern, from the power switch to the walkway leading to the entrance of an adjoined chamber, were color coordinated in the same palette.

"I thought you were Crystal Beth and Rusty Crank?" said the bartender. "You should know where you are." They volleyed a blank stare between each other, then back to the bartender, who groaned and shook his head. "Why me?" He sighed, put his hands on his hips, and shuffled off into the next chamber. Tori and Dean wandered behind.

She was too awed to sense fear, despite the danger, and Dean seemed as beguiled as her.

Within the next chamber was a circular table the size of a swimming pool. At its center, molded into the metal, was a familiar blue logo.

SYNDICATE

Tori didn't know much about the Syndicate, only that they had been the premiere supervillain team in Wonder City, specializing in organized crime, before the Dope Gang arrived. Their roster had changed multiple times; most of their members were now permanent residents of The Cooler, doing life on ice.

"We're in the secret hideout of the Syndicate?" Dean gulped.

"That was the boss up there," affirmed the bartender, pointing straight up. "He put his neck out for you two."

"That was," said Dean with another gasp, "Memento Maury?"

"The same," said the bartender as Dean and Tori exchanged a frightful glance.

Then the bartender scooted over to a fancy metal cabinet and punched a code into a keypad. When the cabinet opened, he stepped in and shut the door. Steam burst from its sides, and a moment later he stepped out, encased in metal.

"Waitaminute," squeaked Tori. "You're the Metal Mobster?"

"The same," said a digital voice. He took two heavy clanking steps away, then turned back. "Wait here. And don't eat anything labeled in the fridge."

The Metal Mobster stepped inside a human-sized pneumatic tube. There was a hissing squeal, like someone attempting to suck clumpy milkshake up a straw. Then he was suctioned up and away like an action figure inside a vacuum, ready for battle.

Once he was gone, Tori howled, "We have to get the fuck out of here!"

Dean nodded. The immensity of their situation had finally, to Tori's relief, stolen all the bad jokes from his brain. Together they chose a direction and scurried from the room, moving deeper into the underground base.

The Syndicate lair had been built into a yawning cavern, with submarine hatches connecting various sections. There were miles of metal pipes, steam rising through grated floors from nowhere in particular, catwalks, ladders, and tunnels branching off from the main room. By the time they had turned twice, it was clear the hideout was several blocks wide with multiple untold levels. They couldn't find an exit—at least nothing labeled with a glowing red sign. And neither of them wanted to follow the Metal Mobster and get sucked through a pneumatic tube.

They entered three closets, a latrine, and a mess hall—the entire place was abandoned, with only reserve lighting illuminating each passage.

"How is this even happening?" asked Dean.

Tori wanted to answer—she had a response cocked and loaded that included a mini-rant about their combined bad luck converging into ultra-rotten misfortune—but she bit her tongue.

Around the next bend, they happened across a room full of monitors. An image on screen caught Tori's eye, and she slowed to a halt within the doorway.

"What is it?" Dean glided to a stop ahead of her.

Tori had thought she saw a ghost on the television. It was another part of her past she would have to explain…*maybe.*

It was a small room, but the wall of monitors tuned to various television networks and feeds was nothing short of overwhelming. Several feeds were updating the chaos around the city from national networks. Others were focused on the tragedy that had transpired in the nation's capital, where half of Congress, all Reformists, had been murdered before voting on a massive power redistribution bill.

"Did that just happen?" Dean pointed at the headline. "What the hell is going on today?"

Tori didn't answer—she was distracted by the other networks, the ones less concerned with the coup d'etat in D.C. but focused entirely on the villains of Wonder City. She turned the volume up on the feed.

"Hello, I'm Rhea Ramsey," said the host of *Supes-Roundup* as Tori backed away to watch the broadcast. "Wonder City, once a shining beacon of the future, today the epicenter of chaos. What brought the city to its knees? Malfeasance? Incompetence? Anti-Supe sentiment? Sympies? Fake news?" She looked into the camera as if invoking spirits from the beyond. "All of the above."

"Total fuckwitted twatface." Tori locked her arms tight across her chest.

Before Dean could ask why they were watching the worst human in the history of media, the broadcast cut to one of Rhea's Supes-Roundup re-enactments. It was shot on an elaborate set made to look like a generic bank interior. Tori swore she'd seen it on an old sitcom.

"It was a typical day in Wonder City," Rhea narrated. "The sky was blue, and the water had never been cleaner, thanks to the Ministry and deregulation.

At twelve noon, the First National Bank was the quintessence of calm." The bank interior was filled with extras in queue to a series of teller stations, passing the time on their cell phones. "Then, terror struck." The revolving door spun, and through the entrance stepped five bloodthirsty lunatics—the Dope Gang—who immediately began to murder everybody in sight.

Of them all, Crystal Beth took center stage, grinning like the Cheshire Cat as she squashed heads and gutted an innocent kid on the end of her crowbar.

"After a harrowing escape from police custody," said Ramsey, "recent coma survivor and known terrorist Crystal Beth was out for blood. This maniac, this anarchist, this psychotic goon, led the slaughter of thirty-six innocents, then framed the Red Defender of Law and Order, Crimson Justice, for the Dope Gang's crimes."

The bloody episode cut to a silly scene with the Dope Gang piling fake bodies into a corner. They sprinkled something that looked like grated cheese on top of the victims from a container that read "Crimson Justice DNA Evidence" on its label.

"I will never understand how people believe anything this woman says." Dean shook his head. "Fucking ridiculous."

"Sensationalist bullshit." Tori turned away the moment Rhea Ramsey invited a popular podcast host on-screen to discuss the Dope Gang's psychology and motive.

She'd had enough bullshit for one day. As she stormed out of the room, she realized Dean wasn't with her. He was entranced by another monitor. She couldn't tell what had caught his attention, but then the shaky, shifting cell phone video stabilized. A montage of violence perpetrated by the Dope Gang, but this time it was actual footage, a highlight reel depicting their greatest hits.

Perc and Oxy bowling down waves of people with energy blasts as they scattered in Indianapolis, tossing them a hundred feet through the air and into the side of a moving semi-truck.

Annie Phetamine stepping into a puddle and zapping a series of Khaki Klansmen with an electrical charge in Metro City.

Moll-E straddling a police officer during an armored car heist in Atlanta. She pumped him full of so much pleasure that he collapsed moments later, clutching his chest.

Dust tossing around the vigilante known as Ultimatum and his V-Boy sidekicks. The black-clad, armored assassin unloaded a whole clip of ammo into Dust's bulletproof chest. Dust grew so large and angry that he palmed Ultimatum's head and crushed him with a parked car in the Burgh's south side.

And lastly, security footage of the infamous event from the streets of Los Dios, Arizona—Crystal Beth battling the Killjoys. This clip was infamous for a reason. The Killjoys vigilante group were known for being more than human, but not as super as most sanctioned supes. They attacked four on one, each armed with a machete and covered from head to toe in black mummy-like wrappings, glowing red mechanical spectacles shading their eyes. Crystal Beth was parrying their attacks with her forearms—the speed of battle a blur of motion and flashing metal—when one of them jumped onto her back with a bomb strapped to its chest. Nobody knew how many times the Killjoys had been broken apart and placed back together—heck, nobody knew if the people under the wrappings were all mismatched arms, legs, torsos, and heads—but they weren't opposed to destroying themselves in the name of their own twisted sense of justice. Beth spun and flung the Killjoy away, where he exploded…in the middle of a Supie mob watching the battle unfold.

All six members appeared to enjoy their swath of destruction. They were violent, crude, powerful, and unstoppable—until Crimson Justice.

"Why Crystal Beth?" asked Dean, but Tori had already escaped into the hall.

"Huh?" She turned back and realized he was glaring at her costume, then shook her head and continued onward. "I already told you, it's for Amanda."

"I know," said Dean catching up, "But why?"

Tori stopped walking.

"I have no doubt that footage was hyperbolic bullshit, but she is a supervillain. She murdered people in Los Dios. Why her?"

Tori wanted to respond with rage, but when she looked at him, the fire blew out.

Subtext traveled between them. Unspoken words that said everything and nothing. There was more to Tori's story, and Dean seemed eager to learn it. Tori could feel his yearning—the probing questions, the interest in her psychology. Sharing her relationship follies was one thing, but she was terrified to share her past—sharing the little she had, took more courage than he could possibly imagine. Couldn't he see she wasn't proud of who she was? Why was he racing so quickly toward disappointment?

The shrieking sound of ripping metal broke the tension, and Tori welcomed the reprieve. There was a bang, followed by a support beam buckling in the distance. It was definitely time to leave.

Together, they passed many oddities within the Syndicate lair—from an empty room labelled *Torture Chamber* to a giant pool filled with vicious piranhas. At the end of another hall, they found a bolted door with an extravagant locking mechanism. It seemed a likely way out—but after turning the crank and sliding it open, they came face to face with a giant hairy orange beast chained to the floor, petting a disembodied doll head with one eye.

They both shrieked. "What the fuck is that!" yelled Tori.

They slammed the door shut and doubled back.

On second inspection of a nearby hall, they found a mysterious ladder leading down through a hole in the floor. It was their last chance. If they doubled back, Crimson Justice was sure to find them.

"It's the only other way out," rationalized Dean, but Tori wasn't sold on that idea. The way the night was progressing, they were sure to run into something ghastly, like more tiny dogs in costume. "Wait here. I'll go ."

Before Tori could argue, he was already descending into the hole. She heard him hop off the ladder and the sound of his shoes scuffing across a dusty floor—there were heavy footfalls, then a series of scuffles, followed by a loud scraping sound that put Tori on edge.

"Dean?" she called into the hole. "Dean?"

It was the first time in hours they had been out of each other's sight. Tori began fidgeting, and pacing, and tapping, and humming. What if he wasn't okay? What if she had to go down there and save him? What if he had finally discovered her secrets?

Why was she so terrified about what *this guy* thought of her?

The answer to that question terrified her even more.

There was silence in the hole. No motion or commotion. Nothing.

She leaned down and said, "Dean?" She could hear the fear in her voice— weak and pathetic—and it bothered her. She decided to give Dean to the count of ten. Then she was going down after him.

By the time she counted to five, her hands had started shaking. By seven, she was beginning to panic.

His head popped up through the hole just as she arrived at nine. "Hey!"

"What the hell!" she growled, hiding her face. She didn't want Dean to see how relieved she was—or how pissed.

"Sorry!" he said, "but I found *something*." His face was enigmatic—mysterious, playful, and kind of charming. If she didn't want to hate him for scaring her, she may have even smiled.

"What did you find?" she asked.

"Just come on down."

Tori followed him down the ladder and through a small pass into a separate underground cave.

And Tori said, "Now that's *something*," with a big cheesy grin.

CHAPTER 21

9:45 PM

RUDY WHINED, "BUT WHAT DOES IT ALL MEAN?" FOR THE hundredth time.

Arthur had tried to answer that question to the best of his ability, but none of it made the kind of sense that Rudy was hoping for. He wanted clarity. He wanted precision. He wanted it explained to him like he was in kindergarten learning his ABCs and 123s.

With Wonder City in a state of emergency, they'd missed the last train. All public transit had been discontinued, even the driverless taxis and subway trains, stranding Rudy and Arthur in Jersey. The Ryde driver who picked them up from the hospital would only take them as far as the bridge. Which meant they had plenty of time for Rudy to understand the situation as they walked home—he just needed Arthur to talk down to his level.

Arthur provided theoretical physics and sophisticated math, with strange science words thrown about that were all gobbledygook to Rudy. Why was Arthur talking about relativity when Rudy couldn't comprehend the family tree?

Arthur examined the cast on his arm, preparing to re-start his explanation from the beginning. His head was foggy with pain reliever after the doctor set and casted his arm, and each time he attempted a restart, he shaved off complexity until it became a simple sentence. A scary sentence that sounded like something out of Dean's novels.

"Alternate realities are disappearing," said Arthur.

"Whose alternate reality?" Rudy tried to wrap his head around it. Rudy loved science fiction—but mostly stories with laser-swords, space princesses, and evil warlords.

One of Rudy's favorite things about Arthur was that they could stay up late talking about amazing things. For Arthur it was science, but for Rudy it was imagination and magic. Rudy didn't care why a black hole existed, only that it did and that something existed on the other side of the event horizon. Rudy didn't understand the fancy terminology or the long-form equations, but he did know when something was fantastically interesting.

"I can't say whose reality," said Arthur. "Luckily, not ours. Not yet, at least."

There was something therapeutic about the cool air and the clear night sky with all the sparkling stars. Usually the city lights were too bright for stars. But the day's chaos had a strange calming effect on those sections untouched by the violence. By turning off the lights, the city could pretend nobody was home, which made the perfect night for walking.

Well, almost perfect…

Pops went off in the distance. Rudy knew what they were, but he didn't let on that he knew. If Arthur knew that he knew they were gunshots, Arthur would start worrying about him—and right now there were too many things to worry about that didn't begin with Rudy.

"Times like these," said Rudy, "I wish I had powers to protect the people I care about."

Arthur thought for a moment, then said, "You do have powers."

"Oh, Arthur," giggled Rudy, slapping him playfully on the shoulder.

It took Arthur a moment to realize why Rudy was blushing beneath his dark complexion. "Oh, no, not that." Rudy's flirty smile vanished immediately. "No, I mean, yes, that—but I meant something else." He sighed, then composed his thoughts. "Ever notice how some people can walk into a room and the whole mood changes?"

Rudy shrugged. "I guess so."

"Or how mothers provide a sense of calm and caring?"

"Not everyone's mother," groaned Rudy. "Mama Rudolph had bite. She once cold-cocked the mailman because he didn't deliver her TV Guide on time."

"Hmmm," Arthur replied. "That may be, but let's just accept my prior statement for illustrative purposes."

"Agree to disagree," said Rudy.

"Regardless, just as *some* mothers exude nurturing emotions, and Dean's hero complex drives him to follow his heart, people feel excitement when attending your parties. They feel transcendent while eating your catered snacks—"

"Oh, Arthur," said Rudy, slapping his shoulder once again and blushing.

"We all have a unique aura that surrounds us. Our innate being." Arthur stared at the sky as he lost himself in his explanation. "Now imagine having that unique aura bonded with the power of a supe."

Rudy eyed him suspiciously. "Arthur, are you telling me you've discovered how supes get their powers?"

"How they get what kind of powers," clarified Arthur. "Yes."

"So, if I were a supe," said Rudy, "I'd be an even better party planner than I am now?"

"Not possible." Arthur put his arm around Rudy. "I call these unique, innate abilities Latent Endowment Gifts, or LEGs. They're the impetus behind all supe powers."

"You called them legs?" Rudy laughed so hard he was having a difficult time breathing. "Oh, mercy, I wish Dean was here right now."

"What else was I going to call them?"

"I get it," said Rudy, "I mean, it's definitely something to *stand on*."

"Ha-ha."

"Was there debate over the acronym? Or did you have to put both feet down?"

"You're incorrigible."

"I mean, it's silly, Arthur. But if I must use the term, I'll just have to toe the line."

"What?" scoffed Arthur. "That's not even a leg joke."

As Rudy's giggles plateaued, a calm settled over him. Laughing made him feel better, even if it didn't solve anything.

They were somewhere east of the Kentsville section of the city, where Arthur lived. It was calm there without a soul wandering the street. Rudy spotted someone watching them from a dark apartment above. It was a paranoid peep, inspecting the streets for danger.

That was the reminder Rudy needed—his friend was out there. Lost, alone, and hunted by a maniac supe.

"How are we going to find Dean? If anything happens to him, Arthur…"

"I know," Arthur replied. "But Dean's a grown man. He can take care of himself."

"Have you met Dean? That boy…" Rudy got choked up thinking about Dean's ineptitude for staying out of trouble. "Remember the fourth of July?"

That year, Dean had showed up to Rudy and Arthur's rooftop party with an un-RSVPed guest. A mystery plus-one.

"Dean, Dean, Deano," sung Rudy, swimming through the crowd to greet them by the stairwell door. "Who's this?" The music was on point, the food was delish, and the weather was perfect—so Rudy didn't need any surprises ruining it. Especially an unexpected surprise with a *facial tattoo.*

"This," said Dean with a big, bold, million-dollar smile that Rudy digested with immediate acid reflux, "is Linda."

"Ohh, thee Linda!" shouted Rudy, despite the fact he had no idea who Linda was, or that there *even was* a Linda. "It's all over your face…*literally.*"

It *was* all over Linda's face, in perfect calligraphy from left ear to eyebrow, accentuated by illustrated sparkles. The girl was a human canvas. She had jet black hair from a bottle, bright blue eyes, and her skin was a collage of ink. She had ear gauges, piercings in places Rudy didn't know was legal to put holes through the skin, and a humongous heart tattoo on her chest—right above the biggest set of plastic jugs he'd seen this side of the dairy section at the grocery store. All of that was wrapped up in a little five-foot package in daisy dukes and a tank top.

Dean's face went cold. Linda glared at Rudy, then said, "Do you have a problem with my form of expression?" Her eyes bulged from her tiny head like a chihuahua, her head moving side to side as she sassed him.

"Not at all," replied Rudy, but his tone said otherwise.

Linda's phone started wailing, her ringtone an obnoxious hamster song. She answered and said, "Yeah, come on up."

"Excuse me?" said Rudy as Dean shrugged.

She hung up and announced, "My boyfriend's here."

"Boyfriend?" questioned Dean.

"I told you, remember? About my open relationship?"

"Oh. I thought you said you were open to a relationship."

"I did. "A second relationship."

That day, Rudy had to uninvite Linda…and her other man, Brock. Both of whom were not too keen on being asked to leave the party. Dean was too distraught to enjoy himself, and Rudy scolded him for inviting a stray he had only met the night before.

Arthur grumbled, "Yeah, I remember the fourth of July."

"Then you know why I worry about him," said Rudy. "He doesn't know what's good for him. He tries too hard to connect—he's got the USB connector upside down, so he keeps jamming it in there, expecting it to fit right in."

"Great metaphor, and accurate," nodded Arthur. "If you were him, where do you think you'd be?"

There was an explosion. Somewhere in the city, something big went boom, and Arthur glared at Rudy, his eyes transmitting—if Dean was anywhere in the city, he was right in the middle of the mess.

"What do you think?" asked Dean.

Tori and Dean were inside a hollowed-out cavern beneath the Syndicate secret lair, and it was full of high-tech gadgets, costumes, weaponry, and vehicles. Most of the weapons and costumes were under glass, like a museum, and ranged from the simplistic to the extravagant. There were costumes of bygone heroes, jailed villains, and some that had yet to be.

Tori was too busy taking in the spectacle to answer him.

There were shields, bows, guns, robotic appendages, swords, axes, hammers, helmets, gloves, and strange objects that appeared to shimmer with power. Some were ancient, others brand new—but all were amazing.

"What is this place?" she wondered. "If this is the secret lair of the Syndicate, why are there so many hero items?" She pointed toward a helmet under glass. "That's Warrior Princess's helmet." Then she gestured toward a utility belt beside an ominous-looking cane with a golden handle. "And that's the Reaping Raven's belt next to The Monocle's cane. Hero and villain, side by side."

"I'm as lost as you," said Dean.

He wasn't sure why Tori seemed so adamant about solving the mystery. There was a psycho supe after them—more than one at this point—and there were no less than fifteen vehicles they could use to escape with the keys in the ignition.

There was a small tank built for speed, a submarine floating in a pool of water that connected with the bay, rocket jetpacks, motorcycles, even a flying hovercraft in the shape of a black skull. They could escape by land, sea, or air—or any combination thereof depending on the vehicle.

"I feel like there's something important here," said Tori as she studied a black crystal resting inside a bell jar made of bulletproof glass. "A mystery I need to solve."

Tori looked at him over her shoulder, and Dean realized she still had mysteries *he* needed to solve. Like what happened with the Grace Falls Seven. And why was she still putting up with him? Any normal woman would've run for the hills by now, and every crazy woman would've dug her claws into him—but Tori, she was neither running nor clinging. Dean couldn't tell if she was enjoying his company or not.

"Can we solve it some other time?" He gently placed a hand onto her arm.

Tori nodded. She backed away from the crystal and looked out over the parked vehicles sitting on motorized pedestals. "Which one should we take?"

Dean studied their options. "I'm going to assume neither of us are pilots, nor qualified to operate a submarine or tank."

"You are correct, sir," she said playfully. "Though I did once stay at a Holiday Inn."

Dean laughed, and Tori glowed.

"Good one," he lauded.

"You enjoyed that, Rusty Crank?" she quipped.

"I did." He grinned, and she laughed. It may have been the first time he heard her full-throated belly-laugh, and it was "the most beautiful thing ever..."

"What?" she whispered. He'd caught her off guard—her eyes were so big and blue, and he was swept away by them.

There were times when Dean said aloud the things he was thinking. Like when he told Peter he smelled like "moldy hard cheese putrefying in week-old unwashed socks" after he attempted to break video game records one weekend. Peter had gone through fifteen bags of Doritos and ten three-liter bottles of Mountain Dew by Sunday afternoon, and Dean had to leave or vomit.

Dean's mental-blurts were legendary amongst his inner-circle, and they made for great stories when reminiscing over a beer. Calling Apollo's Sunnies "a cult" was a prime example—but if he hadn't said that, would he have met Tori?

"You have a beautiful laugh," said Dean, doubling down.

For some reason, Tori gave him courage.

Tori's cheeks grew rosy beneath her galaxy makeup. The bare skin between her neck and chest flushed.

"Thanks," she croaked. Before Dean had the chance to follow up and say something he'd regret, she changed the subject. "What about the motorcycle and sidecar?"

"Sure." Dean strode over to the motorcycle and grabbed the black helmet resting on the handlebars. It was one of the coolest-looking things Dean had ever seen, with big bulky tires, vertical exhaust pipes, and the chassis made entirely out of carbon fiber.

"No." Tori grinned and planted her hands on her hips.

He had the helmet over his head, preparing to slip it on. "No?"

"That's *my* helmet. You're riding in the sidecar."

Dean tilted his head. "Are you serious?"

"Like the plague," she said. "That one's yours." The helmet sitting on the sidecar seat looked like it was meant for a sidekick—most likely a dog or monkey.

"I'm too big to sit in that," he argued.

"Rusty Crank is Crystal Beth's sidekick, remember?"

"But you're not Crystal Beth."

"I am tonight," she said. "If Crimson Justice thinks I am, then I deserve to be the one in charge of my own getaway."

"Fine." He tossed the helmet over. "But if I fall out and hit my head again, it's on you."

She caught the helmet with both hands and was immediately transfixed by the design on its side. It was an airbrushed eagle with the body of a lion. It felt like it meant something to her—like it was destiny.

"It's a Gryphyn," said Dean. "A benevolent mythological creature."

"Does it do anything special?"

"Gryphyns ward against evil," he explained. "They're powerful guardians of good. It's said they mate for life, and if their partner dies, the other will mourn for the rest of its days."

"Where'd you learn that?" Tori seemed to appreciate the romanticism, even if she didn't appear to believe in it.

"Hobby," he claimed.

She nodded, then slipped the helmet over her head as Dean buckled into the sidecar, his legs spilling out onto the hood. When he attempted to put the sidekick helmet on, it was much too small and sat ridiculously on top of his head. Dean knew he looked absurd but gave Tori two thumbs up with a big unapologetic smile.

She was laughing. Even though he couldn't see her face with the helmet shield down, he could hear it, and it gave him warm fuzzies.

Tori lifted the kickstand. "Ready?"

"You're never going to let go of the Rusty Crank thing, are you?"

"Nope," she sang, then hit the kickstart. The cycle roared to life like rolling thunder and knocked the Monocle's cane from its holder under glass.

Dean had a feeling he was going to regret this.

Tori couldn't stop giggling as the motor roared.

The one and only time she'd ever ridden a motorcycle was with Jordan. It was a loud, whiney bike he bought at a garage sale with her money—he couldn't keep a job at the time. She asked to drive, but Jordan refused. "Men don't ride in the bitch seat," he'd insisted.

She had a zinger ready—she was going to say by that logic, the seat *belonged* to him—but she didn't. It was going to start another fight, and they had just ended one that lasted all week.

Tori never had another chance to ride after that.

"Manda," whispered Tori, "if you could see me now."

Tori spotted a ramp at the end of the vault and hit the throttle. When the bike lurched forward, Dean's head whipped backward, but she never let off the gas. The bike hit the ramp at fifty miles per hour and steadily picked up speed as it soared into a tunnel hewn through rock.

The first stretch was fitted with motion sensors on halogen lights set every fifty feet—until they passed an ominous "Under Construction" sign followed by complete and total darkness that gave them both an immediate case of white knuckles.

"Headlights!" shouted Dean, but she could barely hear him over the engine.

Was he sidecar-mansplain-driving?

There were three buttons on the left handle next to her thumb, and she innocently flipped the first one. Process of elimination—maybe she'd get lucky on the first try. When nothing happened, she motioned to flip the second switch. Four simultaneous explosions went off behind them like flash-bombs, brightening the tunnel for the briefest second.

The bike swerved, but maintained course after the blasts as Dean frantically waved—did *she* do that?

She quickly flipped the next button. Two rocket boosters ignited from the back, making the cycle lurch left, then veer right, scraping paint off the sidecar as it ground against the stone wall. Dean shouted, sparks flew, and the tunnel was lit long enough for Tori to swipe the third button, snapping the headlights on—

—just in time to witness the end of the line.

The end of the line, in this case, was a steel reinforced wall surrounded by orange emergency cones and a diamond-shaped sign that said "DANGER"— all of which were going to render them into a burning splatter.

Tori tried the brakes, but the boosters kept the cycle moving forward at fatal speeds. She thumbed at the second switch again and missed, instead striking the first button once more, then braced for impact—

Four explosions went off behind them as the wall cracked in half, splitting open like the jaws of a fire-breathing dragon. Just wide enough for them to pass through and out into the night—belched free surrounded by fire and dust.

They landed with a screech and squeal of rubber tires against asphalt and soared down the highway along the river. When Tori peeked into the rearview mirror, she saw nothing but an abandoned cement factory. No steel reinforced doors, no tunnel or exit of any kind. Just an old building on the corner of an on-ramp to the interstate that Tori was now merging onto.

But something was amiss. There were no cars. There were no lights. There was no nothing—just stars and shadows.

All travel on the interstate was blocked off, leaving them with nothing but open road as far as the eye could see. Tori hit the throttle down the straightaway, free as a bird, when they crested the incline of an overpass and spotted headlights.

Though, it wasn't quite headlights—more like a headlight—singular. It was big, and growing bigger every second, until…

…until it became clear it wasn't a headlight at all. In fact, it wasn't even a vehicle.

By the time Tori realized what it was, she swerved toward the closest off-ramp, but the light was too fast. There was a flash, the sound of snapping metal, and Tori zoomed straight down the ramp. She never saw the sidecar soaring straight ahead without brakes.

The sidecar rolled a whole city block, kicking up sparks, until it ran off the road and smacked into the median. When it tipped over, Dean spilled out onto the pavement like a can of beans. By the time he rolled onto his feet, the glowing ball of light had ripped the helmet from his head, snapping the straps with a quick flick, then shoved him to the ground.

"Where's my hundo, asshole!" growled Apollo. He was so bright, Dean could hardly see him.

"How'd you find us?" squeaked Dean as Apollo grabbed him by the jaw.

"Does it matter, dimwit? I'm a supe! I track down perps. It's what I do."

"I'm not a perp," mumbled Dean through gritted teeth. The pain in his jaw was grinding away at his adrenaline.

"You stole my fucking hundo, asshole!"

Dean reached into his pocket and flipped the wadded hundred-dollar bill at Apollo. The crumpled bill plunked him between the eyes, then fell to the ground without so much as a flinch from the glowing idiot.

"Do you think I want my money back?" growled Apollo. "It's the…the…"

"Principle?" mouthed Dean.

"Fuck you!" yelled Apollo, dropping Dean onto the pavement. "It's the principle, alright." Apollo's luster dulled, and Dean could see the bruising around his left eye and all the scratches. Someone had busted him up good.

"Nice shiner," chuckled Dean. "Get it? Shiner?"

"You really want to suck my dick, don't you?" he taunted, coming completely unhinged.

"Great bully line," jeered Dean. "You guys love bringing everything back to your dicks."

Apollo grabbed Dean by the belt and tossed him into the middle of the highway, like lobbing a duffel bag. The sound of distant beeps and shouts approached, and before Dean could roll away, he was surrounded by crisscrossing headlights, closing off escape.

Six full cars and trucks of Apollo's Sunnies unloaded onto the interstate and chanted his name, led by Kristy wrapped in her own toga.

"Eww, babe! You found him!" said Kristy, skating around awkwardly in a pair of white stilettos. "Did you get your money back?"

Apollo looked furious. "It's not about the money, babe! It's the principle."

"Oh." Kristy pinched at the air. "But isn't it a *little* about the money?"

Apollo's jaw set. "Why are you dulling my shine, babe?"

Dean took their lover's spat as an opportunity to escape and rolled away. Two guys in wifebeaters and jeans, wearing flannel printed bedsheets as togas over their clothes, grabbed him before he could make his break.

"Where do you think you're going?" said the uglier Sunnie.

"Yeah, where do you think you're going?" said the dumber Sunnie.

Dean had gotten himself into a few pickles, but none quite like this. This was an imminent threat of physical violence—no escape, no absolving combination of words. This would be a beating.

Ugly and Dumb dragged Dean back into the center of the car circle and allowed Apollo to take center stage. The glowing supe cracked his neck from side to side as Ugly and Dumb jostled Dean by the collar.

"Damnit!" growled Dean as the stitching of his t-shirt popped. "Can you whackos lay off the shirt, please!" Lil' Pete would never forgive Dean if the shirt he gifted was ruined.

"What shall we do to him?" urged Apollo to his Sunnies, like Maximus inciting a bloodthirsty crowd at the Coliseum.

The Sunnies hurled insults mixed with violent direction—a few highlights were:

"Rip his balls off!"

"Tar and feather the bastard!"

"Rip out the dickhead's teeth!"

One guy even said, "Draw and quarter him!" and Dean wondered if the didiot even knew what that was—

Didiot—

He thought of Tori…

She was probably almost home by now, and despite the violence he was about to incur, it made him smile. The last thing he wanted was for his problems to get Tori hurt. Their day together was a single serving—he was never going to see her again. If this was his curtain call, he was thankful to have felt a connection to someone remarkable.

Just a taste of what he never got to have.

Because why else would he have endured all this pain? Why else would fate have been so cruel? The whole day, everything that transpired, felt like a send-off. One last hurrah in the middle of chaos to prove that he could brush up against something great but never quite have it.

He was so lost in his misery he never heard the crowd of Sunnies agree to "break his face" or the tiny tinkling of a half dozen metal marbles roll to a stop all around him.

"Yeah, I like that." Apollo grinned. "I'm going to break your fucking face."

"Ewww! Hey babe!" shouted Kristy. "What are those?"

"Damnit, Kristy!" growled Apollo. "If you want to be my sidekick, you need to start looking out for number one—*me*! And right now, I'm in the middle of face breaking."

"But—"

"But nothing!" shouted Apollo, as all six metal marbles, the exact things Kristy was desperate to warn him about, sparked and blew up. Each belched a massive white cloud of debilitating chemical gas—

"My eyes!" cried Dumb.

"I can't breathe!" whined Ugly.

—that made the eyes sting and the air unbreathable.

Dean was able to get a lungful of clean air before the mist blanketed him and his captors. When they buckled over coughing, Dean shut his eyes and kicked.

He struck something hard.

"My bulbs!" squealed Apollo, followed by a glitchy flash.

Dean squirmed away, then shoved Dumb aside into Ugly. He limped onward—his foot felt like he had kicked two solid brass fishing weights—as he journeyed through the mist for fresh air.

"Where'd he go?" hacked Apollo. "Where'd that fuck-nut go!" He was affected by the gas, but not nearly as much as the others, and he cradled his sore manhood. "Find that asshole! Find him now!"

Dean blindly bumped his way between the circle of cars, smashed into a rearview mirror, and was spinning away when someone grabbed him.

"Dean, it's me."

Startled—and like a complete and total dummy—Dean opened his eyes amidst a breeze of chemical agent. Before the intense burn settled in, like ramming Tabasco and chopped onions directly into his peepers, he recognized the Gryphyn-emblazed helmet and allowed Tori to guide him away.

"I thought you left." Dean coughed. He could hear the frantic shouting moving further away as they put distance between them and the Sunnies.

"Why would I do that?" Tori's voice was voice muffled beneath the helmet. "You were in trouble." She led him away from the chemical fog and over the highway median, then down the off-ramp back into the city.

"Thank you," whined Dean. "Oh, this stings!" His eyes burned so badly he thought they were melting. He couldn't see, even when Tori grabbed his face and forced them open.

"We need to wash your eyes out," she said as she ushered him at double speed. "This way. Hurry."

"I'll murder you!" shouted Apollo. "I'm going to rip off your nuts and eat them! Do you hear me, Dean! I'm going to slaughter you!"

CHAPTER 22

10:15 PM

"FOR THE RECORD," SAID DEAN, "TEAR GAS IS NO FUN."

"Was it ever recorded otherwise?" asked Tori, as Dean finished washing his face with milk, followed by splashes of water from the restroom sink.

They'd found a small convenience store a quarter mile from the highway ramp. The store remained open despite the city-wide panic, though the owner sat behind the register with a shotgun fully loaded. He seemed like a nice gentleman, wearing a Tin Men t-shirt not too dissimilar from her own. He'd been willing to let Tori help Dean so long as they paid for the milk.

"Hollywood," said Dean, "makes everything look so glamorous."

She smirked. The fact Dean never lost his sense of humor, even when in pain and discomfort, was a good thing. She appreciated the self-deprecation. She had met too many guys who were all ego and bravado, who'd never let themselves appear weak or vulnerable. Maybe they believed they'd appear less manly if they did, but Dean didn't appear any less manly to her. And there was something to be said about seeing someone at their worst and not being repulsed by them—and let's be real, tear gas does not bring out the best in people.

Dean didn't grind her nerves either, which was saying something. She could only ever say that about one other person in her life.

"Is the milk helping?" she asked.

It was the owner's suggestion to use milk. He took one look at Dean and told them what to do—but demanded they only used the skim.

"Leave the good stuff," he said. "Nobody buys that one percent crap."

It helped with the burn, though it was slow relief.

"Yeah," replied Dean, after blinking like he was dropping a beat.

"Good." She smiled.

"Ugh," he groaned, "where the hell are we?"

The restroom was cleaner than it smelled. It was a small one-stall closet with a rust-stained sink and a cracked mirror. The tile was white, but the grout had soaked up every stain committed within those four walls. It made her grimace—but when she looked back at Dean, he was smiling.

"You washed off the face paint."

"I did." She resolved not to show her emotions beyond a nervous smile.

Dean opened his mouth but stifled his words before he could speak them. He eventually asked, "Where'd you get the tear gas?"

"The bike," she explained. "The sidesaddle was full of them. I tested one, grabbed a handful, and went back for you. I didn't know it was tear gas."

"Well, my eyes and throat aren't happy," he groaned. "But the rest of me sure is."

She winked. "It was a happy accident."

He kept smiling.

She smiled back and became aware of how awkward she was acting. It was her own fault. She couldn't turn off her discomfort after removing the face paint and couldn't understand why. She felt exposed. Embarrassed.

"Where's the bike?" he finally asked.

"A few blocks away. Stashed in an empty lot."

"Good," he said. His eyes were still red, but he seemed vastly better. "Would you mind? One last time?"

She nodded and grabbed the milk carton while Dean leaned his head over the sink.

"I hate to ask," said Tori, as she splashed another round onto his face, "but do you have any money?"

"Back pocket," he said.

Tori was surprised by his trusting answer, and politely reached into his back pocket as he hunched over the sink. "I'll be right back."

"You're not robbing me, are you?" His eyes were closed tight with a milk-drenched face and smile.

"For ten stinkin' bucks?"

"There's a rewards card in there for a free slice of pizza. That's a two-buck value."

"If I don't return in five minutes, you'll have your answer." She ducked out of the room to pay for the milk. She caught herself smiling as she left. She was enjoying their banter and allowing herself to live in the moment—to get out of her own doubt-ridden head.

Tori wasn't the kind of person who'd snoop through another's business. In fact, the level of trust Dean had in her to offer up his wallet made her nervous. Why did he trust her? She was still a stranger. A stranger dressed as Crystal Beth—a psycho killer who'd rob you blind and wouldn't so much as piss or spit if you were on fire—though she might toss a can of kerosene.

She was halfway to the register when she removed the ten bucks from his wallet, and with it came an old punch card for a free slice of pizza from Giordano's—her and Amanda's favorite. A coincidence. One that made her smile until the front door opened and a gust of wind blew the card from her hand.

Chance is random. A million micro-actions and interactions must occur to make one tiny event happen. The wind that blew the card from her hand was allowed into the store because the man who entered needed to grab a few items for his pregnant wife. Pickles and peanut butter. Her cravings were inspired by something she saw on TV, and that ad was only running because the station had to evacuate due to the danger downtown. One fallen domino setting off a million other dominos.

And when that card fell onto the floor and landed face down, Tori saw the message scrawled onto the back. She froze. Dots were connecting in her head, and she hadn't yet put the clues together to see where they led. Even the shooting star she'd witnessed earlier that night seemed conspicuous. Yet coincidence seemed too crazy a notion.

"Oscuro?" asked Tori as she stepped back into the restroom with Dean washing off the last remnants of milk from his face and hair.

"Yeah?" said Dean, without a hint of conspiracy.

She asked one more time with clarity. "Your last name is Oscuro?"

"I'm assuming you saw my license. That photo should be burned."

"How did you know Amanda?" Tori demanded.

She was shaking. There was no reason to be this angry without knowing all the details, yet this revelation was the kind of thing that caged Tori within her own head. She couldn't let this go, not after everything…

"Your Amanda?"

Tori nodded, then shoved the dog-eared Giordano's Pizza card toward his face with the final hole punched. She flipped it over, and on the back was a quick message.

Thanks for the slice!
IOU paid in full.
- Hems.

"Wait," said Dean. "Hems is your Amanda? Wow, okay. How's she doing? I haven't seen her since the fire."

Tori blinked as another revelation struck. "You worked together at The Incubator?"

"Yeah, I worked down the hall," he confessed. "I saw Hems every morning and introduced her to Giordano's on a lunch break. I gave her my free slice, so she thanked me with a new rewards card." He smiled. "Small world."

"I wish you would've told me." The knife dug deeper between her shoulder blades with every new scrap of information.

"I haven't seen her in three years. Not since the fire. Everyone at The Incubator went by last names, even Ivanovich and Yastrzemski. I didn't know her first name." He looked mortified. "We all called her Hems."

"Hemmels," she corrected. "Her last name was Hemmels."

Dean was about to reply when he caught on—Tori saw it in the way he stood, like someone was running an ice cube down his spine.

"Her last name," said Dean carefully, "*was* Hemmels?"

"Amanda's dead," said Tori. She put the rewards card back into his wallet and tossed it onto the sink next to him. It had no sooner landed when she spun around, blocking any chance Dean had at explaining himself further.

Then she left.

Crimson Justice was always angry when wearing the cowl and hood. It was like magic—like switching between personalities. One personality was a happy-go-lucky husband, and the other was a dangerous crime-fighting machine. Some might say he was the most powerful thing in the world.

He was.

It was a damn shame that people couldn't see he was making their lives better—he was saving them from themselves!

Every criminal bust, every mobster and supervillain he threw behind bars or put six-feet-under was a thrill. That thrill never changed. There was something addictive about the way they screamed and broke beneath his iron grip. His first bust was just as exhilarating as his last. Even his failures were pretext—eventually Law and Order prevailed.

Some called him a menace. Some called him an oppressor. Some even called him a murderer and a monster.

How deluded were they? The fake news and their "facts" were just trying to make him look bad. Reformist Sympies were the bane of his existence—the very thing tearing down civilization. Did he kill? Yes. Did he destroy public and private property? Yes, but only to do what needed to be done. Evil had to be stomped out before it spread—plucked from the ground by the root— bleached before the stain set in.

The Dope Gang had to be destroyed. Every remaining member. Once he caught Crystal Beth's scent, he tracked her across the city and found her within the confines of villainry—a Syndicate hideout disguised as a laundromat. When he arrived, he found a treasure trove of criminals.

Memento Maury.

Metal Mobster.

Terry Cloth.

Jack the Rapper.

Gabba-ghoul.

Tommy Gun Timmy. And more!

The list was impressive. Maybe, if he hadn't been so intent on crushing Crystal Beth into a red smear under his boot, he could have taken them all down. But they were only a distraction. By the time the dust had settled, the establishment had imploded, and Crystal Beth was gone.

"Where is she?" growled Crimson Justice. Memento Maury's yellow silk tie was wrapped so tight around his fat neck that his head looked like it was about to burst.

"Who?" croaked Maury. His feathered fedora was going up in flames, along with the rest of Mooks.

"The felon known as Crystal Beth!" shouted the Red Hood of Justice. "She is a symptom of a plague that has gone unchecked for far too many years in this city."

"Unchecked?" croaked Maury. "You've been prowling this city for half a decade. You've upended crime at every turn. You've beaten and killed almost every supe, hero, or villain that showed up in town. If Crystal Beth is a symptom, you're the disease!"

The silk tie around Memento Maury's throat snapped right along with his neck.

Crimson Justice chuffed. "Fake news."

Crystal Beth couldn't have gotten far. In fact, he could already smell her.

10:30 PM

When Dean stepped out of the convenience store, Tori was sitting on the curb. It surprised him. He'd expected her to be long gone. The look in her eyes, the betrayal, made him feel awful. It was a good sign she had stayed, but Dean wouldn't press his luck.

The bell above the store exit announced his presence, but Dean took his time approaching her. "Mind if I sit?"

Tori shrugged. He joined her on the curb—not too close, but not too far. Just the right distance between them. Because that's where they were, right? There was something growing between them—*maybe?* But it needed space.

"Giordano's was our favorite," she said. "She came home one day, all excited. Said she finally found a good pizza place in the city. Said Oscuro from work showed her." She sniffled. "I always thought, what a strange name. Must be foreign. Never thought it might be someone's last name."

"When did it happen?"

"Recently," she said.

"The last time I saw Hems—Amanda," said Dean, "she was running into a burning building." Tori didn't tell him to stop, so Dean kept talking. "My office was down the hall, and every day I'd say *good morning*, and she'd give me a smile and ask about my evening. I'd often say something snarky, probably stupid, and she'd giggle and continue answering phones. Eventually, we became friends, recommending restaurants, beer, music, movies, and books to each other."

"Did you like her?" She watched him with tears, listening closely.

"I thought Hems was pretty. I thought she was someone special," he admitted. "But I wasn't ready for someone like her. Not then. My heart was still too broken."

Tori nodded.

"The day of the fire," said Dean, "it happened after lunch. I remember walking back into the office and Hems wasn't at her desk. I thought it was odd. By the time I sat down, there was an explosion followed by the fire alarm." Dean paused, remembering it like a fever dream. "We tried to evacuate, but the building was burning like it was purposely spreading to block us from the exits. My team and I got out, but I was only a step outside the building when I saw Hems running back inside with a fire extinguisher."

Tori laughed sadly, covering a happy but painful thought. "Sounds like her."

"I followed her inside," he continued. "I thought to myself, if Hems was going in to help people, I should too."

Tori was stunned. "You went back inside? What happened?"

"We got separated. I tried following her, but instead I found a group of people who couldn't find their way out. I helped them."

"You're a hero."

"No," He shook his head emphatically. "'Hero' doesn't mean what it used to. I'm human."

They looked at each other for a moment.

"I can see the similarities," said Dean.

"Huh?"

"Between you two," he clarified. "You and Amanda are a lot alike."

Tori felt a rush of tears. She scooted over and placed her head onto his shoulder. "I can't believe she's gone."

Tori grabbed hold of him, and he held her as she cried. He waited patiently for the sorrow to pass, quietly mourning the woman who connected them both.

"Do you think he was here?" asked Arthur.

Rudy inspected the wreckage from a distance. There were bodies, and it took some mental gymnastics to turn everything he was seeing in real life into faux-celluloid within his mind—only when it seemed fake, like a movie, was he able to look.

There was a burning helicopter and a demolished laundromat. It was a disaster.

"Absolutely," said Rudy. "This reeks of Dean."

"I can smell it too," admitted Arthur.

Rudy groaned. "I told that boy to go easy on the cologne. A little goes a long way if worn properly."

"What has he gotten himself into?" said Arthur. "How many supes can one guy piss off in a single day?"

"Considering the time? At least three."

As they walked around piles of brick and burning wood, they came across a body. The man was massive. Rudy imagined it'd take a lot to bring down a man that size.

Arthur crouched and took the man's pulse.

Rudy danced back and forth, like he had to pee. "Is he dead?"

"Very," said Arthur. He stood up and paced over to Rudy, turning him away from the body. Rudy had an overactive imagination, and this was surely going to compound his nightmares on top of nightmares.

After all, it was at this point in a horror movie when the body would sit up and say, "Can I help you?"

And it did.

Rudy and Arthur froze.

"Arthur," said Rudy, "I thought you said the man was dead?"

"He is dead," replied Arthur.

"Correction," said the dead man, "I was dead."

They slowly spun toward the not-so-dead man. Rudy's knees wouldn't stop shaking.

Dean always wondered why Rudy liked horror movies when they scared the beejeezus out of him. To Rudy, being scared over something fake felt like a roller coaster without the weightless freefall of riding one. He could scream, sometimes squeal, then laugh at himself afterward.

The problem was, this dead man wasn't a character in movie. He was standing with his neck slung at an odd angle until he grabbed his head with both hands and reconnected his broken spine.

Rudy screamed on cue. It was a high-pitched screech that rattled eardrums.

"Allow me to introduce myself," said the dead man. "I'm Memento Maury."

CHAPTER 23

10:50 PM

"I LEFT IT OVER THERE," SAID TORI, POINTING THE WAY WITH helmet in hand.

Crickets chirped in a chorus of sound, and the sky was as clear as ever, displaying a kaleidoscopic arrangement of brilliant stars. Despite everything, the whole day felt like magic.

They were five blocks from the convenience store in a narrow, abandoned lot between rowhomes. Originally, there had been a rowhome right where they were standing, but it had long since burned down. Some of the old timbers were still there, which made the perfect cover for Tori to stash the bike.

"Are you okay with me as a back warmer?" asked Dean.

"A what?"

"You know," said Dean, "I'll be riding behind you."

Tori marveled at him for a moment. He really was so different than any man she'd ever met. "I just blew snot bubbles crying into your shoulder. I think we're past the point of respecting personal space."

"Fair enough," said Dean as he discreetly checked his sleeve.

Tori laughed and said, "Kidding," then winked and added, "Sort of."

Dean helped pull the bike out of the tall grass, and they walked it over to the curb. He looked at Tori and caught her stealing a glance—her gaze lingered. Words didn't need to be spoken.

Maybe this wasn't a single serving of excitement. Maybe it could go on.

"What's that?" asked Tori, peering past him.

"What's what?" Dean looked over his shoulder.

The crickets went silent.

"Crystal Beth!" said an electronic voice. "Stay where you are!"

A drone scooted overhead, followed by a second and third. A spotlight hit them from a larger fourth with a suspicious-looking red V painted onto its underside.

"V-Boys," cursed Dean.

And it wasn't just the drones that found them.

From the left came a blinding light as a caravan approached. The motorcade slammed their brakes to a screeching halt. They honked their horns and cursed—red-eyed, miserable, and angry, with a beaming Apollo riding a makeshift throne tied onto the back of a pickup driven by Ugly and Dumb. Kristy was at his feet, yelling, "Death to dull Dean!"

From the right marched an angry mob of V-Boys and Khaki Klan—one of them shouting, "There she is!" Most carried crowbars, bats, and chains—weapons of the street—and a few held semi-automatic rifles. They'd brought signs with slogans like "Crimson Is Justice" and "Death to Sympie Anti-Patriots!"

The odds were already stacked. But then, from the sky came a red streak, hovering above them like a scarlet reaper.

Crimson Justice had found them once again.

The walls were closing in, and there wasn't enough runway to freedom.

Tori threw a leg over the bike, and Dean ripped her away from the seat just in time. The Justice Beams destroyed it in a shower of sparks, tossing the wreckage into the burned-out rowhome.

"There is only one escape…" said Crimson Justice. His words were met with rousing cheers from the V-Boy fanatics and jeers from Apollo's Sunnies. "…Death."

"Oh, go shine it out your asshole!" raged Apollo.

Crimson Justice turned his attention to the supe on the makeshift throne. It was an easy boy nailed to a piece of plywood and tied onto the back of a pickup.

"Do not get between Law and Order," threatened Crimson Justice, naming both fists with a shake from each.

Apollo jumped onto the pickup cab and pointed at his floating rival. "You suck."

Tori and Dean exchanged a glance, and an unspoken plan formed. Nobody was watching them. Not the Sunnies, the V-Boys, Khaki Klan, nor their drones, which had pulled away to get better video of the supe showdown.

"I do not suck," growled Crimson Justice.

"Oh, you totally suck," spat Apollo. "You suck azzzz."

"I do not suck ass."

"No, I said you suck azzzz."

"What's the difference?"

"The difference is your mom!"

"Leave my mother out of it," growled Crimson Justice.

"Hey!" shouted Kristy.

"Not now, babe!" growled Apollo.

She pointed. "They're escaping!"

Tori and Dean had already jumped the chain-link fence at the back of the abandoned property when everyone realized they had slipped away. At the corner, a rusty van came to a skidding halt, blocking their path.

"This way!" Tori dashed down a side street of old brick rowhomes—many of which had decayed over time, with collapsed roofs and walls, and weeds that had reclaimed the property. The growl of the angry mob followed close behind, keeping pace.

They sprinted ahead, scaled another fence, and were almost to the end of the empty block when Crimson Justice lowered himself into view straight ahead, hovering ten feet above the street. He placed a hand straight out before him—a cursory ask for compliance—and flashed a wicked smile as the breeze caught his crimson cape. It was a smile made from nightmares.

Dean was afraid. There was no telling what Crimson Justice might do. Would he grab them by the collar and stuff them into a jail cell? Maybe stuff his fists down their throats and rip out their spleens?

A barrage of red-hot bullets smacked into the pavement in glowing streaks, pulverizing the blacktop. The line of fire narrowed around Dean and Tori as they ducked and covered their heads, skidding to a stop in each other's arms. The barrage of gunfire continued until it centralized on its target and smacked Crimson Justice sixty feet backward. When he slammed into a parked car, he was instantly chased by concentrated fire from three separate police helicopters until the car exploded and melted in a bloom of light and heat. The helicopters continued to circle, spilling buckets of rounds into the place where Crimson Justice landed—the pavement beneath him like molten lava.

"Leave at once, citizens!" said Robo-Lad, soaring past them toward the fiery wreckage. "This is no place for the innocent of heart!"

"C'mon!" yelled Dean, snapping Tori out of a trance. He almost had to yank her arm to get her moving as the mob closed in.

"Get her!" someone shouted.

"Death to Crystal Beth!" yelled another.

Being chased made Dean run faster than he ever had in his life, and at the same time, more exhausted. The adrenaline acted like jet fuel, but the tank was half the size. However, no matter where they raced or how fast they ran, the crowd seemed to find them like a blob swallowing the space between them. Even the drones could be heard buzzing overhead, constantly tracking them down. Dean and Tori zigged and zagged, crossed a pedestrian bridge over a massive, but empty, six-lane highway, and forced the crowd into and through the tiny choke point. Still, the mob found them, closing off escape after escape.

At the end of the next intersection was the Wonder City Market—three hundred vendors selling fresh meat, produce, dairy products, bread, and other locally sourced goods, as well as a hundred different food vendors with tastes from all over the globe. It was packed every day from noon till 4 PM with tourists and locals. Dean had visited multiple times, but there was something about entering the dark abandoned building after hours that creeped him out— yet the stitch in his side wouldn't let him run much further.

"In here!" shouted Dean. The outdoor section of the market had never properly shut down due to citywide panic, and they entered through an open vendor door into the dark building, slipping away into the shadows.

They snuck into the third row, then down past a produce stand, where they found cover beneath a bin full of bananas next to the cash registers. It wasn't the best hiding spot, but it was smart, with plenty of exits should the mob find them.

They were both gasping for air, and Dean was feeling his thirty-three years in his lungs. He wasn't a smoker, nor unhealthy, but this was the kind of manic "run for your life" sprinting that even a soldier couldn't maintain.

This was terrifying. This was no longer magic.

"You really need to take that costume off," said Dean between gasps.

"If I wasn't so scared," said Tori, pausing for a gulp of air, "I would've found that flirty."

"Seriously. They're not going to stop until they realize you're not Crystal Beth." Dean peeked over the pile of bananas and spotted shadows moving through the darkness. One of them dragged a metal pipe, screeching like a horror movie monster intimidating its prey.

"Come out, come out, wherever you are!" they sang.

"Boo!" shouted another, laughing like a maniac before doing it again. By the sound, Dean guessed they were about four rows over.

"I think we can slip out behind them," suggested Dean as he turned back to Tori and discovered another lollipop from the vault in her mouth—a red one. "Do you have a blood sugar problem or something?"

"I have a mouth fixation," she mumbled, the candy stick bobbing around.

"A what?"

"It helps me think," she explained. "Besides, I'm hungry."

Dean pointed up at the bin of bananas above them, and Tori shrugged, like she hadn't thought of that. He was smiling—he was being chased by a bunch of psychos and he was *smiling*. His life wasn't all doom and gloom, but there was something happening that made him feel brand new...

But first, they had to escape before the entire market was surrounded.

Dean crept to the aisle as silent as one might expect from an untrained lookout. The coast was clear, not a shadow in sight—a straight shot toward the glowing red exit sign in the distance. He crawled back to Tori and asked, "Are you ready?" just as a metal pipe smashed between them, splattering banana.

"Lookee what we found," said the pipe-guy, dressed in army surplus with a red V patch attached to his chest. He was accompanied by four others, one of them aiming a gun.

The gun-guy said, "It's Crystal Beth and her new boyfriend."

"He's not my boyfriend," replied Tori, and Dean couldn't help but feel stung, even in such dire circumstances.

"I don't care if he's your *girlfriend*," said pipe-guy as others arrived from all sides, some of them painted up like they were going to war in a jungle. "Let's go."

As the men escorted Tori and Dean from the market, they noticed most of the mob were barely V-Boys, like cheap knockoffs dressed in whatever almost-tactical gear they could find. One wore football pads and a hockey mask like he was straight off the set of *Mad Max*; another wore fishing gear with a shirt made of duct tape. Some aimed assault rifles or military grade knives and bear-repellent, as if Dean and Tori were ninjas or human weapons they needed to watch with extreme prejudice.

The men led Dean and Tori into the street, where they were enveloped by the mob. Dean was hoping Apollo might show up—at least Apollo was dumb enough to cause enough chaos to let them escape. Tricking a few hundred people was a different story.

"Kill her!" screamed a toothless woman.

"Make that bitch pay!"

"Burn the Reformist pedos!"

"Stone that Sympie villain bitch!"

It was almost too much for Dean to take.

Dean shouted, "She's not Crystal Beth!" and the butt-end of a rifle battered his guts. He doubled over, the wind knocked clean from his lungs, but that didn't stop him from trying again. "She's not…Crystal…Beth…"

"Leave him alone!" shouted Tori, kneeling next to Dean to check his breathing.

"She sure looks like Crystal Beth to me," said one of the V-Boys who captured them. His southern accent had Dean pondering how far he'd driven to be part of the chaos. These people had their guns loaded and ready to roll a thousand miles in any direction, like killing Reformists was a hobby.

The lollipop was still in her mouth, but Tori's eyes were wide, and Dean swore she looked like she was about to vomit.

"She's cosplaying!" shouted Dean.

"What's a coz play?" asked some dude from the mob. There was a rousing rumble of agreement.

"It's when people dress up, sometimes as supes," explained Dean. "For enjoyment."

"That's a good coz play," said some-dude.

"I thought so too," smiled Dean, still hunched over and holding his ribs.

"Thanks," muttered Tori.

"But why would someone go around dressed up like a *supervillain*?" asked another.

"Yeah," agreed gun-guy, "why would you do that to yourself?"

"Why would anyone willingly dress like a slut," spat toothless-lady.

Somewhere in the back of Dean's head, Rudy groaned, "Oh no."

"What is wrong with you people?" growled Dean. "Calling a woman a slut because of the way she's dressed is as demeaning as me calling you a bunch of dumb fucking rednecks."

There was a pause.

Then someone popped Dean over the head with something hard, and he nearly saw stars.

"Stop!" yelled Tori. She removed the lollipop from her mouth and put her hands up, stepping in front of Dean to protect him. Pipe-guy wound up, ready to throttle her, when Tori halted him with a simple question. "What are Crystal Beth's powers?"

Pipe-guy scowled at her.

Toothless-woman said, "You're Crystal Beth. You tell us."

"None of you know Crystal Beth's powers?" asked Tori, while Dean tried to shoo away the stars that buzzed across his vision.

"I always thought she was as nutty as my Aunt Betty's fruit cake," said a gentleman in a *Crimson Justice 4 President* trucker hat.

"You thought she was crazy," nodded Tori. "Okay, what else?"

The crowd was entranced by her. Mystified. Did Tori have a plan, or was she stalling? Dean's head throbbed, and his vision blurred, and there wasn't much he could do to help her.

"She can fly?" guessed someone nearby.

"Can she though?" replied Tori facetiously.

"She's super strong," said someone else, and Tori nodded along.

"She's really fast."

Tori kept score, holding up three fingers for *crazy, strong,* and *fast.*

"She can breathe fire!"

"Nope," she answered, shaking her head.

"She can teleport?"

"Nope, not a thing," she sang.

"She's super strong."

"Yeah, we got that one," nodded Tori. "Anything else?"

"And she's bulletproof."

"Uh huh," she confirmed, and everyone around them took a cautious step back as Tori added a fourth finger. "All of that is true. Crystal Beth is a serious badass. She's crazy. She's strong. She's fast. And she's bulletproof." Tori spun toward the people behind her a shade faster than expected, and everyone ducked and scurried aside. "You." She pointed toward a guy wearing an "Only Good Reformist is a Dead Reformist" t-shirt, who had a giant knife sheathed into his belt with a buckle the size and shape of Texas—the vendor from Supes-Con.

"Me?" he whimpered.

"Yeah, I remember you," she said. "Give me your knife."

"Nuh uh," said Texas-buckle, but when Tori stepped toward him and held out her hand, he drew it as quick as a six-shooter, handing it to her properly by the blade.

"Thank you." Tori took the blade by the handle and held it up to the crowd like a ringmaster. "Crystal Beth is one heck of a fucking badass! The thing is, I'm not Crystal Beth." Then she took the knife and cut a tiny gash into the outside of her forearm. The cut grew rosy, then streaks of blood rushed free. She held her arm up to the crowd as the blood dribbled down her forearm to her elbow. "See? Crystal Beth is bulletproof, and I was able to cut my arm with that dingbat's knife. I ask you, if I can bleed so easy, how am I Crystal Beth?" Nobody moved. "Would the real Crystal Beth bleed like this?"

"How did you do that?" asked Toothless.

"I did it like any of you," said Tori. "Cut me, cut my friend, and we bleed. We're just human, trying to get home because it's late, and quite frankly it's scary out here tonight. Would you please just let us pass? Let us go home so we can get some sleep and you all can go about doing whatever it is you were planning to do tonight until you found me and thought I was someone else."

It was quiet. The crowd of hundreds said nothing. It looked, in the very least, like they were considering it.

Then pipe-guy said, "Sorry ma'am," before turning to the others. "C'mon now, ya hear? We got the wrong gal."

As the crowd numbed and turned away, a few arguing amongst themselves, someone kicked Dean in the gut with the sharp end of a cowboy boot. "I'm no redneck, no sir-ee," then spat a wad of tobacco juice on the ground beside him.

Once the crowd had moved on, Tori knelt at Dean's side.

"Are you crazy or just stupid?" she asked, cradling his head.

Dean looked at her and grumbled, "Both."

"C'mon," said Tori, helping him stand, "We need to get you cleaned up, again."

Dean was woozy, but he climbed to his feet with her help. "We need to get something for your arm first."

"I'll be okay. Just hungry. I think there's a Supe Burger around the corner. They're always open."

As they walked the street, the last of the mob dissipating behind them, Dean was struck with a thought.

"You know, when I first met you," he admitted, "I thought you might be the real Crystal Beth."

"Sorry to disappoint." She smiled.

"I'm glad," said Dean. "I really, really hate supes."

Tori grinned, and it was quiet between them.

"Have you ever read the Supe Achillean Theory?" he finally asked, breaking the silence.

Tori shook her head as they rounded the corner. The Supe Burger on the next block was open, a shiny beacon in a city of scared, hungry people. "What's that?" she asked.

"It's a scientific principle that states the fallacy of every supe having a weakness," said Dean. "As powerful as they are, as a human they probably had a fear of heights, or maybe a bad knee playing sports. When they became a supe, their entire body fortified the strong healthy things about them but left their one weakness—their Achilles Heel—unaffected. Perhaps, in some cases, it even exacerbated it. Made that one thing their weakest link."

Tori nodded along. "Like the thermal exhaust port on the Death Star."

"You amaze me." She'd made him dizzy all over again. *Did she just talk nerd to him?* "The rest of the theory tries to identify the weakness in everyday people, and how we all have that one thing that brings us to our knees. But it's only when we're invincible that we truly recognize how much we could be hurt by its exploitation."

"I think that's probably true," said Tori. "I have a thing for assholes—and rats."

"And tiny dogs in costume," added Dean with a chuckle.

"Shut up." She laughed. "You know as well as I do, those weren't dogs." They took a few more steps toward the Supe Burger. "What's your weakness?"

"Rudy thinks I have a hero complex."

"So you've said."

"But I know my real weakness." Dean stopped walking. Tori didn't notice, so Dean grabbed her hand before she got too far away and pulled her toward him. "My weakness is that when I think I've found someone worthy of what I have inside me, I give them everything."

Tori's eyes widened. Dean knew his words had impact, but he wasn't sure how deep they struck until he threw caution to the wind, said *fuck it*, then leaned forward. When her eyes started to close, he was sure—and he kissed her.

It was the kind of kiss that was soft, electric—like a paradox—both painful and blissful. His heart thumped so wildly he thought she might hear it. The wounds on the back of his head throbbed, and he knew he was bleeding. He knew he was in serious need of a seat and something cold to drink. But he didn't care. He didn't want this to end.

Eventually Tori pulled away. "We need to get you an ice pack. I think you might be concussed."

"Oh, I'm concussed alright," he slurred.

"Come on, concussion boy," she said. "Let's get a bite while we're at it."

CHAPTER 24

II:25 PM

NEW LOVE WAS LIKE A RIVER AFTER A STORM. THE SURGE OF novelty creating a rush of excitement, washing away the dirt of the past, and in some cases, eroding the foundation of the riverbed. After the deluge, the flow withers, and the calm of the current sets in.

At times, old love was as much about keeping the river flowing as it was about finding new ways to capture the rain after the storm.

All her life, Tori had looked for someone who wanted to stay and catch the rain with her. There were plenty of men, but none of them wanted to fight for her. They had fight, sometimes a lot of fight, but it was aimed at conflict—not her love, not her affection.

She had been fooled too many times. Men who seemed honest were sometimes the most deceptive. At least she knew what she was getting into when the edges were rough and the ambition one-dimensional. She didn't have to guess their priorities.

Dean, however, mystified her. He was a Boy Scout until he wasn't. He had an arsenal of dad jokes until he cut her deep with a sharp sense of humor that made her laugh, even when she was intent on being grouchy. He was kind, non-violent, and stuck his neck out for her—even took on a mob to defend her honor—and he had multiple gashes at the back of his head to prove it. He was good. Decent. Honest. Sincere. Loyal. Trustworthy. Funny. Kind. Brave. And he was everything her past loves weren't.

He seemed too good to be true.

When he kissed her, she wanted it. She didn't realize how much she wanted it until he leaned in, and her lips magnetically found his.

With that kiss, she saw things.

She could see it all, as if he was already a part of her. She saw a lifetime. She witnessed it. A love that did not wilt, catching the rain together. He was the one.

Was she imagining things? Maybe. Probably. Most likely. But…what if?

Was it destiny? How does one know if that feeling in their gut is real, or just the river after the storm? A deluge that inevitably withers…

And by the time they stepped foot into the Supe Burger, she knew what she had to do.

She was in too deep. Her self-loathing resurfaced.

Tori demanded that Dean sit at the booth while she went to the register to order fries and a couple large sodas, as well as a cup of ice and plenty of napkins. The skinny teen at the counter behind sheets of bulletproof glass looked her up and down, then proceeded to fill her order despite his disdain for having to work to midnight in the middle of a riot.

Then Tori slipped away into the restroom to wash the self-inflicted wound on her forearm. It bled worse than it appeared, but was already looking better than it had minutes ago. She had almost left the restroom when she caught a glimpse of herself in the mirror—the hair, the costume, the remnants of face paint. She didn't like what she saw.

She had gotten Dean caught up in her complicated mess. Her life wouldn't be fair to Dean, and when she returned to the register to pay for their order with the remainder of Dean's ten-dollar bill, she thought about all the awful things that poor guy had been through today.

The bank heist. The vault. Chased by a psycho supe. The sewer monsters. The angry mob. Mooks. The Syndicate lair. Crashed sidecar. Chased again by the psycho supe. Chased by two psycho supes and an angry mob. Then bashed over the head by an angry hillbilly.

That was a lot for one day.

She was responsible for all of it. It was time to come clean, even if it meant ruining whatever this was between them.

With a plastic tray of food in hand, she arrived at the booth by the window.

"Scoot over," she said, and Dean complied. She sat next to him on the red vinyl seat, pinched the top of the waxed paper cup filled with ice to create a pack, and began dabbing at the wound on his head with napkins. "Does it hurt?"

Dean was too busy giving her cutesy eyes to notice if it hurt or not.

"I'm okay," he said, though he was having a difficult time remembering what transpired. "Did I get hit on the head again?"

"You did." She placed the icepack against the wound. "Hold this here."

He nodded, but his starry eyes wouldn't leave her. He was drinking her in. Soaking up every detail as if it might be the last chance he had.

"This was a really weird day. But I think it might just be the best day of my life.

Either he had brain damage or—

"You can't mean that." Never mind her own feelings, what Dean just said was ludicrous. He only just met her! She just met him! How could he have feelings? How could either of them have feelings? This wasn't the plan! This wasn't what she intended to do when she woke up that morning.

She was honoring Amanda. Today was for Amanda.

"I do mean that," asserted Dean, as the door to the Supe-Burger opened with a bell chime and three new customers walked over to the register. "Maybe I'm being naïve, but—"

"You are," she argued. He pushed her too far. Now *she had* to say it. She had to come clean. "Dean…" She took a deep breath—this was going to be hard. "You don't know me."

"You're Tori." He smirked.

"I'm serious. You don't know me."

"But I do," said a voice.

Tori froze.

"Little rat likes her late-night cheese. Rats are creatures of habit. They return to the same place over and over. Easy to predict."

When he sat down opposite Tori and Dean, she visibly shook. Her stomach turned. She felt like she had seen a ghost—three ghosts to be exact, as the other two customers gathered around, both dressed head to toe in black.

Dean said, "Who're you?" and the guy in the leather jacket smiled as if Dean had just invited a vampire into his home.

"I'm Tori's fiancé," he said.

Dean side-eyed Tori, and she made no attempt to correct that statement.

One of the guys standing beside the table gestured with his hands, and the other guy laughed.

When Tori peeked at Dean, she could tell that his concussed mind was spinning, piecing together the situation.

"Are you all part of a cosplay team or something?" asked Dean, noting their costumes. He may have been concussed, but he was growing sharper by the minute.

"Fucking hell, Tor," growled the big guy. "Where did you find this shithead?"

"Jordan," she cautioned, her face mustering the most angry glare she could possibly conjure, "leave us the fuck alone."

"Sorry, Tor, can't do that." Jordan held out a hand to Dean. "I'm Jordan."

To Tori's horror, Dean shook it.

She knew if Dean hung around long enough, something bad was going to happen. They had dodged some bullets today—literally—but this was going to be rough. It was the way of her universe. Everyone betrayed her, or they lasted long enough for her to betray them…or worse, they died.

She didn't want any of those things for Dean.

Jordan introduced the others. "That's Grant, and that's Geoff—he's mute and I never know what the fuck he's saying with his hands."

Geoff responded with a sign like he was dipping a finger into a hole, then pointed at Jordan with a smile.

"What do you want?" fumed Tori. The grin on Jordan's face went slack, then vacated his face entirely, exposing a faint scar across his scruffy chin.

"You know what I want," said Jordan. "But right now, I want you to tell this poor dope what you've obviously neglected to tell him, *or I will*."

Jordan meant it. He was going to sit there and watch her tell Dean everything, and there was nothing she could do about it.

She could tell Dean was spinning. The fact that there were more secrets beyond the scope of her entanglement with Jordan, who happened to be a big asshole of a man, made Dean look sick.

"Go on," said Jordan, helping himself to their fries and even snagging one of the sodas.

Tori sighed. "Dean, I haven't been completely honest with you."

"No shit," he muttered, and the boys laughed.

"Seven years ago, I joined a support group for people who had gone through terrible tragedies in their lives," she said, and Dean nodded. "It was a very specific group: the children who survived the Mum Murders, the Grace Falls Seven. The thing about support groups is that when you start baring your soul to people, when you finally let down that guard, sometimes you allow things back in."

The first few meetings of the Grace Falls Seven were relatively lame. There were seven of them: Tori and Amanda, as well as Jordan, Geoff, Cyndi, Grant, and Bert. They sat in a circle sipping coffee and eating donuts—the only enjoyable part for Tori—while everyone shared their thoughts and experiences…everyone except her.

Bert had attended Milton State University there in Grace Falls and received a degree in therapy and social work. He claimed he was inspired by their collective childhood traumas and wanted to find a way to heal their minds.

Bert was goofy, lighthearted, and a little weird. He was very specific about certain things to the point of eccentricity. Some of the odder aspects of Bert's meetings were:

- They could only meet at 7 PM sharp on Wednesdays, lasting for exactly one hour, never a moment longer.
- They were only allowed to have donuts during their meetings, never bagels.
- They could only drink the provided coffee, never water or any other kind of refreshment.
- Everyone had to wear comfy shoes.
- They all had to use hand sanitizer before and after the meeting

To Tori, it was a waste of time. She only attended because Amanda made her—but there was something else that bothered her. Maybe she didn't trust digging up the past, or maybe it was the way Grant put his hands on Amanda like they were rushing toward a hotel room—or maybe it was the way Jordan leered at Tori.

The years had been kind to Jordan. He grew up big and strong and good-looking. It was Rick all over again, and Tori put up her defenses—which included being anti-social with a nasty case of ABF.

It wasn't until the fifth meeting, when Bert pressed Tori to share her thoughts, that anything significant happened.

"Tori," said Bert, catching her mid-coffee-gulp, "why don't you start us off today?"

"Why don't you?" She leaned back in the cold metal chair with her arms crossed.

"I can," said Bert, "but we've all been waiting for you to share *something*."

"I don't want to share my thoughts."

"I get that," noted Bert, running a hand through his bushy hair. "But we experienced something awful together. Unless you're willing to share your thoughts, to help fill in the gaps, we will always have missing pieces stirring up unanswered questions. What happened that night? How did we survive? When we get those answers, we'll all be set free."

There was a collective nod from around the room, even from Amanda, Grant's disgusting palm resting on the inside of her thigh.

"You want to know what happened that night?" snarled Tori.

"We do," agreed Bert.

"You're the only one who knows," added Jordan. "We were locked up. Bert escaped and called the cops. You and Amanda were taken. An hour later, the cops arrived."

Tori knew Amanda didn't remember much. After all those sleepless nights with Amanda volleying questions at Tori into the wee hours of the morning, Amanda would've brought it up. Maybe she had blocked it out of her memory. Maybe her eyes were closed.

But Tori? She knew more than anyone.

"C'mon, Tori," pleaded Bert. "We're all broken, just like you, except we're willing to admit it."

She glared at him as if daring Bert to call her that one more time.

"You're broken, Tori. And it's time to unburden your mind and let yourself be healed."

Broken. Why did they always call her that? She'd heard it so many times.

"Please?" asked Amanda. "I want us to get better. I want this nightmare to end, once and for all."

And that did it. Tori sighed, then relented.

"They took me and Amanda." The audience nodded, willing her to continue. "The killers, *the supes*, there were three of them. They dragged us to the falls. We were screaming for them to leave us alone. They brought us to the observation bridge. Our mothers were already there, on their knees, in front of their leader—the old man—and where his eyes should be, was nothing. Just empty holes."

Cyndi was in tears. Geoff scooted over to take her hand, whispering that everything was okay.

"And then?" nudged Bert.

Tori didn't like being pushed. Especially when digging up memories she'd tried to forget. Repressed memories she was only now remembering, like a secret door inside her mind she could open and close.

"They killed our mothers. Your mothers too. Lined them up, slit their throats, and kicked them off the bridge into the falls. My mother died looking at me." She swallowed. "But I wasn't sad. I was angry. I hated them. I hated them so much.

"I know what the police report said," she continued, staring at the tile pattern on the floor. "It said they were bulletproof. It said they could walk through walls and disappear into shadows. It said that they couldn't even do a proper autopsy because the coroner's tools couldn't break the skin. I have no idea if any of that is true. All I know is that the angrier I got, the more I wanted them dead.

"They were going to kill us," she said, her whole body shaking. "Amanda begged them to let us go, and the old man said something I could never remember, but now, I can hear it perfectly in my head." Tears rolled down her cheeks. *"He said close your eyes child. He who sleeps beneath the waves will need your eyes to wake and wander."*

"What happened then?" mumbled Jordan.

Tori lifted her eyes from the floor. "I killed them."

"I don't understand," said Dean.

"My whole life," explained Tori, "I've had this block in my head, like I

don't even know myself. I've suffered with PTSD and survivor's guilt. I always feel like something's weighing me down, holding me back."

"Yeah, yeah, you're broken, it sucks," groaned Jordan, rolling his eyes. "Finish the story. We've got places to be."

Tori cried for days.

It was the kind of revelation that changed the dynamic of her relationship with Amanda. All their lives, Tori had protected her. But now, it was Amanda's turn to take care of Tori.

Bert, however, had a plan.

"I'm a licensed therapist," he proclaimed at the next meeting. "However, I've also been studying alternative ways to heal the human mind. I tried it once at a party with friends, but it didn't work out the way I intended. There was a lot of pain in them, as I see a lot of pain in you. Out of chaos must come order."

"What are you suggesting?" Amanda leaned forward into the circle from her cold aluminum chair.

"We came here to find answers," said Bert, adjusting his seat. "We got those answers but found new trauma. Trauma that unites us all, despite the years we've spent apart."

"Oh yeah?" said Geoff. "And what's that?"

"The end of all that plagues us," consoled Bert. "Humanity is being threatened by an evil scourge that is infecting our daily lives. Every day, there are more of them. Every day, there are more of us dead." He got up and stood at the center of the circle, like he was about to give an inspirational speech. Only what came from his mouth was as shocking as it was agreeable. They had been through so much, and it was clear where all their problems had originated. "All supes must die. And I know a way to make that happen."

Over the course of the next few months, they met twice a week. Their usual session on Wednesday, and a second meeting on Saturday to plan. As wild as it sounded, Bert made them believe in him. There were jokes that maybe he had slipped something into their coffee to make them believe the absurd. However, they agreed to everything, every step of the way.

"Our past was intertwined by ritual," explained Bert. "A dark ritual orchestrated by the old man. Through similar ritual, we will be set free."

Nobody questioned him. Tori knew something was wrong. She wasn't herself as they plotted. Bert found a way to summon fear and manifest it into motivation. Her conscience never spoke loud enough for her to hear its warning, though it protested, like a whisper beneath a stormy wind.

When that beautiful fall night arrived, the leaves a vast array of color and the full moon filtering through the sparse forest canopy, it was hard to believe they might be on the path to something foul. Their plan was already in motion.

Amanda and Tori led Rick up the path toward the falls. It wasn't hard to convince him to follow them. All they did was giggle a few times and exchange a few silly looks, and Rick forgot all about his fiancée.

At the top of the falls on the observation bridge was a small gathering of people. Bert said it would look like a party, and he didn't disappoint. Their whole group was there, with guests, music, food, and a reddish-brown punch they knew to avoid.

Bert was wearing a red and black checkered blazer and sunglasses, dancing to the music like it was the party of the century. Jordan was dancing with a petite brunette but couldn't take his eyes off Tori—she wondered if his *friend* would notice. Geoff brought his childhood best friend, and Cyndi was getting cozy with another girl. When the time came, a cup full of punch was handed out to every guest.

Amanda said, "If this works, you'll be different. Whatever you've struggled with your entire life will be gone."

Tori knew the ramifications. There was nothing she wanted to hold onto. It would be a relief to be rid of the pain. Bert's promises would reinvent her— make her a brand-new woman.

They drank the punch until the bowl was nearly empty. Once the guests tried it, they couldn't get enough. Before the hour was up, they were drunk.

By the time the clock struck midnight, Bert had taken off his blazer and sunglasses and turned the music down. "Listen up!"

Amanda, Cyndi, and Tori took their places beside Bert, while Jordan, Geoff and Grant flanked them on either side of the bridge.

Jordan's guest, the brunette, whined, "I'm not feeling well."

"Aw, honey," comforted Bert. "It must've been all that punch you drank. You see, within that punch was a very special ingredient. A recipe I learned from an old friend."

It would all be over soon. Amanda reached out and took her hand as Rick smiled. He really thought he was getting them both later that night.

When a kid named Duncan fell to his knees and retched all over the bridge, things went downhill fast. Bert stepped forward and said, "Tonight, you'll be a part of something that changes the world."

He removed an object from his pants, and someone screamed.

Tori couldn't see what frightened them. She didn't care. Her mind swam with warmth and love…

…Maybe Bert had put something into their coffee.

In the screaming chaos, Rick ran. He collided with Grant and Geoff, then split in two—one of version of him was wrestled to the ground while the other bolted into the forest. Bert didn't need to command Tori to go after him. Rick was her guest, and she wasn't about to let him ruin their plans. She chased him through the woods, down the steep rocky slopes, and caught him as he stumbled into a dead end—he had to face Tori or leap into the falls.

"What is this?" cried Rick, buckling over, his stomach roiling with pain.

"The end of all that's wrong with the world," she insisted, but somewhere inside she knew those weren't her own words.

"Why do you want me dead?" he sobbed. "I'm sorry for what I did to you and Amanda." Tori thought his wailing seemed odd. She wasn't trying to harm him; she was trying to save the world.

Something flew past them, soaring over the falls and splashing into the roaring mist below. Tori almost didn't see it. Then another went by in a flash—a body. Duncan, screaming as he fell into the mist.

"Tori," pled Rick, "Please, let me go."

Tori was malfunctioning, her conscience fighting the warm haze. When he recognized the apprehension in her eyes, Rick slipped away and ran.

When he was gone, Tori returned to the observation bridge.

Her mind was burning off the hazy remnants of a thick fog. She was disoriented, confused, embarrassed—but most of all, she felt guilt. Tori had spent all her life running from a dark past, and suddenly, she found herself the demon in someone else's story.

Bert had a knife—a long, hooked blade, and with a single slash, he sent the Rick-copy over the falls. Amanda and the others watched, under the same mind control that prompted Tori to chase down the other Rick. She watched them from afar as they gathered.

"Join us," called Bert, waving her over.

She crept forward, watching the knife like a trinket dangling from the hand of a hypnotist. Her heart pounded as she prepared to grab Amanda's hand and flee into the woods. The closer she came to Bert the more she felt it, like gravity pulling her, dulling her mind.

"Thank you, friends," said Bert. "Thank you for making this happen and setting yourselves free." He was motioning the bloody knife like a conductor's baton, helping to enunciate his words. It was entrancing.

Tori was within five feet when Bert swung the knife and gracefully slashed Geoff's throat. Before Geoff fell to his knees, Bert tossed Cyndi from the bridge and ran his blade through Grant's chest. Jordan smiled as Bert approached, and never ceased even as the blade sank into his belly. Then Bert swung Jordan and Grant from the bridge, after Geoff fell into the abyss while absurdly attempting to put his own spilled blood back into his throat.

When Bert turned to Amanda, Tori's rage went red hot.

"Ladies. Without you, this night wouldn't have been possible." Tori stepped forward, blocking Amanda as Bert's mind-control wormed back in. "Now now, our savior goes last. The ritual won't work any other way."

Tori's lips sharpened into a scowl. She was fighting back, and Bert knew it.

"I guess a tiny scratch won't hurt." He reared back and stabbed Tori in the shoulder. When the blade hit the skin, it shattered, breaking apart like glass. "Wow, you are a special one, aren't you?"

Tori wanted to give Bert a great big "fuck you, fuckwit" but her mouth wouldn't move. Instead, she gave him the finger and smirked.

"You know, evil geniuses often take moments to tell the victims their ultimate plans. The problem is, I'm not evil," said Bert. Tori wanted to hit him but flipping the bird took all the strength she had. "I'm just a man doing what needs to be done to bring peace to this world. A sacrifice of pain from those who wronged you—like your gentleman friend—represents your childhood trauma. It's like telling the old gods what parts of your lives to focus on. Then a sacrifice of many to benefit the one—a transference of your own lives into mine.

"You see," continued Bert, "I found a way to create my own origin story—to make myself a supe. It's what I've always wanted. My fiancée will be quite impressed when I come home tonight as powerful as the gods themselves."

Tori tried to move, to slug him, to maim him with her mind, but nothing happened. Nothing at all. She was weak. She had never amounted to anything, and she'd never live up to the potential within her.

"Oh my," gasped Bert, "I wasn't supposed to tell you everything. I guess I am the villain of this story. Ironically, I'm also the hero of my own."

Then Bert grabbed Amanda and shoved her off the observation bridge.

Like magic, Tori's desperation broke Bert's spell. She dove over the edge after Amanda. As always, if Amanda fell, so did she.

Tori caught Amanda's arms just before the crash. Together at the end.

When Tori opened her eyes, she found herself washed ashore near the Elm Way Bridge, several miles downstream. The sun was high, and Amanda was beside her, coughing water from her lungs.

Jordan was there too, running toward her as she wiped the clay from her face, trudging through the muddy bank. Grant was nearby, fishing Geoff from the river with Cyndi's help.

"What happened?" asked Amanda. "Are we alive?"

There was too much pain and too much coughing for them to be dead. They shouldn't have survived their wounds, let alone the falls. And there was a collective feeling amongst them—they were fundamentally different.

They each described waking from a terrible nightmare while floating downstream—recollecting flashes of the observation deck the night before and a glimpse of horror from somewhere in between...

Then came the awful realization that what had transpired for them the night before had been a whole year for everyone else. Jobs and careers were lost. Personal belongings were gone. Even poor Aunt Susan had passed from grief. They didn't belong to this world. They were remnants of a different time. They were refugees without a home.

One by one, they discovered new abilities. Nobody knew where they came from. An unexpected part of the ritual? Or had Bert planned this all along? Regardless, they had gifts, and they were going to use them.

They made a pact: Find Bert. Kill him. And oppose all supes everywhere.

Calling themselves supervillains seemed preposterous after everything they had been through. The Tin Men uprising had started small, but it was gaining steam—it just needed energy to change the world. It was an abandoned collective—an idea from the Third World War, to stand up to a corrupted philosophy, to oppose the malfeasance of those in power, and protect those who couldn't protect themselves. That group unanimously agreed to become the face of the movement—standing up to Ministry oppression and their twisted fascination with supe power.

The Supies called them anarchists, but their sign—the alchemical symbol for tin—was a symbol of hope, peace, unity, freedom, protection—and when push came to shove, violence. They would wear the symbol proudly, but the movement needed to be larger than them—they needed their own identities to protect themselves as well as the movement.

All they needed was a name.

It was Jordan who came up with their infamous moniker.

As each member of the Dope Gang took a new identity, Tori kept a secret. She didn't feel different—she felt off balance. Like an open door left ajar. What she was capable of and how far she could go depended on her—but she feared who she was. Tori, the little girl who stood up to murderous supes, became the woman afraid of her own shadow. But she played along and adopted a new name. A name that never felt like hers. A name that became infamous. A name she tried to escape even when there was nowhere left to go.

Especially now, without Amanda.

Geoff and Grant finished off the fries while Jordan cradled his head like a pillow and grinned.

"Dean," said Tori, gathering her strength for the punchline. "I am Crystal Beth."

CHAPTER 25

ONE YEAR AGO...

"DEANO," HISSED RUDY, "WHAT'S YOUR PROBLEM?"

They were at the premiere of the newest Stephen King adaptation. Fifteen minutes into the movie, Dean had already checked his phone six times—the light from the screen distracting everyone in the surrounding four rows.

"Nothing," he claimed.

"If you don't tell me what's going on," threatened Rudy under his breath, "I'm going to toss your phone into the first row."

Dean sighed. Moviegoers slung murderous scowls at him from the surrounding five rows—even the older lady beside him, to whom he offered a handful of popcorn.

"Sorry." He shoved his phone into his pocket. "It won't happen again."

And it didn't, at least not until the screen faded black and the credits rolled. The names of the top two leads hadn't even ascended to half-screen when a burst of light distracted Rudy, emanating from the reappearance of Dean's phone.

"Oh, c'mon," growled Rudy as he bolted from his seat.

Dean finally caught up to him at the corner outside the theater. He appeared to be cooling off when Dean asked, "Why are you so angry?"

"What's so important on your phone that you'd ruin the movie for me?"

"Nothing," Dean replied, but Rudy gave him the O.E.Y.I.F. and Dean knew he couldn't lie. "Brie. She posted something cryptic on FriendSpace."

"Which was?" Rudy asked, hand on hip.

Dean was almost too embarrassed to read it, but he reopened his phone and recited the words carefully. "Been thinking about someone. I'll see you in your dreams."

Rudy laughed. "You're a sucker."

"What?"

"You're a sucker, Deano." Dean was too confused to respond, and Rudy didn't give him the chance. "That girl's going to torture you till the day you die. You hang on every word, every post, every scrap of information, and analyze it like a detective, looking for clues."

"That's not entirely true," mumbled Dean.

"Oh, but it is," argued Rudy. "Tell me, Deano, have you checked the comments?"

"There aren't any." He peeked at his phone once more. A single comment had just been posted. "Wait."

"And what does it say?" sang Rudy, as if he could see the future.

"Be seeing you in my dreams too, darling," said Dean. "Posted by Lawrence. He's away on business, apparently."

"And now how do you feel?"

"Disappointed."

"Exactly my point," said Rudy. "You get your hopes up so high, all the time, for a teeny, tiny, microscopic chance that she's talking to you. If she wanted you to know she was thinking of you, she would text—she would call—she would visit. Dean, you gave her the bloody blade she's slowly butchering you with."

"I know." Dean looked down at his feet.

"Then why are you doing this to yourself?"

Dean didn't have an answer. This was his fatal flaw. Even when the truth was staring him right in the face, he ignored it until it became so obvious, so undeniable, that it destroyed him like an avalanche.

"I don't know," said Dean, hanging his head.

"C'mon, you softy," said Rudy, throwing his arm over Dean's shoulder. "Let's go to Hooters."

"What?"

"Yeah, you heard me," said Rudy. "Isn't that what sad straight men do? Leer at hot women in tight clothing? Or no clothing at all? C'mon, Deano, before I change my mind."

NOW...

"Great talk, guys," grinned Jordan, as he leaned forward inside the Supe-Burger booth. "Though, you kind of glossed over the fact you've been fucking me for the last five years, including last night." Tori glared at him as he inspected her left hand. "Where's your ring?" It sounded rhetorical.

Dean's head hurt. His body hurt. His soul and pride were hurting too. He felt betrayed. Looking at Tori was like eying up the last bite of cheesecake after stuffing himself beyond capacity—he could either avoid the pain or take that last bite and live with the consequences.

It was a horrible analogy, but Dean was, after all, concussed.

"So, when I was knocked out at the bank?" asked Dean.

"Oh," laughed Jordan, "That was me. Surprised you're still alive after that."

"And the bank vault?" asked Dean.

"We had a disagreement," admitted Tori. "He hurt you to scare the hostages. I grabbed you and barricaded us inside the vault."

"We're still trying to figure out how you managed that," said Grant, with Geoff nodding along. "Have you been holding out on us?"

Tori shrugged.

"You've been lying to me this whole time?" accused Dean. Rudy was right, he had a faulty picker. Clearly there was something wrong with him. He should've known better. Of all the women he'd dated, this one just happened to be a liar, a murderer, a vicious criminal, and the one thing he hated most—she was a super.

"Well, boys," said Jordan, hopping from the booth. "I think it's time we let them talk it out." He leaned over and whispered into Tori's ear. "You'll always be mine. Until I decide you're not." Then he kissed her on the head and backed away while Geoff and Grant walked to the door. "We'll be in the van out back when you're done."

They left.

There was silence.

"I hate supes," mumbled Dean. How come all the assholes got powers? And guys like Dean were supposed to sit back and take their bullshit? He'd had his goddamn fill. "Do you even feel guilty?"

Tori sat there silently—she let Dean vent before attempting to explain. "Of course I feel guilty," she finally said. "You were just some guy I was stuck with until the danger passed and—"

"*Just some guy you were stuck with?*" He slid away, deeper into the booth. He didn't want to be near her.

"That's not what I meant," she said. "Let me finish."

"Why? So you can lie some more? I almost died for you, and you could've just flown away or walked out of there without a scratch."

"I can't fly," she grumbled, like it was absurd.

"How'd you cut yourself?" he asked, eyeing the gash on her forearm. Tori hid the wound away when Dean attempted to poke at it with his forefinger.

"Never mind how I did it," she said, rolling her eyes. Then she scooted out of the booth and stood, crossing her arms. "I didn't mean to lie to you."

"Are you trying to say that you purposely didn't lie to me?" asked Dean, twisting her words. "Because purposely not lying means you told the truth, and that's not what you did."

Dean scooted out of the booth after her, and they stood face to face. He may have been angry, but she was beautiful—the kind of girl who would've made him forget everything, even Brie. She was the kind of woman who would've brought out the best in him. He would've made her breakfast, bought her favorite flowers, and romanced her with words, with gifts, with affection, with everything he had to give and more—anything to make her smile. He thought she might've been "the one"—as if that wasn't the most foolish, stupidly awful idea ever.

Tori, as it turned out, was just another waste of time. Another waste of effort—and in this case, a waste of blood, sweat, and probably some tears.

She'd become another story—the supe girl who locked herself inside a bank vault with him, etc...etc...a "date" filled with danger and lies.

"What do you want from me?" she asked. "Am I supposed to tell complete strangers my business? Hi! I'm Tori, a.k.a. the notorious Crystal Beth, nice ta meet ya! Say, don't listen to the media, I'm not a fucking psycho!" She finished with a sarcastic uppercut and a cheesy grin.

"Aren't you though?" said Dean. "Just because you're not the person they portray you to be in the media doesn't absolve you from the things you've done."

"What've I done? Do you even know my crimes?"

"I've seen the video. Crystal Beth tearing shit up, laughing, hurting people. Los Dios, Arizona—you killed fifteen innocent people tossing a Killjoy with a bomb."

"I was defending myself!" she shouted. "When you're a target, everyone and their crazy fucking jerkoff uncle wants to take a shot at you—literally! If I wasn't bulletproof, do you know how many times I would've died? For whatever fucking reason, these days everyone has their goddamn cameras out recording, hoping to take the next viral video instead of running for cover. I had no idea they were there, and trust me, I still haven't forgiven myself. I carry that around with me every fucking day! Every. Fucking. Day. I never swung first. I would never—"

"—Never?" interrupted Dean. "You were involved in a bank robbery earlier today that killed a ton of people. I know that for sure. You instigated those riots in Los Dios—I read that in the Gazette. *Supes-Roundup* might be an over-the-top crock of shit, but if you're so honest, why are you palling around with a bunch of violent supervillains anyway? *Who* is the real you? Tori? Or Crystal Beth?"

Her shoulders slumped. "Just because I was with them didn't mean I agreed with their methods," she said. "That's not what I believe in. That's not what we set out to do."

"That's not what you believe in?" he scoffed. "What about the armored car heists? The bank robberies? What *do* you believe in, Tori?" His heart was pleading to her—to give him a reason to forgive, to move on, to forget about the deception. "Tell me what you believe in." His voice was wracked with emotion. He desperately wanted to ignore the bad and see the good—but how was that any different than chasing after Brie for a decade?

Tori took two paces away, then stopped and spun around. Dean wondered why she even cared to explain. What exactly was she fighting for? Wasn't she engaged? Dean was owed an explanation, but he was too wise and experienced to know that just because he deserved one didn't mean he'd get one.

"Does it look like I kept that money? I live in the Dire District, dumbass. It was Ministry PAC money being used to bribe judges. We gave it to the families of those affected by supe violence." As she finished, her anger seemed spent—until she caught Dean shaking his head. "You want to know the real me? You want to know what I believe?"

A pool of frustrated tears collected below Tori's eyes. "Fine." She ran an angry hand through her hair, wiping a strand away that had snuck into her vision. "I grew up a poor orphan girl nobody loved or liked, except Amanda. And honestly, sometimes, I believe she put up with me because nobody else would. And now she's gone. I don't expect you to know what it's like to have nothing, but sometimes you make stupid decisions that aren't in your best interest, because you're trying to protect someone you care about.

"I believe in human rights," she continued. "I believe in truth. I believe that supes are out of control and need to be held responsible, and that sometimes, in extreme situations, you must bend the rules to expose the real crooks. I've been a pawn in someone else's game for so long, but I can't do it anymore. I want to believe in something more than...*this!*" She bitterly gestured to her hair and clothing. "I never wanted to be Crystal Beth. I thought it was a means to an end. It was about payback and fighting for an idea. I did things I'm not proud of, but I'd never hurt innocent people. Believe me or don't believe me, I would never, ever, kill someone. I would never take away someone's mom, or dad, or brother, or sister. Not after what I've been through."

Dean was torn, but he was too hurt to feel anything other than betrayed. "Give me one reason to believe you."

"You're not making this easy." She was backing away from him like a frightened stray.

"Am I supposed to make it easy?" he protested. "You hurt me. I am hurting. You did that." Then he looked down at the tiled floor and gathered his thoughts. "You know, did you even like me? Or was I just a game? Did you use me to make that asshole jealous?"

When he looked up, she was already through the door.

Tori entered the night, exiting the Supe Burger with the same dreadful feeling from that morning. She was thinking of Amanda. She was thinking of the pain inside her. Dean made her forget, if only for a while, but she got too attached. She stood on the drive-thru curb and peeked around the back, where she saw Rusty parked by the dumpsters. She hated that van. She hated Grant and Geoff. She wondered where Cyndi was. And she despised Jordan—love and hate were separated, at times, by the thinnest line, and he'd consistently blurred that line since the day they started dating. She deluded herself into thinking Jordan was only person who'd ever understand her—not because he actually did, but because he had the same life experiences. She now understood that was not, and never would be, the same thing.

She returned his engagement ring with a punch to the jaw. She thought it was mutual—after all, he'd left her a message at the First National Bank.

"It's Over," it said in runny gold spray paint.

And yet, here she was, going back to him…again.

Why'd it have to be Jordan or nothing else?

And why'd she walk out on Dean? Why didn't she fight for what she felt? She was a supe, wasn't she? She could do almost anything except tell Dean how she really felt because she might get hurt by someone honest and good?

She looked up at the sky.

A white streak lit the heavens, flashing from east to west, here to there in a half second before disappearing forever.

"Fucking Amanda." Two shooting stars. Twice in one night. "Why? Why are you making me do this?"

Tori took a deep breath and held it. When she exhaled, she spun on her heel and re-entered the Supe Burger—just in time to see Dean collide with the bulletproof glass by the register.

"You thought you could get away from me?" growled Apollo. "That wasn't very bright."

Dean rolled onto his knees. He was tired of getting beat up, and so very tired of Apollo's puns—the same ones over and over.

"Get some new material," groaned Dean. "Your brain's like a photon."

"What's that supposed to mean?"

"It's traveling light," quipped Dean as he unloaded an uppercut to Apollo's chin that nearly broke his own hand. He buckled over, bracing his wrist. This was it—he was going to die in a Supe Burger—*what a way to go.*

"Tomorrow they're going to open this store and start flipping slices of Dean on the griddle. Nobody will ever know what happened to you."

"Leave him alone!" yelled Tori, bursting through the door.

"Oh!" teased Apollo. "Here comes the *girlfriend*."

Dean wasn't sure which he hated more—Apollo's big asshole grin or him referring to Tori as his girlfriend.

"She's not my girlfriend," said Dean—

—at the exact moment Tori professed, "I'm not his girlfriend."

They looked at each other.

"Friends with benefits, a booty call, I don't care what you are," mocked Apollo. "Let me illuminate you both with a lesson."

"What lesson is that exactly? You keep saying you need to teach me a lesson based on principle, but so far I have no idea what that principle is."

"You know, Dean," said Apollo, stalking toward him, "when you tried to hit on my girl, I let that fade." Tori glanced at Dean, and he shrugged in return. It was true—he had flirted with Kristy before realizing she was Apollo's sidekick—or maybe his agent? Social media manager? *Cheerleader?* "But then you really tried to pop my fuse. You couldn't break my hundo, so you stole it. You tried to give it back, but only after I caught you red-handed, and you kicked me in the bulbs. I cannot in good conscience let that fade. If I did, every jerk and joker would try and screw my bulb too tight. Call me stupid, but—"

BOOM!

Apollo was mid-soliloquy—a self-serving rant nobody wanted to hear—when the roof collapsed right on top of him, like a comet crashing into the center of the dining area. When the dust settled, Crimson Justice stood from a perfect three-point landing.

The Supe Burger staff clamored through the drive-through window, screaming, "Minimum wage ain't worth this shit!"

Tori and Dean may have been on different pages, but they simultaneously ran for the door. Crimson Justice blasted it with the Justice Beams, melting the metal and glass.

"There's no escape from Law and Order," growled Crimson Justice. They ran for the other exit, but Crimson Justice zipped from the center of the room and barred their path in the blink of an eye. "Seriously? I just said there was no escape."

"Fuck off, Bert!" Tori slugged him.

"Tori," consoled Crimson Justice, his voice transformed. Gone was the gravelly growl, replaced with a tone akin to a sitcom lead. "That was the most pathetic punch you've ever thrown."

"Bert?" questioned Dean. "The cult killer? The Charles Manson guy from your story?"

"Cult killer Charles Manson guy?" squeaked Crimson Justice. Tori and Dean retreated as far as they could, their backs to the bulletproof glass. "What kind of bullshit stories are you telling folks?"

"So, you didn't ritually sacrifice those people, brainwash and attempt to murder us?" she accused.

"Oh," he sang. "I did do that, and I did murder you. Not sure how you survived."

"What part are you arguing?" asked Dean.

"I wasn't anything like Charles Manson," Crimson Justice protested, throwing his hands into the air in disgust. "I'm a good guy! …Waitaminute. *Dean?*" His giant jaw dropped open.

When Crimson Justice removed his hood and cowl, Dean had front-row seats to the biggest revelation since the Villains UnMasked special aired last spring, when they unmasked The Dubious Brothers live on television.

This was monumental.

This was something nobody else might ever see.

This was a big load of horseshit.

"Lawrence?" groaned Dean.

"Dean? That *is* you! Hey buddy, long time no see."

"I thought your name was Bert Rose?" questioned Tori.

"Bert is short for Lawrence," explained Crimson Justice—Lawrence—Bert.

"It is?" questioned Dean. "I thought Larry was short for Lawrence."

"That's true," Lawrence agreed, "but so is Bert."

"No, it's not," argued Dean.

"Uh huh," said Lawrence. "My maw-maw used to call me Bert all the time."

"Maybe it's because you look like Ernie's roommate," said Tori, noting the shape of Bert's head and the unibrow.

"Good one," chuckled Dean, and Tori smirked.

"Ha, ha," mocked Lawrence. He lurched and hurled Dean into a corner by the fountain drink station. Then he turned to Tori.

"Wait," she said. "Your full name is Lawrence Rose?"

"Yeah, what of it?"

"Lawrence Rose. Law Red," said Dean from the floor. "Red Law? Crimson Justice?"

"That's so lame!" yelled Tori.

Dean always wanted to find a woman he could communicate with telepathically. Not actual telepathy, like the Reaping Raven, but to find someone he could anticipate and understand with just a look from across a crowded room. The look Tori gave him then was a plea to cast aside their differences. Too bad it was coming from someone who lied to him…but if they were going to survive, they needed each other.

"Wait," Tori stopped to think for the second time. "Lawrence? As in Brie's husband?"

Dean nodded.

"How do you know my wife?" Crimson Justice demanded. His eyes darkened, and his hands bawled into fists.

Dean wondered if Brie was aware of her husband's twisted origins. According to Dean's math—a struggle under normal conditions, let alone concussed—they were together for years before he got his powers. And Crimson Justice had only arrived in Wonder City five years ago.

"I don't know her," said Tori. "But Dean told me *all* about her."

"Oh, did he now?" Lawrence snickered. "Did he tell you he professed his undying love for her at my wedding reception?"

"He did, actually."

Dean took note of the way Tori was inspecting the room. Looking for an escape? A weapon? Anything…

"Funny story," said Lawrence. "I wasn't sure you were going to make a fool of yourself that day till I nudged you in the right direction."

"What?" asked Dean, taking a step toward Lawrence.

That day was biblical to Dean. Everyone had moments in their lives that became the structural pillars of who they'd become. That day summed up his entire existence and defined his sense of self. It was a badge of courage and shame—the day he finally told Brie, even if it was too late.

But this one statement by his rival—his *nemesis?*—put all of that into question.

"One of my secret abilities," explained Lawrence. "I was born with it, and once I learned to control it, oh boy did it come in handy." He smiled at Dean. "I call it the Crimson-Poke."

"That sounds dirty." Tori was still studying the room.

"It can be." Lawrence winked. "I'm no Clooney, so anything that gets me a leg up—or two, if you get my drift."

Dean and Tori glanced at each other, again passing mental notes.

Tori asked, "Are you telling us you can control people's minds?"

Lawrence laughed. "Nah, nothing so intrusive."

Suddenly, Tori stepped toward Dean and took his hand, threading their fingers together.

Dean shook her away immediately—*why'd she do that*?

Tori looked embarrassed.

"You see?" Lawrence snickered. "I can only *make* people do something they *want* to do. It's just a nudge—a poke. However, over time, and with some chemical assistance conveniently added to a caffeinated or alcoholic beverage, it can be a powerful tool for obedience."

"You did it," Tori accused. "You drugged and mind-controlled us, you fucking wankfaced piece of fucking shit!"

Lawrence laughed.

"Did you use it on Brie?" asked Dean.

"What?" Lawrence looked surprised.

"Did you use it on Brie?" Dean demanded. "Did you manipulate her?"

"I've used the Crimson-Poke on her thousands of times," gloated Lawrence, and Dean felt red-hot rage. "Oh, hold on, you mean the mind control. C'mon, Dean, Brie's a supe groupie. She banged me the first night because I had a few minor powers. She was never going to be interested in a normie like you. Hell, we got engaged after I came home with super-flight one evening. Never even asked how I got it. I guess boning at fifteen thousand feet scrambles the brain enough to deter those kinds of questions."

Dean imagined himself clocking Lawrence with a left hook for his disgusting, loathsome behavior—as well as comeuppance for Dean's last five years of pain and suffering.

Instead, it was Tori doing it for him.

She launched forward—a blue lollipop jammed into the corner of her mouth and a plastic wrapper gently floating to the floor behind her—and swung.

The sound was like a thunder crack, and Lawrence's head spun to the right.

Lawrence chuckled. "Now, that's better."

Tori seethed. "You're a fucking scumbag. A real asswipe."

"And you're pathetic."

Lawrence decked her. It was a half-hearted swipe one might use to shoo a fly, but the impact sent Tori up and over Dean and through the bulletproof glass. She landed behind the register and skidded across the greasy floor to the soft-serve machine at the back.

"Wait," said Lawrence, "What's that smell?" He took a big whiff around Dean and laughed. "Hah, all night I thought I was tracking Tori, but it turns out I got a whiff of your girly cologne."

"Better than your cheese-musk," snarled Dean, and a trove of old memories flooded back to him. That was the other reason they couldn't stand Lawrence— he always smelled like the neon arcade "cheeze"—even now.

"But I'm the one fucking Brie," Lawrence taunted. "You know, funny story, bro—Brie and I hooked up for the first time on Halloween, remember? Immediately after my first failed attempt at godhood. You were a total dick that night, so I snagged your girl."

"What?" Dean choked. He recalled the events of that night perfectly, having just recited them to Tori hours ago. He was reminded of the green glow emanating from Brie's window, and the tainted punch…

…the punch!

"Yeah." It was as if Lawrence sensed the moment Dean finally figured it out. "My mentor taught me a thing or two about alchemy. I turned people into actual werewolves, man! Ain't that a howl!" Then he sidestepped Dean and stalked toward Tori.

"You know," said Dean, blocking his path. Both fists clenched and ready. "I always thought you were a tool."

"Bro, what's up with you two?" asked Lawrence, gesturing back and forth between them. Tori was still recovering on the floor and had gotten to one knee. "If you're not banging, what's the deal?"

Dean ignored him. There was nothing he could do to stop his old pal from slaughtering Tori and mopping her remains with Dean's face. It was desperation time and—

"—Hey! What's that?" shouted Dean. His eyes went wide as he pointed over Lawrence's shoulder.

"What?" said Lawrence, turning his head—

—as Dean kicked him square in the nuts.

It was like Dean had dropped a fifty-pound kettlebell onto his foot. The pain rumbled from toes to temples and swelled into every joint.

Lawrence turned back to Dean and smirked. "Balls of steel," he bragged. "I'm not the same idiot I was in college, bro. I don't fall for sophomoric shit."

Dean smiled through the grimace—because he knew something Lawrence didn't.

"You—*bzzt*—are—*bzzt*—under arrest."

A one-armed cyborg, formerly known as Robo-Lad, arrested Lawrence from behind. The gears and servos in its robotic arm and hand whined as it clasped down on Lawrence's neck between cervical vertebrae 2 and 3. Any other creature would've been paralyzed, but Lawrence?

Lawrence wasn't any other creature.

"Give it up, man." Lawrence punched Robo-Lad through the chest. The robot-body broke into pieces, and when the head fell off and rolled away like a tin can, it came to a stop under Tori's right boot.

"Heads up," she warned, a moment before booting Robo-Lad's noggin off Lawrence's own with a loud metal clang, like a ball-peen hammer striking solid metal. Tori dropped the wax paper handle of the eaten lollipop onto the floor, crunched loudly on the candy inside her mouth, then bounded over and struck Lawrence in the gut. The wind that escaped his lungs knocked Dean backward into the grill and toaster, sending an avalanche of bagged buns onto his head.

Each punch sounded like a wrecking ball crashing through solid cement as Crimson Justice and Crystal Beth exchanged blows. At one point, Tori took Lawrence down with a leg sweep, then smashed an elbow to his solar plexus in mid-air, cratering him into the tiled floor. She was on top of him in a flash—

his throat crushed under her knee as she pummeled him with lefts and rights, his head bouncing off the crumbled floor with every shot.

A blink later, she was thrown past the drive-thru window toward the storage closet at the back and embedded into the wall with an audible crack.

"Well, guys," said Lawrence, dusting himself off, "it's been fun catching up, but I have four other members of the Dope Gang to kill tonight."

Tori was crying. "You killed her."

Dean put the pieces together and said, "You killed Hems?"

"I kill a lot of people," admitted Lawrence. "Especially criminals."

Dean took the metal spatula from the grill and flung a frying beef patty at Lawrence. The sizzling wad of grease and meat slapped him across his ugly butt-chin.

"A food fight? Have we really sunk this low?" Lawrence stalked toward him like a slasher savoring the kill. "I didn't want to do this, Dean, but you leave me no choice."

Dean grabbed a mustard bottle and squirted Lawrence in the eye from long distance.

Lawrence carefully wiped the mustard away with the back of his hand and cracked his supe knuckles. "Brie will just have to forgive me—if she ever finds out."

When Lawrence gathered Dean by the t-shirt and lifted him into the air—it all happened in slow motion. Lawrence aimed to punch Dean's head clean off his shoulders, but Dean wouldn't stop squirming long enough for him to line up his fist with Dean's face.

Dean expected his life to flash before his eyes, but he was too busy fighting to notice. He only sought to make this as uncomfortable an experience as possible for Lawrence. After all, Dean was no supe. He was a germ, and Lawrence was the bleach.

Dean's hand grappled with the last thing he touched before being yanked into the air and smashed it into Lawrence's grinning mouth. It wasn't a spatula, a searing hot greasy slab of meat or anything particularly troublesome—not that any of those things would affect Crimson Justice like they would've affected Dean. The item in his hand, the one he stuffed into Lawrence's gritted teeth was a soft, pliable bun. A stale sesame seed bun that broke to pieces the moment it wadded itself into his mouth.

Lawrence dropped Dean and staggered back. "What was that?"

Dean looked down at his hands as if they were magic and found them coated in sesame seeds. He grabbed another sesame seed bun and tossed it in Lawrence's direction. The supe spun away, using his cape to deflect the toss as if Dean had launched a flaming bag of poo, and slammed into the side of a metal counter holding all the fixings—mayo, tomato, lettuce, and rehydrated onions. The whole shelf toppled as he slipped on the condiment-covered floor.

Lawrence staggered and coughed into his gloved fist as Dean removed the toaster tray filled to the brim with browned sesame seeds.

"Easy, bro," warned Lawrence. "Let's not do anything rash." He was scratching his neck as it turned bright red, matching the shade of his costume.

"Funny you should say," replied Dean. "I think I've already done something *rash*."

Then, like a catapult, he slung the tray full of sesame seeds at Lawrence. Each and every seed that struck him erupted into a welt, whether hitting bare skin or not.

Tori removed herself from the wall and limped over to Dean's side while Lawrence started to swell. It was a full body bloat. He looked like a week-old beached whale.

"The sesame seed bagel. The hummus with tahini," recalled Tori. Lawrence's weakness was hidden within the details of Dean's story. She remembered his refusal for anything other than donuts—no bagels—at their group therapy sessions. "He's allergic to them."

Dean nodded as Lawrence reached into his utility belt and retrieved an EpiPen, but his swollen sausage fingers couldn't pop the yellow cap.

"Guys," croaked Lawrence. "Please, guys. Little help here?"

"You were going to kill us," said Dean as Tori drifted away.

"Was not," croaked Lawrence. "C'mon, man, I'm your best friend's husband."

"No, you're not," said Dean, as Lawrence's swollen hand crushed the EpiPen in two.

When Tori returned juggling a twenty-five-pound plastic bag of sesame seeds, she wasn't smiling. She stepped over to the bloated sack of human flesh writhing on the ground—eyes swollen shut, purple lips like a Botox accident gone horribly wrong—then tore the plastic bag open with her teeth and said, "This is for Amanda."

She emptied the whole bag onto Lawrence's inflated head.

The reaction was immediate.

Veins protruded from Lawrence's neck as his body surged into an allergic meltdown with nothing to stop it. His supe histamine production went into overdrive as he quickly inflated to double his size. Lawrence's face disappeared, and his mouth looked like an open sphincter.

"I don't think he's going to stop," warned Tori.

"Aw shit," whispered Dean, simultaneously awed and frightened.

Dean was tired of running. He ached all over, and there was a blister on his right heel. But, as he'd found previously that night, it didn't matter how tired he was or what part of him hurt—once there was something threatening his life, running was as simple as breathing.

There was only one place to escape to before the inevitable. The same place Tori had found the twenty-five-pound bag of Crimson Justice's only weakness.

Together they dashed for the storage closet and slammed the door shut just as Crimson Justice exploded. There was a sound like squealing flatulence, then a pop followed by a gust of foul wind. A series of meaty chunks sprayed the door. Boxes of supplies fell from shelves and burst open on the closet floor, and then everything went still.

Neither of them spoke.

Eventually, Dean found a pull-string attached to a light and clicked it on.

Tori had maneuvered herself into the corner, as far away from him as possible. Her body language reminded Dean of when they first met, locked inside the bank vault earlier that day. With her defiant expression and folded arms, it was like she was protecting herself from him. Unapproachable. Unavailable. Uninterested.

"Why'd you lie to me?" he eventually asked.

"Because." She didn't elaborate.

"If you locked us inside the vault, why didn't you get us out? Where were your powers? One minute you're bleeding and running, and the next you're throwing haymakers with that asshole?" He pointed toward the door.

"I'm not sure." The look on her face said she knew exactly why. Dean felt like a stranger once again.

"Why are you acting like this?" he asked.

"Acting like what?"

"Like someone who doesn't give a shit about me."

"Why do you even care what I give a shit about?" she barked. "You don't like supes! I'm just another one of your stories. One of those *broken* women who hurt you."

Her words were a mirror that made Dean grimace. Was that how others viewed his dating life? She made him sound like a monster.

"Yeah." Dean surrendered. "I guess that's all you are."

Dean walked over to the door and grabbed the handle.

"Where are you going?" she asked.

"Home." He pushed the door aside, smearing bits of Lawrence as it swung along its arc. "You don't need an escort home. It's obvious you can take care of yourself, Crystal Beth."

Then Dean stepped over a chunk of Lawrence by the door and never looked back.

CHAPTER 26

11:50 PM

WHEN TORI LEFT THE SUPE BURGER, SHE FELT LIKE SHE HAD lost something. Her keys, her wallet, her phone, were all left behind at home—but this feeling went deeper.

It felt like she had lost all hope.

She meandered over to the rusty white van parked by the dumpsters and knocked three times on the side door. A second later it slid open, and the three men inside laughed like she was wearing a clown nose on her stupid, funny face.

Were they high?

The van was littered with empty snack bags and soda bottles, with the emergency blanket wadded up in the back next to the toolbox and car jack. The blanket looked like it had been tossed over a secret payload—probably the cash they stole from the heist.

"What took so long?" Jordan's eyes were glassy. He was fist deep in a bag of Doritos while the others hoovered half gallon slushie drinks in radioactive blue and green.

Tori shrugged. "Crimson Justice is dead."

"Fuck off," spat Grant, spraying Geoff with a splatter of green slushie.

"You killed him?" scoffed Jordan, like he'd never heard something so dumb. He always underestimated her. They all did.

Was it so difficult to believe she could've gone toe-to-toe with Crimson Justice? She had before. They were the ones who retreated, who left Tori and Amanda to die.

"No," said Tori. "Not exactly."

"Then who did?" mocked Jordan. "The twerp?"

Dean wasn't a small man, but Jordan was much larger. In fact, every few months Jordan grew. He was already six-foot six-inches but was only six-two when they first met. At his current rate, he'd be over ten feet tall if he died at the average age.

"Actually, yes."

"Wait," said Grant, "are you serious?"

She nodded. They gasped.

Geoff threw his arm around Grant and excitedly shook him. He hooted and hollered—albeit silently—as Grant shouted, "The big red curse is over!"

Jordan, however, looked skeptical. "No way."

"Let's check it out!" Grant beamed and leapt from his seat.

"We don't have time, dumbass," growled Jordan. "We have ten minutes to get to the drop."

Geoff looked like someone had stolen his favorite toy, while Grant moped, stirring his slushie. "Okay, whatever."

"You have the stuff?" asked Jordan, glaring at her. He was suddenly serious. The way Jordan shuttled from one emotion to the next tied her stomach in knots.

"No," she confessed.

"What do you mean, no?" snarled Jordan. Geoff and Grant looked murderous. "You locked yourself inside that fucking vault and didn't take the stuff?"

"No," she said. "I ate it."

"You *ate* it?"

She nodded.

Geoff shot Grant a disgusted look, then performed a series of signs that ended with the word "poop"—a sign they often exchanged for the fun of it.

"Always a fucking bitch." Jordan swiped her by the hair. With his mighty strength, he brought Tori's face to his, dragging her into the van and torquing her neck. "No wonder you and Amanda stuck together all those years. Two catty, broken broads."

Tori batted his hand away and fell to the floor.

Was this the love she deserved? Cold, rough, and cruel? Jordan may have been passionate, but not in a good way.

"What are we gonna do?" asked Grant.

"Take her in," replied Jordan. "They never said nothing about *how* we deliver the package. Let them extract it from her guts."

"Fuck off," spat Tori as she tried to get up from the dirty van floor but was suddenly overtaken by a sluggish warmth spreading from her chest into her arms and legs.

Jordan retrieved something from his pocket and placed it onto the floor beside her. "You forgot something."

Her ring.

She wanted to take it and shove it up his ass, but her mind swam in a pool of warm water. A haze had settled between her eyes.

Geoff hopped into the driver's seat while Jordan closed the sliding door.

"Bro, you got her?" asked Jordan.

Grant said, "Easy peazy," and held out his hand.

"What are you doing?" she asked. "Are you using your powers on me?"

"Sorry, Tor," said Grant. as Rusty's engine started with a gurgling roar. "We've got a payday coming our way."

Grant's powers were sucking away her energy, but she felt something else. The warming pleasure behind the tiresome zap. The pleasure sensations traveled up and down her spine—Moll-Energy—which brought one question to mind. "Where's Cyndi?"

She wanted to run, but her body wouldn't even crawl if she needed to. Once their powers had sunk in, it was hard to pull away.

"Cyndi can't hear you," said Jordan, as Geoff pulled out of the Supe Burger parking lot and hit the gas.

"Why?" Her sight was dimming. "Cyndi, stop…"

"Because," said Grant, as he lifted the emergency blanket—the one that looked suspicious, like it had been thrown over a payload—"she's kind of vacant at the moment."

Cyndi was heaped into the back of the van. Her eyes rolled back, and a streak of blood oozed from the top of her head.

What had they done?

Cyndi's powers projected throughout the van, snaring all four of them in its web, like she had been uncorked. They *were* high, after all—high on Moll-E's ecstasy.

The combined attack made Tori fade into a deep sleep.

"Sweet dreams," Jordan sang, laughing.

It was after midnight when Dean arrived at the doorstep to his apartment. He unlocked the door, stepped over the threshold, then sighed. He dropped the Supe-Burger bag by the door, then began the ritualistic removal of the contents in his pockets. He tossed his keys onto the entry table, followed by his wallet and something else wedged next to a wad of lint. It was a flash drive labeled "ENZYME."

Dean couldn't remember pocketing a flash drive. In fact, it seemed highly unlikely that a flash drive would happen to fall into his pocket, though the thought did cross his mind despite the impossibility—they *were* living in the age of supes...

Did it teleport?

Was telekinesis involved?

Could it phase through solid objects?

What about dark matter and black holes?

Maybe it manifested into existence within his pocket?

Was he the unwitting recipient of stolen information?

Oh shit.

He was the unwitting recipient of stolen information!

Dean tried everything to forget Tori. The idea that she was a cat-burglar, though on brand, frustrated him even more. Add yet another lie on top of the lying heap. He'd spent all day with her, and she'd told more lies than the President.

Well, that wasn't true, but it felt that way.

His mind was so tied up with thoughts of Tori that he never heard the approaching voices from down the hall until the door to his apartment sprung open and bashed him on the head—for fucksake, could people stop bashing him on the head?

From the floor, Dean half-expected to find Apollo standing above him—or even Dust—or, worse still, the spectral zombie remains of Crimson Justice— Bert—Lawrence himself, looming to eat his brains with all his super strength.

None of that came to pass, but someone did dive on top of him.

"Dean, Dean, Lady Machine!" cried Rudy into his chest. "You're alive!"

"Barely." With every sob, Rudy's visor bopped him on the forehead, causing Dean's many head wounds to throb. The floor of his apartment was as unforgiving as the pipe he'd taken to the head, or the vice grip of Crimson Justice strangling him with his own t-shirt.

"C'mon, Rudy," said Arthur. "Let the man up."

Rudy removed himself from Dean and crawled to his feet. Then both men reached down, grabbed an arm, and lifted him.

"What happened to your arm?" asked Dean, noting Arthur's cast.

"What happened to your head?" Arthur gestured to the walking head wound that was Dean's noggin.

"That's a long story," said Dean as he paced further into his apartment. He noticed they'd left the door wide open, which was strange, but it didn't matter. Dean was home, and he was with his friends.

"Why didn't you let us know you were okay?" scolded Rudy.

"Because you had my phone," snapped Dean.

"And whose dumb idea was that?" he roared. "Don't you ever let me do that again." Rudy pulled Dean's phone from his pocket and handed it back to him. "You received quite a few *messages*."

To Rudy and Arthur's surprise, Dean took his phone and tossed it onto the couch. He didn't even look at it. The look on Rudy's face was questioning whether or not this was the real Dean. The real Dean would've immediately checked that phone for one specific messenger—but nothing. Not a glance.

"Deano," said Rudy, "what happened today?"

"Yes, Dean, what did happen tonight?" said a big man in a gray suit entering his apartment. He ducked through the door and placed a charred fedora with a bright yellow feather onto his head. "Or shall I call you Rusty Crank?" It took him only two steps to cross the room, then he held a meaty hand out for Dean to shake. "Memento Maury. We've met."

"Deano," questioned Rudy, "who's Rusty Crank?"

While Dean recounted his day in detail, Rudy put the news on the television, letting it play in the background. Dean prided himself on his storytelling ability, but he was all nerves as he narrated his tale in a mass of disjointed adjectives and verbs. The mob boss of mob bosses was on his couch, drinking all his beer, and the story came out in rambles. Maury's wide frame filled the entire couch, so Rudy and Dean each took an armchair. Arthur, however, was too nervous to sit, grabbing Maury a new beer every five minutes.

Dean glossed over Memento Maury's secret Syndicate lair beneath Mooks, and how they stole the motorcycle from the cavern full of supe tech and weapons. He continued with Apollo and their confrontation on the highway surrounded by Sunnies. When he got to the part about Crimson Justice and their standoff inside the Supe Burger, he only said they got away and finished his tale prematurely. Dean didn't trust Memento Maury, and that kind of information seemed best left on the down-low.

Rudy was quiet, digesting the tale like he had just finished one of Dean's novels. Eventually someone had to speak, and Rudy was usually the first to do so.

"What are you going to do?" he asked.

"About what?"

"*About what*?" shouted Rudy, his face crinkling like something stunk. "About Tori? About Crystal Beth? She's a supe! A supervillain! But based on everything you told us tonight, does she really sound like a villain to you?"

Dean took a moment to compute Rudy's ramble. It made *some* rational sense.

"What am I supposed to do?" he asked.

"Tori's not responsible for your hatred of supes," said Arthur. "That happened a long time ago."

"How can I be with someone who could tear me apart at any moment?"

"How is that any different than Brie?" replied Rudy.

"Brie didn't have powers," added Arthur, "and *she* managed to destroy you, Dean." Maury nodded to Arthur, and he left to retrieve another beer from the fridge.

"Do me a favor," insisted Rudy. "Close your eyes." Dean complied, but not before rolling them with a grunt. "I want you to think of Warrior Princess." Nothing happened. "Now, I want you to think of Brie." Nothing—not a twitch. "And now, think of Tori."

A smile formed. It was slight. It was conflicted. But it was definitely a smile.

"Aha!" shouted Rudy. "A-HA!"

"If you start singing "Take On Me," I'm leaving my own apartment," quipped Dean.

"That's totally unfair," whined Rudy. "You know how much I like my classics."

"Oh, I do," groaned Dean as Arthur accidentally kicked the Supe-Burger bag by the door—when something else caught his attention.

"But not as much as you like Tori," teased Rudy.

"Okay, whatever," said Dean.

"Deano," said Arthur, standing by the front door after retrieving a fresh beer from the kitchen. He had the flash drive in hand. "Where'd you get this?"

"I found it in my pocket," Dean explained. "I think Tori put it there."

"This is my research," said Arthur, bringing the flash drive and the Supe-Burger bag back to the living room with him. Maury took the beer from Arthur's hand, then threw back an enormous swig before clearing his throat.

"That's where I come in," said Maury. He set the fresh beer down next to the other six empties on the coffee table and leaned forward on the couch. It groaned against his weight as he shifted. "Dean, do you know what happened to Amanda Hemmels, a.k.a. Annie Phetamine?"

Dean shook his head. "Tori only told me that she died. I know Crimson Justice killed her. I read it in the papers."

"Amanda worked for me," Maury explained. He removed the fedora from his head and scratched at the thinning hair beneath. "But it's not what you think."

Amanda's alarm went off at 6 AM sharp every morning, playing "The Warrior" by Patty Smyth. It was her favorite song—not because it was a classic, upbeat tune, but because it had meaning. It was their song—hers and her best friend's. They had survived together. Through thick and thin, sickness and in health, they were everything to each other. Every morning when her alarm clock played that song, it was a reminder of their friendship—of all they had gone through, and why every day was a blessing.

By quarter past seven, she peeked into Tori's bedroom. Tori was a chaotic sleeper and was so twisted under her covers that Amanda thought she was fighting demons in her sleep.

"Hey, Tor," said Amanda. Finding the right volume to speak to someone still asleep was an art form. Too low and they'd never hear it—too loud and she was sure to have the nearest object flung at her head. "It's after seven. Are you meeting me downtown later?"

"Uggggggghhhhhhh nnnnnnnhhhnnnn," groaned Tori.

They'd been up late the previous night, drinking and watching the skies for shooting stars. They saw number six—a streaking fiery piece of cosmic rock and ice that lit up the sky for a half second, then disappeared. It was a blink-and-you-miss-it event, and last night's was special.

She needed all the luck she could get.

On her way out, Amanda stopped by the mirror to check her makeup—she looked like a librarian. The glasses. The sweater. The long skirt. She tossed Tori's leather jacket on to break the innocence—today she had to be tough.

It was early autumn—the sun was warm, and there was something she loved about this time of year. Halloween was around the corner, and that meant horror movies! She and Tori would sit around and watch them into the early hours of the night on Halloween. Nothing was too scary, too gory, too campy for their tastes.

They were two peas in a pod.

Amanda smiled thinking about it as she hopped the train for downtown Wonder City.

She arrived at the Wonder City First National Bank with five minutes to spare and grabbed two coffees at the Java Joe's on the corner. There was a sonic boom and a streak of crimson in the sky. Everyone around looked up and cheered—Wonder City's defender was on the prowl, keeping the streets safe—or so they believed.

Amanda wouldn't let that ruin her day—she said "good morning" and provided smiles to everyone she encountered. She said hello to Ed, the bank security guard, and entered with an anxious twist in her gut.

Was today the day?

"Morning!" sang Amanda, walking to the teller booths.

"Morning, sunshine!" said Misty as Amanda handed her a coffee with extra cream. "Oh! Just how I like it. Thanks, darling."

"You're welcome!" said Amanda.

Misty had worked at the bank for twenty-five years and had taken Amanda under her wing. Amanda was still new, having only worked there the last few months, but she had ambitions to move into an office one day. First things first, however…

"Another bright and sunny day in Wonder City," said Misty. "And Crimson Justice is hot on the trail of Memento Maury."

"Really? Does anybody know what Memento Maury looks like?"

"If anybody does, it's Crimson Justice."

"Yeah," agreed Amanda as she opened her drawer and counted money—as she did at the start of every shift. There was catharsis in counting. There was peace in numbers. It helped her relax and to concentrate on anything other than her life, and the double—now triple—nature it had fractured into.

Misty was staring at her.

"What?" asked Amanda.

"Girl, you need a man," sassed Misty.

"Why's that?" Amanda giggled while stifling the urge to roll her eyes. "I have no time for a man. Too much to do and no time for love."

"Mmm hmmm," said Misty. "What about him?"

A gentleman entered the bank—good-looking and wearing a blazer with red suede shoes.

The man approached Misty with a smile. "Good morning. I need access to my safety deposit box, please."

"Identification and deposit box number?" asked Misty.

He slid his identification under the glass. "Doctor Arthur Ravine, box number 42."

Amanda absentmindedly said, "The answer to the meaning of life."

"The universe and everything," added Arthur.

"Do you two know one another?" asked Misty.

Amanda shook her head. "It's from a book."

"Oh, look at you two, something in common," said Misty in a suggestive tone.

"Sorry," said Arthur. "My boyfriend wouldn't approve."

"Oh, I see," noted Misty. Once she finished verifying Arthur's identification, she left the teller booths and waved for the man to follow. "C'mon back. I'll take you to the vault."

Arthur said, "Good day," to Amanda.

"Take care!" She smiled. Once they were gone, Amanda dramatically groaned and said, "Oh darn, untied again," and quickly bent over to re-tie her shoe before the panic set in and the nervous shakes took over.

Today was the day, and she wasn't ready.

Amanda's first opportunity to go to the vault came three hours later. Misty was on break, and a woman in red needed access to her safety deposit box. Amanda grabbed both sets of keys—one to the woman's box plus the key to box number 42.

By the time the woman finished stuffing a wad of cash into her safety box, Amanda had used her gift of speed to open box number 42 and snag its contents. While moving faster than perception—not even the grainy, ten-frames-per-second security cameras could accurately capture her image—Amanda nearly lost her connection to the speed. She double checked the number on the metal box to make sure she was taking the right stuff.

Inside the safety deposit box, she found two lollipops—one blue, one red—and the mystery of her task became even more perplexing.

She pocketed the candy and returned the box before the woman or the security cameras could catch her.

"All done?" asked Amanda, and the woman nodded. Amanda took her deposit box and placed it safely back into its spot along the vault wall, then escorted her to the entrance.

"Do you ever get tired of Supe Burger?" asked Amanda.

Tori could eat a whole cow and not gain a single pound. While Tori scarfed down a Double Supe Burger with cheese and a large order of fries, Amanda was stuck with a Supe-Slim Salad and a side of dressing.

It was a bright, sunny day, and warm enough to sit outside in the sun at the picnic tables. However, Amanda was feeling distressed, like she might be over-exposed. It was probably paranoia after what she had done, but the task weighed heavily on her conscience, making every shifty character that passed their table into a possible spy, or worse.

"Never," said Tori. "Do you ever get tired of your salads?"

"Always," groaned Amanda. Her hands were shaking.

"Are you okay? We can go somewhere else for lunch," suggested Tori. "I'll toss the burger and we can get you something other than fucking rabbit food."

"This is fine." There was something eating at Amanda, and it wasn't the salad. She needed to vent, but where would she even start?

"What's wrong?" Tori asked around a mouthful of burger.

"Have you ever questioned if you're doing the right thing?"

"Sure," she said. "I question my engagement to Jordan every day."

Tori may have said that tongue-in-cheek, but Amanda hated Jordan. She hated his ego, his moral decay, his powers—he behaved like he could get away with anything. In fact, she hated them all, every member of the Dope Gang except Tori. Tori was the one who said they were trouble from the beginning. Tori was the one who thought a life of being labeled a supervillain was a bad idea. Tori was the one who steered them toward activism and away from crime—but these days, it felt like even Tori was slipping further from herself. From the beginning, Tori only went along to protect Amanda. Amanda had a trust problem—she gave it to people who didn't deserve it, from Rick to Grant to Bert and on and on. And now, Tori was losing her ability to avoid the toxic people who had infected their lives.

Just last night, Tori had said she and Jordan were over, and now? She was wearing his ring again…

"I'm not talking about relationships," said Amanda. "Not really. I meant our jobs. Our *other* jobs."

"We've come this far," asserted Tori. "I have to believe we'll figure something out. If we don't fight back against the supe fascists, then who will? We were gifted with abilities to stand up for the little guy. We have a responsibility to do all we can to unmask the corruption."

"Yeah," mumbled Amanda. "But are we doing it the right way?"

"Sometimes you have to go fist for fist," said Tori. "Why?"

She shrugged. "I thought, maybe, there was another angle. Something we haven't tried."

"Sorry, Manda." Tori set her burger down into its cardboard container. "I'm not in the mood for one of your question-capades. We do what we do because we're trying to make a difference."

"The only difference I see is how much this whole thing has changed us,"

Amanda protested. "Geoff and Cyndi are lunatics. Jordan's a rage freak and could go off the deep end at any moment. Grant's not even Grant anymore. That's why I dumped him years ago. We've all become so obsessed with revenge and distracted by power that we've lost sight of why we decided to do what we do.

"I mean," she continued, "I know we decided to cause chaos to bring the supes to us, to lure them into a fair fight on our terms, but we weren't supposed to rob people. We weren't supposed to risk lives and destroy property. Damnit, Tor! I know you and I are careful, but people have still gotten hurt."

"Okay," sang Tori, but it was clear Amanda's argument had rubbed her the wrong way. "What should we be doing?"

"I'm still working on that," admitted Amanda. "But I need you to trust me."

"Are you doing something stupid?" asked Tori.

Amanda bleated.

"Oh shit fudding fuck, you've done something stupid, haven't you?"

"No," she argued. "Well, maybe. I-I-I don't know."

"Fuck," groaned Tori and pushed her burger away. It was a bad sign when Tori lost her appetite. "Why didn't you tell me?"

"Because I knew how you'd react."

"How am I reacting?" asked Tori.

Amanda sighed, then sealed the salad container. "You always tell me you worry how people perceive you. That you put off a vibe that scares people away. That maybe that's why you ended up with Jordan and guys like him. That the good ones pass you by because you're too afraid show them who you are—you slip on a mask and refuse to let people in. Sometimes not even me. When you're masked, I don't even like to be around you."

"When I'm masked?" spat Tori. "At least I'm not weak like you. You come crying to me about everything." Then she crossed her arms and went for the kill. "I'm tired of hearing about your feelings every moment you have a new one."

Amanda took her salad, then stood to walk away.

"What?" sneered Tori, "not going to tell me how that feels?"

"Why bother?" said Amanda. "I'm not the nerdy child who needs your approval anymore. See you at home."

CHAPTER 27

12:15 PM

RUSTY PULLED UP TO THE ABANDONED WAREHOUSE FIFTEEN minutes after midnight. Perc put Rusty in park and cut the engine as Dust prepared for the drop. This was it. This was their payday, and Dust was feeling confident—though the Moll-Energy was certainly providing a buzz.

He never imagined squeezing Moll-E's neck would've turned her into a pleasure vegetable, but as Dust always said, "you're either with me, or you're against me."

They had the research. Though it was inside the belly of a nearly impervious supe, there were always ways to extract it. A laxative or even a diamond sawblade could do the trick. Tori was strong, but she was always second fiddle to Jordan, which was how he liked it.

"You two grab Tori," he demanded.

"What're you gonna do?" asked Oxy. "You're the strong one and you're asking us to drag her all the way to the rendezvous?"

"If this is a trap," said Dust, "I'll have both my hands free to throttle them. With Crimson Justice out of the way, I'm the new alpha in town."

"Good point," said Oxy, rolling his eyes.

Dust had always been arrogant, even before he was blessed with powers. When it came to strength, he was legitimately in the top three—Crimson Justice, Blue Anvil, then Dust. Forget Major Rager and the Russian, the Cossack Kid—Dust beat them both single-handedly. The whole gang was there, but he had landed the final blow. The others were just riding his coattails.

After tonight, Dust was going solo. It was time for him to spread his wings and fly the coop. Maybe he'd keep Tori around as a sidekick.

However, extracting the package by diamond sawblade might change his mind—he wasn't keeping damaged goods. There were hundreds of smoking hot candidates willing to fill the position. He heard good things about Cowgal Jezebelle, and there was nothing like good ole' American pie.

Dust snuck over to the old building and peeked inside for trouble. It was as empty and smelly as it had been earlier in the evening.

"Why are you smiling like that?" asked Oxy. Tori was slung over his shoulder, and Perc already looked ragged after helping drag her to the entrance.

"Nothing," said Dust, unable to wipe his grin away. "Just imagining the future."

They entered the building like elephants, the floorboards whining with every step. Dust wasn't afraid of anything. He had fought all the toughest, scariest supes in the country—from brawlers to gadget wielders to elementals and human weapons. So, when it came to stealth, Dust didn't see the need.

In the corridor ahead, he spotted a light. Two dancing sparkles followed by a drifting shadow. Dust let the rage swell his body to seven feet tall and clenched his fists.

"Y'all big boys," said a female voice. "Y'all know what they say, the bigger y'all are, the harder y'all fall!"

There was a zap and pop, and before Dust knew it, he hit the floor. The whole room spun like a tilt-a-whirl. Perc fell and hit his head, and Oxy crumpled with Tori unconsciously pinning him to the floor.

"We're here to see the Benefactor." Dust had never been so dizzy. He thought he might vomit and felt himself shrinking to normal size for the first time in years.

It was magic. He sucked at fighting magic. Magic was cheap because it didn't take muscle to cast spells, and it annoyed Dust that he could be beaten so easily by something so…*pretty*.

"I know y'are, hun," said a blonde gal in pigtails wearing daisy dukes and cowboy boots.

"You're Cowgal Jezebelle," groaned Dust.

"Indeed, I am, sugah. I'm also the welcome wagon, The Cooler's new head of security and special task force to the President." Then she snapped her fingers, and everything went dark. "Nighty night, y'all."

"When Amanda showed up at my *laundromat,* perhaps I should've taken better precautions," said Memento Maury from Dean's couch.

"You mean Mooks?" contended Dean.

"What's Mooks?" asked Arthur.

"It's a speakeasy," said Maury, "a safe place for the criminal underground to obtain services, seek refuge, and grab a drink. It's been in operation for thirty years, but over the last few we've had a change in service."

"What do you mean?" asked Dean.

"I've been working as an agent of S.O.S.A.D. Force."

"S.O.S.A.D.?" questioned Rudy—his eyebrows at full mast.

"Supe Operations Supply And Demand Force," boasted Maury.

"That does sound forced," quipped Dean.

"So, so sad." Rudy and Dean turned to each other with a subtle glance to gauge their mutual amusement, which then ignited into fits of laughter.

Maury glared at them.

"Sadly, I've never heard of them before." Dean snickered.

"I don't know about you," giggled Rudy, "but that acronym makes me sad."

"So sad!" cracked Dean, and they laughed until they couldn't breathe. Rudy fell from the armchair and Dean started crying—his head throbbing with every joyful sob.

"You two," scorned Arthur, smirking, "have a serious problem."

The more they tried to stop, the harder they laughed.

"What's next?" asked Maury. "Are we gonna spell I-CUP?"

At that, Dean and Rudy ceased laughing and exchanged a befuddled frown. They both spelled it out in their heads, ending with an audible "see-you-pee!" and started cackling all over again.

Maury glared and shook his head at Arthur.

"So immature," said Arthur, suppressing a laugh.

"Are you done?" They weren't anywhere near done, but when Maury leaned forward threateningly and slammed his fist onto Dean's coffee table, busting all four legs, they immediately stopped.

"I'll shut up," said Dean. He added a "sir" for good measure.

Rudy nervously readjusted the visor on his head to appear like he was taking the conversation seriously.

"Good," said Maury. "S.O.S.A.D. Force is responsible for legally supplying supes with weapons, vehicles, and supplies. Eventually, the federal government got greedy and decided to expand the operation. It didn't matter if they were a supe or supervillain. S.O.S.A.D. Force provided them with anything they needed…for a price.

"Being a mobster and part of the criminal underground," continued Maury, "was quickly becoming a failing business model. So, I applied for a license, and S.O.S.A.D. Force was happy to acquire the Syndicate lair as a distribution center. Then, one day, I was visited by an F.B.S.I. agent." Maury glared at them and waited. "What? Nothing funny about the Federal Bureau of Supe Investigation?"

Rudy looked at Dean, then back to Maury and said, "No sir. It is not funny."

Maury pursed his lips, then nodded. "The F.B.S.I. has been investigating the Constitutional Crisis surrounding Supes. You see, it's one thing for a supe to do good of their own accord—to stop a robbery or save someone in trouble. It's another thing for it to be sanctioned by the government, especially when the resulting chaos destroys property, businesses, and lives. And what if a supe decides not to help? Afterall, they're people too," explained Maury. "Have you heard of Penelope Lincoln?"

"The Supreme Court Justice who recently passed?" asked Arthur.

Maury nodded. "She was murdered by supe assassins."

"What? Why?" asked Dean.

"Next month, the Supreme Court will be hearing a case on this very topic. Are government-sanctioned supes and vigilantes unconstitutional? The court had four Ministerium Justices and four Reformist Justices. With Justice Lincoln, it was deadlocked. With President Haines already nominating her replacement, and nearly all the Reformist congressmen and women dead, the nominee will be sworn in within days and stack the court in their favor. Then, the horrific reality of supes will become a nightmare for generations to come."

"How does this all connect with Amanda?" asked Dean.

"Because Amanda was our inside guy," said Maury.

Amanda was unsure what to expect when she entered the laundromat, but she wasn't expecting Mooks. It reminded her of the Cantina from Star Wars, only more depressing.

"What is this place?" asked Amanda as Maury ushered her into a quiet booth at the back.

"Safe refuge," answered Maury. "Did you see a red streak in the sky?"

Amanda shook her head.

"We have to be careful. Crimson Justice doesn't know this place exists, and I'd like to keep it that way."

Amanda was frightened and felt like she was betraying the person she cared for most. Her family was gone, the Dope Gang was falling to pieces, and all she had left was Tori. Their plan to take down Crimson Justice had turned the Dope Gang into angry husks, and Amanda worried it was happening with Tori too.

Amanda loved the idea of being a crime fighter. She loved the idea of dressing up in costume and ridding the world of evil, even if that evil was glorified by endorsements, politicians, and propaganda into making everyone believe it was on the side of creating a better world. What she didn't intend was for it to get so twisted, so dangerous, so utterly insane that she was willing to work with a crime boss to end it before it ended them.

"Am I doing the right thing?" Amanda didn't expect Memento Maury to tell her anything other than his interpretation. However, he surprised her with a thoughtful response.

"Annie," he said. He didn't know her real name. "I spent a lot of years doing unethical things in the name of making money. Then supes came along, and what was once about money became survival." Maury then removed his hat and scratched the thick mop beneath. "You see, I ran a straight business. We never killed nobody. Organized crime was organized for a reason. We don't want to make messes. When things get messy, people get hurt, and we wind up behind bars. Problem was, when supes arrived, we ended up in pine boxes—and that's only when they had enough remains to scoop off the ground and toss into one of those boxes.

"Then, one day, not too long ago," continued Maury, "an F.B.S.I. agent came to me with an offer I couldn't refuse. Instead of fighting the law, we maneuvered to help secure it. Our means are still illegal, but in the name of taking down supes and restoring balance. Nobody deserves to die because supes can't restrain themselves.

"I was tasked," he explained, "to find someone with the ability to smuggle information out of the First National Bank. Someone who could do it undetected. Grab the information from the informant, place it into my hands, and from my hands to the F.B.S.I. I chose you because you have those unique abilities. You're going to be a hero, Ms. Phetamine."

Amanda reached into her purse and placed the contents of the security box onto the table.

"What's this?" asked Maury.

"This is what was in lockbox 42."

When Amanda left Mooks through the front door of the laundromat, she never saw the crimson streak across the sky.

The warehouse wasn't a palace, but it was theirs. Six of them, living under the same roof, made for tight living conditions, but the abandoned partly finished luxury apartments were the kind of place they could live under the radar. There were discarded supplies in the halls and across the property— piping, rebar, and mounds of dirt beside bulldozers and dump trucks that had been parked and left behind when the funding was pulled. The industrial lighting, open walls, and ducts gave the place a hipster vibe.

Jordan called it a dump, but Amanda called it home.

When Amanda entered their apartment after a long day at the bank and her secret visit to Mooks, she immediately removed her shoes by the front door. The place was empty, and she loved it when nobody else was home. She could play music and dance while washing a full sink of dishes or making supper.

She loaded a playlist on her phone and let the music bleed through the Bluetooth speakers. In twenty minutes, she finished the dishes, swept the floor, and tossed a few cartons of old Chinese food spoiling on the counter, then disinfected everything before she felt the growl of hunger.

She'd never finished her salad at lunch—she was too upset—and was suddenly dying for a bite.

After searching the fridge and pantry, Amanda weighed her limited options and pondered ordering takeout, but decided on preparing macaroni and cheese from a box. She placed a pot on the stove, set it to boil, and had just opened the box when her phone chimed. "Hello?"

"Hey." Tori's voice blasted over the Bluetooth speakers. "Are you home? Can we talk?"

"Yeah," said Amanda. "I'm making dinner. Your favorite."

"Ugh. Mac and cheese, again?"

"I'll add some hot sauce," she said.

"Ooh, give it some bite, baby."

Amanda laughed. "Mama knows what gets you hot," she teased.

"Who are you talking to?" growled Jordan from the other end of the line. He didn't sound pleasant—though Amanda couldn't remember the last time he was pleasant.

"Manda," groaned Tori to Jordan. "Leave me alone, okay?"

"Maybe you should marry her instead," he snapped. "You two deserve each other."

"Are you guys fighting again?" It seemed like a constant. He and Tori fought every day, and she wondered how often Jordan got physical with her best friend—his rage frequently got the better of him.

"Same old, same old," grumbled Tori. "I'm outside. Be right up." There was a tone, like Tori hit the wrong button to disconnect, and she grumbled about how much she hated her "shitty phone" when there was a loud bang at the door.

"That was fast," said Amanda as she dumped the dry macaroni into the boiling pot.

"What?" said Tori over the Bluetooth speakers, realizing her phone was still connected.

"I said, that was fast. Need me to get the door?"

"I'm still outside," answered Tori.

Amanda had seen this moment a thousand times in horror movies—the rising dread that the person outside the door was the monster they had tried so hard to avoid.

Amanda stopped cold. Shadowy feet shifted beneath the door, followed by a hiss and a crack as her body shifted into high gear. When the front door splintered and blew off its hinges, Amanda's speed allowed her to dodge most of the debris, but not all. What initially felt like a small nick at her side turned into a real gusher when she slowed down to look.

Through the dust came a red-hooded figure, stalking into her home…and smiling. "When Law and Order comes knocking at your door, answer it," said Crimson Justice.

Amanda darted to the kitchen and returned with a knife in under a quarter-second, but the metal snapped at the handle when she arrived. The Justice Beams broke the blade and punched a hole through the wall behind the sink, missing her by inches. She threw the handle and three washed dishes, then made a run for the door.

The handle smacked Crimson Justice on the chin, and each plate collided with him from various angles, slowing his reaction to her speed. When she got to the open doorway, she was only a single stride from escaping—just three feet and she was gone. Three feet and she could race away, and join the others—safety in numbers—when something smashed her in the back so hard it propelled her off her feet…

…and into Tori's arms.

Pain shot up and down her back, followed by a numbness that spelled trouble. It was the kind of resolute numbness that quickly invaded her entire body, an urgency that swiftly dissolved into a warm embrace. She only had time to look up at Tori and say, "Love you," before she died.

"I never saw nothing like it," confessed Maury. "Crystal Beth took Crimson Justice on, mano a mano, and lasted fifteen minutes before the police arrived. Eventually, Crimson Justice flew off, having murdered two members of the Dope Gang."

"Two?" questioned Dean.

"That's the miraculous thing," said Maury. "When they found Crystal Beth inside the rubble, she was all but dead. Beaten to mush, broken—she should've died. She had organ failure, massive head trauma, and nearly every bone was broken or shattered. Two hours later, she woke up in a hospital bed."

"How do you know?" asked Dean.

"I was there, kid. I saw the whole thing."

When Tori opened her eyes, she awoke from a dream of another place. She was happy there, at least for a time. But as the seconds passed, she forgot all about her dream and began to remember…*everything.*

Every part of her burned like it was on fire. With a quick tug, she snapped the handcuffs on both wrists tethering her to the hospital bed and sat up. An alarm went off, and it was so loud, Tori thought her head might explode. She was shivering, and with each sensor she ripped from her body, a machine started to wail, adding to the noise. Doctors flailed around in the next room, rushing to observe her through the reinforced glass windows, and a nurse burst in covered from head to toe in a hazmat suit.

"I know you're scared, but you need to calm down," said the nurse.

"Where's Amanda?" she demanded.

The nurse looked at her blankly.

Tori felt like she was having a nervous breakdown. "Where's Amanda?" she asked again. Then Tori corrected herself. "Where's Annie Phetamine?"

"Oh," said the nurse.

"She's dead." An old man entered the room wearing a police officer's uniform, but with way too many badges and pins to be a beat cop. He waved off the nurse, who quickly left the room.

"Dead?" A lump formed in Tori's throat, and her eyes stung with tears.

"She died," he repeated, his mustache tremoring as he delivered the news. "Do you remember what happened?"

Tori shook her head. "Some of it."

"Crystal Beth—"

"That's not my name."

"What is your name, dear?" he asked.

"You can call me Tori."

"Tori." He nodded. "I'm Commissioner Dudley. You've been through a lot tonight. Two hours ago, you were rushed into emergency surgery. You had catastrophic organ failure, and there were parts of your body where the bones had been pulverized. The doctor's attempts to save you failed when they realized they couldn't pierce your skin. They found an open artery and gave you a sedative to ease your passing.

"Only," he continued, "you didn't pass. The nurses watched as your body miraculously put itself back together, bit by bit. I imagine you must be experiencing terrible shock."

"You have no idea." Tori wanted to scream. She wanted to rage.

"You're right, I don't have any idea."

"Are you arresting me? I'd like to see you try."

"I'm not arresting you, dear," said the commissioner, and there was something about the way he spoke that triggered memories of her father.

Tori looked around and caught the eyes of a big shadowy man standing in the hallway, watching through the window. There were others, too. She felt like a science experiment, a slide under a microscope.

"Then what are you doing here?" she asked.

"We need your help," he explained. "Were you aware that Annie Phetamine was working for the F.B.S.I.?"

"Amanda," said Tori. "Her name was Amanda, and no. I mean, yes. I mean, kinda. I knew something was up, but I didn't know what exactly."

Tears sprang from Tori's eyes. This was her nightmare—losing Amanda. It had been just the two of them since forever, and the idea that she would have to spend that moment forward without Amanda was as terrible as the end of the world. It was her own personal apocalypse.

"Tori," said Commissioner Dudley, "can I trust you?"

"Your mistake to make," she said, shaking her head.

The commissioner interpreted that as a yes and continued. "I believe, and the people I work with believe, that Crimson Justice is a menace. They believe that supes and their abilities should be neutralized. We've been working with an individual who has put his own life and career on the line to smuggle research that could make that a reality."

Tori waited for more information. When none came, she asked, "What does that have to do with me?"

"Amanda, with her gifts, was helping us accomplish this by extracting useful information from this individual through her employment at the First National Bank." The commissioner stepped toward the bed, unafraid. "Would you help us finish what Amanda started?"

"What you're saying is that Tori has been working for you?" asked Dean.

"And the commissioner, the F.B.S.I., and S.O.S.A.D. Force, yes," listed Maury.

"And I was the mole," admitted Arthur.

"All that just to take down Crimson Justice?" asked Dean.

"Yes," said Maury. "And those like him."

"Well, I don't think that'll be a problem," said Dean as he stood up to exorcise the nervous energy. Maury finished his beer and spotted the Supe Burger bag on the floor by Arthur's feet. He snatched it up and rummaged about inside like he was looking for a double-patty snack.

"Dean," said Rudy politely, "are you experiencing hallucinations? You've been struck on the head quite a few times tonight. We're talking about taking down Crimson Justice, the most powerful being on the planet."

"What is this?" Maury dug deeper inside the bag. "There's no food in here."

"That's interesting…" said Arthur, as he paced over to assist Maury in removing the contents of the bag. When the golden scales logo appeared, it was time to tell the truth.

"Deano," asked Rudy, looking from the scales to his best friend and back again. "Are you telling us that…"

"…Yes," admitted Dean, his shoulders slinking to his sides.

"You're Crimson Justice!?" he shouted.

"What?" scoffed Dean as Arthur took a step backward. "No! Crimson Justice is dead."

"What do you mean, he's dead?" asked Maury.

"I killed him," Dean confessed.

Rudy laughed a big, full-throated belly laugh that sounded awfully fake. "Oh Dean, such a kidder."

"I'm not kidding." He shook his head and sighed. "I may have omitted a few details from my story."

"Why?" growled Rudy. Arthur wore his own puzzled expression.

"Because I didn't know if I could trust a mobster," he said, gesturing to Maury. Dean paced the room. "Crimson Justice confronted Tori and I at the Supe Burger down by the Wonder City Market. Crimson Justice is—*was*—Lawrence Rose."

"Why do I know that name?" asked Rudy.

"Brie's husband," explained Dean. "Lawrence and Brie Rose. He was allergic to sesame seeds. I stuffed some buns into his mouth and he had an allergic reaction."

"You did *what*?" blurted Rudy. "Oh, you mean hamburger buns. You did *what*!?"

"You're not joking, are you?" asked Arthur.

Dean shook his head.

"You actually killed the big red asshole?" asked Maury.

"Yeah," said Dean. "He blew up. There was nothing left, so I grabbed the evidence and ran."

The television flashed, and a "Breaking News" report started playing on screen. Dean grabbed the remote control and turned the volume up.

"This Breaking News Report is brought to you by Supe Burger, home of the Supe-Sized All-Beef Patty on a sesame seed bun," said the news anchor.

"Oh no," anticipated Arthur.

Dean silently read the bold headline displayed on screen before the anchor's words began to form meaning in his head. "DOPE GANG ARRESTED BY MINISTERIUM GUARD. MANHUNT CONTINUES FOR UNKNOWN CO-CONSPIRATOR."

Security footage was introduced, along with a disclaimer that the F.B.S.I. were looking for "this unknown man." It was video of Dean and Tori leaving the bank vault together, hand in hand, as Apollo stalked the halls after them. It paused when Dean looked up at the camera and zoomed in on his blurry, grainy face.

"Ohhhh," groaned Rudy, his nose and eyebrows scrunched up into his I-Smell-Dirty-Booty-Face. "Oh, Deano. That picture is not flattering, like at all."

12:45 AM

"My fellow Americans," said President Haines into the microphone, his eyes glistening like glass. "This evening's unrest in Wonder City has become a flashpoint for the growing divide in this country." He was speaking from the East Room with an American flag behind him displaying all eighty-two stars.

Cameras flashed periodically, but the president kept speaking, reading from his teleprompter. "I promised earlier today that I would not sleep until those responsible for today's unrest were brought to justice. I am happy to announce that with the help of the great V-Boy militias and their second amendment rights—not the Wonder City Police Department—we were able to flush out the Dope Gang and take all five of them into custody, as well as those responsible for today's false flag operation implicating Crimson Justice in the death of three dozen crisis actors." He held up a shaky, aging fist to the camera, as if to illustrate strength. "While our country has been shaken by today's events, our resolve to crush our opposition has not. Some say the words I use are un-presidential, but I insist, that only the toughest words backed by the most stringent force, can *be* presidential. When our enemies punch, we must not punch back. We must pull the trigger and rid the world of their deviancy, for only true patriots shall inherit this great land.

"With that in mind, I am asking for peace tonight on the streets of Wonder City. To all the terrorist Tin Men with your weapons and your belligerent ideals, go home. Go home and wallow in shame that you have failed, your purpose has failed, and that you are nothing but a bunch of losers.

"To all the V-boys who came from far and wide and stood up to the terrorist Tin Men—thank you, and please return home. Put away the tools of freedom, but reload. Peace can only be achieved through firepower. Bless all of you, true patriots."

Haines didn't blink, not once throughout his speech. His eyes seemed wrong, but most viewers couldn't articulate why.

"Tomorrow, I will be traveling to Wonder City to enact swift justice by sentencing The Dope Gang to life imprisonment within the state-of-the-art Supe-Max prison, The Cooler. They will be frozen and spend the remainder of their days injected with a nightmare-inducing serum, sleeping until death. I urge all Americans to tune in tomorrow at 8 PM, prime time, must-see-tv, to witness the urgency of true justice. Witness the end of the Dope Gang's reign of terror. Witness the execution...*ahem*, I mean, the sentencing on live TV. It'll be huge and unlike anything you've ever seen before. I promise.

"At this moment, I urge all Americans to decide what is best for their future. Shall you be true patriots? Or shall you become an enemy of democracy? Will you stand up and fight for law and order? Or shall you oppose the Ministry?

"From this day forward, the president will have a new title. Those elected to this office will receive the title of caliph, a title bestowed upon only the greatest rulers of the greatest civilizations that ever existed. The title of president has become synonymous with weakness. But where there was once weakness, there shall now be resolute strength.

"I am Caliph Haines of these United American States, and blessed are the righteous patriots of this land, from sea to shining sea. Good night."

CHAPTER 28

12:50 AM

"GOOD MORNING," SAID THE NEWS ANCHOR. "I'M PHILLIP Phillips, and welcome to *The AM Buzz*." He was a handsome man, mid-fifties, with salt-and-pepper hair and steely blue eyes. He was the kind of man that fifty percent of the population could trust. The other fifty percent swore he was the devil.

"Tonight's breaking news: the notorious Dope Gang has been apprehended by the newly formed Ministerium Guard and have been escorted to the state-of-the-art supe detention center known as The Cooler, created by the geniuses at Amycus Labs." The broadcast cut to live footage of Dust, Oxy, Perc, and an unconscious Moll-E surrounded by masked soldiers with high-tech weaponry. At the back was Crystal Beth, prodded along by the barrel of a gun. She gazed directly into the camera—her face, sad and stoic, a far cry from the typical media depiction of her and the Dope Gang as raving lunatics.

"Their charges? Attempted robbery, burglary, aggravated assault, and more than forty counts of first-degree murder, in addition to conspiracy and sedition." Phillip Phillips shuffled his papers as the camera shifted, superimposing a new image on screen. "More breaking news: a search is underway for this man—his identity unknown." The blurry image on screen depicted a man in a black t-shirt with a large U and M on his chest. He had a scruffy beard and dark hair—with very little to identify him from the unfocused photo. "The Unknown Man, as dubbed by online Chatter users because of the logo on his chest, is suspected to have helped the Dope Gang rob the Wonder City First National Bank and take thirty-six innocent lives."

The broadcast immediately cut to Commissioner Dudley, surrounded by Ministerium Guard watching his every move. "I maintain that Crimson Justice should be held accountable, in part, for those deaths, and I will be working with the district attorney to make sure those charges stick."

"Sir!" shouted a reporter, shoving a microphone into Dudley's chin. "There are reports that the Dope Gang had assistance from an unknown man caught on security footage. Do you have any reason to believe this Unknown Man is a person of interest?"

"No comment," said the commissioner.

Phillip Phillips returned on screen. "For more on this story, we go to Robin Robinson, our intrepid beat reporter, live on the scene."

"Thank you, Phillip," said Robin, a plucky blonde braving the city streets amidst the riot that had finally ceased after the President's speech. "I'm here with Apollo, Wonder City's newest defender, having only recently won his Supe-License with the conclusion of this season's *American Supe* final. Apollo, what's it like out there on the streets this evening?"

"Robin," said Apollo, his glow nonexistent, "I have to say it's a real dimmer. I came to Wonder City expecting a bright welcome. I attended Supes-Con this morning, but everything burned out from there. I'm not sure Wonder City is the place for me."

"What happened today?"

"Well, Robin," he moaned, "my Sunnies and I were accosted earlier this evening."

"Your Sunnies?"

"Yes, Robin. "My Sunnies—my fans, my groupies, whatever you want to call them. We were accosted by Crimson Justice and a foul-mouthed little prick named Dean who stole my hundo."

Robin appeared as if she were acquiring a migraine. "Why did Crimson Justice accost you?"

"I don't know, Robin," he whined. "Maybe he's jealous of my shine? He wears a mask, and I don't, which says it all."

"Says what exactly?"

"Are you even listening, Robin?" Apollo snatched the microphone from her hand. "There's a real dark menace out there, and his name is Dean. He's a writer, and…and…" Then the epiphany hit, and Apollo began to shimmer. "…and I think I just discovered my first nemesis." He reached out and grabbed the camera, aiming it directly onto his face. "People of Wonder City, your newest protector will save you from people like dimwit Dean. Dean represents everything I shine against, and I will stop at nothing to make sure he burns for stealing my money. And another thing—"

"Excuse me," said someone off screen. "Apollo?"

"Yeah?" he growled, turning toward the voice. "Who wants to know?"

"My oh my," said Cowgal Jezebelle, "I have been waitin' fer this moment. Y'all under arrest."

"Me?" laughed Apollo. "What for?"

"Criminal trespass," started Cowgal. "First-degree assault, failure to openly display your Supe-License, and obstruction of justice—that is, obstruction of Crimson Justice, ya hear?" She stepped into the shot, flanked by men—or robots, maybe something in between—wearing white masks.

"Like hell I am!" spat Apollo. "I'm not scared of you. I kicked your skanky ass all over the American Supe Arena—oh! Ow! Ow! My bulbs! Let go of my bulbs you b—"

As a scuffle broke out, the camera spun through the air, and a long string of verbal obscenities made it onto the live broadcast before cutting away to Phillip Phillips in the studio.

"Thank you, Robin, and we apologize for the salty language," said Phillip Phillips, a rosy hue rising in his cheeks. "Next up, weather with Stormy Stevens…"

Dean paced his apartment so vigorously that Rudy thought he might hurt himself. Over the course of their friendship, he had never witnessed Dean so worked up over anything. He was mumbling, sweaty, and pale—on the verge of a breakdown. The poor guy had been through the wringer and taken enough dings to the noggin to put most normies down for the day. Make no mistake, Dean wasn't a supe, but when he cared about something, he exhibited super-human anxiety.

"Dean," Rudy began. "Why don't you come sit down. I can make sliders and we can talk this out."

He didn't stop pacing. It was almost as if he didn't hear Rudy. Dean never turned down a chance to savor Rudy's sliders.

"Is the kid always like this?" asked Maury.

"He has his triggers," said Arthur, adjusting his glasses.

"How long is this going to last?" Maury checked the tiny watch attached to his massive wrist.

"Well, it helps to try and understand what he's thinking," explained Rudy. "Sometimes we can jog him out of it." Rudy stood beside the path Dean was wearing into the rug. "For example, Dean is probably ruminating over how he killed Crimson Justice, who happened to be married to Brie, the love of his life."

"Fuck," groaned Dean—his mumbles clarifying on cue. "I totally killed Brie's husband. I killed Lawrence."

"And he's probably wondering whether or not he's still concussed," said Rudy.

"Shit, my head hurts," grumbled Dean. "How do I even know I'm thinking straight?"

"And I'm sure there's a teensy, eensy, tiny little bit of him freaking out over being a potential suspect in the First National Bank robbery."

"I could go to jail, and I didn't even do anything."

"That's a good trick," said Maury.

Rudy held up a cautionary finger, as if to say, "hold my hard seltzer."

"But what he's really struggling with," said Rudy, "the thing that's *really* digging into him, is that he doesn't know what to think or feel about Tori, and the fact that she's been caught and about to be stuffed into The Cooler."

"Damnit, Rudy!" shouted Dean. "What am I going to do about Tori? Everyone's going to believe she murdered all those people."

"Deano," said Arthur, "People are going to believe what they want to believe. You could show them a smoking gun and they'd still only see it in their preferred Tint."

"But what am I going to do?"

"What do you want to do?" asked Arthur.

"I don't know," said Dean, still pacing.

"What *are* you struggling with?" prodded Rudy. "I only know one woman who's ever gotten you this worked up. She left you three messages today and you still haven't even glanced at them."

"But Tori's a supe," said Dean. "A supervillain, of all things!"

"Hey!" groaned Maury, "Easy on the moral dichotomy, lover-boy."

"But Dean," argued Rudy, "according to your story, it sounds like gal-friend hates supes too! She may not wear a Tin Men pin secretly stashed onto her collar like you—but she's been actively operating as part of said Tin Men. The anti-fascist, anti-commie, anti-*all-the-evil-stuff* Tin Men that *even you* believe in. You said she wore the symbol on her t-shirt, right?"

"Are we really weighing her morality on a freaking t-shirt?" asked Dean.

"*UMMMMM*, I don't know, *Unknown Man*," sassed Rudy, over-pronouncing the UM. "Can a t-shirt really illustrate someone's personality? Or maybe their taste for bad puns?"

Dean looked down and saw the words "Element of Confusion" on his chest.

"Dean," said Arthur, "sometimes people lie to protect the people they love." It was obvious Arthur was speaking of his own untruths. "Nobody likes to put their faults on display. The poor girl was an orphan, and based on the story she told you, she's used to being abandoned and betrayed. So she's a supervillain. That doesn't mean she's any less worthy of love."

Rudy placed a loving arm around Arthur. He may have hidden secret things from his partner, but even Rudy realized he had good intentions.

"Deano," said Rudy, "that girl is alone right now facing life in The Cooler. There's not a lonelier place in all the world. You've found a reason to ditch almost every crazy girl you've ever dated but stuck to the one who couldn't be bothered to love you, let alone see you for the honest, loving gentleman you are. You're a good man. You and Arthur are the two best men I've ever met. You spent a day with Tori and you're pacing like a madman in your own living room. Nobody's perfect, but I believe this gal, with her one extraordinary fault, might just be the most perfect gal for you."

Dean took a deep breath and closed his eyes. When he opened them, he appeared as sharp and resolute as ever.

"So, what do I do?" asked Dean. "How do I get her out of there?"

"*You're* not doing anything," said Rudy. "*We* are going to do something."

"We are?" stammered Arthur.

"I'm not sure how that's even possible," said Maury. "You want to bust into a Supe-Max Prison, fight off Ministerium Guards, grab the girl and make a clean escape? To where? How? It's not like you guys are supes with any kind of serious power."

Rudy felt nervous for a variety of reasons. First and foremost, he hadn't thoroughly thought his role in this escapade all the way through. Second, the violence. He preferred his action on the television from the comfort of his own couch, watching hot actors brandishing futuristic weapons and fighting off bad guys and monsters. He wasn't particularly happy to be in the middle of it, in person, with the people he loved…

…but he couldn't let Dean do this alone.

"But *you* do," said Dean, grinning at Maury. "You have a whole network of supes and vigilantes. You have a whole cavern full of weapons and tech."

"Kid," groaned Maury, "you want to take on the Ministerium Guard? They ain't the Secret Service. Hell, they ain't even Green Berets. They're cyborgs—half man, half machine!"

"Dean," said Arthur, "even if we all had supe powers, even if I could get us inside The Cooler, how far could we get before we're caught?"

Dean smiled. It was the kind of smile that spelled trouble.

"What if we were Crimson Justice?" he asked.

The handcuffs around Tori's wrists burned. They weren't made of metal, but of something else, perhaps infused with magic, draining her strength like she was covered in leeches. She could hear her own heartbeat, slowly thumping, the sedatives pushing her in and out of a bad dream.

There were soldiers in masks. White faceless masks that were less human than they seemed to be. They were man and machine, cybernetic killing organisms with human brains. She could've taken them down if she weren't so weak…or so hopeless.

Everything was shit.

Her best friend was gone. After spending the last several years of their lives tracking down Bert, finding out his super identity, and devising plots to destroy him, Tori was left alone. After all of that, in the end, Crimson Justice had ended Amanda.

To add insult to injury, she'd met someone—a really great someone. A guy who was different than any guy she had ever taken an interest in—and he was almost a victim…

EARLIER THAT DAY…

"What time are we meeting Dust?" asked Tori as she settled in next to the others.

She needed time alone and ended up walking through Supes-Con, browsing vendors until a confrontation chased her from the convention hall.

She could still see look on that poor girl's face, and the tears resurfaced.

"Twelve thirty," said Oxy.

"It is twelve thirty," said Tori.

"Twelve thirty-ish?" Oxy shrugged.

The midday sun was high in the sky, and the First National Bank was resting in the shadow of skyscrapers, wardens standing watch over Wonder City. The entire block was filled with Supes-Con attendees in costume or hauling swag. It was a festive celebration of supes—families, best friends, big smiles, and Tori was anything but in the mood for celebration.

"Amazing," groaned Moll-E as she adjusted her wig. "Look at all the fools. Fucking sheep!" They were huddled on a shady corner, discreetly watching the bank while sipping coffee. Perc lit up a cigarette while he had the chance.

"Hey, cool it, Moll," said Oxy. "Right now, all these moron supe-worshipers think we just have bad taste in supes. Don't give them a reason to believe we're the real thing."

"They'd shit themselves if they knew," said Moll-E. "Beth, get your fucking head out of the clouds, would ya?"

Tori wasn't daydreaming. She was monitoring the sky. Every time she saw a flash of red, she felt traumatized. There were enough cosplaying Crimson Justices around to make her feel sick, but she knew the only one they needed to worry about would be coming from the sky.

"Fuck off, thundercoot," growled Tori. "Remember why we're doing this."

"Bitch," sneered Moll-E, "what's gotten into you?"

"My best friend is dead," stated Tori with complete apathy. "Where's Jordan?"

"Scoping out the joint. He'll be here soon…ish." Oxy shrugged again as Perc frantically signed a message into his face. "What do you mean *did I grab the jammer?* Of course I didn't! That's your job!"

"You mean to tell me we don't have a cell phone jammer?" sassed Moll-E. "Shit, you lunk-headed assholes! What're we supposed to do now?"

"We go in as planned," said Dust, strolling up from behind them. "We're doing things a little different today."

"What do you mean?" asked Tori. "We go in, grab lockbox 42, and get out. A simple smash and grab."

Dust avoided her question. "Listen up. People have been pouring into the bank since Supes-Con opened. There are at least three dozen people inside. Oxy, Perc—you guys take the door. Don't let anybody in once things go down. Moll-E, you keep the hostages nice and calm. Beth…" Jordan glared at her, as if to threaten her with harm if she stepped out of line. "…you come with me to the vault. Anybody gets in our way, put 'em down."

As they entered the bank, Oxy and Perc went straight for the ATM by the door and got in line while Moll-E asked to open a new account with a manager. Dust and Crystal Beth got in queue for a teller—a much longer line than either of them anticipated. There were more than five dozen people inside, and more people flooded in every minute.

"I thought you said there were only three dozen people inside?" whispered Tori.

Dust winked. "More leverage."

He was smiling—not because someone said something funny or because he was getting drunk or high. Tori couldn't remember the last time he smiled because he was happy, which made her immediately more suspicious than she already was.

"Why do I have a bad feeling you've done something dumb?" she whispered.

He raised an eyebrow. "Why do something for free when you can get paid?"

"Get paid? We're already doing this to clear our names. We made a deal."

"I may have posted the gig on SupeHeistFinder.com last night," boasted Dust. "I said we had an inside scoop on supe-stuff being smuggled out of the First National Bank. Asked if anyone out there was interested in outbidding our client for our services."

"Are you fucking joking?"

"We're getting paid, babe," said Dust. His affectionate pet name was extra painful. He only ever referred to her that way when he was belittling her feelings. He was an extraordinary gaslighter, always dismissing her needs, feelings, and thoughts while elevating his own with a passive-aggressive victimization that took her many years to decode.

"This was bigger than a payday," she argued. "Amanda died for this."

"And we'll get paid for our loss," he sneered.

"Do the others know?"

"I told Oxy and Perc that our benefactor was going to reward us."

"What if we're being double-crossed?"

"What if we're going to be rich?" Jordan leered at her. "Why are you always so dead set on right and wrong? On ethics over power? Maybe you're okay being poor and broken, but I'm tired of begging for scraps."

There it was. That word that followed her everywhere.

Broken.

Did he know how much that word hurt? Did he realize how often he used that word to describe her, his own fiancée? This day was supposed to be for Amanda. It wasn't about getting rich! It was about finding a way to make everything right.

While Tori stewed, a random guy entered the bank. He looked nervous and wore a t-shirt that probably would've made Tori and Amanda giggle under any other circumstances. The guy meandered around, searching for the end of the line.

The guy stood out. She didn't know why she noticed him. She should've been preparing to do her job—for Amanda, not the payday Jordan had arranged—but she couldn't help herself as she tracked him through the bank.

"Hey buddy," said some guy dressed as the Green Falcon, "the line ends back here."

Dust groaned in agreement and grew two inches.

The lost guy moved to the back of the cordoned, zig-zagging line and ended up standing right beside them—separated by a thin strap of nylon. Tori could feel the rage emanating from Dust like he was on fire. It didn't matter that the poor guy wasn't purposely attempting to cut in line—a line they weren't intending to stay in—Dust's rage would've killed a baby if it had started crying that very moment.

From his leather jacket, Dust pulled a gun.

Tori sucked in a breath. The Dope Gang never used weapons. They had no use for them.

Dust cocked the hammer and placed it directly behind lost-guy's head as he peered out the window.

"No! What are you doing?" yelled Tori.

She grabbed the gun by the barrel and crushed it as Dust pulled the trigger with an impotent click. They exchanged a glance—it lasted only a second, but the chasm between them widened. They were on irreconcilable continents, an ocean of differences between them.

This was it. Tori was done.

Dust wound up like he meant to murder. He had a bemused grin on his face, like he was teaching Tori a lesson, and swung. Lost-guy was out cold before he hit the floor—hit in the back of the head with a partially blocked left hook.

Tori tried to stop it, but Dust was just too powerful.

She thought lost-guy was dead.

The resulting commotion sent the Green Falcon-knockoff tumbling, and the bank devolved into chaos. Security guards, defense systems, and drones were deployed—but Oxy and Perc cut them down with power blasts siphoned from the terrified crowd. One blast sent a security guard through a safety-glass shield that had been installed to prevent super-powered heists. Moll-E pumped so much pleasure into the room, ten people immediately fell asleep mid-stride for the exit.

"What the fuck are you doing?" growled Tori, and Dust backhanded her. She hit a stone pillar, then rebounded, flying from one end of the lobby to the other. She saw stars, and by the time she got to her knees, Dust was lifting his boot above lost-guy's head, ready to stomp out his brains.

She was a hundred feet away. She had less than a second to prevent an innocent death.

A lot can happen in a second, especially within the mind.

Tori had been torturing herself with the same question since it happened weeks ago: why couldn't she have arrived sooner to save Amanda?

Just a second sooner, and she could've caught the glass picture frame that impaled her best friend. It was a framed photo of the two of them—a prom photo, their dates overwhelmed as the two girls laughed at something hilarious off camera. Crimson Justice had plucked the frame off the wall and flung it at over two hundred miles per hour. Glass and metal, tossed at that speed, may have even severed Tori's own hands—but Amanda would have survived. She'd still be there with Tori. Best friends forever.

This time, Tori would make the impossible happen.

She darted toward Dust, his foot rapidly approaching lost-guy's head, and hit him so hard he flew like a beanbag through the air at Annie Phetamine-level speed. His head hit the top of an office door, but his momentum corkscrewed into a trajectory that would've made even the most iron-stomached supe, like The Bottomless Pit, vomit his dinner.

Tori grabbed lost-guy and tossed him over her shoulder.

Oxy blasted her, making her stumble off balance. "What are you doing? You're going to ruin this for everybody!"

Tori spun, shoved Moll-E out of the way, and ran deeper into the bank, searching for an exit with lost-guy in tow. She slid around the next corner, avoided a powerful blast from Perc, and saw the bank vault ahead—a behemoth of reinforced anti-supe alloy and alien technology.

She ran for the vault, still lugging lost-guy over her shoulder like he was nothing but a baby—but she wasn't thinking straight. If she had been, she would've tried to punch a hole through the side of the building.

"You bitch!" yelled Dust. "Get back here!"

With one hand, Tori ripped the vault door free—snapping ten two-foot-thick deadbolts and whisking it open like a kitchen cabinet. She dashed inside with lost-guy and watched as Dust turned the corner, a raging eight-foot monster—a sad, sadistic version of the man she begrudgingly called her fiancé.

Until now…

She tossed his engagement ring at his head, then blew him a sarcastic kiss and waved. With a feat of strength beyond anything Dust could've done at his strongest, largest, most enraged, she slammed the vault door shut and crushed it into the wall beyond repair.

Dust spent the next ten minutes attempting to break the metal door down, but he was running out of time. Every bash against the vault door cracked the ceiling open and sent deposit boxes squirting from their designated spots embedded into the walls.

Tori found lockbox number 42, filled with four lollipops—two red, two blue—and a flash drive, which she stashed into lost-guy's back pocket. Then she waited.

She wasn't sure what she was waiting for.

To be captured?

To be rescued?

For lost-guy to wake up and keep her company?

Did she even want his company?

She cried. Everything was such shit.

Hours later—with a few fun moments in the middle—and everything was back to being shit. She was chained to the others—Cyndi, Grant, Geoff, and Jordan—in a disgusting stone hallway somewhere beneath The Cooler. She was last in line. There was a howl up ahead and flashing lights. It sounded like someone was being tortured.

"Keep moving," demanded a Ministerium Guard with a digital voice. He prodded her with something that felt like an electrified ham-fork jabbed into her lower back.

"Easy, fellas," she groaned, feeling drunk. "You're gonna give me a fucked-up tramp-stamp."

"Where are you taking us?" shouted Grant. He was at the front of the line, right behind Cyndi in a wheelchair. A guard slugged him for asking.

"Holding cell," said another. "Your trial is in nineteen hours."

"That's some kind of due process." Grant spat a wad of blood.

"Clean them up and prepare them," said a figure from the shadows, its voice disguised by an electronic device. "This is going to make some great television."

CHAPTER 29

SUNDAY EVENING. 7:45 PM

WHEN THE PRESIDENT ARRIVED, HE WAS GREETED BY THE Ministerium Guard on the rooftop helipad of The Cooler. His armored helicopter with the presidential seal on the side appeared like a flying tank. The Ministerium Guard saluted him, dropping to their knees and bowing their heads in reverence. It had become the preferred way to profess allegiance to the president, ending two hundred years of military salutes, in preference of a gesture more…*divine*. He demanded their loyalty, and a simple salute wouldn't do.

"Rise," said the president. The Ministerium Guard got to their feet. As he walked past, they fell in line, escorting him from the helipad into an armored elevator where his chief of staff awaited him.

"Welcome to The Cooler, sir," said the president's chief of staff.

"What did I tell you, Harden?" scolded the President.

Harden squirmed in his too-tight suit. "Uh, not to call you sir?"

"That is correct," said the president, adjusting his cataract glasses. "And what did I inform you to call me instead?"

"Caliph Haines. You said the Caliph title is more suited to your position."

"Correct," said Haines. "The Ministry has given its full power to me. The radical Reformists have been squashed, and absolute authority is mine." As the elevator doors closed, Caliph Haines reached out and knocked three times against the chrome reinforced doors. "Hear that, Harden?"

"I do. Strong doors." Harden smirked nervously.

"No," corrected Haines. "Three knocks. The doorways are opening. The membranes are thinning. We are coming home, Harden. The Ministry shall welcome them all with open arms."

"Right." Harden nodded. He had no idea what the old man was saying. More and more he appeared unhinged, cranky, and senile. The chief of staff feared the Caliph and the power he now held. Harden had sold his soul for that power.

But now they were all going to burn.

8:00 PM

The Cooler was built and maintained by Amycus Industries as part of their supe research in coordination with the federal government. There were two other supe prisons—The Pit, built into the side of the west-coast sea-cliffs after most of California fell into the ocean—and The Black, built into the dark side of the moon, where inmates were forced to live in total darkness.

If Tori had her druthers, she would've chosen The Pit for the ocean view, even if the death rate was eighty percent. Only supes with non-flight abilities were permitted. It sounded like a place where she could find distraction amongst the danger.

The Black sounded awful. She imagined wasting her days away in zero gravity and total darkness. It was a permanent sensory deprivation chamber, which drove the inmates to madness.

But The Cooler was the place of nightmares. She was minutes away from being frozen, where she'd live out her days in a perpetual slumber, unable to move inside a small, refrigerated unit while being pumped full of literal nightmare fuel.

The Pit and The Black may have sounded hellish, but the Cooler was hell frozen over.

Maybe the freezing process would kill her? Although that seemed unlikely.

Tori was stripped and showered via high-powered hose spouting ice cold water. Her lips turned blue before they jammed her into an orange jumpsuit, then strapped her onto a cart, like a UPS driver delivering packages. Two dozen guards then carted all five members of the Dope Gang into separate cells, where they were left in darkness for hours.

When the guards returned, they were wheeled into large marble room with futuristic medical apparatuses attended by doctors in lab coats. Rows of purple cloth stadium seats, three rows deep, began twenty feet into the air at all sides on a mezzanine, with automated television cameras stationed at every angle. At the front was a judge's bench draped in purple, emblazoned with the Ministry emblem—a torch surrounded in white.

There were five open freezers—each the size of a torpedo—branded with serial numbers that matched those sewn into their jumpsuits.

It was surreal. It was terrifying. She hadn't been so scared since she was standing on the observatory bridge, watching Bert slice and dice her friends and toss them over the falls.

A parade of people in fancy suits and silk ties, pantsuits, and pencil skirts entered the room through the mezzanine level doors. They filled up every purple chair. One of them looked vaguely familiar—a blonde woman.

These people were bearing witness to their sentencing.

Jordan fought against the magical shackles. "Let us go, or you'll pay." He was trying to wield his anger, but the power-dampening restraints wouldn't let him.

"Funny you mention that word," said someone with a voice modifier. A figure wearing a red overcoat stepped into the room through a door beside the judge's bench. She looked familiar too—Tori had seen her on TV hours ago.

"You're the Benefactor?" asked Grant, while Geoff struggled against his shackles, signing something urgent nobody could see.

"I am," said the Benefactor. "I've always been the man in charge."

"Rhea Ramsey," grumbled Jordan. "I did not see that coming."

"We were set up," said Grant.

Rhea smiled. "The president has asked me to personally preside over this court. He will be here momentarily."

"The stakes have never been higher," said Ted Nougat. He was seated at a broadcast table wearing a star-spangled suit. His voice sounded like someone stuffing a chalkboard into a blender.

"What the fuck is this dog and pony show?" whined Jordan.

"This is your trial." Rhea smiled.

"And the stakes have never been higher," repeated Nougat into a microphone.

"You already said that," groaned Scott Rio, standing beside him with his own mic. "Focus, Ted."

"Right," said Nougat. "But what if the stakes get higher?"

"For christsake!" growled Rio.

"You always do this!" Nougat pointed at Rio, spittle flying from his mouth like shrapnel. "You always tell me how to do my job. I'm broadcasting this event, just like you! And I'll do it the way I want to do it!"

Two men entered the court in the middle of Nougat's rant. Everyone but Nougat knelt to acknowledge them, even the Ministerium Guard. It was the kind of entrance that, although ordinary, took the warmth out of the room. The short old man wore a pair of cataract glasses that completely shielded his eyes, as well as a wide-brimmed black hat from a bygone era. The sight of him sent tingles up and down Tori's spine, but she couldn't find the focus to understand why it made her nervous—it was hard to hold a single thought with all those pills in her stomach.

"Get a hold of yourself, Ted," scolded the old man.

Nougat turned, then immediately sank to his knees and bowed his head. "Forgive me, Caliph Haines. I was merely—"

"Merely being a neurotic lunatic, Ted?" said Caliph Haines. "Shut up, please."

Nougat nodded—a fearful sweat moistened his brow—and allowed Caliph Haines to preside over the court with his chief of staff behind him. All heads within the court were bowed, and Tori jostled against her constraints— now was the time to do something if she could.

"Rise," said Caliph Haines, and those in attendance unbowed their heads and stood. "I am Caliph Haines, and I have the power to preside over this court."

"You don't have that kind of power," shouted Grant. "I was a political science major, and—"

"—and you made awful life choices," scolded Haines. "Including such a vile statement. Absolutely vile. How dare you say something so awful." Then he nodded to the guards.

Tori didn't see it, but she heard the pop and felt the spray.

The president ordered Grant shot dead with a simple nod. Grant was never bulletproof, not like Tori or Jordan, even without the power-dampening shackles.

"As I was saying," said Haines, "I will be presiding over this court. Doctors, have you completed the tests?" He looked toward the group of men in lab coats checking dials and sensors. There were four of them—two nondescript doctors wearing glasses with the same dark hair and beady eyes. The third was an Asian man who stunk of menthol. The fourth was wearing red suede shoes and a pair of darkened rubber goggles that magnified his eyes.

One of the lab coats had finished moments ago, prodding a strange device up to each of the prisoners' left eyes. Tori hated the blasted thing—its effects felt like an ice-cream headache, simultaneously sharp and dull and lodged right behind the eye. The contraption looked like a handheld ray gun, with a long tube that forced the eyelid open, collecting data.

"The numbers don't make sense, sir," said the administering lab coat.

"What do you mean?" spat Rhea, pacing toward them with a frustrated but curious gait. The crowd silently watched as the host of *Supes-Roundup* sauntered over to Dust, Perc, the unconscious Moll-E, Crystal Beth, and a very dead Oxy. She took a wide, safe berth around them as Rio and Nougat gave the play-by-play to the TV audience.

"Let me see," said Rhea. After a moment, she scoffed. "That's impossible. Run the tests again."

The lab coat jumped to it while the others stayed out of his way. He hastily jammed the tool up to each of the prisoners' left eyes and collected the data again. Then he showed Rhea the results on a monitor, and her forehead creased into something that looked like constipation.

"What is it?" asked Haines. The audience held their collective breath and exchanged speculative whispers.

"Her," said Rhea, pointing at Tori. "Do her again."

And the lab coat complied.

"Crystal Beth? Again?" said Rio, commentating for the audience.

"I smell something foul," said Nougat.

"I think that's you, Ted," said Rio.

"One man's musk is another man's cologne," added Nougat.

Tori was fed up with having the device jammed into her face, and the way it forced her eyelid open wasn't exactly fun. But it seemed to be making Rhea very uncomfortable, which meant she would keep doing it just to see the woman sweat and squirm like the fucking worm she was.

"Unbelievable," said Rhea.

"Holy hell, would you tell us what's going on?" shouted Nougat. He looked like he was about to climb over the broadcasting booth to see what was causing all the drama. His long nappy hair appeared to frizz with its own anticipation.

Rhea took the readings loaded onto a hand-held device directly to Caliph Haines at the bench, who read the results for himself.

"Interesting," said Haines. "Omega 5."

"What does that mean?" asked Nougat.

"It means we freeze her and throw away the key," proclaimed Haines from atop the bench. "But first, Crystal Beth—or shall I refer to you by your given name? Tori Jane O'Neill. Daughter of Joseph O'Neill and Lillian Martin of Grace Falls, Pennsylvania." The discovery of her real name and past would've angered her if she weren't so sedated. "We have reason to believe you're holding on to valuable information."

Tori didn't answer. They were going to freeze her for the rest of her life. What good was compliance? She hung her head in silence and waited for this farce to end.

"Set me free and I'll tell you where it is," offered Jordan.

Geoff tried to sign his own acquiescence, but nobody was paying attention.

"I thought you gentlemen were about the money?" asked Rhea.

"Information for freedom sounds like a good trade to me," said Jordan.

Tori glared at him from beneath her curls. If she had laser eyes, she would've carved out his genitals and laughed while watching them burn. He was a creep, and she hated herself for ever loving him. When the chips were down, Jordan showed exactly who he was—a callous, self-serving, sociopathic egomaniac who wasn't half as smart or interesting as he thought he was.

"Agreed," said Haines.

"What?" scoffed Rhea. Haines grinned, his old yellow teeth like a creepy jack-o-lantern that made Tori shiver. Rhea sighed, then nodded and turned back to Jordan. "Fine. Tell us."

"The package is in her stomach," said Jordan. "She swallowed it."

One of the lab coats groaned.

"Is that true, Ms. O'Neill?" asked Haines. When Tori didn't answer, Haines laughed. "I would imagine, my dear, that if you know where the research is, you may wish to confess prior to our scientists sawing you open."

Tori closed her eyes. She had nothing to say. If they wanted to open her up, so be it. Let them. She deserved the pain. Maybe they'd clip an artery and she'd get lucky.

"Doctors," ordered Haines, "open her up." Then he gestured for the guards to release Jordan, and they did so with a series of key fobs to unlock his shackles.

The nearest lab coat, the one with the red suede shoes and goggles, kept his head down and grabbed a scalpel.

But menthol-lab coat scolded him. "What are you doing? That's not going to work."

Another lab coat rolled her into position. The cart readjusted into a stretcher, and computerized medical equipment was wheeled into place around Tori. It looked like a personalized guillotine, positioned over her stomach with a mean-looking diamond sawblade.

Menthol-lab coat hit the trigger on a joystick, letting the sawblade whirl with an angry growl before placing a pair of safety goggles over his eyes.

Tori braced for excruciating pain.

An unannounced breeze crept into the courtroom and blew aside stacks of papers that tumbled and drifted around the room. The sudden, ominous blast of air stayed the doctor's hand. All eyes slid away from Crystal Beth and toward the side entrance, attracted to a bright crimson cape.

He was dead. She'd seen the pieces of him at the Supe Burger, like whole cuts of beef at a butcher shop.

But there he was—Crimson Justice stalking into the courtroom.

FORTY-FIVE MINUTES AGO

Dean was certain they were doing the right thing.

They had a plan, and Dean knew it was going to work, just like he knew the A-Team would always pull it out in the end. Rudy was chewing on a stogie he had saved for special occasions and was doing a half-decent Hannibal impression, except that he was punching holes into the plan every time he opened his mouth.

"But what if they don't do what we expect them to do?" he asked.

"We have to be ready to improvise," said Maury. They were stuffed into the back of Maury's limousine as his driver, a half-dead-looking chap, ferried them to their destination. Maury had the front seat to himself, facing the three of them wedged together in the back.

"Aren't we already improvising?" asked Rudy. "Isn't this improvisation?" His voice screeched into pitches that only dogs could hear.

"Technically speaking," said Arthur, "since we're discussing it before we act, it is indeed a plan. It only becomes improvisation when the plan is being enacted—"

"—baby," Rudy interrupted, "don't make me slap you."

"What *if* it doesn't work?" asked Dean.

"We end up in jail," Maury deadpanned. "Which was where we were all going anyway."

"Speak for yourself," said Rudy, folding his arms.

"Rudy," said Arthur, "he's right. We've all either done something illegal or are being accused of it."

"Oh really?" challenged Rudy. "What exactly have I done?"

"You live-streamed within a top-secret lab," explained Arthur. "You exposed many of the company secrets I was working to expose through my contact."

Rudy wilted.

"One way or another," said Maury, "we're all going down."

"Amanda," said Dean, thinking of the friendly face who used to greet him every morning. "She was trying to do the right thing, and she paid for it."

"Deano," said Rudy, "I don't want to pay for doing the right thing."

"Tori saved my life," he replied. "More than once. I owe her."

"Are you sure that's your entire reason?" asked Rudy with a suspicious stare. If Rudy was going to go through with the plan, he needed to know why. Dean kept flip-flopping, and it was vital that his best friend admit why he had to save Tori.

It was time to unleash the nuclear news he'd been saving—especially since Dean hadn't checked his phone's messages since he got it back last night. In fact, Rudy had spotted it still sitting on the counter when they left.

Rudy pursed his lips. "Brie called while I had your phone yesterday. Did you check your messages?"

Dean shook his head. "I left my phone at home."

Rudy expected Dean to obsess over Brie's intent and beg for all the details of what they'd discussed—but he didn't seem to care.

"You don't even want to know what we discussed?"

"I need to get Tori out of there, Rudy," said Dean. "I can't think straight until I do."

"One day," gushed Rudy, "one day around this Tori, and you're already a changed man." Then he looked at Arthur with the same unflinching resolve that he saw in Dean. "Alright. Let's do this. This Tori-girl must be something special, because she did what nobody could do in thirteen years." He gestured at Dean. "She got my best man here to forget all about crazy, Brie."

"Sounds like a perfectly good reason to attempt a daring rescue." Arthur smiled. "And, while we're at it, expose the Ministry conspiracy to take over the world."

"That too," agreed Rudy.

"I put my life on the line to bring them down," Arthur continued. "They have to be stopped."

"Whatever floats your boat." Maury looked bored. "It's not like any masked do-gooders are coming to save the day. Blue Anvil's toast and Robo-Lad's a junk heap."

"I feel good about this," said Rudy. "It's for a good cause." But his leg had suddenly developed a nervous tick.

"Are you okay?" asked Arthur.

"My best friend and business partner fell in love with a supervillain who's about to be locked up on ice forever." Rudy started to hyperventilate, choking out his words in between breaths. "We're planning to bust her out of supe-jail and take down the Ministry, even though we've already recovered Arthur's research and handed it over to the secret agent mobster who can put these assholes away and expose the conspiracy to build a government controlled supe-army—*and* the truth about how supes are created—*and* there's an existential crisis brewing where alternate earths are dying off one by one! It's like going for extra credit on a test even when you know you've already passed. If I'm not alright, what am I? Heh-HA-ha!"

Dean took every word to heart.

"Guys," said Dean, "let me do this alone. I can't have you getting hurt on my account."

Rudy sighed. "Don't listen to my nonsense. You're my family. This is how I cope. Besides, the plan, *although improvisational*, needs all of us doing our part to pull it off."

"I can't ask you to do this," said Dean.

"Oh, I know. You'll just owe me a big fat one. Like taking me to Moulin Rouge at the Revival Theater next month while Arthur's away."

Dean groaned.

"See?" said Rudy. "A really big fat one. So big and fat you won't be able to squirm your little ass out of it—like skinny jeans without the stretch."

8:10 PM

"Crimson Justice," said Rhea. "We heard you were dead."

"What a turn of events," added Rio, turning to his broadcasting partner.

"The stakes have just gotten higher!" said Nougat.

"Reports of my demise have been greatly exaggerated," said Crimson Justice. His voice was scratchy and strained, and he limped into the room with his cape wrapped around his huddled form.

"It's an honor, as always," said Rhea, gliding over to shake his hand.

"Stay back!" warned Crimson Justice, his hand extended like the Heisman trophy.

The sedative they'd forced down Tori's throat dulled her fire and gave her the sensation she was floating. But when she saw Crimson Justice, the sedative burned away with rage. If there was one thing that made her pending incarceration tolerable, it was knowing she had helped end Bert's reign of terror.

Crimson Justice glowered at Dust, noting his lack of shackles, handcuffs, chains, and other secure fasteners.

"Why have you unbound the criminal?"

"Asshole," grumbled Jordan. "I knew you weren't dead."

"Dust has provided valuable information," explained Haines. He appeared bemused, like he was enjoying a sunny spring day at the park—not presiding over a court in a subterranean prison level at 8 PM on a Sunday night.

"Mr. President," said Crimson Justice, "Dust is a vicious criminal and—"

"—How odd," interjected Haines, "that my own protégé would not call me by my proper title."

The witnesses leered at Crimson Justice while Jordan sneered.

"You're not the president?" asked Crimson Justice.

Haines twitched suspiciously.

"Ha-ha! I was just testing you. Of course you are!"

A door opened to the witness stand on the mezzanine floor, and Tori's eyes tracked the noise.

"Refreshments!" sang a man in a purple shirt and sunglasses. His arms were full of soda cans and candy. "Get your refreshments! I have Twizzlers and orange Fanta—and, really, anything out of the vending machine down the hall."

It was a spectacle, the kind that made Tori's eyes wander. She caught sight of the lab coat with the red suede shoes and goggles, giving her a magnified wink while everyone watched the refreshments guy handing out sodas. What was at first bizarre quickly became absurd when the blonde woman Tori recognized stood up and shouted, "I know you!"

"Me, sweet thing?" said the refreshments guy.

"You're Moody Rudy," she accused, stalking down the aisle and through the doors to the witness stand.

"That is preposterous! I have no idea who that Moody Rudy is!" said the refreshments guy, dropping his payload and throwing his hands into the air— then waving them around like he was providing a discreet mayday.

The blonde reappeared seconds later through the courtroom doors, her heels angrily clapping the cement as she soared past the Ministerium Guard, past the bench with Caliph Haines and his Chief of Staff, past Tori, Jordan, and the lab coats, and approached Crimson Justice like she was on a mission.

"Young lady," scolded Haines, "what do you think you're doing?"

The Ministerium Guard raised their weapons.

"I'm sorry, Caliph," she said, "but Crimson Justice is my husband."

The room filled with gasps.

Haines smiled. "Proceed."

Crimson Justice shrank at the sight of her and turned away like a beast, hiding his hideousness from beauty.

"Stay back," he whimpered.

But the woman wasn't fooled. She lunged forward, grabbed the cowl, and tore it back.

"Dean?" she asked, less surprised than she should've been.

"Hey, Brie," squeaked Dean.

5 MINUTES AGO...

When the sounds of an angry machine fired up, Dean's imagination got the better of him. He imagined all manner of insidious torture devices closing in on Tori. It was now or never—the anxiety coursing through his system should've been crippling, if not for the hero complex daring Dean to save the day. This was a do-or-die situation.

Five years ago, when he confessed his feelings for Brie at her wedding reception, his conscience had scolded him for not confessing earlier. He had thousands of prior opportunities to speak from his heart, but he never did. It wasn't that he didn't have the guts, and it wasn't that he didn't feel the immense need to profess something his soul wanted to sing from mountaintops. It was because he didn't want to live with the ramifications of his actions. Losing her would devastate him—so he'd waited until the last possible moment. And even then, as Lawrence had explained, he needed a little Crimson-Poke to complete the task.

And he lost her anyway.

This was different.

Dean was still sorting through his feelings, but he refused to allow this unfair world to get any crueler.

Tori didn't deserve this fate.

She deserved to be happy.

Dean didn't know how long he could uphold the charade, but if he could last five minutes, it would give them a chance. Just five minutes—three hundred seconds—to make them believe, within reason, that he was Crimson Justice, the scariest supe on the planet. Then Arthur could slip away and finish the plan.

When Dean slipped on the Crimson Justice costume, there wasn't much of it left. The hood, the cowl, and the cape were in good condition, but the rest was shredded apart, as if something had exploded from within.

That was problem number one.

Problem number two was that Dean was only half the size of Lawrence. The guy was well over six feet tall and as wide as a commercial oven.

Arthur got them into The Cooler with his Amycus badge and escorted them inside without anyone noticing. They parted shortly after, and Dean and Maury hid away in a storage closet.

"How the hell am I going to pull this off?" Dean asked once they were inside.

"Carefully," warned Maury. "You're pretending to be the most powerful being on the planet. Tell people to stay away and they will."

"Okay, but what if they don't?"

"They will," said Maury, "because everyone's afraid of him."

Memento Maury didn't know Lawrence's wife would be in the audience as a witness. Rudy wasn't prepared to be recognized as Moody Rudy from his broadcast. Arthur had no backup plan to prevent a diamond sawblade from attempting to split Tori open like a Pez dispenser.

And Dean? Dean had no idea there was going to be a third problem striding toward him in a skirt and high heels.

He froze at her approach. He'd spent the last five years imagining what it might be like to see her again. But this was not how he'd envisioned it.

"Dean?"

"Hey, Brie. What's uuuuup?" He was acting like they had randomly bumped into each other at a supermarket or gas station. A casual, unplanned meeting—completely happenstance.

"I thought you were dead," she said. "I was watching Rudy's livestream, like everyone else in the city. I thought you died at the First National Bank. I called you, like, a hundred times."

He shrugged, unable to speak.

"What are you doing here? What are you doing with Lawrence's costume?"

Dean's silence was unusual. It was like he was operating against his base code, malfunctioning. Everything she said sounded like it was coming from a boiling teapot and turning to gibberish inside his head.

All the while, he avoided looking at Tori. He knew where she was within the room, and he spotted the hostile apparatus above her with the diamond sawblade, but he couldn't bear to look at her.

Maybe he was worried about what Tori thought of him?

Maybe he didn't want to see Tori's expression while she witnessed Dean and Brie together. What would Tori think was happening?

Or maybe he was afraid how he'd feel when he saw Tori wearing an orange jumpsuit, tied down, a diamond sawblade dropping methodically toward her abdomen?

"Who is that?" shouted Rio.

"I imagined Crimson Justice would be, ya know, bigger." Nougat shrugged.

And that's when Dean realized he didn't need to sort through his feelings. Yesterday, something magical had happened. From that moment on, Tori was the one.

Dean sidestepped Brie like he was avoiding a land mine. He paced at Tori and shouted, "I'm sorry!"

Tori turned her head to him, and their eyes locked. She looked defeated, like all the hope she could ever feel was gone. She looked at him like there was nobody else in the room.

"What the fuck are you wearing?" Her voice was cold and hollow.

"I'm here to rescue you."

"Why?"

"Because," said Dean. He wasn't going to avoid confessing his feelings just because he feared what might come to pass if he did. "Someone like you doesn't come around every day. You feel like a Friday night, like every 80s ballad, like magic, like anything can happen when I'm with you. I've spent my entire adult life wanting to be seen by someone special, and you see me. You've unmasked me. You see who I am, and I know I see you. You're funny, sweet, silly, and tough, and I find it exhilarating when you laugh. I adore you, Tori. I'm sorry for the things I said. You're not broken. You're perfectly imperfect, and I'm falling for you."

Rudy raised both hands into the air like Dean had just scored a touchdown. He grabbed some unwitting man's hand, then raised and high-fived it all in one motion.

"Would you like me to shut that wimpy little fuck up, Mr. President?" asked Jordan, cracking his knuckles and awaiting orders.

"Please." Haines nodded.

"Tori, I've gone through a lifetime of disappointment. I can't let go now that I've finally found someone who can be everything to me."

"What are you guys doing!?" shouted Rhea, startling the lab coats. "Open the girl up already!" The lab coats scurried into position around Tori.

Jordan stepped forward, his orange jumpsuit straining against his growing mass, and his fists grew to the size of Dean's head. The lab coat operating the saw pulled the trigger and guided the roaring sawblade down onto Tori's abdomen before Arthur in his red suede shoes could pull the plug.

She screamed.

There were sparks, then a snap—Dust winding up. Dean lunged forward, pressing a red button on a small box Maury had given him. The lights went out, and everything electrical within the room went dead, including the cyborg Ministerium Guard, who fell lifelessly to the floor.

"Somebody turn the lights back on!" shouted Rhea.

When the lights finally returned with a mechanical whirl, Tori was standing defiantly at the center of the room—unbound, unharmed, and smirking at the audience.

And she wasn't alone.

Feelings.

Tori was tired of feelings, but feelings weren't tired of her, not yet—as much as she wished that weren't true. She was fine being numb, wallowing in the empty void, on her way to living like a freezer-burnt fish stick in a dark avoided corner of The Cooler, right next to Jordan, forever.

When she heard Dean's name, she had a whole-body reaction, like she was waking up from a nightmare. Hope was an unfamiliar friend, and it came knocking for the first time in years.

Then she heard Brie's name, and jealousy warmed her fingers and toes.

She didn't want to feel jealous. She didn't want to feel anything. She didn't understand why Dean was there, why he was dressed like Crimson Justice, or why the mere sight of him made her ache.

She'd opened her heart to Dean for only a moment, and he'd slipped inside. Made himself at home, feet up on her coffee table and sipping milk straight from the carton. She tried to evict him, to toss him out on his ass and slam the door shut, but she failed. He kept finding his way inside, like he had keys copied when she wasn't looking.

She was a loner—her heart operated better when she was alone.

Except, deep down inside, she wanted love. She may have tossed Dean out and locked the front door, but she left the back door, the basement, and the second-floor bedroom window next to the trellis wide open.

No. She didn't need to have feelings. She was tired of falling and feeling and feeling and falling. She felt like she'd never stopped tumbling down into a chasm of despair. She'd lost everything she ever cared about.

…But it was fun falling with Dean…right up until he learned the truth. She knew he'd be upset. What she didn't anticipate was how devastated he'd been. He was really hurt. She saw it in his eyes.

So why was he there in the courtroom? To celebrate her incarceration? Did he hate her that much?

"I'm sorry," he said, sidestepping Brie.

Wait, was he talking to Brie, or to *her?*

"What the fuck are you wearing?" asked Tori, strapped horizontally to the supe-dampening cart with the diamond sawblade lingering above.

"I'm here to rescue you," he said—a movie quote that almost made her eyes roll.

"Why?" He should've been home, safe and sound, away from the awfulness.

"Because," said Dean, launching into a soliloquy that brought her to tears. But it wasn't until his last few sentences that her heart nearly burst inside her chest. "I adore you, Tori. I'm sorry for the things I said. You're not broken. You're perfectly imperfect, and I'm falling for you."

Jordan said something, but she hardly heard him. Her attention was solely focused on the only person in the room who mattered.

"Tori, I've gone through a lifetime of disappointment. I can't let go now that I've finally found someone who can be everything to me."

"What are you guys doing!?" shouted Rhea. "Open the girl up already!"

Two of the lab coats scurried to either side and unzipped her orange jumpsuit, then rolled her undershirt up to expose her midriff. One of them drew a red X in marker above her navel as the technician hit the trigger and the sawblade spun free. The shackles were so tight, she couldn't even thrash about to make the process difficult.

The sawblade methodically lowered, and she wondered if it could break her skin. When the blade grazed her belly, the flare of pain caught her off guard. It was so intense that she heard an audible snap, and the lights went off as the pain subsided.

Moments ticked, and the lights remained off. The whole room was silent.

After half a minute passed and nothing happened, Tori grew suspicious. When she finally caught her breath, she lifted her head to investigate. The room was dark, but she could see everything and everyone...*paused in place.*

She saw President Haines standing at his bench.

She saw the crowd of witnesses in various states of excitement and confusion.

She saw the soda and candy guy with the sunglasses, yelling something from his perch behind the witnesses.

She saw the friendly lab coat wearing the red suede shoes and goggles who winked at her, pulling the plug on the saw.

She saw Rhea Ramsey yelling and pointing.

She saw Brie, looking confused and jilted.

She saw Jordan raising a gigantic fist.

And she saw Dean, racing to her aid wearing a saggy Crimson Justice costume and carrying a weird gadget with a red button in his hands. He appeared like he would have jumped in front of the sawblade to save her. She had no doubt that if time hadn't gotten stuck, it would've happened.

But strangest of all, amidst this peculiar pause in time, she saw a familiar face.

"Hey Tor," said Amanda. "I've missed you."

CHAPTER 30

WHEN DEAN WOKE UP YESTERDAY MORNING, HE WOULD NEVER have guessed the trouble he'd find himself in that day, or that it would culminate at The Cooler thirty-six hours later, face-to-face with Brie—and that he would be striding past her, professing his growing sentiment for another woman. Another woman who just happened to be a notorious supervillain.

He watched in horror as the supe-cutting saw blade lowered toward Tori's power-suppressed abdomen—the president and his goon squad cutting her open in search of a flash drive that was once in Dean's possession—all while a seven-foot-tall menace of human rage stalked toward him with raised fists, ready to smear Dean like a fly across a windshield.

Dean retrieved a gadget from his pocket, a tiny black plastic box with a red button that Memento Maury had given him. Dean would have preferred a more powerful weapon, like Robo-Lad's sonic-disruptor or The Green Knight's massive mystical axe. But this would have to do. He pressed the red button just in time, the blade within microns of tearing through Tori's perfect skin.

Then the lights went out, the Ministerium Guard fell like action-figures… and everything *stopped*.

Was that supposed to happen?

When nothing moved, Dean responded with the first thing that popped into his head. "Welcome to the Twilight Zone."

"Not quite," said a female voice.

"Hey Tor, I've missed you," said Amanda.

Tori was dead.

She knew it.

She knew she was going to end up dead sooner than later—not in a sad, "oh boo-hoo, mourn for me" kind of way, but like a snappy punch line. "Aw shucks, I'm dead."

She'd squandered her youth, dated asshole after asshole, lost her best friend, found a man, then lost her life. It was like a run-of-the-mill country single or a tragic Hallmark movie. All she needed now were some sleigh bells and fake snow.

"Motherfucker," she growled, noting the glowing sparks dangling on the air next to the sawblade that had only glanced her skin.

"Nice to see you too," sang Amanda with an amused grin.

"I died? How? The fucking blade hardly touched me!"

Tori was furious. If she was going to die young, she wanted to go out big—explosion, decapitation, evisceration—the kind of stuff that made her cringe and squeal with uncomfortable glee while watching slasher movies with Amanda—so long as it was quick and painless.

"What the fuck is going on here?" Tori was still inside the courtroom, but the lights were out, and everything was frozen in time—Rhea Ramsey was in the middle of shouting orders, and Nougat looked like he was crapping his pants. But the president—Samuel Haines—was staring at her with a frozen grin.

And Amanda? Was Tori supposed to believe her dead best friend was actually there? This was a bad trip. This was an illusion—a head game.

"What happened to *hey Manda, missed you too?*" sang Amanda. Tori glared, urging her to cut the bullshit immediately. "What do *you* think is going on here?" Amanda unstrapped Tori from the cart that bound her and somehow popped open the supe-dampening shackles on her arms and legs with a flick of the wrist.

"How'd you do that?" asked Tori, gesturing to the shackles that fell away and clanked onto the floor.

"Do what?"

"Do you have the key or something?" Tori asked.

"You really don't have any idea what's happening, do you?"

"Do you always reply to my questions with a question?"

"Do you?" asked Amanda with a straight face. Then she giggled. As Tori scowled, ready to unfurl a clever retort, Amanda quickly replied. "I want you to think about your surroundings. I want you to examine what's happening here."

Tori scoffed, then looked around the room with the kind of annoyed indifference between siblings when one had a good point the other refused to acknowledge. It was a casual glance at first, until she identified the common expression shared across the many faces in the room.

It was fear. A lot of it. Many were afraid of the failing power. Some were afraid of her. The snack guy and red-suede-shoes were afraid of what was happening to *her*. However, there was one person in the room who looked like his whole world was collapsing.

"Yeah, okay," said Tori. Her gaze fell on Dean and lingered. Amanda noticed straightaway.

"You like Oscuro, huh?" Amanda smirked.

"*Like* is a strong word—"

"—Tori," Amanda interrupted, "you've been fighting your whole life. Running up that hill. Trying to keep everything afloat. And the one moment someone good comes into your life, you build an impenetrable Tori-shield to force him away. Why?"

Tori's voice was weepy. "I don't deserve him. And I don't think he'd like the real me." She avoided looking in Dean's direction, despite her desire to admire his dorkiness in the Crimson Justice costume that was four sizes too large. "I'm not his type."

"What is his type?"

"Actually, the girl right there."

Brie was tall, slender, sophisticated, and beautiful—with the kind of long straight blonde locks Tori always wished of her own. The two of them were similar, but opposites—mirrored versions detailing the differences between a charmed life and one that went off the rails.

"Riiight," replied Amanda sarcastically. She walked over to Dean and Brie, their bodies frozen in time, and pointed to his face. "This man doesn't give two shits about that girl. He's running toward you. And didn't he profess his growing affection for you a minute ago?"

Tori sighed, like Amanda was making it up.

"Listen, Tor! He's not a supe. He's putting his own life on the line for you.

He broke *into* a supe-prison to break *you* out. Think about that."

"Are you trying to tell me he's insane?"

"I'm trying to tell you that he's fallen madly in love with you," said Amanda.

Tori looked away. "Why would he go and do a stupid thing like that?"

"Welcome to the Twilight Zone," said Dean.

"Not quite." It was her. He could have picked Brie's voice out of a crowd. "You know, Dean, time is relative." Her voice sounded like it was everywhere all at once, maybe even within his own head. "A whole lifetime can pass within a moment."

Their surroundings changed. They were sitting on the ratty futon in Dean's old dorm room from a decade ago.

"Hey man," said Peter, entering the room with a sheepish smile. "I'm going over to Tammy's for the night. You kids have fun!"

"See ya!" Brie waved as Peter opened the door and left.

Dean was amazed. The room was exactly as it was back then. From his Goonies poster with the nick on the corner to the sticky patch on the futon armrest where Peter spilled Mountain Dew. It even smelled the same—like wet socks. Dean had always wondered why Brie put up with it, even though he was glad she did.

"*They Live*?" asked Brie. "*Or Better Off Dead*?" She was holding a DVD in each hand.

"What?" asked Dean.

"What are we watching?" she asked. "You always told me these were must-see movies. So, which one?"

Dean stood up and paced behind the couch. Everything felt real. The floor creaked and his mouth tasted buttery, like he had just finished eating a handful of popcorn from the bowl in Brie's lap.

It was freaking him out.

"We never did this. You never liked my movies," he said.

"Would you prefer a memory instead?" Suddenly, they were making out in the back of Dean's parked car, the stereo blasting something garbled—as if he couldn't remember the tune.

Dean pulled away from her and fell into the space between the seats in an awkward position, like getting his ass stuck in a wooden barrel.

"What's wrong?" she asked. "Did I bite your lip too hard or something?"

Dean felt like he was spinning in a centrifuge—the force pulling the sour bile from his guts into his throat. He dove for the door, pulled the handle, and spilled out onto the frosty ground in the frigid night air. He crawled away and stumbled onto his feet, only to find himself back inside The Cooler, staring at Dust's fist creeping toward his face as if it was an old VHS playing while paused, advancing frame by frame every few seconds.

"Did you get my messages?" Brie approached him from behind, moving at normal speed. She was wearing her old Milton State University sweatshirt off her shoulder and those skimpy workout shorts that gave Dean fantastical fits of lusty discomfort.

"What messages?" he asked. "And why are you barefoot?"

"The ones I left on your phone, silly." She rolled her eyes playfully, ignoring the rest.

"Oh, sorry. I didn't have time to check."

She winced.

"For someone who makes a lot of bad decisions," said Brie, "this might be the worst you've ever made." She gestured at Tori like she was eyeing up a rival at the bar.

"Doubtful," Dean replied. "I spent over a decade chasing you." In all those years, Dean never saw the waving red flags—but now the veil was lifted, and he was seeing them all on arrival.

"Come off it, Puppy," she grumbled. "I know where your heart is."

And then he heard it. It was faint, but growing in volume like an orchestra rising from silence to crescendo. It was a song. One that elicited memories he'd rather have forgotten.

"Where's that coming from?" asked Dean.

"It's our song, silly," said Brie, "and it's coming from our hearts."

Dean could hear the wailing guitar opening to "Angel." Brie had always referred to it as their song, even though they were never actually together. It was a sick joke, a song that held meaning for a couple that never was. They'd had one night together—a fleeting memory that Dean could only recall in fragments—her bed and a classic rock station that coincidentally played that song at the right moment.

Dean felt a strange lovesickness overwhelm him. A feeling like things were spinning out of control. A heavy head, tired eyes, and a warming sensation like he was being slowly dipped into a steamy hot bath.

"Why are you doing this?" Dean fought his growing sentiment. Years of heartache returned. Years of clutching onto fleeting moments, bad dates to distract himself from the aching void, and years of reaching for something that seemed so tantalizingly close, yet out of reach.

He felt lost again. He felt hopeless.

"Face it, Puppy," said Brie. "I'm aces."

"Why would he go and do a stupid thing like that?"

Seriously, why would Dean go and do a stupid thing like *fall for her?* Didn't he realize she was a fuck-up? Didn't he realize she was doomed? She couldn't even save herself!

Tori hopped off the cart and examined Dean from afar. His expression was full of absolute terror as he lunged forward…to do what, exactly? Save her? Jump in front of the blade that could saw through power-dampened supe skin?

She had never once witnessed Rick or Jordan show interest in her well-being. In fact, Jordan was right there striding *away* from her to pound on Dean's face.

"*You're broken.*" They all said that. They all meant it. They were all right about her.

"You're the best person I've ever met," said Amanda. "Sure, you're not perfect. You nibble around the outside of all finger foods like a disgusting chipmunk, and you secretly drink pumpkin spice lattes every fall and loathe yourself for it. You hate cake, which is kind of infuriating, and you can be a real grump. But you're my best friend, and you gave me a life."

"Rude, but you're being dramatic. I didn't *give you a life,*" said Tori, air-quoting Amanda. "I kept you out of trouble. I followed you into danger. Then I let you get involved in something that got you killed."

"That was my choice," said Amanda. "But that's not what I'm talking about."

Tori knew exactly what Amanda meant. It was written all over her guilt-stricken face. She was talking about the observation bridge over the waterfalls, twenty-seven years ago.

Tori could hear the rumbling falls in her mind's eye. Then they were there, standing beside their younger selves, and the whole scene came sharply into focus. The hot summer air under a crescent moon sky, a cooling mist lingering on every draft. Three masked killers, the Old Man—their leader—and the two of them as kids with knives to their throats. Blood drenched the wooden planks, their mothers cut and tossed over the side.

"Why are we reliving the past? I don't want to see this."

"Why are you talking to me?" said Amanda. "I didn't bring you here."

"Then who did?" Tori spun, searching for the culprit. Was Amanda the Ghost of Christmas Present, visiting her in death as judge and jury—like Anubis weighing her heart against a feather?

The falls were flowing over the sheer drop and crashing below in a thundering mist, but everything else was frozen still, as if waiting for Tori to make a connection.

"Tori," said Amanda, preparing to answer the mystery by placing a comforting hand onto her shoulder. "You did."

"I don't understand," said Tori.

"You blocked this out," explained Amanda. "Who'd want to remember this? The problem is, you built so many walls to protect yourself, you never realized the first brick was a lie."

"What do you mean?" Tori looked down at her feet to make sure she was still standing, because it felt like she was falling.

Then some asshole unpaused the scene.

The old man, cloaked in shadow under the moonlight, snuck up behind little Tori. His foul breath tickled ear.

"Close your eyes, child," said the old man. "He who sleeps beneath the waves will need your eyes to wake and wander."

The three killers—like triplets, with long, straight, jet black hair and white masks—nodded, as if the old man's words were directives.

The stroke was quick and violent. The blade raked across young Amanda's throat as she tried to scream, and a gush of blood rushed through the open wound. Another blade was pulled across young Tori's neck, but nothing happened. The killers tried again and again as Amanda's life drained away, with Tori kicking and screaming and diving toward her friend—to touch Amanda's outstretched hand like a lifeline.

"No," cried Tori. "This is *not* what happened!"

"But it is what happened," said Amanda. "You were the last one alive."

There wasn't a day that went by where Dean hadn't fantasized about seeing Brie again. Those fantasies ranged from a variety of romantic tropes spread across his many years of watching too many movies, from the *10* fantasy—running toward each other on an abandoned sunny beach like Bo Derek and Dudley Moore—to the *Serendipity* fantasy of coming across a long-lost message written on the "Permanent Vacation" liner notes of a used Aerosmith CD. Dean was a hapless romantic, destined to be disappointed while waiting for something that would never come to pass. Dean was so obsessed with the idea of being reunited with Brie that he never stopped to examine how it was affecting his present. Until he was locked within a bank vault with someone so unlike Brie that he was forced to pay attention.

Cruel fate had brought Brie back into his life the moment he met someone who brought out the best in him.

Or maybe he had just been plunked on the head too many times.

Brie was the past. She was still married to a psycho, albeit a dead one. And Brie wasn't the woman he thought she was. Maybe she'd always been this other person.

And maybe she'd always been a supe too…

His head thumped, and all he saw was Brie—whether his eyes were opened *or closed*.

He saw memories—the greatest hits of their times together. As he fought the incoming imagery, he felt nauseated while "Angel" played between his ears—he wasn't just hearing it, but thinking it—and it blared to uncontrollable volumes that made it impossible to think.

"Puppy," whispered Brie, "I'm disappointed in you." One moment, she was stroking his cheek—the next, she was strutting toward him from a distance. He couldn't tell if he was experiencing time in chronological order or losing his mind. "I happened across Rudy's broadcast yesterday and I became concerned.

"I always check up on you, ya know?" she continued, nuzzling against his shoulder like a cat looking for a place to nap. "I know everything about you. Always have.

"I can sense you from anywhere," she whispered from his other shoulder—two of them, cozying in from either side. "Like an eternal flame burning within a lighthouse on the shores of a perpetual storm. But, suddenly, yesterday, you started fading from me. In fact, you blinked out there for a moment."

The other Brie said, "I left you messages, but Rudy had your phone. He told me you were missing."

"You could sense me?" His thoughts were heavy, like they were soaked in honey.

"Did you really believe I'd let you get away? Just because I was married to Lawrence didn't mean I was going to let you go." Then she wasn't just on either side of him, but standing right before him as well, sucking the air from his lungs as if she were kissing him from a distance. It was hard to breathe and think. "Your adulation is intoxicating, Puppy. You're like a battery, fueling me up with your thoughts, your passion, your fantasies, *your love*. You're inexhaustible. A hopeless romantic to the end. I can't have you dreaming about anyone else but me."

Even in his current stupor, Dean couldn't help but feel angry. There was something hidden in her words—*motive?*—that made him cringe.

"I need you, Puppy," she moaned, while her copies nestled closer.

"Why?"

"Because you give me purpose."

"Why?"

"Because I can't be what I am without you."

"Why, damnit!" growled Dean. "Why?"

Her copies disappeared. She moped, and sighed, and whimpered, then finally admitted, "Because you keep me...*regular*."

"Are you saying I'm like a fucking laxative?" growled Dean. "Is that what I am to you? I've spent the last fifteen years of my life chasing after someone who needs my love like a daily fucking dose of fiber!?"

"If you want to be dramatic about it." Her blonde hair brushed his cheek as she leaned to his ear. "You're important to me, Puppy. Why are you being so difficult?"

"What the fuck does any of this mean?" The music in his head cut off with a cymbal crash, and Dean shook Brie free, keeping her at arm's length. "Are you a supe?"

"Kinda." She rolled her eyes.

"You used me," he growled. "You never had any interest in me or cared for me. You even used *our song* to keep me hooked after you were married. That's why you played it at your wedding." The words *our song* felt like a betrayal—she was the one who called it that. She manipulated him into believing he meant more to her than he actually did. "Why do you need me to like you? And stop fucking calling me Puppy!"

Brie shrugged. "I just like the way you taste."

Brie changed before Dean's eyes at the exact moment he realized he didn't love her anymore. She was no longer the leggy blonde he had fawned over, but a pale, vapid monster with demon eyes. She had fangs, boils, even a mustache.

Dean gasped. "Either the spell is broken or you just got *real ugly*."

"What?" She felt along her body, then her face. When she discovered the teeth and mustache, she wailed. "What did you do, Dean? What did you do?!"

"Nothing!" he shouted. "I swear!"

"Love me, Dean!" She stretched out her arms, looking for a big, repulsive kiss. "Make me beautiful again!"

"No," cried Tori. "This is not what happened!"

"But it is what happened," Amanda pressed. "You were the last one alive. After spending a day weeping together with the other children in the crossbase of the old mill, Bert escaped. He ran away and found the police. Then they dragged me and you out here to the bridge, along with our mothers.

"They murdered them in front of us," she continued, "and then they killed me. But not you."

The killer: a big hulking beast of a man, his face hidden behind a featureless white mask. He'd taken his knife and repeatedly raked it across young Tori's throat so many times, he looked mechanical. But the outcome was always the same. The blade couldn't scratch her.

"You've always had powers, Tori," said Amanda. "You defeated three supe serial killers."

As Amanda spoke, Tori witnessed the will to survive awaken inside her younger self. Watching the blood drain from Amanda's throat ignited an innate urge. She broke the beast-killer's blade with her bare hand, jammed part of it through his eye, then swiftly tossed Amanda's murderer away from her dying body. The murderer's ribs crushed as he slammed into the railing.

Then the masked woman lunged at Tori with her knife. The two grappled until Tori found leverage and snapped the woman's neck—the bone burst from the skin and blood ran like a rushing river.

With busted ribs, Amanda's killer attacked Tori, landing a skull-crushing punch. Shock waves sent the river rushing up stream, and little Tori fell from the bridge.

"But, the Old Man…" said Amanda as the scene progressed.

"Lars!" shouted the old man, his eyes as vacant as two black holes. The hulking killer turned to him, awaiting orders. "Some flowers may die so that others may flourish. Rest soundly with he who sleeps beneath the waves." Then he tipped his hat and walked away without a care in the world.

"…he ran away," Amanda finished.

While the Old Man escaped, the killer approached the edge of the observation bridge. Little Tori was there beneath the railing. She snatched him up and over the rails, and they fell together into the falls, disappearing into the mist below.

"Ran away, you say?" said Caliph Haines, approaching them from the other side of the bridge. "I prefer to say I recognized your talents and decided to let them blossom."

"You?" Tori pointed, shaking with anger. "You're the old man."

Haines took a bow. He appeared quite spry for someone as old as dirt. "You look surprised, my dear."

"And you look like the Crypt Keeper." Tori sneered.

"How are *you* here?" asked Amanda, speaking on behalf of Tori's total lack of awareness. They were inside Tori's mind, weren't they? Reliving her memories, the ones that she had purposely forgotten?

"Ah, the figment has consciousness," said Haines. "Truly remarkable."

"Answer the fucking question, prick," growled Tori.

"The question is not how, but why, my dear," said Haines.

"*Why* the fuck are you fucking here?" snarled Tori.

"Because," said Haines with a creepy grin. "I can be."

"What kind of asshole answer is—"

"—Hush now, child," interrupted Haines. "Your reverie continues."

Little Tori returned alone to the observation bridge, soaking wet. She wept and rocked Amanda's lifeless body until the police arrived.

"I found them!" cried an officer who stumbled upon them amongst the broken bodies. "Two of them…alive!"

Then, over the officer's radio through crackling static: "I found the other four in the cross-base of the old mill. EMTs en route. Fifteen minutes."

"It'll be okay," said the officer, kneeling to look little Tori in the eyes. "My name's Officer Blaise, and everything's going to be okay. I promise."

Amanda and Tori clung to Officer Blaise and cried. They cried so hard, Tori thought they might stop breathing.

"I don't understand," said Tori, watching it happen like a three-dimensional, fully immersive movie.

"What cannot you accept, child?" asked Haines.

"You couldn't accept our deaths, Tor. It was a bridge too far, you could say," punned Amanda—a little whimsy to soften the moment.

"But how?" cried Tori.

"Reality is like fine china," said Haines, "Apply trauma, and it fractures. It is still china. Perhaps not as fine as it was before the trauma, but now with sharpness of its edges."

"What does- that- even mean- you crazy- shitmagnet!" The words spilled from her mouth as if she were fighting them.

"In order to grasp your true reality," explained Haines, "you must first let go of the false, Ms. O'Neill."

"You brought us back to life," said Amanda, explaining what Haines would not. "You're the reason we all lived. You're the reason we all have powers. We're pieces of you. And it's time for you to take it all back."

"This can't be happening." Tori grabbed handfuls of her hair. "I'm hallucinating."

"You are hallucinating," said Haines, "but that does not mean it is any less true."

"You," said Amanda. "You brought us back. You gave us new lives, Tori."

"That's impossible," she sobbed. "I'm not capable of that."

"You're the one of most powerful supes that has ever existed. Didn't you hear what they said? You're an Omega 5, and I don't think they mean fatty acid."

"You were the reason I was in Grace Falls, my dear," said Haines. "I was searching for you. A girl born with great power. I found you like a fire in the darkest night. The young daughter of a staffer who worked tirelessly, day and night, on my campaign for Governor. A young girl capable of things never before witnessed. Just a simple little thing without comprehension of her true potential."

"No," shouted Tori. "No no no no no!"

"I murdered them all to unlock your powers," Haines continued. "They were sitting right there like an unused book of matches. Strike it just right, and the whole book would flare like tinder."

Tori swung a fist at Haines. Her punch was fueled by rage, hot and furious, a wide arc hissing through the air. It would've taken his head clean off—but he disappeared with an ugly, vicious smile. Her fist passing through him like a phantom.

Tori let out bone-rattling scream. She was angry: at herself and Haines, at the world and the truth. What did Haines want with her? Weren't there a thousand other supes he could've fucked with? He had ruined her life. Everyone she ever loved was dead.

And what did that make Amanda? Had she always been a ghost?

Tori looked at her best friend and believed the worst—that Amanda was never real. That she was only a figment of the person Tori imagined she'd be.

"I know what you're thinking," said Amanda. "And it's hard for me to answer."

"Are you really Amanda?" asked Tori. "Or are you just in my head?"

"If I was a fantasy, why'd we fight all the time?" asked Amanda with a loving smirk.

"You're really Amanda?" Unrelenting tears sprang from Tori's eyes.

"I believe so," said Amanda. "I mean, how would I know?"

Tori spun away, suddenly doubtful.

"Tori, I am Amanda. I am the person you knew. I have all her memories, even the ones from before the murders. What is a person without their memories? I'm as real and independent as anyone." She stopped for a breath. "Amanda never became an adult. But from the moment her heart stopped, I became Amanda Hemmels. Does anything else matter?"

Tori turned back to Amanda and looked her over with new eyes. She took two steps and flung her arms around her best friend.

"How can this be real?" asked Tori, her face buried into Amanda's shoulder.

"I'm sorry, Tor," said Amanda, holding her tight. "But this is very real."

Then they were back inside The Cooler. The dark courtroom was lit by hot sparks flying from the sawblade and hung on the air like holiday lights.

"I missed you so much," cried Tori.

"I love you, Tor," said Amanda. "You gave me life. But it's time for you to move on. Take your wish and be happy."

Tori pulled away from Amanda. "How did you know?" Earlier that night she had seen two shooting stars, her first without Amanda, and made a wish.

"I was there," said Amanda. "I never left."

Tori let out a deep, soul-rattling sob. It took the breath from her lungs and shook her body until she was a shivering mess. Amanda had shown her the truth she'd buried since she was six years old. She spent years believing she was a fuck-up, a second-rate supe, impenetrable and impervious to physical pain—a basic supe power she'd received after tussling with Bert on the observation bridge.

But it was inside her all along.

Was she born with her abilities? How powerful was she and what could she do? And now that she knew what she had done, could she live up to her own potential?

"What am I supposed to do?" asked Tori, feeling a bloom of strength inside her.

"Kick some ass?" suggested Amanda.

"Somebody turn the lights back on!" shouted Rhea Ramsey.

A mechanical generator groaned to life, and the lights flickered. The darkness lifted to reveal Tori standing at the center of the room—beside a dead woman.

CHAPTER 31

SOME FANTASIES WERE BETTER LEFT IN THE IMAGINATION.

Once Dean's love for Brie had vanished, she became a hideous monster. He'd been under a spell this whole time, feeding her with his affection. Had she always been like this? An illusion?

"Puppyyyyyyyyy." Brie presented a pair of withered lips, ready to smooch.

"Stay away." Dean ducked and scooted aside from her grasp.

"C'mon," she whimpered. "We're running out of time!" She launched herself at him—clawing and swiping for a hold—and Dean stumbled away, his foot catching the cape as he dodged her. "You can't leave me like this!"

His surroundings seemed less surreal, as if the wall between reality and unreality had been fortified. When the dreamscape finally collapsed, it was abrupt. Everything snapped back to its proper place, like elastic.

"Somebody turn the lights back on!" shouted Rhea.

A mechanical generator groaned to life, and the lights flickered on. The darkness lifted to reveal Tori standing at the center of the room—beside a dead woman…

…while Dean was left staring into the windup of a cold knuckle-sandwich served up by a psychotic supe.

"Who's that?" shouted Rio as Jordan snagged Dean by the crimson cape, ready to clobber. The reality snap was so disorienting that all Dean could do was squint and brace for impact, dropping the little black box with the red button.

"What's up, Oscuro?" Amanda appeared, popping her knuckles.

"Hems?" Dean was dangling two feet into the air as Jordan spun at the sound of her voice.

Amanda winked. "I hear you dig my girl?" She was in the full Annie

Phetamine costume. The shorts, the domino mask, the fishnets, the streaks of blue in her hair—she looked like a roller derby girl without the skates and helmet.

"What the fuck is this?" growled Jordan as Tori strolled up beside him.

"Put him down," she demanded.

"Like hell I will," said Jordan, tightening his grip on Dean.

Tori replied by backhanding Jordan, and he released Dean like a pneumatic press, slowly placing him onto the floor. By the time Jordan regained his wits, he had grown three inches, a seething angry bull with steam exiting his nostrils. He swung for Tori's face—all power and rage without speed or precision—and she caught his fist like a ping-pong ball and crushed it like an aluminum can. When he screamed, she elbowed his throat, stifling the noise with a sickening gargle.

"Hey fuck-twats!" shouted Tori, snatching Jordan by the hair. When she realized she had the courtroom's undivided attention, she shoved Jordan onto his hands and knees. "Want to see a neat trick?"

"What the fuck are you doing?" choked Jordan.

"Yeah," agreed Rhea as she glanced toward the exit. "What the fuck *are* you doing?"

"What I should've done a long time ago," said Tori.

Jordan fought against her grasp like a snot-nosed brat against his mother's iron grip.

Rio looked stunned, Nougat cringed, and the audience trembled without the Ministerium Guards to protect them.

"Little broken Tori," snarled Jordan through gritted teeth. "What are you gonna do?"

She glared at Haines and smiled. "Hey Jordan," she said, leaning over to impart one last thought. "It's over, shitbag."

She knocked him out cold with a left hook—though impressive, that wasn't the trick. Dust was a rage monster, and Crystal Beth was considered a psychotic sidekick. The kind of power it took to knock Dust out was on par with Crimson Justice-level badassery—and the crowd knew it.

The trick, however, was much more impressive.

Tori made Dust disappear.

She put her lips together and blew. One moment he was a sorry sack of shit on the floor, and the next, he'd turned into dust. Broken into miniscule particles of matter that drifted away into nothing. Followed by every other wicked member of the Dope Gang—obliterated Moll-E, dead Oxy, and Perc screaming at the top of his mute lungs.

"Finally," said Haines.

The courtroom erupted into chaos.

Nougat yelled, "Oh shit!" He tripped over Rio vacating the room like he was fleeing poison gas or consuming hot lava.

"Where you jerks going? It's just getting good!" Rudy sat down with an armful of orange Fantas. He crossed his legs and popped one open to enjoy.

Into the room flooded every available Ministerium Guard. They carried electrified batons with power-dampening shackles at their waists. Their white featureless masks were empty, cold, and emotionless—tin cans with human brains at the wheel.

Amanda made quick work of the lab coats, herding them together and tying them up using the cords of their own scientific devices in a whooshing blue blur. The lab coat with the red suede shoes shouted, "Wait! I'm with Dean! I'm on your side!"

"Don't I know you?" A static aura crackled the air around her.

Arthur removed his goggles. "From the bank?"

"Yeah! Small world, man. Annie Phetamine. But you can call me Amanda."

"Doctor Arthur Ravine," he said, taking her hand. "But you can call me Arthur."

"Are both you guys with Oscuro?" She gestured toward Rudy, who was hurling cans of orange sodas at the cyborg guard.

"Rudy's my partner. And yeah, we're Dean's backup."

"Nice!"

One moment Arthur was speaking to Amanda, and the next she had flitted away three feet to his right, followed by a Ministerium Guard swinging his baton through the space she had vacated a blink before. She smiled at the guard, waved, then bopped him on the shoulder, zapping him with so much juice that his head fell off and rolled away with a loud metal thunk.

"So," said Amanda, "I'm gonna go beat some tin cans and give the lovebirds time to talk. If you have a plan, now's the time."

"You got it!" Arthur beamed. He turned to Dean and Tori as they crashed into each other's arms. "Awww, look at them."

"Ahem, now's the time to make those moves, Doc!" shouted Amanda, having already busted three guards with her super speed.

"Right! Yeah, good luck!" Arthur leapt over a crumpled guard and ran toward the exit, passing Dean and Tori as he left.

"What are you doing here?" asked Tori.

Dean never answered. He took her in his arms, and it felt like destiny.

When she finally pulled away, she couldn't stop laughing. "You look like a dickweasel."

Dean was about to answer when a cluster of gunshots fired. Tori caught a stray bullet without looking, like she was swiping a mosquito.

He flinched.

She beamed.

"You look amazing," he said.

"No, I don't," she giggled. His words disarmed her displeasure with his idiotic attempted rescue—she fluctuated between wanting to sear his brain with so many cusses that his pubes went gray to swooning over his sweet gestures and obvious flattery. "I'm in an orange prison jumpsuit."

"I'm in an asshole jumpsuit," he replied, gesturing to the oversized Crimson Justice costume. "Same difference."

"Except you look a dickweasel. I look like a con."

He kissed her.

She could spot stray bullets out of the corners of her eyes, catch them in place like light-tossed tennis balls, but she never saw that kiss coming. It made her feel lighter than air. She floated on cloud nine, her chest bursting with joy—a feeling she thought she was incapable of…

Until she heard a whimper. It sounded like an animal—a throaty whine and gargle, distracting Tori from the perfect moment. She opened her eyes and saw the woman with the long blonde hair cowering in a corner.

Tori asked, "What's up with her?"

Dean looked over his shoulder. "She's having a cosmetic issue."

Arthur Ravine was not a man of action.

He was out of shape, scared, frantic, and unsure. Arthur's early thirties had seen the energy of youth slip away while spending days tapping keyboards and squinting through the eyepiece of a microscope.

His physical condition wouldn't be an issue if not for the immediate life-or-death situation. His friends, his partner, his career, his entire world were on the verge of collapse. It was up to him to save the day.

With the flash drive in hand, Arthur soared through hallway after hallway and down a flight of concrete stairs to the Amycus Labs in the lower levels. His mind dashed back and forth, considering all the variables.

As he laid in bed that morning, the sun peering through his bedroom window while Rudy nestled in close, he'd felt miles away.

"Arthur," said Rudy, "you're being quiet, and that means you're thinking, and when you're thinking, that means you're analyzing things, and we all know what that means."

"Oh," he mumbled—his brain catching up. "Sorry."

"What's wrong?" asked Rudy.

"It's a lot," said Arthur.

"What is?"

"The plan," he explained. When Rudy didn't reply, Arthur elaborated. "It's not bad, but it does rely on way too many variables."

"Like?" Rudy revolved his hand in a circular motion.

"What if my badge doesn't work?" Before Rudy could answer with positive reinforcement, Arthur continued. "What if they recognize me? What if they don't believe Dean is Crimson Justice? What if I can't get to the lab?"

"Wait. You're the one who suggested we use the lab, Arthur!"

Rudy was right. It had been Arthur's idea. The lab was the only way to take it all down—to expose Amycus Industries from the inside.

"I know," said Arthur, "but all plans are based around best-case scenarios. There are too many human factors to predict what could happen. The perfect plan doesn't exist, in which case we would need to have multiple plans from multiple points of failure. The exponential results are endless."

Rudy groaned. "I hate it when you get brainy."

"The lab is our best hope now that we have this." Arthur held onto the flash drive like it was the One Ring—it was a fair analogy.

The lab below The Cooler was built for testing frozen supes. It was how scientists identified Deus Particles and their link to alternate Earths. It was those experiments that forced Arthur's hand when he was approached by the F.B.S.I. agent. He'd only wanted to make the world a better place. If that hadn't happened, would any of today's events have transpired?

Arthur knew the lab would be abandoned—it was Sunday, after all— but that didn't mean it wouldn't be guarded. Arthur hoped the chaos in the courtroom above would draw all the security from their posts, and he was right—no guards, no checkpoints, just smooth sailing.

All he had to do was swipe his ID badge to obtain full access to the lab and enact his portion of the plan.

Except when he grabbed the lanyard, the plastic card with the magnetic strip was snapped in half.

Arthur looked between the ruined ID badge and the security reader at least three or four times before he realized how completely "effed" he was. He kicked at imaginary rocks on the ground until panic set in. Without his contribution, everything was lost.

A rumble. A smash.

Something big was going down in the courtroom above. The blows cracked the door right off its steel reinforced hinges. It fell away into the lab with a big whoosh and bang, triggering motion detectors that sparked lights and loaded computers with an audible whirl.

Arthur didn't believe in destiny or luck. He was a man of science. But Rudy believed, and maybe there was something about his fortuitous situation that went beyond science. Maybe there was someone looking out for them… somewhere…

"Let's get to work," Arthur said aloud as he jogged into the lab, the flash drive resting in the palm of his hand. It was the only existing copy of his research.

Rudy was left alone to watch the chaos below like he had front-row seats to an off-Broadway show. He hated theater—sans *Moulin Rouge*, of course. It was a bad stereotype that because he was gay, he had to enjoy seeing grown adults dressed like humanized cats. Or rap-infused historical events. No, Rudy hated those things as much as he hated Miracle Whip. In fact, Miracle Whip and musicals were his two most hated things.

Well, those two things and candied yams…

…those two things, candied yams, and basic-bitch Ugg boots—

—ahem, those two things, candied yams, basic-bitch Ugg boots, and *HOT TAKE* Grease—oh, he loooooaaaaathed Grease.

These were the thoughts zipping through Rudy's mind when he noticed Annie Phetamine tied up in limbs. Things were looking bleak. One of the cyborgs wrapped a chokehold around her throat, and Rudy felt a mounting anxiety attack. He tried to help, but tossing the remaining cans of Orange Fanta wasn't doing anything to stop them.

Then he fainted.

Rudy fell out of the sky and landed in the middle of the pack. He smashed a few cyborgs with his backside, releasing their grip on Amanda's neck. Once free, she busted heads and disabled them in a zipping blur, like beating on steel drums—she even managed to help Rudy onto his feet.

"Thank-ya, sir," said Amanda.

"Oh honey," said Rudy, "It was the least I could do. Besides, I think I fainted on the way down." He took note of the butt print stamped into the metal head of a disabled cyborg and immediately decided on a diet. "Where's Arthur?"

"Went that-a-way." She smiled and pointed to a door on the far side of the room—

—when everything shook.

It was a violent shake. A quake. Like the whole building had been struck by a missile.

Several layers of rubble crashed through the reinforced concrete ceiling, with protruding arms and legs of poor saps caught in the meteoric smash. Then a fleshy mass dropped through the hole in a not-so-perfect three-point landing—like a drunken gymnast.

From the rubble strutted a naked meaty cadaver. It was missing chunks of flesh from its body, with rashy hives flourishing across its remaining skin. Parts of him flapped and waddled. Vast sections of muscle and sinew were missing, exposing vital organs.

"I cannot…be…stopped," growled Crimson Justice, wearing only his red boots.

"Fuck, Bert," gasped Tori. "Are you okay?"

Seeing him in such a state really made her feel sorry, even though she'd spent years wanting revenge. But what did that revenge look like? A good pummeling? Putting him behind bars? Turning him into a horror cliché?

Killing him? They'd already done that.

"You little twats," he gargled, pointing at Tori and Dean. "I'm going to disembowel you both, swap your guts, stitch you up, then stick my boot up your a-holes."

"That's creative," said Rudy, who accompanied Dean and Tori at the center of the room and joined their gaping, gawking stares at Zombie Justice. Amanda zipped beside them in a flash surrounded in crackling static, followed a moment later by the breeze she dragged along with her.

"Grody." Amanda gagged. "Or gnarly. I can't decide which."

Tori turned to her bestie. "Staying or going?" She didn't understand why Amanda hadn't evaporated like the others. Was Amanda making this happen? Or was she?

"Wait," grumbled Bert. "Didn't I kill her?" He glared at Amanda with a single eye, his other socket as vacant as the room.

"What did you wish for?" asked Amanda, ignoring Zom-Bert.

Earlier that night, when Tori saw the shooting star—the first she had ever seen alone—she wished to never be alone again. She didn't want to live without Amanda. But she believed Dean should be a part of that future too, whatever it might be.

"You *do* know what I wished for, don't you?" asked Tori.

"Do you always answer a question with a question?" replied Amanda, smiling. "I'm here as long as you need me."

Bert raised a mangled eyebrow. "I guess I'll have to kill her all over again."

"Try it, fuckstick," threatened Tori.

"You're such a bitch."

"Cumbubble," she sneered.

"Fucknugget," he spat.

"Dickfucker."

"Twatwaffle!"

"Spunktrumpet!"

Bert's only eye narrowed before he flung one final insult. It was the insult of insults, made more insulting merely by the tone and pronunciation. "You cu—"

"Whoa!" shouted Dean. "Don't you dare!" His fists were balled, and Tori thought it was cute—her fearless normie, willing to defend her honor against an undead supe.

"Or what?" scoffed Bert. "What are *you* going to…" That's when Bert caught sight of the blonde weeping in the corner, and the wind vacated his lungs—literally, because they could see them. "Babycakes?"

Brie looked up.

"Babycakes! What are you doing here?"

As a member of the Dope Gang, Tori had seen some real shit. She once saw Fat Mama, the supe from Sheboygan, swallow the Inedible Man. Watching Brie prance over and leap into Bert's arms ranked right behind that shitastrophe for pure nightmare fuel.

"What are we looking at?" asked Amanda in equal parts awe and disgust.

"When Zombie met Ghouly," quipped Dean.

Tori laughed.

"I volunteered to be a witness," cried Brie, her head buried into the rashy part of Bert's chest. "I wanted to see them pay for hurting you. It was all over the news. Crimson Justice was missing, and Moody Rudy posted to his followers that you were dead."

Rudy shrugged. "Deano, you know I couldn't sit on that fact-nugget."

"Babycakes," coddled Bert in his deepest baritone, "what did they do to you?" Then, after further examination, he said what they were all thinking. "You got real ugly."

"That's what I said!" shouted Dean.

Brie grimaced. "Can we not discuss this right now? You're not so hot yourself, Mr. Rose, and it looks like you're missing a few *key* pieces, hun." She gestured below his non-existent belt, then rolled her eyes and groaned. "Not that I'd ever notice."

"Sunnuva bitch!" he roared. "They exposed my vulnerability, babycakes. They threw benne at me, and I blew up. I blew up bad."

"Who's Benny?" asked Rudy.

"Benne," said Dean, "It's another word for sesame seeds."

"That's his super weakness?" Amanda laughed. "Sesame seeds?"

"And soon to be my fist," added Tori.

"Did you have your EpiPen?" scolded Brie. "I told you! Keep it stashed in your Utility Belt!"

"I did," Bert groaned, rolling his only eye. "Go eat a Snickers or something. You'll look better when you've had a bite."

"Actually, I think I'll grab a Puppy snack," said Brie. "There's more than one way to feed off my favorite client. A more direct way."

When she opened her mouth, a hairy green tongue slithered out, like it wanted a taste before the meal.

"I told you, Dean," bragged Rudy. "Brie's a Suk-You-Bust."

"You mean a Succubus?" Dean's face contorted like he was suffering through a migraine.

"Don't correct me, Deano! I told you she was a demon! A Suk-You-Bust!"

"Yeah, yeah. What do you want? A pony?"

Rudy shrugged. "If you're offering…"

"Wait, babe," said Bert, holding Brie back from prematurely pouncing on her meal. "Before you ruin my best suit." Bert took a confident step toward Dean, then gestured at his nakedness. "Do you mind, bro? How about helping an old pal regain some modesty here, huh?"

Tori scrunched her face but gave Dean a nod of approval. "Please? I'd rather not fight him with half a ding-a-ling flopping around."

"Yeah, sure." Dean quickly stepped out of the massive costume, like removing a hospital gown, and tossed it over.

"You were fully clothed under there?" asked Rudy.

"Yeah. No way I was going commando in something Lawrence previously commandoed."

Tori nodded, along with Rudy and Amanda in complete and total agreement.

"Thanks, bro," said Bert, slipping the suit over his battered frame. "But I'm still gonna rip your dick off and make you eat it."

"Careful," warned Tori. "Don't give me any new ideas. Though there's not much left for you to chew, am I right?"

"Law and Order will always prevail." Bert pulled the cowl over his massive melon, opened his mouth, and unloaded the Justice Beams.

Tori took the brunt of the blast, crashing into the wall fifty feet away. Amanda dodged, but Dean and Rudy were blown aside and skidded on their asses across the polished cement floor. Amanda flitted from the room and returned a blink later with a length of rebar, twirling it like a staff.

"No." Tori removed herself from the rubble. "He's mine, Manda. Go get help." Amanda dropped the rebar and disappeared with a static breeze. Then Tori nodded to Rudy and Dean. "Get away from here. I've got this."

Dean climbed back to his feet. "Are you crazy?"

"C'mon, Deano," said Rudy, tugging at his shoulder. "You heard the lady."

"Trust me," Tori whispered, placing a hand against his cheek. "You came here to save me, now I'm going to save you." Then she smiled just for him, and he returned a smile that was just for her. "Bert has no idea what I'm capable of."

"To be continued?" he asked.

"After this commercial break." She winked. "Now go."

Dean backed away, his eyes like malfunctioning tractor beams unable to disengage. He looked like he was wondering if this might be the last time he'd ever see her.

Brie howled, then pounced toward Dean and Rudy, like a cat. The dynamic duo ran from the room with the succubus in tow, leaving Tori alone with Crimson Justice…or so she thought.

"This will be interesting," said Haines, walking up beside her.

"Master!" Bert genuflected.

"Oh, yeah, like I didn't see that coming." Tori rolled her eyes. These two *would* be in league with each other—the League of Creepy Fuckers? The Dastardly Knobgobblers? The Ugly Fuckfaces? She could name them all night long…

"Crimson Justice has been my most faithful acolyte," bragged Haines. "I helped him ascend to what he is today."

"An undead jizzfaced loser?" Tori tied the top half of her orange jumpsuit around her waist.

Bert unbowed his head and stood. "The Caliph let me survive when we were kids. He orchestrated the whole thing. He let me go and killed the others, igniting your latent powers."

"Sounds like he went out on a fucken limb," growled Tori. "Why don't you both jump off onto something fucking sharp?"

"The Caliph," Bert continued, "taught me everything I know. Ritual sacrifice to the Old Ones granted me my tremendous powers."

"We'll see how tremendous they are," Tori taunted.

"Indeed, we will," said Haines. "And I have you to thank for all we've accomplished."

Bert got ready to charge.

"Aw, don't I feel special," said Tori, as she wound up.

Arthur was nearly finished synthesizing the glucose enzyme when someone came stumbling into the lab, searching for a place to hide.

"What are you doing here?" asked Rhea Ramsey.

"Oh," mumbled Arthur. He searched his mind for any plausible reason why a doctor would be in the lab on a Sunday night during a prisoner uprising. But an answer suddenly appeared from behind the host of *Supes-Roundup*. "I'm here to stop you and the other fascists from locking up my boyfriend's best friend's new girlfriend."

"Ah, the gays." Ramsey sniffed. "Step away from whatever it is you're doing over there before you infect the terminal with your disease."

Arthur would have fired back with a righteous retort, but instead he smiled and waited for the massive man behind her to tap her on the shoulder. When Rhea turned, she was looking directly into the chest of a gigantic mobster.

"Shut up, Ramsey," said Memento Maury, who shoved her into the room with a loaded gun aimed at her face. "Almost done?"

Arthur nodded as he checked the computer terminal and typed a new command. "I've synthesized enough for the entire prison. A few more minutes, and we'll have the rest." Behind him, in the center of the massive lab, was a tube the size of a swimming pool filling with red liquid, like a giant vat of Kool-Aid.

"Good," said Maury, as he removed the gun from Rhea's face and aimed it at Arthur.

"What's going on?" he asked. Arthur peeked over his shoulder—maybe there was a bad guy behind him, waiting to pounce.

"S.O.S.A.D. Force thanks you for your service," said Maury.

CHAPTER 32

CALIPH HAINES FOUND HARDEN HIDING IN THE BREAK ROOM between two vending machines. He hadn't been there long and was surprised to see the President wandering around The Cooler completely unescorted.

Not that he needed protection—it just appeared odd. Very un-presidential.

"Harden," greeted Haines.

"Yes, sir," said Harden, who immediately ejected himself from his hiding space, then corrected his greeting while straightening his tie. "I mean, Caliph."

"I have something I need to do," said Haines. He appeared to taste the air. It was an odd gesture: his mouth slowly parted, his old pink tongue flitting in and out before he found the *flavor* he was looking for. "Meet me in the supply room within Cellblock Ten-B in no less, *nor more*, than fourteen minutes from now. Can you do that for me, Harden?"

"Yes!" shouted Harden. "Yes, Caliph."

"Good," said Haines as he walked away, as slow as an old man without a care left in the world. He stopped at the break room door and turned back to Harden. "Be there on time. Not a moment too soon. Not a second too late. Do not let your new *friend* down."

Tori had been an underdog all her life. She lost her parents, grew up the poor orphan girl in school, unjustly earned an unflattering nickname for hurting the wrong boy's feelings, and bounced from loser to loser. She thought she'd turn her life around in college, but once Bert derailed her life, she could never manage to make anything of herself.

She was always fighting an uphill battle. Against an unseen force.

Today, she'd realized she wasn't fighting Bert, the Old Man, Jordan, or an unjust world.

The only person holding Tori back…was Tori.

Power rippled through her from head to toe. She couldn't help but wonder *why now?* If this power had been there all her life, why was she only now coming to realize it? Was it because she had hit absolute bottom? Was it because of Dean? Was it the near-death experience? Or maybe something else had opened the valve inside her mind that had kept her full ability blocked for so long.

"I'm going to pluck off every digit," growled Bert. "Then your eyes, ears, then each tooth, one by one."

"Hey fuckbucket, does this kind of banter do it for you?" Tori ducked under a right hook and slugged him in the ribs. She felt them flex under her fist and wondered how much harder she could hit on the next swing—

—when Crimson Justice clobbered her with a right, then left, and sent her spiraling through the wall and two weight-bearing pillars. Tori rolled over and popped onto her feet just in time for Bert to hit her with everything he had.

"If you like," said Haines, appearing beside her, "I can call Crimson Justice off, Ms. O'Neill. All you must do is ask for mercy." No matter where she landed, what angle or direction she looked, Haines was there. Was it a mind trick? Was he a telepath? A teleporter? A speedster? Was his power to be really fucking annoying?

"Go suck a turd." She wanted to zing Haines with a better insult, but her repertoire had been spent. She extricated herself from the splintered remains of the judges' bench. Her orange jumpsuit was torn and dirty, and the sentencing room was all but destroyed.

"Suit yourself." Haines shrugged as he removed his cataract glasses for the first time. To Tori's horror, there were two black holes where his eyes should've been, like the light had died in those empty sockets.

This man, whatever he was, had been the source of all her nightmares— the bogeyman watching over her shoulder.

On cue, Bert unleashed the Justice Beams, then followed them up with an explosive punch that could've lit the atmosphere on fire.

When Bert was done unloading, he found Tori—a woman less than a third of his overall mass—smirking like he hadn't just unleashed his entire arsenal at her.

She'd absorbed it all, every last bit, like a sponge.

His jaw dropped.

Anyone else would have been vaporized in that furious tornado of combos, but not Tori—not *this* Tori. She grinned, then approached him while dancing through a volley of kicks and punches, swatting them aside like they were buzzing gnats.

"My turn," she said.

"Puppyyyyy!" squealed Brie. "Come back here and let me taste you!"

Dean and Rudy ran for their lives. It took all Dean's courage to dash away and leave Tori behind to face Lawrence alone. The moment the heavyweight fight started between Crimson Justice and Crystal Beth, Dean knew he was out of his league. Tori was on her own, and he was more scared for her than for himself—which was saying something, considering the hideous creature chasing them.

Brie was a bloodthirsty succubus cannibal creature, chasing them while salaciously licking her blood-red lips with her rancid, hairy tongue. Dean wanted to turn around and plug her hairy-mouth-hole with his fist, though that would be the quickest way to lose a hand.

Being chased by succubus Brie was an inverted fantasy—an upside-down dream—a twisted nightmare of everything he had yearned for the last thirteen years.

All Dean wanted was to end this awful weekend—to get out of The Cooler alive, take Tori home, set a date, exchange numbers, and sleep till his alarm went off for work on Monday morning. Even if he had to run to the nearest Supe-Burger himself and return with all the sesame seeds he could find.

First, they had to escape Brie and avoid Cooler security. But every hallway in the supe-max prison looked exactly the same.

"Where are we going?" shouted Dean, once it became clear that they were running in circles without a plan.

"I'm following you!" shouted Rudy.

"But I was following you!"

"Why would you do a dumbass thing like that?"

"Because you ran first!"

"Because we're being chased by a suk-you-bust!"

The walls were stacked with rows of pipe, and LED lights were embedded into the ceiling, fading on panel by panel when they sensed approaching motion. The halls were silent and dark, only coming to life as they sprinted through, perpetually rounding a bend that never seemed to end.

Behind every locked door were stacks of freezers full of frozen supes or temporary holding cells for supes yet to be sentenced. There were no exits, just endless incarceration, as the entirety of The Cooler went into lockdown.

There was a loud bang, the kind that could only have been caused by supes. Dean wondered if Tori was alright. It wasn't the first explosion, and every structure-rocking blast rendered the whole building more treacherous.

The Cooler was coming undone, brick by brick. What had taken two full years to build was cracking apart level by level as Tori and Lawrence battled. Dust fell in perpetual leaks from the ceiling, and the lights flickered—the typical, clichéd, run-of-the-mill disaster scene as they fled through the halls.

"C'mon, Puppy! Give mama a little sugar," Brie keened. "Let me lick it up, baby!"

Rudy groaned. "Deano. What is wrong with you? This *woman* had you chasing her milkshake for a baker's dozen?"

"Gimme some sweet Puppy piiiiiieee," she sang.

Dean ignored him—as well as the sudden realization that Brie was a closeted hair-metal freak.

All he wanted was to see Tori again. Every structure-jostling slam made him feel less confident that would ever happen—but then Tori erupted through the concrete wall ahead and soared through the adjacent wall. Lawrence followed, his fists clenched. The eruption set off a chain reaction of flashing red lights and power failures—but that wasn't what stopped them dead in their tracks, despite Brie's inevitable approach.

Rudy and Dean were glued to the floor.

From the cracked rubble ahead came a light, followed by a shimmering tremble before a secondary explosion filled the hall with luminescence. It was so bright, it stopped Brie's advance.

They shielded their eyes against the overwhelming brilliance.

"Oh! Look, it's. Dimwit Dean!" said Apollo. "My nemesis."

The hall was so bright, they couldn't see him. It was like staring directly into the sun.

"Oh shit," groaned Dean.

"I always thought I'd take my last bow under the bright lights," whispered Rudy, "but not like this."

"Knock knock," said Apollo.

"Who's there?" questioned Rudy.

Dean elbowed him.

"Watt's up?" said Apollo, laughing menacingly. "Get it? Watt's up? Like, electrical watts in a light bulb?"

Dean rolled his eyes. "Yeah, we get it."

Brie laughed. "Oh my god, he's so funny."

"Supe groupie," grumbled Dean.

"If we die, I want you to know I appreciate you," said Rudy. "Even your jokes aren't that bad."

"Oh, Dean," sighed Apollo, fading into a pleasant glow. He was wearing an orange jumpsuit like a toga. "I'm going to light up your life, bitch."

"I already paid you back, psycho!" yelled Dean. "Leave us alone!"

"It's not about the money, it's—"

"Yeah, yeah! We get it," shouted Dean. "It's the principle. That's the fucking word you're fucking trying to remember, you fucking psychotic asshole!"

"No," said Apollo, shaking his head. "It's not about the money. It's about defeating my nemesis."

The Cooler jostled with another heavy blast, widening the hole Tori and Lawrence had crashed through. Rudy flipped Apollo off, then pushed Dean through the hole and into an adjacent hallway.

"We're supposed to be subtracting enemies, not acquiring them!" shouted Rudy as they raced away with two angry supes on their trail.

"S.O.S.A.D. Force thanks you for your service," said Memento Maury.

Arthur Ravine had never seen a real gun before, let alone one pointed at him. It was a surreal experience he would rather not repeat if given the chance to continue living.

The gun itself looked like a toy in Maury's massive mitts, and Arthur wondered if he pulled the trigger, would a cheap plastic flag shoot out the barrel with a cartoony "BANG"?

For a man with a genius IQ, Arthur wasn't as scared as he should've been. He was a man of duality—the emotional man couldn't exist in the same place and time as the logical scientist.

This ordeal, however, was the first time his life had been threatened with a deadly weapon, and he didn't feel a thing. Arthur took his pulse, sliding fingers over his wrist.

Normal.

No panic. Just a steady line that allowed Arthur to use his greatest weapon: his brain.

"Just shoot him already!" said Rhea Ramsey, her beady eyes flaring.

"Why do you think I'm on your side?" grumbled Maury.

"You're pointing the gun at him, not me," she said with a snooty, irreverent tone, like nothing could ever touch her.

Maury scoffed. "I'm pointing my gun at the only real threat in the room."

"Hardly!"

"That man," said Maury, poking the gun in Arthur's direction, "created a way to turn supe powers off and on."

"Oh, I'm well aware of Doctor Ravine's discoveries," said Rhea.

"How do you know about my work?" asked Arthur.

Even Maury was surprised.

"Simple," said Rhea. "I was your F.B.S.I. contact."

"No," said Maury, "you couldn't have been. I was working with the F.B.S.I. too and—"

As Maury explained himself, Rhea Ramsey changed shape. She was no longer the host of *Supes-Roundup*, but instead she was Scott Rio. Then she shifted again and again. With each manifestation, she became an infamous celebrity known for controversial Ministry rhetoric.

"Great," groaned Maury. "She's a fucking shapeshifter."

"Do you only take the form of washed-up fascist actors?" asked Arthur.

Rhea, returning to her original form, gave him a humorless smile. "Crimson Justice was dispatched to find Annie Phetamine and kill her after the drop. Once she contacted you, he paid her a visit. However, Crimson Justice made the mistake of killing her before we had all of Doctor Ravine's research in hand. When you contacted us about a plan to retrieve the final drop with all the research, we were willing to let you handle it. But then that big dumb dope, Dust, posted the gig onto SupeHeistFinder.com—a site the government runs, by the way. We were quick to intervene."

Maury pinched the bridge of his nose.

"And the commissioner?" asked Maury. "Was he in on it too?"

"The Commissioner believes he's working for the F.B.S.I.," said Rhea. "What a fool."

"So you hired the Dope Gang to break into the vault and steal my research?" asked Arthur.

"They were already going to do it, but I gave them additional incentive. I offered five hundred million dollars. Besides, I don't trust mobsters, and neither should you."

"I was scammed," said Maury.

"Not that I was actually going to pay them." Rhea smirked. "Once the research was in my hands, I was going to turn the Dope Gang over to the police. And maybe Crimson Justice too—that man has a serious vendetta against those Tin Men pricks."

"What would the host of *Supes-Roundup* need with my research?" asked Arthur.

"Oh, honey," said Rhea, "*Supes-Roundup* is state-sponsored entertainment, and the president has appointed me as Secretary of Supe Affairs. With your research, we could control the course of human events. We could ensure the United American States has the most powerful supes. We could topple governments. Americans will be the chosen ones. We will be kings and queens amongst men—well, when I say *we*, I don't mean you gentlemen. The future of America does not include the ugly, the un-patriotic, the brown, the Sympies, the poor, the unclean, or the sinners."

She looked directly at Arthur when she said *sinners*. Arthur felt like he had accidentally popped a piece of watermelon candy into his mouth, which was the most unfavorable experience he could imagine—watermelon candy was the worst.

"Why's that?" asked Maury.

Rhea puffed her chest. "You're both impure. Obviously."

"Fucking fascists," groaned Maury.

"Why do *you* want my research, Maury?" asked Arthur. He was almost finished. They hadn't even noticed him typing out the algorithm into the keypad.

Maury laughed. "Money, of course. With your research, I can get back to business. Since supes started popping up like weasels, organized crime is barely legit. The Syndicate will be back on top, and I can continue to provide weapons and supplies to supe and supervillain without consequence. I'll corner the market."

Arthur as he hit the return key, starting the algorithm. "So one of you did it for money and the other for world domination."

"Hey kid," said Maury, "don't lump me in with her. I'm a capitalist."

Tori had been in a lot of fights in her life. Her first came at the age of seven, shortly after her mother's funeral, when Kevin Thomas called her a "stupid orphan." Tori called Kevin a "booger-loving ho-ho" and followed that with a left hook. The fights got progressively harder from there.

Crimson Justice was the kind of un-hurtable, unconscionable creature with the growing reputation of a terrorist. Supes like him had free reign to hurt and destroy. If they stepped out of line or lost favor with the government, a loyal supe would apprehend them—dead or alive. Apprehended supes were tossed into a prison like The Cooler and inhumanely disposed of. All the while, scientists experimented on them, searching for what made them tick.

The scientists of Amycus Industries may have discovered the source of supe powers, but nobody knew exactly why some supes burned, others flew, and so on. Doctor Arthur Ravine had developed a sound hypothesis, but he'd been unable to prove it thus far.

Supes had destroyed Tori's life. She didn't care why they were or what they were. She only wanted the nightmare to end.

Tori knew she was fighting for what was right. She was fighting for the little guy, the Tin Men, the people who wanted to live free and happy without the worry of being oppressed or hated or even murdered in pursuit of their happiness. She was fighting so that no little girl would ever have to grow up without family, friends, or stability. She was fighting for people of every color, race, creed, and orientation, so the world would be a better, more peaceful place than the one she was born into.

Bert was not fighting for the same future.

He unloaded every power he had in his arsenal. Their fight was like a video game, complete with specialized windups, poses, and catchphrases like "Surrender to the Long Arm of the Law!" Bert hit her with everything he had, but nothing slowed her down. In a way, Tori hadn't yet begun to fight back.

First, she wanted to know that she could take his best.

They were inside a supply room, with rows of crates housing unused supe-freezers and other scientific gear. The exposed rafters were a hundred feet above, surrounded by vents and open ducts. It was a massive structure and yet one tiny part of The Cooler.

"Young lady," said Haines, "you may capitulate the fight." He furrowed his eyebrows and removed his hat, holding it over his heart to show he cared.

"Give it up, Tori," said Bert. "I can do this all day."

"Is that it?" She picked herself up off the floor once again.

Bert seemed confused. "Is what it?"

"Is that all you can do?" she clarified. "I mean, do you have any other powers? Any super-secret ones you save for emergency situations?"

"What are you on about, Ms. O'Neill?" asked Haines, but Tori ignored him. In fact, she walked right past him on her way to Bert.

"No," said Bert, "that's everything. Except the Red Mist, but I seem to be missing a few intestines and a sphincter to properly eject it."

Tori attempted to stifle her laughter.

"You're sure?" she asked. "Nothing else?"

Bert counted out all the powers he used on his fingers, whispering to himself the half dozen options, and reported back that he had indeed used everything. "What about you, Crystal Beth? Got anything hidden up your sleeve?"

He smiled arrogantly, and Tori couldn't wait to bust out his remaining teeth.

"Oh, I haven't used any yet. I don't even know my limits, to be honest."

Haines watched silently.

Bert side-eyed her. "What do you mean?"

In a half second, she spanned the fifty feet between them, reared up, and clobbered Bert so hard his remaining teeth cracked. He hit the far wall and bounced off, landing in a heap on the floor. Before he had the opportunity to react, she was on top of him. She tossed him into the air and slammed an elbow into his sternum before he had reached the apex of his travel, thundering his body straight down into the concrete floor. She pummeled him over and over, beating on him like a boxing dummy at the local YMCA.

When enough bones had cracked, she stopped.

"Let's walk through it. Super speed? Check. Super strength? Check. What else?" Tori lit her hand on fire while the other turned to solid ice. Then she took each of Bert's hands and did the same to his—and despite its initial resistance, Bert's flesh eventually burned and froze.

"Jeebus almighty!" screamed Bert.

Then Tori let him go.

"Fire? Ice? Check and Check. What else can I do?" In a blink, Tori had Bert by the crimson collar. In the next, they weren't in The Cooler at all.

They weren't even in the Earth's atmosphere.

She held him at arm's length while he struggled against her grip, unable to breathe as the lack of oxygen and pressure caused havoc across his body. They were in outer space. As she held him there, she could feel the skin surrounding her eyes draw shades of blue and purple, painting an image of the galaxy—like a mask.

After a few seconds in orbit admiring the view, Tori whisked them back to where they came—there one moment, gone the next.

"Teleportation? Check." She puffed out her chest. "I guess the hillbilly was right."

Bert fell to his knees, gasping for air, and looked up at a goddess. She was no longer wearing her prison jumpsuit, but her favorite knee-high boots and leather jacket—her hair was brilliant platinum, pinned up like a cascading wave of curls falling off the side of her head, and her high-cut t-shirt was emblazoned with a new logo. But there was something else—the gold and black pants, the star earrings—she was going to be a symbol, fighting for little girls like Sally, whom she met at Supes-Con the day before.

"What…are…you?" he asked as her imagination continued to create a new vision for herself. Her new costume came to completion with a satisfying snap.

"I'm no longer Crystal Beth," she said. "I can tell you that much." Then she remembered the bike helmet. There had been a majestic beast airbrushed onto its shiny surface.

The same beast now printed onto her brand-new t-shirt.

"*It's a Gryphyn,*" Dean had said. "*A benevolent mythological creature.*"

"*Does it do anything special?*" she'd asked him.

"*Gryphyns ward against evil. They're powerful guardians of good. It's said they mate for life, and if their partner dies, the other will mourn for the rest of its days.*"

Then Tori looked at Bert and said something profound.

"I am the Gryphyn," said Tori.

"My, my," said Haines, "that you are."

Rudy was beginning to curse the fact that he and Arthur had ever went along with this cockamamie plan to break some supe-girl out of supe-prison for his supe-hating best friend who had somehow fallen for said supe-girl, despite all the supe-hating and supes in a supe-fucking-prison.

And he was beginning to feel that all of them were going to end up dead.

What had happened to Arthur? Was he alive? Did he make it to the lab?

"Puppy!" sang Brie.

"Dimwit!" sang Apollo.

The two had become fast friends, ganging up to take down their common enemy. And they were fast. Weren't villains supposed to be slow? That's how it was in the movies. Jason Voorhees was as sluggish as dry mud. If those idiot kids had chosen one direction and power-walked without tripping over shit, they would've made it to safety every time.

But this was the real world, and long-legged Brie kept pace with Apollo's Olympian jog. Rudy wasn't cut out for this. His lungs felt like they were on fire. He would just as soon duck into a maintenance closet and wait it out if he could.

But then he looked at Dean and realized he couldn't let his best friend down, even if he didn't know how to get them out of this jam.

"There has to be an exit," gasped Dean.

Rudy could tell he was worried—not just about escaping, but about Tori. She was fighting the most powerful supe on the planet, one that could survive with only half his organs, and even Rudy felt that wasn't a good sign for her survival.

Then, when all hope seemed lost—when their legs and lungs seemed heavier than they'd ever felt before—Rudy recognized the massive man in the big gray suit standing in the doorway ahead.

He gathered up the extra breath required to shout, and as he did, several events transpired at once:

1. Rudy shouted, "Maury!"
2. Apollo caught up to them from behind.
3. Brie jumped onto Dean's back and took a big honking bite into his right shoulder.
4. Maury turned as they collided with his big, bulging frame.
5. A gunshot went off.

Haines was slow-clapping—the kind that only worked in dramatic coming-of-age movies about undersized football players or Jamaican bobsled teams.

Bert was a shivering mess. Sections of skin and muscle were missing. He was scalded and frozen, depressurized and broken apart by pure force. Was this revenge? Was inflicting this level of pain equal to Bert's transgressions? Equal to losing her best friend?

Had Tori taken her pound of flesh?

She was still clutching fistfuls of his uniform, watching him gasp for air through a collapsed lung and shattered ribs.

"My dear, that was impressive," crowed Haines. "Tell me, how did you know you could accomplish such feats?"

"I didn't," she replied. "I just imagined what I wanted to do, and it happened."

Then she imagined something else—something different and amazing, starting with a warming glow emanating from her hands. When she released Bert's uniform, he stood up and removed the hooded cowl.

"What did you do to me?" asked Bert, blinking with two whole eyes. He felt around his body, even checking on the family jewels and finding all the plumbing intact.

"I healed you. Don't thank me."

"Why?"

She refused the urge to slap him upside his dumbass head. "Because nobody should suffer. Ever."

Tori felt suddenly dizzy, like her blood sugar was low. Had she overexerted herself? Haines had stopped clapping and was looming somewhere behind her. She took a breath, cast aside her dizziness, and turned to him, unafraid.

"Mercy is for the weak," said Haines.

"What are you, Cobra Kai?" She imagined Dean laughing. He would have gotten the reference.

"You still do not realize what you are, Ms. O'Neill," said Haines.

"Enlighten me."

"In order to keep me and those I serve from destroying this dimension, reality itself was fractured into thirteen equal but different interpretations. One by one, I have worked to destroy them all. This world was doomed to self-destruction, its people infected with powers they could never comprehend. A power, my dear, that has chosen you as its prime vessel.

"They call you many things," he continued, "in other realities. Different names, different lives, but always the same face. The same defiance. This world would have crumbled beneath its own sin, given time. However, I am on a schedule."

"What kind of quacky, bullshit fucking wack-a-doo nonsense are you on about?" growled Tori. He sounded like Dennis Hopper delivering a madman speech in any number of roles, from *Waterworld* to *Speed*.

"Would you like to see?" asked Haines. "I'll show you what exists behind the veil."

There was a shadow behind Caliph Haines. Yet it was connected to him. Like the hellish doxie triplets from the sewers—as if his old, frail body were the protective clothes of the real thing stuffed inside.

"No, thanks," said Tori. It seemed proper to maintain some level of cordial discussion. He was without a doubt a scary sunnuva gun, and there was something about his shadow that gave her the kind of heebie-jeebies reserved for serial killers or the creepier episodes of *Dateline*.

"I should have been more clear," said Haines. "I was not asking."

The man who had accompanied the president appeared, entering through a cargo door, and stepped up beside Haines.

"Harden." Haines checked his watch. "Fourteen minutes. Not a second sooner, nor later."

"You're welcome, Caliph," said Harden with a sheepish smile.

"I wasn't thanking you," said Haines. "Harden, I would like you to show the young lady how I altered you."

He hung his head, then apprehensively removed his red tie. He rolled it up before stuffing it into his pocket, then continued to unbutton his white shirt.

"What is this?" asked Tori—like she was caught in the middle of the most heinous bachelor party ever assembled.

"Please, Harden," said Haines, "show her your secret. Do not be shy."

Harden's face was shiny with sweat. He forwent the casual unbuttoning, grabbed hold of his shirt, and tore it open, sending the remaining buttons scurrying across the floor. What he unveiled upon his chest sent shock waves through the room, and Tori gasped in terror.

Ricochets are unlikely, but not improbable. A bullet of the right caliber hitting a hard surface at the right angle could cause a ricochet. However, like skipping rocks across the surface of a lake or pond, the number of bounces beyond the first descended into extreme levels of impossibility.

This day, for whatever reason, impossibility took an encore.

Dean rolled into the room with Brie grappling onto him for another bite. Apollo and Maury slammed into the far wall, and something clanked onto the ground and bounced several times. Rudy slid into the room face-first and came to a stop just two feet from the clanking, smoking object as Rhea Ramsey screamed obscenities.

"Rudy?" Arthur's white lab coat was slowly staining red above the cast on his arm, and a series of sparks showered from the terminal behind him.

"Arthur?" cried Rudy from the floor.

"We've been double-crossed," said Arthur, clamping his hand over the wound to staunch the bleeding.

Rudy looked up into the green eyes of his partner, the man he loved, and decided his feelings of fear and insignificance had perpetuated long enough.

"Put your hands up!" Rudy waved the gun with a slight tremble that forced him to use his other hand to steady his aim. When nobody listened, Rudy fired a shot that struck the wall between Maury and Apollo, gathering everyone's attention—even Brie's. She stopped nibbling on Dean.

"What're you going to do with that?" asked Maury. "You're pointing a pistol at four supes. I can't die, Rhea's a shapeshifting fascist bitch, bright-boy over there's bulletproof, and I don't know what the hell Blondie is."

"You don't strike me as someone who packs heat just to protect himself from normies," said Rudy. "Something tells me these are special bullets."

"Special bullets?" asked Brie, providing Dean an opening to slip away from her grasp.

"There's no such thing, dumbass," said Rhea.

"Go ahead, be a total B, Brie," teased Rudy. "Yuck it up, rude Rhea, but I don't see Memento Maury making any moves to stop me."

Maury closed his eyes and pinched his nose.

"Whatever!" shouted Apollo, "I'm a star, not a coward." He advanced on Rudy.

A pop sounded, and Rudy's bullet ricocheted off Apollo's chest and embedded into the wall above Rhea's head.

"Ow!" Apollo rubbed his chest. The bullet had left a dent. "Once I'm done with Dean, I'm gonna to knock your lights out too!" His glow grew until Arthur jumped forward with a hose.

"Cool off, bright boy." Arthur turned the valve and coated him with a sticky red liquid. Apollo's light blacked out.

"What the fuck is this?" shouted Apollo, wiping the sticky fluid from his eyes. He looked like a candy apple as it coated his hair and skin—smelled like one, too, as the room filled with a fruity scent.

"It's a glucose enzyme," said Arthur, as Apollo struggled to reignite his glow. He looked constipated and strained—even less ripped than before.

"What the fuck is going on here?" roared Apollo.

"Shit," groaned Maury—eyes wide with a gleam of sweat along his brow.

Arthur cleared his throat and gestured to the giant vat of red liquid at the center of the lab beyond the busted terminal. "I coated your cells in an enzyme that prevents your body from accessing the Deus Particles they're entangled with."

"In other words, geek-stain?" growled Apollo.

"In other words," said Dean, "Arthur snipped your balls."

Then Dean did something he clearly had been wanting to do all weekend. He had taken too much abuse, too many bumps and bruises, and Rudy couldn't blame him when he balled his fist and slugged Apollo square in the nose. Blood burst from Apollo's nostrils, and Dean's knuckles went bright red. Both men screamed, but Dean smiled through the pain.

Apollo stared at the puddling blood resting in the palm of his hand. His other hand cradled his broken nose as involuntary tears scrolled down his cheeks. "What the hell did you guys do to me?"

"We took your powers," said Rudy. "It wasn't like you were doing anything good with them."

"C'mon, boys," said Maury. "Let's talk this out."

"Too late for that," said Dean. Rudy handed him the gun, then began to staunch the blood leaking from the wound on Arthur's arm. Dean took the hose in his other hand and aimed it at the remaining supes but kept the gun on Rhea.

"Pupppppyyyyyy," whined Brie. Dean glared at her, angling the nozzle of the power-stealing-hose in her direction. She flinched. "I mean, Dean! Just Dean, hehe." She had licked the last few drops of his blood from her chin and miraculously looked like her old self—only plain. The luster had gone out of her hair and skin, but at least she no longer looked like a monster. "This is silly. Why don't you let me go?"

"You tried to eat me," said Dean.

"Yeah, but—"

"She tried to eat you?" asked Arthur, wincing as Rudy dabbed at his wound.

"She's a suk-you-bust," said Rudy.

Arthur's eyebrows elevated.

The terminal behind Arthur buzzed and snared his attention. He pulled his arm away from Rudy before he had properly staunched the graze and appeared lost in scientific thought.

"What's going on?" asked Dean. The vat of red liquid darkened.

Arthur furiously typed away on the terminal keypad as Dean's head swiveled, twisting back and forth between the buzz and warding off their captives.

"You assholes," sobbed Apollo. "I'll never shine again!"

"Shut up, dumbass," groaned Maury.

"You're the dumbass," growled Rhea. "You got outwitted by a nitwit."

"All of you!" shouted Dean, "cool it!"

"Arthur," said Rudy, "I know you're in the middle of science-ing that keyboard, but there's a nasty buzzing sound, like the time my Gram forced me remove a hornet's nest from her attic." Rudy then looked to Dean. "That's why I hate *Grease*."

"What?" asked Dean. It was one of the many Rudy-riddles Dean had yet to decode—why did Rudy hate *Grease?* He was loading a follow-up question when—

"This is bizarre," said Arthur.

"What is?" asked Rudy.

Arthur turned to everyone in the room with a worrisome expression as the vat of darkening liquid began to empty.

Maury laughed. "Looks like your leverage is going down the drain."

"You can give me my powers back, right, bros?" begged Apollo. "Please?"

Arthur looked pale—he had either lost too much blood, or…

"What's wrong, Arthur?" asked Rudy.

"The bullet hit the terminal," explained Arthur.

"I see that, Captain Obvious," said Rudy.

"It started the distribution process," said Arthur.

"The distribution process?" asked Dean.

"Yes," said Arthur, "and I can't stop it."

"What is the distribution process?" asked Rhea, looking concerned.

"Shut up, asshole." Dean turned to Arthur. "But yeah, what is the distribution process?"

"Oh," said Arthur, as if the question had jump-started his thoughts. "The plan was to break in and disrupt Tori's sentencing. Dean would pretend to be Crimson Justice so he could get far enough into the room to use Maury's tiny black box to fry all the circuitry—cyborg Ministerium Guards included. Then from the lab, I could use the flash drive to synthesize enough enzyme to power down all supe opposition. If we made them believe we had the power to de-supe a whole prison, they might just let us leave, and the world would know what Amycus and the president were planning. And we could use the distribution process to disseminate the enzyme if they called our bluff."

"Uh huh," said Rudy, "which is?"

"I'm sorry, was that not clear?" Arthur blinked. "If there was ever a supe insurrection, these tanks would drain and start the distribution process... Through the sprinkler system, obviously."

"Wait," said Dean, "all of that red de-supe stuff is going to start spraying every supe within this building."

"Yes," said Arthur. "I thought all of you understood that?"

"You said you'd use the enzyme to stop supes," said Maury.

"How else was I going to do that in a two-hundred-million-square-foot underground facility?" Arthur rolled his eyes at the ridiculousness of their logic.

"Can we stop it?" asked Maury.

Arthur typed something into the terminal, then turned to face them all again. "No, we cannot."

"What?" cried Brie. She looked terrified. "I can't lose my powers looking like this!"

"Don't worry, Brie-Brie," said Rudy. "Arthur has an antidote in a tasty shade of blue."

"Oh, thank gawd!" said Apollo.

"Well," said Arthur, "Yes, that is true. The repellant enzyme was only ever temporary. Topical application has a shorter half-life. If consumed, the body would naturally metabolize the enzyme and powers would gradually return. Furthermore, there is—or rather, was a second, blue-tinted glucose enzyme that reacted as a counter-agent to the repellent."

"*Was* a second glucose enzyme?" Maury didn't appear to like where this conversation was going.

"I created an algorithm. I couldn't let my research fall into the hands of anyone who'd use it to hurt others." He looked at Maury. "Or for profit."

"What does the algorithm do?" asked Brie.

"After the enzyme was created and the distribution process was started, the algorithm was designed to erase my research once and for all," said Arthur.

"That's good news, right?" asked Dean.

"It is," agreed Arthur.

"Good job, Arthur!" shouted Rudy.

"Well," continued Arthur, "it was."

"Arthur," scolded Rudy, "Let's try and get on the same page, shall we?"

"Sorry," he said.

"Wait," interrupted Brie. "Why is the red stuff turning purple?"

"Ah, yes," said Arthur, checking over his shoulder. The vat of red sticky liquid was indeed turning a deep shade of purple. "That is the *not good* news. My research wasn't just about turning supe powers off and on—which was why I began working with the F.B.S.I.—which we now know was just Rhea Ramsey in disguise."

"When did we know that?" asked Rudy.

Rhea smiled, and Dean shrugged.

"But Amycus wanted me to go further. They wanted me to find a way to turn supe powers off." Arthur swallowed heavily. "Forever..."

"What the fuck!?" growled Apollo.

"...hence the purple hue," finished Arthur.

"Forever and ever?" asked Rudy.

Arthur nodded, and the supes in the room shrieked.

"Arthur! How is this bad news? This is spectacular! This is—"

"Hey!" shouted Apollo, "you can't leave me like this! Give me the antidote so I can get out of this shithole before that purple stuff starts flying."

"Calm down." Dean turned to Arthur. "How long do we have before the distribution process starts?"

Arthur looked frazzled. "Once the tank fully drains, it'll start distributing from the upper levels down. About five minutes."

"Five minutes!?" shouted Brie.

"We need to get out of here!" yelled Rhea.

"Is she a supe too?" asked Rudy. "I can't keep track anymore!"

"C'mon kids," pled Maury. "I'm not going back to being Sleazy Moe. Memento has a ring to it."

"Fix me now and let me go!" Apollo was losing his cool. The red sticky liquid dried onto his skin like a crunchy candy crust. A small blink of luminescence peeked through, but Apollo never saw it as he lurched forward, demanding his powers be returned—launching himself at Dean.

Even though Peter was the video game guru back in college, it was

Dean who held the 3rd Floor, Classic Video Game Championship two years running before surrendering his title to The Tank before Graduation. Dean was unbeatable at certain games, his best being the classic NHL '94 for SNES.

After Lawrence started dating Brie, Dean made sure to embarrass the big doofus by running up the score that final year, beating Lawrence 21 to 2 in their semi-final match. It was a small consolation, but it still felt good to get one over on the man who stole Brie.

These details were crucial to explain what happened next.

When Apollo lunged at Dean with his supe-abilities returning, allowing him to move faster than a normal man, Dean spun on impulse. He may have been a normie, but Dean's eye-hand coordination was stellar—a key piece of information that Apollo would wished he'd known before he attempted the foolish endeavor.

Before Apollo arrived within three feet of Dean, he squeezed the trigger—not of the gun, but the hose attached to the vat of purple sticky liquid.

The result was as messy as it was shocking.

Apollo's glimmer flickered and popped, like a burned-out lightbulb.

"You dick! Why'd you do tha—"

"Oh my god!" shrieked Brie. She nearly crawled up the wall to prevent the pooling purple goo from touching her.

Rhea squealed.

Maury pinched his nose.

Rudy's eyes flared while Arthur did calculations in his head.

"What just happened?" asked Dean.

"Total molecular incompatibility," mumbled Arthur.

"What?" asked Dean.

Apollo went poof. His light blinked and flashed, then discarded his flesh like Dean stepping out of Crimson Justice's four-sizes too large costume. What was left of him hit the floor like a puddle of wet playdough.

"Apollo's most basic supe abilities weren't his super-strength or invulnerability," said Arthur, scratching his head. "His most basic ability was creating light. All supe abilities are based on the individual's cellular structure blending with their superpowers—the Deus Particles—in homeostasis. His Latent Endowment Gifts, LEGs for short, were unraveled. The purple glucose enzyme rendered this equilibrium with the body's basic latent abilities as suddenly incompatible, and Apollo's body shed the incompatibility immediately."

"Like I'm five!" shouted Rudy, reminding Arthur not to science over his head.

"In other words," said Arthur, "his light and his body became incompatible."

The room went silent.

Eventually, Rudy noticed the sick look on his best friend's face. "Deano? Are you okay?"

"Tori," Dean whispered under his breath.

MASKED

CHAPTER 33

TORI AND DEAN HAD LIVED THIRTY-THREE YEARS. THIRTY-three years of highs and lows—

Mistakes and successes—

Lessons learned and desires—

Triumphs and failures—

They were both flawed but innocent. They were victims of the world, and it was hard to imagine their happy ending.

Sometimes the hottest, brightest flames are the ones that blow out quickest.

The unknown truth of their past was that Tori and Dean were never more than mere moments from each other. Since the day Dean stepped foot into the town of Grace Falls, attending Milton State University, their lives had crisscrossed again and again.

The night Dean met Brie, Tori was sitting at the booth with Amanda and their new friends, giggling at the guy with all the hot sauce on his face devouring buckets of wings. That night was the beginning of Peter's "wingman" obsession.

The evening Amanda went missing? Tori and Rick were kissing outside the restaurant where Dean was contemplating an escape plan during a date gone wrong.

Dean's fateful run-in with Brie at the bookstore? Tori was filling out an application for the mini-café in the back.

And so on…

They were always moments apart. Two lost souls searching for the other, out of sync, and now they were running out of time.

Dean ran from the lab like he was shot out of a circus cannon, Memento Maury's suit jacket in his hand—a 74w special, gray, pinstripe jacket with a yellow satin lining. Maury parted with it exactly two seconds after Dean threatened to hose him with the purple sticky stuff.

"Do you want to find out what happens to you?" threatened Dean, and Maury immediately surrendered. It was already a pressurized room, and Dean's intensity was broiling.

"Go get her, Deano," said Rudy. Dean sprinted from the room with only a nod to Arthur and Rudy as a parting gesture.

Brie begged for Dean to stay—to play the hero and escort her to safety—but there was nothing, not even hypnotism, that could've fooled him into falling for her trickery ever again.

He sprinted to the end of the hall, then turned left, retracing the path he and Rudy took when escaping Brie and Apollo. Despite the burning sensation in his legs and chest, Dean never slowed down, not even after tripping over piles of rubble.

Emergency lights strobed, while angry, buzzing alarms reminded Dean that he was running out of time. He had five minutes to find Tori in a massive ultra-security prison before the distribution process coated everything in a sticky purple spray—a spray that could very well end her life.

Dean chased his chaotic thoughts up an accessibility ramp and jumped over the railing onto the level below. He blasted through a pair of security doors, shouting her name.

As he passed from section to section, he noted a growing hiss, sounding like a serpent nipping at his heels. It was only after he rounded the next bend and peered back through the previous hall that he saw what was following him—pairs of nozzles lowered from the ceiling had begun spraying a fine purple mist. Dean caught a whiff of the sweet-smelling liquid and ran faster, pushing himself right to the edge of an anxiety attack as he blew through an abandoned security checkpoint.

"Where y'all think y'all goin, hun?" said a woman in pigtails and daisy dukes. She stepped out of the checkpoint office crammed with frightened witnesses seeking refuge while weaving a marvelous display of jazz-hands. Sparks of light danced from her fingertips.

"That's him!" shouted Rio as Dean soared past, ducking through the metal detectors.

"That's the guy!" shouted Nougat. "The stakes have never been higher!"

Dean never slowed. He left them far behind, racing through two additional lengths of hallway. Nothing was going to stop him. Nothing and nobody—not Apollo, not Ministerium Guards, not even Lawrence—except the woman in pigtails with the southern twang who suddenly swept his legs with a spinning backheel kick.

"I said," repeated the woman, "where y'all think y'all goin, hun?"

"I'm getting really sick and tired of getting hit in the head!" shouted Dean.

"If y'all hadn't noticed, I'm Cowgal Jezebelle." The woman sauntered over and put the heel of her cowboy boot into his chest, flattening him against the ground. "*American Supe* Season Five runner-up? I'm head of Cooler security, and y'all tresspassin'."

"Let me go." Dean swiped her foot away. There was no snappy retort worth exchanging. He had to get moving. He couldn't slow down.

She laughed. "Y'all feisty in the northeast. My daddy always said, Cowgal, northerners are ornery, but them northeasterners? Y'all unpatriotic heathens with—"

As Cowgal droned on, Dean heard it coming. The motorized nozzles lowered from the ceiling, and the high-pitched hiss signaled the mist being deployed in the previous hall.

"What in tarnation is that?" said Jezebelle, noticing the nozzles lowering above.

"Get out of here!" shouted Dean, slipping away while she was distracted.

"Boy, don't make me come after you!"

Dean stopped at the next bend and looked back. She was waving her arms around in a ridiculous pattern—*was she spellcasting?*—when the purple mist deployed.

The dancing sparkles sprang loose from her fingertips and zipped around the room trailed by phosphorescent dust. The perky, petite Southern blonde disappeared—but not magically. She was swallowed whole by a full-figured woman—her cowboy boots splitting wide open to accommodate her enormous calves. Her bare midriff became a flood of flesh, while her hair darkened ten shades.

"What the gosh darnit's happenin' to me!" she screeched.

Dean didn't stick around to witness the final stages of her transformation. He ran to the end of the next hall, checked the following room, then turned right, racing deeper into The Cooler. He was light-headed and gassed, his lungs burned, and he didn't know how much farther he could go. He was on the verge of physical and emotional collapse, and the urge to give up grew louder with every stride.

Dean knew there were things in life worth fighting for. Many virtues were worth risking life and limb, but there was only one thing worth risking one's soul.

Love.

Dean had never had love.

To clarify, Dean was never loved by someone he loved too.

The pursuit of that love was the one thing that motivated him the most throughout his life. It was the one thing he could never catch.

Weddings may have been for assholes, but Dean always wanted to be that asshole. He wanted his special day. He wanted a special bride, smiling just for him as she walked down that aisle.

The panic in his chest told him one thing. As he raced the halls looking to prevent Tori from a terrible fate, possibly death, he realized he didn't want to live without her.

He *could* live without her, technically. And he *would* live without her if he had to.

But he didn't *want* to live without her—and damnit, it was about time he got something he wanted.

"Tori!" he shouted.

He shouted it over and over as if her life depended on it.

"What are you?" gasped Tori.

Her terror blunted the sharpness of her tongue. She wanted to unleash a string of curses that could accurately capture her feelings, but there was nothing loading into the chamber except that single question.

It was a great question, however. To the point. She didn't care who answered first—Haines or Harden. She wanted an answer from both the old man with the black hole eyes and his chief of staff—*whatever the actual fuck he was…*

Harden was vertically split across his dad-bod tummy—and from it came an appendage, disgorging itself from a fleshy pocket until it stretched at least five yards long. Then it sprouted four legs—like a crustacean—as it opened its yawning mouth.

Sharp spindly teeth lined the opening and projected a ray of warm light, as if beyond those needles was the doorway to a vast volcano. Harden and the creature were connected and yet separate as the wormy thing took command of his body, utilizing Harden's human legs as its own back set. The creature was in total control, except for Harden's head, which flopped around and averted its gaze from the horror growing from his own abdomen.

"That," said Haines, wagging a forefinger, "is a difficult question."

"Then give me a difficult answer," said Tori, "you geriatric fart-bag."

Haines smiled, his old, parched lips stretching apart to reveal a set of yellowed teeth with retracted gums. "I am merely an emissary of the great beyond, child," he said. "We want what is yours, what was once ours, and I have come to ensure we take it back." He gestured to his chief of staff like he was a loveable fuck-up. "Harden, as you see, has been altered. His biology has been adapted to take vast power and transmutate it from one form to another."

"What in the fucking lunatic speak does that even mean? He's a walking crab-penis!"

"I thought it was obvious, dear," said Haines. "You are a vessel of vast power that you have no capacity to understand and even less capacity to control. Once you're consumed, your matter will become a valuable tool."

He had no sooner finished speaking when a broken piece of metal—a long section of sheared steel from the earlier battle—erupted through Harden's chest like a javelin. The man and the creature screamed in unison. "Ow, lady! Cut that out!" cried Harden's head.

"Crimson Justice?" prompted Haines.

"Sorry, Tor," said Bert, theatrically protruding his lower lip. "I appreciate you healing me, but he is the boss."

When they surrounded her, three on one—Haines, Crimson Justice, and Harden the crab-penis—Tori smiled. It finally seemed like a fair fight. All her life, she'd felt surrounded by enemies. She spent the last several years playing the part of a supervillain in the media. The walls had been closing in since she was six, and for once she had the power—the real power—to fight back and control her destiny.

Bert lunged first, like an Olympic wrestler grappling for a leg. She backhanded him as if swatting a shuttlecock with a badminton racket. He collided with Haines and bounced off the old man without a flinch.

Then the Harden-crab-penis came rumbling to devour her, the heat from its mouth an inferno. She sidestepped the creature, snatched the steel from its chest, and swung like a bat, knocking the six-legged thing forward into a heap.

Next, she moved on Haines.

"I assure you, Ms. O'Neill," said Haines as she stepped closer, "I'm not as weak as I appear." The old man never lifted a finger, but the dim shadow looming behind him swung and connected. Tori hit a rafter or two before she began her descent, right into Bert's fist.

The angle of her propulsion sent her on a collision course with Harden. The creature's maw widened, ready to catch her whole like a dog snatching an airborne treat.

But this dog treat bit back.

Before Harden's jaws could snare her, Tori used her momentum to smash a fist into its monster head, knocking the beast out cold. Harden flopped to the ground, unable to move. Just a conscious human head atop a limp crab-penis body.

"Bang bang," said Tori, "The Warrior" playing in her head.

"This is highly uncomfortable," whined Harden with a face full of cement floor.

Bert primed and fired the Justice Beams, winding up like a sumo wrestler stomping his foot. Tori took it, then fired back with something she immediately coined the ABFS. She seared half of Bert's right side with the nastiest Automatic Bitch Face Stare she had ever presented in public. The first two layers of Bert's skin flayed from his arm, and if it wasn't for the leather costume, it may have gone clean to the bone.

"I was not expecting you to be so…" said Haines, searching for the right word. *"Pesky."*

"Thanks," said Tori, bouncing on her toes.

"It was not a compliment. You're making the inevitable difficult."

"Spoken like a true sex offender," growled Tori. "You know, people have underestimated me my whole life. Called me broken, since I was old enough to know that sucked. I had dreams of something more. I had a family. I had a best friend. And I'll be damned if I don't take it all back, with interest, starting with your manky face."

She unloaded a left hook. The breeze alone from her fist passing through the air toppled a forklift several yards away. When it hit Haines across the chin, it was like hitting the vault door without her powers—right after she ate that red lollipop and discovered what it could do.

Haines turned his head and spat a wad of blood onto the floor. The blood hissed as it burned into the polished cement while a red trickle dribbled down his chin. He was otherwise unfazed. The ancient old man accepted her punch like she was blowing him a loving kiss, and all he had to show for it was a busted lip.

"Perhaps, child," said Haines, "you're not as powerful as you believe."

Beside Haines appeared a door out of thin air. A plain white wooden door and frame with a basic silver knob. It was standing in the middle of the room like some display inside a hardware store. It was unclear whether the knocks were coming from inside her own head, or if she could hear them with her actual ears, but those three knocks repeated over and over, never louder than a polite rap.

Knock. Knock. Knock.
Knock. Knock. Knock.
Knock. Knock. Knock.

"Go on, my dear," said Haines. "Answer it."

Tori's tongue went bitter, the taste like the time Amanda made chocolate chip cookies with unsweetened chips—she declared Amanda unfit for baking after that fiasco and put her into culinary jail until further notice.

That was less than a month before Amanda died.

Her anger toward Haines' twenty-five-year-plus conspiracy to ruin her life went nuclear inside her chest.

"I think not," she sneered.

"So be it," said Haines. "I've always appreciated the hard path. The outcomes are more conclusive."

The shadow around Haines spun and slapped her across the room—and Tori nearly blacked out. When she collided with the wall, an unseen force captured and pinned her forty feet into the air. With a snap of Haines's fingers, Harden roused and crawled back onto its six tittering legs—and Tori thought maybe she bit off more than she could chew. Her powers took a lot of thought to control. It was like hitchhiking on a super-highway with a skateboard and a big hook—trying to snare a ride with the energy that equipped her with miraculous abilities.

Even as the probability of her walking away and reuniting with Dean and Amanda plummeted, Tori was preparing to do anything to end the nightmare. President Haines was responsible for so much death, destruction, manipulation, and twisted machinations beyond her limited understanding. Whatever he really was, behind those black hole eyes, did not matter. What he wanted with her, with the country, with supes, did not matter either. The only thing that did matter was that Tori put an end to it, right here and now.

Except her plan to thwart Haines was looking like her engagement to Jordan—a total failure—and the smothering nature of their relationship seemed like an apt metaphor too.

Being crushed against a cinderblock wall within the supply room of a supe prison was as fun as it sounded. Tori felt her ribs bow under the growing pressure and ground her teeth. She couldn't move, and the pain filled her ears with white noise.

"Tori!"

Did someone shout her name?

"Tori!"

She thought she'd imagined it.

"Tori!"

From the corner of her eye, she saw movement—a shadow that stumbled around the far corner of the hallway and came to a sliding stop at the bay doors of the storage room.

"Tori!" Her eyes connected with Dean's as the wormy, phallus creature growing from Harden's abdomen crept up the side of the wall and opened wide. The heat billowing from its molten gut engulfed her like dragon's breath.

She had very little time to react—in fact, it was less than .0125 seconds before Harden swallowed her whole—but it was long enough to witness a whole lifetime.

With their eyes connected, she witnessed a new life. She saw stolen kisses, the laughter, the birthdays and holidays. She saw music, and performing in front of her fans, including her biggest—the man who watched from backstage. She saw picnics together with friends, a puppy, their first night in their first home. She saw fights, make-ups, passion, and comfort—she saw a baby, a family, and a forever she cherished more than life itself.

And from the look on Dean's face, he witnessed it too…

As the creature widened its jaw, savoring to digest her into something else—a terrible way to go—Tori decided she had no plans nor patience for that ending.

When Harden's maw snapped shut, Tori was gone. She disappeared, and the thing protruding from Harden's body gurgled its displeasure as it crawled back down onto the floor.

"Ms. O'Neill," said Haines, "If you do not show yourself, I shall be forced to kill the young man." With a wave, Haines pulled Dean toward him. He slid across the floor like he was scooting across a bowling lane in nothing but his socks.

"Oh hell, the president's a supe too?" shouted Dean as he tried to break free to no avail. "No wonder you're such a douche."

When Tori reappeared within five feet of Haines, the illuminated panels across the ceiling switched off, replaced by flashing red lights and a buzzing alarm. The Cooler was going into emergency lockdown, and by the look on Dean's face, there was serious danger to follow.

But Tori couldn't stop smiling.

"Now I see," she said. "I see what you are."

In those ten seconds, she saw the shadowy thing behind the old man for what it really was. It was awful, and it was terrifying, and it was worse than the doxie-triplets, mutants, Nergal, and any horror movie monster she and Amanda had ever watched on VHS, way too late at night, the covers pulled up to their noses—but as frightening as it was, the shadowy thing was more afraid of her. She could smell its fear as it played the old man like a marionette.

Tori gestured at Dean, and he stopped sliding, canceling Haines's command—and in that split second, a hot breeze glanced across the back of her neck.

"Look out!" yelled Dean.

But Tori never moved. She never flinched. She knew what was coming, and she was unbothered. Harden the crab-penis dove for her and missed—though, not quite *missed* as much as it *phased* straight through her, stumbling with its frothy, dribbling mouth snapping closed. Its needle teeth sank into Haines' midsection.

The old man's black hole eyes widened, and Tori saw a spark—a glimmer of panic. The creature missed its target, but the hungry volcano in its gut could not resist the taste of flesh. It hesitated, then bit down, attempting to chew its master and feed its hungry core.

Tori stepped over to Haines. His pained shivers froze him in place. She reached out to the shadow, as if her eyes had adjusted to seeing the darkness, and grabbed hold.

"Bye-bye, bad man," she said, ripping the shadow away from the old, crusty husk. The body wilted to the floor in sync with a mechanical sound beneath the buzzing alarm.

Tori hadn't fully grasped what she had done when Dean threw Maury's massive sports coat over their heads, just as a purple mist began to fall.

"Wait a minute," said Bert from his knees, finally recovered from the incendiary flare of Tori's ABFS. "Did I let one slip?"

As the purple mist coated his body, Bert shrank. His shoulders and chin narrowed, and his crimson abs fled the scene forever. The third-degree burns on his arm flared with pain—as did every blow, punch, kick, bullet, rocket, explosion, death ray, blade, claw, throttle, and whiplash—and his un-supe body was overwhelmed. He'd be crippled for the rest of his days.

"What's going on?" asked Tori as they lowered themselves to the floor, creating a small tent just for two.

"Stay under the jacket," warned Dean.

Tori nodded. She trusted him. She trusted him with her whole life.

"Did you just save me?"

"You saved me first," he replied. "In more ways than one."

"My hero," she whispered.

They kissed. She felt the whole world and all its promises finally live up to her expectations. Years of struggle, heartache, and pain, all gone.

"What is this?" cried Bert from somewhere beyond. "Master! Caliph Haines! Help me! Help me!"

But Haines was gone—

"Tori," said Dean as their lips parted.

"Yeah?" Her indefensible heart thumped wildly in her chest as she smiled.

Dean was smiling too, shyly, as if he was about to say something deep and profound from the very depths of his soul. She wanted to hear it. She wanted to know his fathomless self, to explore all he had to offer, and she would give him all of her. All of who she was. Her vulnerability was in his hands.

And then he was gone.

One moment they were holding hands, and the next, hers were empty.

Her arm, exposed, was coated with the purple liquid that dripped onto the floor and puddled around her foot beneath the tent. She searched for Dean, ignoring Bert's painful wails, and stood up as the mist finished falling.

Harden popped to his feet beside her as the entirety of the creature fell away, severed from his abdomen forevermore. He couldn't have looked happier.

"Thank you," said Harden. "Thank you!"

"Freeze! Get your hands up!" shouted the police, raiding the room like a drug bust. Dozens surrounded them, waving guns in every direction—and Tori hardly noticed.

"I didn't do anything!" shouted Harden. "I swear! It was all the president!"

The last of the mist had drifted to the floor. Tori dropped the jacket and stood up to survey the room.

Bert was face down on the ground in a fetal position, his muscles and body contorted like a dried-up mummy. A few officers gathered, attempting to understand the old-man-mush on the floor next to the giant phallus with its legs still twitching, while the shirtless chief of staff continued to profess his innocence.

"Crystal Beth," called Commissioner Dudley as he entered the supply room and forced his men to lower their weapons. She hadn't realized they were aimed at her—

—like she was sleepwalking.

Tori didn't know she was crying, only that she stopped when she saw the familiar face. She looked at the sweet old man with the bushy white mustache as if he were someone who could help her find Dean.

"To my surprise," said Dudley, ignoring her tears and taking her hand in his, "Annie Phetamine showed up at the precinct and told us everything. Then, a minute ago, she disappeared."

Tori shook her head. None of it made any sense.

"Where did he go?" she cried.

Dudley didn't seem to know what she was talking about, only that she appeared distraught. He knelt beside her as she sank to the floor.

"They're gone," she cried. "I can feel it. They're gone forever."

Then she sobbed into his shoulder for a very long time.

Grief was like a snowflake. It was unique to the sufferer. No two people react to it alike. The pit in Tori's stomach was so wide and awful, she didn't know how she was going to take her next step, let alone the fifteen-minute walk to the fleet of ambulances parked outside The Cooler. She fell into Rudy's arms and told him everything between tears and quaking sobs.

It took all fifteen minutes for her to understand, in part, what had transpired.

It took all fifteen minutes to find ways to articulate it so that others might understand.

Arthur received a phone call as she explained her story. It was the coroner.

They'd found another body at the First National Bank inside the vault. He was wearing a t-shirt just like the one they had described—the Element of Confusion with a big "UM" on the chest. Rudy and Arthur had been inside that very room last night and never saw that body. It was a mystery.

A mystery they slowly unraveled together.

Commissioner Dudley arrested the mortal Memento Maury—the big man screaming, "I was framed!" while being escorted into a paddy wagon covered in a purple candy crunch.

A permanently-shaped Rhea Ramsey was booked for numerous crimes, the least of which, impersonating a police officer, and many, many more.

A plain un-suk-you-bust Brie hung around, listening to Tori, Arthur, and

Rudy attempting to understand the tragedy from the back bumper of an ambulance. She appeared sad, never spoke a word, then eventually drifted off after the EMTs wheeled Bert into the back and drove away. They never saw her again.

After several days of mourning and piecing together information, they realized that Dean had died the previous day while locked inside the First National Bank vault with Tori. When Jordan hit Dean during the heist, he'd suffered a catastrophic head injury. Tori, unbeknownst to her, brought Dean back—as she had every member of the Grace Falls Seven except Bert. Dean was inextricably tied to her latent powers, manifested by the great fear of abandonment that had crippled Tori throughout her life. Those passive abilities stayed active as she consumed the red and blue lollipops, but the purple mist took everything away. Permanently. Those powers were gone forever, along with Arthur's research. He'd been terminated from Amycus Industries.

Ironically, Dean's attempt to save Tori was also to save himself.

He lived and died for love.

They cried for hours.

They cried for days.

They mourned for weeks and months.

Tori mourned a full year and she kept mourning, and she never forgot his smile, his bad jokes, nor the way he looked at her—like she was the most perfect thing he had ever seen.

MASKED

CHAPTER 34

TWO YEARS LATER

HARDEN BISHOP WALKED THE NATIONAL STATUARY HALL, making his way through the crowds of reporters, security, Capitol Police, television cameras, and flashing bulbs. He approached the statue of Captain John Monaco, legendary hero of the second American Civil War, and bowed his head. The inscription at the foot of the lifelike sculpture said, "The Deadliest Weapon Is The Truth."

Harden had just finished giving televised testimony to the Senate Intelligence Committee and left knowing he had changed the world. The partisan divisions within the press would write whatever suited their audience, but there was evidence. President Haines was dead, and with him the stranglehold over the Ministry Party, but the divisions within the country ran deep. As much as Harden wanted to believe those responsible for the chaos two years ago would be punished, he had his doubts. Some called him a traitor. Some stopped just short of calling him a hero. Others claimed he only did it to save his own skin. In truth, Harden testified because the truth needed to be told.

After all, Harden knew where all the bodies were buried…literally.

And now, so did the world.

Two hard years in jail gave him perspective, and as he prepared to turn himself in for the remainder of his four-year sentence, he did so with a clean conscience. Unfortunately, someone behind him pulled a trigger and excavated his conscience all over the marble floors and walls of the Capitol.

MASKED

Christopher Dudley retired to a small island off the coast of Spain with his wife of thirty-eight years. He did so with a full pension and lived out his days sipping drinks from tiny straws and big wedges of tropical fruit, some with tiny paper umbrellas. In the days following the Wonder City Riots, Dudley and his men took back the city from the V-Boys and Khaki Klan, doing so without the help of supes.

He was praised as a hero one last time.

Every Wednesday for nearly two years, Tori visited Rudy and Arthur at their apartment. They played board games or watched movies, and sometimes Peter and Tammy would join them. They'd laugh. Sometimes they'd cry. And always before she left, she'd promise to call and text more often, and even offer to have them over to her place next time. Then, every week after a tearful goodbye, she'd disappear until the following Wednesday.

Tori never talked about her life. She never talked about her job or what she was doing to stay afloat. All they knew was that she was depressed and that there was nothing they could do to help, outside a miracle.

They spent Christmas Eves together. New Years, Fourth of Julys, Thanksgivings, Halloweens, birthdays—even Dean's and Amanda's—and they became family. They were thankful to have each other, but that didn't mean it wasn't difficult. It was a friendship built upon common loss and sadness. That sadness seemed to get buried over time for Rudy and Arthur, but Tori's remained just below the surface.

It took eighteen months. Arthur promised under two years, and Rudy was confident he'd deliver. He was, after all, a brilliant scientist, and Rudy was his biggest fan—though the project didn't come without its frustrating days.

Rudy knew when Arthur came home after work and went straight to his office that he was to be left alone at all costs. On good days, he could hardly make it through the threshold of the apartment door before he started rattling off his progress—all of which flew over Rudy's head like a spy plane zipping silently above the clouds. But he'd smile and tell his partner he was doing a great job.

Unfortunately, there were nearly twice as many bad days as there were good days. Rudy decided it was best, for himself and their relationship, to understand the breakthrough might never come to pass.

It was late October when Rudy texted.

Tori had just returned from a quick trip to the bodega down the street for groceries when her phone cried, "It's me!" Most days, she left her phone behind when she left the apartment. It had become a distraction, a heavy ball-and-chain that was dragging her further underwater when she was already drowning. When her hands and mind were idle, she'd somehow find her way onto Dean's FriendSpace page to look at his pictures and read through old posts as if she were trying to get to know a ghost.

Then again, wasn't that all she ever knew? A ghost? He was dead before she even knew his name.

She would read the in-memoriam posts from friends and family. Her online meanderings always ended with a bottle and tears, re-opening the wound every time.

She read his books, multiple times. They became so dog-eared that she bought new copies to read when she needed to feel close to him.

She spent hours, night after lonely night, looking to the stars. She never once saw another shooting star to wish upon. It was as if all the magic in the world had fled forever.

She spent her days writing music and her nights bartending at the new and improved Mooks. After all the felons on-ice were de-suped at The Cooler, those who survived the transformation made Mooks a popular place for former supes and supervillains to drown their sorrows and reminisce about former glory.

On the weekends she'd volunteer, leading a support group for people who'd survived traumatic experiences at the hands of supes. She imagined Amanda and Dean were somewhere watching over her, pushing her forward—even when it hurt.

Tori suffered with nightmares of President Haines—and took no pleasure or solace from the memory of his demise. There were doors in her nightmares, and three knocks coming from beyond—but Tori always managed to wake up before she opened them.

It was a difficult life. She was getting by. She was surviving one day at a time.

After she unloaded her groceries into the fridge and cracked open a can of sparkling water, she grabbed her phone from the counter and checked the message.

What are you doing tonight, Ta-dore-i?

Rudy had given her that nickname because he "adored" her. She thought it was a stretch, but it stuck, and she didn't mind—she adored Rudy too, like a brother.

Part of her wanted to ignore the message, like she always did, six days a week. It was Monday, and the one day she dedicated to Rudy and Arthur—the two men she loved more than anyone alive—was more than enough to make her feel again. That day, Wednesday, was still forty-eight hours away. She spent the other six days a week being numb, desperately attempting to avoid alcohol and chemicals that could aid her obliteration. She kept imagining what Dean and Amanda would say if she sank that far—and those thoughts were enough to keep her away from the edge.

Still, she was creeping closer to it every day.

She sighed, then texted back. *Nothing. Dinner. PJs. Bed.*

Tori had no sooner set her phone onto the counter when another message came through in Rudy's voice—"It's me!"

She snatched up the phone, read the message, then groaned.

Be there in five.

She didn't like company. Her apartment was small. It was messy. And she didn't appreciate unannounced visitors—nor visitors who announced themselves with only minutes to spare. She had no sooner rearranged the pillows on the couch and threw a few dirty plates into the sink when she heard the three knocks on the door.

She froze.

A wave of anxiety overwhelmed her.

She shrank to the floor next to the sink, and her forehead moistened. Her stomach turned.

"Is she home?" asked Arthur.

"I texted her five minutes ago," said Rudy.

"Did she say she was home?"

"She didn't say that *exactly*."

Hearing their voices through the door helped provide Tori enough strength to stand and pace the floor. She listened to them bicker and smirked.

Would she and Dean have been like that?

She could only dream…

"Hey," she said, answering the door as she tracked Rudy's eyes—they brightened when they saw her, then immediately darkened at the sight of her hair, her clothes, and the wild state of her apartment.

"Oh honey," groaned Rudy. "I knew things were bad, but I didn't think they were this bad."

He shooed her aside and entered, while Arthur remained in the hall, politely waiting for an invite.

"Come in," Tori said with a defeated smile. Arthur nodded and stepped inside, then proceeded toward the windows, where he drew back the shades to a beautiful autumn sunset. The sky was several shades of orange, pinks, purples, and blues—reminiscent of her old supe makeup, when she used to prowl the streets for supe-justice.

Wonder City was beautiful that time of year. There were ZepNews balloons crawling through the skies, and everything appeared at peace. Maybe that's why she always had the shades drawn—she wasn't at peace. She was chaos.

Rudy searched for a place to sit but leaned against the wall instead—he seemed anxious. "Is it always this dark in here?" he asked. "Or have you officially become a creature of the night?"

"I just don't like brightness," she admitted. She was feeling self-conscious about everything, from the state of her apartment to the jeans she had worn three days straight, and decided to beat them to the punch. "Why are you here?"

"We're here because we're worried about you, Ta-dore-i!" whined Rudy.

Arthur was smiling. He only smiled like that when they played card games—it didn't matter if they were playing poker, rummy, or war, the guy could not summon up a poker face, even after practice. Rudy once gave him a Halloween mask to wear, but it reminded Tori too much of the Ministerium Guard, and she had a small but terrifying nervous breakdown.

"I'm fine," she said. "Really, I am."

"Tori, honey," consoled Rudy, "there is no way I believe that."

"I am! I'm bartending at Mooks. I've written two dozen songs. I've been working with a producer. I'm volunteering. Things are looking up."

"Do you have friends?" asked Rudy. "Besides Arthur and me?"

She shrugged. "Friends are overrated."

"Have you dated?" he asked. "Have you gotten out of the apartment to do anything fun other than hang out with your two gay-best-friends once a week?"

"I don't need to," said Tori. "I don't want to."

"Did you see the news yesterday?" asked Arthur, wiping the smile from his face.

"No," she said. "Why?"

"There's a gang out there," said Arthur, "causing havoc across the city."

"They call themselves The Dope Gang," said Rudy. "They're hurting a lot of innocent people."

"Obviously, I have nothing to do with that."

"We know," assured Rudy.

"So, what do you want *me* to do about it?" She was beginning to feel like this was not a friendly visit, but an intervention.

Rudy and Arthur glanced at each other. Neither of them seemed comfortable starting what they intended to say.

"What?" she growled. "Just tell me."

"You see," blurted Rudy, "everyone has LEGs. And these LEGs can do great things..."

"They'll help me walk right out of this conversation," said Tori.

Rudy sighed. "I waltzed right into that one."

They both wanted to say that Dean would've appreciated the comeback, but neither of them did. They couldn't. It was the two-ton elephant in the room every time they were together.

"Okay. Show's yours, Arthur," said Rudy theatrically.

Arthur took a deep breath as Rudy stepped back, giving him the stage.

"Crimson Justice killed more than six hundred people while attempting to *save* this city. Six hundred sixty-three people, to be exact, and that's only those they know about," said Arthur. "He was a terror to be sure, but he was a deterrent. Since that day, there have been more than fifty-thousand reported supe-incidents in Wonder City, including assault, murder, robbery, and more. The city needs a *real* hero."

"So?" grumbled Tori.

"It's been twenty-four months," said Arthur, "since, you know, The Cooler."

"Yeah," said Tori, fighting back tears.

"I lost my research twice that weekend," explained Arthur. "The same research I tried so hard to smuggle out of Amycus Industries. We smuggled it back in because it was our only hope of rescuing you and taking down the president."

It was also the same research that took everything she thought she finally had away from her. She had survived Crimson Justice and Harden—she'd even got revenge on the old man with the black hole eyes, President Haines, for shoving her onto that supe journey to begin with.

Amanda was back from the dead.

Dean was holding her hands.

Her life, the one she imagined lying in bed at night with Amanda as kids, wishing upon shooting stars, was finally about to start—she saw it all with Dean. And she knew he saw it too. Their whole lives flashed before her eyes. It was real, even if his life was leased by her abilities—the strange latent abilities she didn't understand.

Then, in a blink—or rather, a falling purple mist—it was gone.

"I'm sorry," she said, wiping away tears. "I don't want to think about that day, ever again."

Arthur nodded and reached into his pocket.

"Don't be sorry," said Arthur. "Neither do I."

"We all lost something that day," added Rudy. "But we gained something too. You became like family to us."

Tori sobbed, and Rudy threw an arm around her.

"I would do anything for my family," said Arthur. "I'd even put my life and my career on the line for them, like I did that day." Then he held something out to her. "And I did it again."

In Arthur's hand was a small paper stick attached to a clear green orb, wrapped in plastic.

Tori shivered and looked up at him, noting the tears behind his glasses.

"This time, however," said Arthur, "it can't be undone."

Tori examined the candy and experienced a rush of various emotions all at once—she was scared and excited, sad, happy, frightened out of her damn mind, and too hurt to dare to be hopeful.

"It's your decision," said Rudy. "The world could really use the Gryphyn, among others."

Tori took the lollipop from Arthur's hand and studied it, like it was both a gift and a curse. She knew what it was like to hear a cell phone chime and suddenly find herself filled with hope. A chime carrying the message that she had imagined all the pain of the last two years. Tori shook so hard, she had to use both hands to hold onto it, fearful the lollipop might fall away and smash like glass.

Rudy helped to steady her shakes as Arthur took an old wooden chair and helped her sit.

"Suckers," she said with a chuckle, remembering the joke.

"Hmm?" asked Rudy.

"Nothing," she said as the tears fell uncontrollably.

She removed the plastic, and with all the strength she had left, she placed it onto her tongue and closed her mouth. She sat there with Rudy's arm around her and Arthur looming nearby, pacing and calculating all the possible outcomes in his mind, as if he hadn't already double, triple, quadruple, and quintuple checked his work.

After a minute, Tori asked, "How long is it supposed to take?"

There was a crackle in the air, like static.

"Not long," said Dean. "We never left."

THE END...

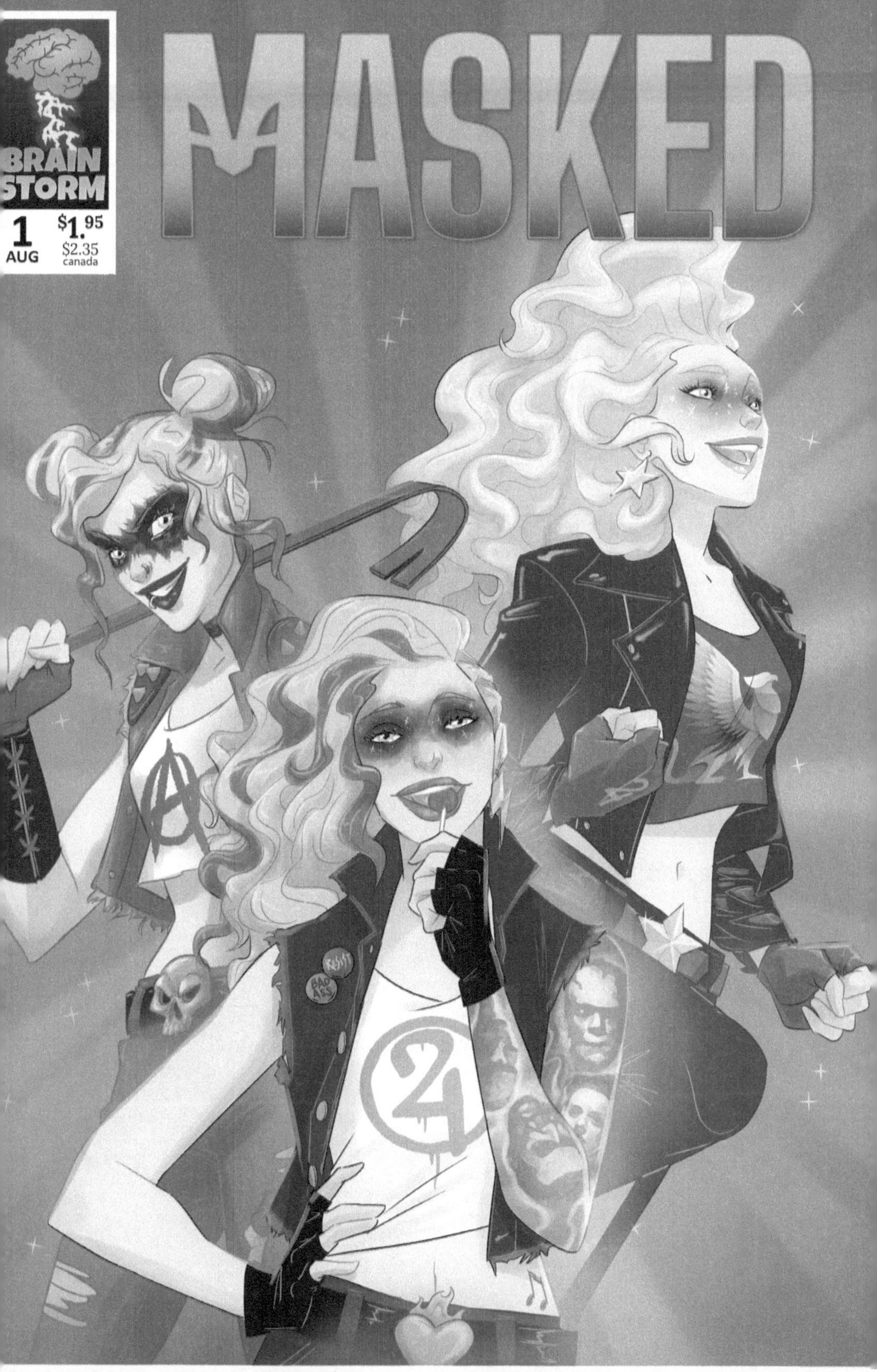

MASKED

AFTERWORD

WITH OSCAR "RUDY" RUDOLPH

Hello friends—boyfriends, girlfriends, and all you other sexy Masked psychos out there!

@MoodyRudy here, giving y'all a quick reminder to navigate on over to your favorite book purchasing site and leave an honest review of this masterpiece of storytelling, if I can be so humble.

Whether or not G.A. is as good as my main-man, Dean-Dean, the lady machine, or even the king of fiction—the mastermind of blow your mind—the breath-taking, scene-stealing, heart-beating Einstein of super-fiction—do it anyway, because that's what one does in a civil society. They leave reviews.

That's right, clap it out with me:
👏 They. 👏 Leave. 👏 Reviews.
👏 They. 👏 Leave. 👏 Reviews.

Again!
👏 They. 👏 Leave. 👏 Reviews.
👏 They. 👏 Leave. 👏 Reviews.

One more time for the stylish homies in the back—you sexy things!
👏 They. 👏 Leave. 👏 Reviews.
👏 They. 👏 Leave. 👏 Reviews.

By golly, oh gee, I think you've got it. In closing, remember, take care, comb your hair, peace, love, and pogo-sticks, and all that jazz.

Off like a prom dress,

Rudy

ABOUT THE AUTHOR

G.A. Finocchiaro resides in the Philadelphia suburbs, with no pets, lousy neighbors, and a porky groundhog that sneaks into his yard to to feast on weeds. G.A. refuses to use TikTok, listened to way too much 80s music while writing this novel, and has a contentious relationship with plants that self-harm despite his watering techniques.

MASKED is his fifth novel.

Don't forget to sign up for his newsletter!
GAFINO.com/Newsletter/

Or follow him on Twitter!
@G_A_Fino